After I flew clean over Oparal and her stupid unicorn, I figured I'd hit the saint hard enough to drive the knife clean through her bird skull.

I figured wrong.

Whatever the thing was—and it sure wasn't a saint—it had a skull plenty harder than bone. The knife scraped deep into the side of its face. It would have taken off an ear if she'd had any. Instead I just sheared off some feathers.

Saint Birdface didn't appreciate the free shave. She opened her yellow beak and let out one hell of a screech. She didn't sound half so much like an eagle as a banshee. Before jumping in, I should have asked the boss what his Shadowless Sword showed him she really was.

The crusaders didn't notice the—what's the boss's word?—the incongruity. As far as the knights knew, I'd just stabbed Iomedae's messenger in the face. They drew their swords and came at me.

"Hey, I'm not the bad guy here!" I shouted. "Come on, boss! Show them what we got."

I expected to hear his magic message again, but he was busy trying to wipe out the illusion. I heard his riffle scrolls snapping off across the room. The illusion over the room and the bad guys stayed in place, but all of a sudden I could see little Alase.

She knelt with an open hand on the floor, like she was feeling for tremors. Instead, a blue circle of light formed all around her, and the paint across her eyes blazed under her sh⋯ black bangs . . .

The Pathfinder Tales Library

King of Chaos

Dave Gross

paizo

Cover art by Tyler Walpole.
Cover design by Andrew Vallas.
Map by Crystal Frasier.

Paizo Publishing, LLC
7120 185th Ave NE, Ste 120
Redmond, WA 98052
paizo.com

ISBN 978-1-60125-558-7 (mass market paperback)
ISBN 978-1-60125-559-4 (ebook)

Publisher's Cataloging-In-Publication Data
(Prepared by The Donohue Group, Inc.)

Gross, Dave.
  King of chaos / Dave Gross.

  p. : map ; cm. -- (Pathfinder tales)

  Set in the world of the role-playing game, Pathfinder.
  Issued also as an ebook.
  ISBN: 978-1-60125-558-7 (mass market pbk.)

  1. Lost books--Fiction. 2. Imaginary places--Fiction. 3. Good and evil--Fiction. 4. Pathfinder (Game)--Fiction. 5. Fantasy fiction. 6. Adventure stories. I. Title. II. Series: Pathfinder tales library.

PS3607.R67 K56 2013
813/.6

First printing August 2013.

Printed in the United States of America.

For Liane Merciel and Robin D. Laws,
with thanks for letting me borrow their toys.

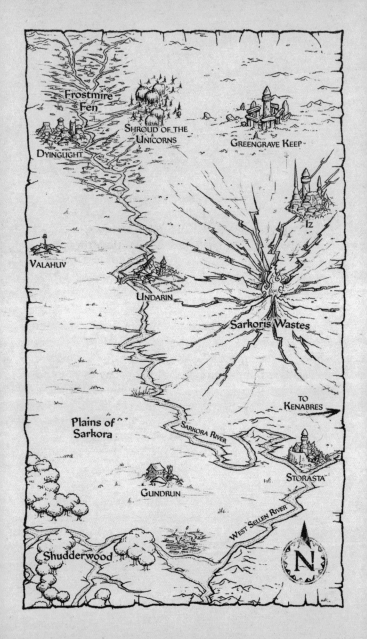

Chapter One
The Watchtower

Oparal

"Faster."

Bastiel lowered his horn. His sooty mane whipped my faceplate as I rose in the stirrups to lean over his neck. The thrum of his hooves traveled up through the saddle grips and shuddered through my enchanted armor. Bastiel required no bridle, no reins—only a word.

The unicorn galloped down the wet hill, his hooves plunging deep through the moss. The mud spattered against my greaves. A cold snap had laced the thawing earth with frost.

Before us, demons swarmed the watchtower.

Above them all hovered a trio of wrath demons. Their raw humanoid bodies and vulture-like heads loomed over the combatants as they shook noxious spores from their bodies down onto their foes. One demon tried to land, and the crusaders rushed to drive it back into the air before it could begin its storm dance. Surrounding them all, tiny fiends teemed like minnows in the foul miasma around the filthy black wings.

On the tower roof, naked demons leaped upon steel-clad defenders. The Mendevian crusaders stood shoulder-to-shoulder along the crenellated wall. Their valor sang to my heart, but against the combined packs of fiends they were far too few.

"Faster!"

Bastiel galloped more swiftly than any horse, but within his great heart he found even more speed. We sailed toward the tower, the sodden earth churning like waves beneath us.

At the tower's base, a gang of brimoraks assaulted a pair of knights. One glance at the fiends left a sick trembling in the vault of my stomach. Every paladin experiences a different reaction to the presence of evil. I once described the sensation to an irreverent friend who dubbed it "the butterflies of evil."

Barely more than half the height of the men, the brimoraks threatened their foes with flaming swords. Their red-hot hooves left prints in cracked mud.

The crusaders stood fast. Behind them, their squires freed horses from the stable abutting the tower. The penned animals bucked against the walls, terrified by the sulfurous vapors emanating from the little arson demons.

One of the defenders caught a flaming sword on his shield and tried to shove it aside, straining against his foe's surprising strength. Before the fiend could bring the brand back into line, the knight—no, the paladin— called upon Iomedae and sliced open the demon's belly with his gleaming longsword. The brimorak dropped its fiery blade with a bleat and fell.

"Sergeant!" The other knight pointed at me and Bastiel. His sergeant saw me. So did the brimoraks.

So much for the element of surprise.

I drew the Ray of Lymirin. Pure light flared from the thrice-blessed steel as the saint's choir sang in voices audible only to me—and, judging by his twitching ears, also to Bastiel. The sword trembled in my grip, eager to strike. I sat deep in the saddle, hugging Bastiel with my legs. The brimoraks braced themselves.

Bastiel caught the first demon on his spiraled horn, tossing it aside. The point of my sword sparked off the curling horns of the second. The blow was nothing in itself, but the holy aura of the blade burned the fiend. It scrambled through the mud, howling and clutching at its head.

Anticipating Bastiel's next move, I grasped a saddle grip and braced myself. The mighty unicorn trampled two more brimoraks before planting his front hooves. Momentum turned him around, pivoting him on his front legs. I clung to the saddle only by virtue of the fantastic strength my magical belt imbued in me.

Bastiel kicked with his own considerable brawn and mass. The resulting sound told me his hooves found their target. Out of the corner of my eye I saw a goatlike head tumble across the yard.

Bastiel danced himself back into balance. I straightened to survey the scene.

Only one brimorak remained, the one whose horns I had creased. It had thrown itself to the ground, screaming and clutching its horns in a tantrum of agony. The sergeant ran after the fiend and stamped upon its neck, severing its spine with a single blow.

The squires finished releasing the terrified horses, calming them with strokes and whispers.

"My lady." The knight who spoiled my surprise attack doffed his helm and fell to one knee, gazing up with an all-too-familiar expression on his face.

Bastiel snorted.

"Stand up, soldier," barked the sergeant. The younger man stood. He could not have seen more than eighteen years before joining the crusade.

The sergeant raised the beaver of his helm. Beneath it lay a battered face fringed with a red-brown beard. He saluted me properly and addressed me by the rank he saw upon my pauldron. "Captain, there's no time to report. They're overwhelmed on the parapets."

"Follow me," I said.

Bastiel's hooves struck the base of the tower stairs. Twice he barreled into vermleks, shoving them off the steps. The infected host bodies burst as they struck the ground, releasing their wormy contents. Behind me, the sergeant bellowed at the squires to cut down the escaping parasites.

The sound of battle grew louder as we reached the spacious roof. Worse than the cries and impacts was a mad jabbering that came from everywhere at once. The sound battered the edges of my thoughts.

Two dozen crusaders remained standing. Ten or so had already fallen, and twice as many fiends lay dead. Everywhere I saw deep gouges in the watchtower stone and in the shields and weapons of the defenders. Blood stained their white-and-gold tabards, and one or two clutched bleeding stumps. They were being eaten alive.

I spied paladins among the common soldiers and low templars. One paladin lifted her warhammer to call down the radiance of Iomedae. The holy light scalded the nearby fiends, but didn't reach as far as I had expected.

The shadow of the wrath demons fell across us. Their sickening spores fell upon us. Those that touched flesh began burrowing in. I felt one upon my face, but its tendrils recoiled as they touched the Inheritor's radiance—one of Iomedae's many gifts to her anointed paladins.

The common soldiers were not so fortunate. The spores grew instantly upon setting root in their skin. Some screamed as green-black vines sprouted from their limbs and heads. A quick-thinking paladin sheathed his blade and produced a flask of holy water from his pouch. Sprinkling the afflicted while calling out a blessing, he vanquished the unholy spores.

Eyes wet with revenge, the fiends turned on the paladin.

I lifted the Ray of Lymirin and shouted, "Iomedae!" The longsword sang, its blinding radiance casting stark shadows across the watchtower. A holy breeze dispersed the remaining spores that drifted down from the hovering demons.

In the light of the Ray, the lesser demons shrieked in agony, while the worse fiends gobbled curses at me. The veteran crusaders took the chance to cut down the confused mob. The sight of me astride Bastiel distracted only the demons and the novices.

And one other.

With his helm torn away, I recognized Ederras Celverian fighting across the tower roof. Our gazes met for an instant. As I turned back to the fray, I saw him do the same, jaw set in anger.

A group of four crusaders forced a tusked demon toward the tower's edge. It grunted as they shoved all their might into their shields. The demon squealed as it slipped from the parapet and fell to the ground.

Bastiel leaped over the nearest group of defenders, and we plunged into the battle. I guided the Ray through the demons' bodies. Their dismembered limbs streamed black ribbons, and they fell.

"Stay back!" A fur-clad sorcerer cried out a warning as we approached. At her hip hung a quiver of icy javelins. Ice caked the tower roof all around her. Demons slipped and fell as they tried to reach her.

I batted away a gibbering bat demon and cut another in half as Bastiel stopped short of the ice.

A scythe-clawed demon managed to stand erect on the slippery roof. A crusader thrust a spear through its chest. The fiend chortled, perhaps at the crusader's ignorance of demonic anatomy. It pulled the spear through its own body, drawing the soldier close.

The sorcerer uttered arcane words. Four snarling bolts of force shot from her outstretched fingers into the demon's head, blasting away an eye and half its face.

Even that wasn't enough to slay the demon. It snapped its jaws at the spearman, spraying his face with ropes of bloody spittle.

I leaped from the saddle and onto the ice, knees bent, sliding in a crouch. As I reached him, the spearman released his weapon and fell onto his back.

He could not have timed it better.

Hopping over him, I added strength to momentum and swept the Ray clean through the demon's neck. Its ichor steamed upon the ice as I slid to a halt beside the sorcerer.

She intoned another spell while reaching for her javelins. I couldn't understand the words, but I heard Thuvia in her accent. She had crossed the Inner Sea and all of Avistan to join the crusade.

Near the center of the watchtower roof, Bastiel gored what looked like a seven-foot-tall flayed man. Throwing the fiend back, he bucked and turned to bring his powerful hind hooves to bear. He battered the demon half to death before a pair of crusader spears finished the task.

I guarded the sorcerer while she cast her spell. Warm winds rose around us. She tossed the icy javelins one by one, letting the whirlwind fling them high, up into the suppurating flesh of the hovering vulture demons. The fiends shrieked and bled, and we held up our shields to cover our heads as a rain of gore and spores fell upon us.

"Paladins, with me!" I ran to the tower's edge, turning the Ray of Lymirin pommel-up before me. "Blessed Saint, let me be a window to your light."

Paladins joined me on either side, murmuring their own prayers. One was the sergeant I met below.

Iomedae's radiance suffused our bodies and made a beacon of the tower. Demon mouths gaped in agony, but I could not hear their shrieks.

I heard only the choir.

A few of the tiny bat-fiends fell flaming to the ground. The vulture demons screamed again, then vanished, teleporting to safety.

My fellow paladins went at once to tend to the wounded. Bastiel picked his way delicately through the bodies, lowering his horn here and there to bestow a blessing.

Sometimes I wondered whether his magic came directly from the Green. If so, it was a wonder he could hear the choir. Had the Inheritor touched Bastiel after the unicorn chose me? Or had he always walked in the radiance?

Miracles are not mysteries, I reminded myself. I need not question them.

I went to one of the dying. I removed a gauntlet and lay my hand upon his brow. When he was safe, I moved to the next. When I had healed all I could, I rose and said, "Who's in command here?"

I looked to those who were not tending the wounded. They looked at each other, counting the absences until the sergeant made a final calculation. He walked to Ederras and saluted. "You are acting captain, sir."

Ederras nodded with obvious reluctance. "Thank you, Aprian."

I drew the paper from my gauntlet and took it to Ederras. "Your orders."

He glanced at the captain's insignia on my shoulder. His eyes hardened. "You joined the crusade less than a year ago." It was not a question.

"Queen Telandia commended me to Queen Galfrey, who invested me with the rank upon admittance to the crusade." That should have been enough to satisfy anyone. I certainly had no obligation to say more, but an unbidden regret made me add, "Last summer I fought against the hordes of the Witchbole."

Sensing my unease, Bastiel came to stand beside me.

"A unicorn," scoffed Ederras. "Of course."

Aprian winced, perhaps embarrassed by his commander's discourtesy. While I had learned to place little trust in first impressions, my opinion of him was only improving.

Ederras's scowl deepened as he read my orders. Before finishing, he snapped, "We don't answer to the Silver Crusade."

A few of the soldiers muttered disparaging phrases about freelancers.

"No, *we* don't," I said, emphasizing the pronoun more than I intended. "We answer to Queen Galfrey." I drew the seal of the queen of Mendev from my pouch and held it up for all to see. Raising my voice, I announced, "Her Majesty commands cooperation in this matter. I need your sorcerer and twenty knights."

"We just lost half our strength," hissed Ederras. "And you can't have Jelani. I need her."

I understood his anger. If I had known I would find him here— No, it didn't matter. I had my orders.

Stepping closer, I lowered my voice. "Listen, Ederras, I know the circumstances couldn't be worse, but my mission is critical. The queen herself—"

"She's sent you fishing," he said. "I've seen this fool's errand a hundred times before. 'Search the ruins surrounding the Worldwound for any materiel useful in prosecuting the war.' It's a snipe hunt, Oparal."

"Not this time. The entire Silver Crusade has been dispatched for the same purpose, but Queen Galfrey wants our own people on it, too. She would not have summoned me for a routine effort."

"Because you're so very special." He made no effort to disguise his scorn, or his anger. His cheeks flushed red. There was a time when I welcomed that sight, the rising of the blood as we fought side by side in the alleys of Westcrown. If he remembered those days, it was not fondly. There was only bitterness left in his voice when he said, "Why didn't you stay in Kyonin with your people?"

"The same reason as you," I said. "I go where I can do the most good."

He clenched his fists. I stepped back out of sorrow, not fear. He still hadn't forgiven me for what I had done all those years ago. Perhaps he never would.

"I don't want to leave you empty handed," I said. "I will take ten, plus the sorcerer."

Jelani said, "Don't I have any say—?"

Ederras and I turned simultaneously, silencing her with a look.

According to my brief, Jelani had been in the field for well over two years. If she hadn't learned discipline by now, she never would. Unfortunately, she was the only sorcerer I had permission to take into my command. Fortunately, I had recent experience with freelancers in Kyonin. She could hardly be more trouble than they had been.

"I need every remaining soldier to hold this tower," said Ederras.

"You need to withdraw. This tower is on the wrong side of the wardstones. What was your captain thinking to station you here?"

Exasperated, he gestured to Aprian. "You tell her."

"He was thinking we needed a better view," said Aprian. He pointed northeast toward a line of storm clouds hovering over a low line of corrupted hills. "Look closely."

It wasn't the clouds alone that darkened the sky. More flying fiends hovered above a pustulant ridge.

Sickly green-black motes floated around them, swarming like gnats.

"How long have they been there?"

"Days. We rode out from Kenabres, over there." Aprian's finger moved slightly east, indicating a city just barely visible on the horizon. "The captain led us across the wardstone line to this tower, hoping to draw off some of the horde."

"More came than you expected?"

"Many more." Aprian nodded. "The worst part was the first wave. Those swarms of bat demons around the floaters, they're half wings, half jaws, all insanity."

The sorcerer stepped forward and picked up a half-pulverized carcass from the watchtower roof. It was as Aprian described: an eyeless maw about the size of an ogre's fist. Its spiny wedge of a body formed wings. "Vescavors," said Jelani. "They can bite through almost anything: wood, stone, even steel. But the worst part is the gibbering. It's maddening."

"The troops held as best they could, but the confusion alone almost broke our lines," said Ederras. His tone had shifted to that of the younger man I had known in Cheliax. "It's good that you arrived when you did. You saved lives."

Ederras sighed and turned away. I knew that sound. He had accepted the need to turn over his troops, but he would no longer look at me. Instead, he addressed the survivors.

"Into the Worldwound. Volunteers?"

The young crusader I encountered before the stables stepped forward. He drew his sword and knelt before me. "My lady, if you will have it, my sword is yours."

His unmilitary gesture broke the dam of propriety. Another man stepped forward, and then another. A few moments later, four dewy-eyed youths and two grown men who should have known better had stepped forward to pose like knights from romantic paintings.

Masking my displeasure, I said, "My writ grants me the choice of your troops. I choose Jelani and Sergeant Aprian." I turned to the sergeant. "Your first order is to select nine more troops for me."

"Oparal, listen to me." Ederras pulled me aside. Strong as he was, my enchanted belt made me much stronger. In deference to our friendship, I allowed him to draw me away.

"You're making a mistake," he whispered when we had moved out of range of human hearing. Out of the corner of my eye I saw an elven crusader turn away discreetly. "Aprian is a good soldier, but you need to know he's been compromised."

"How?"

"Demonic possession."

"He wouldn't be in the field if he hadn't been exorcised."

"With his record, he should be commanding a legion. But every time his name appears on the rolls of valor, someone at court strikes it off. There must be a reason."

I knew something of the prejudice of those at court, although my persecutors were elves, not crusaders. "Aprian stood with me to channel the light. I saw him healing the wounded."

Ederras's expression turned to stone as he realized the implication: I had not seen *him* channel the light or heal the wounded.

"Listen, Ederras, if it's a question of my taking your best man, just say so."

"I wasn't trying to deceive you, Oparal. I was just telling you the facts so you can decide for yourself. You're the one who needs everything to be perfect."

His words stung because they were just. I had at times refused to yield to imperfect answers in the face of difficult problems. The past year had begun to open my eyes to some of my personal failings, but he couldn't have known that.

I tried a different tack. "It seems a very long time since Westcrown, Ed."

"It seems like yesterday, Captain." With that he turned to look west, where infection roiled through the wounded land. When he looked back, resignation filled his eyes. "Take them and go."

There was a time when we would have embraced before parting. Instead, I saluted. He returned the gesture without looking me in the eye.

Aprian made his selection. None of the volunteers stood beside him—another encouraging sign of his competence.

I signaled Aprian and Jelani to walk with me. Bastiel followed without the need for a sign. In our months together, the unicorn had learned to read my moods and body language. At times I almost believed he could read my mind.

At the tower's base, my troops gathered their horses. Thanks to the squires, none of the steeds had fallen to the brimoraks. Some of the mounts would carry their riders' bodies back home.

"Ten minutes." I pointed to a nearby hillock. "I will address the troops up there."

"Yes, Captain," said Aprian.

Bastiel carried me away while my crusaders said their farewells. Some waited at the base of the tower stairs to touch the faces of the dead as they were carried down. I saw prayers upon their lips, mourning in their eyes.

Others traded equipment or tokens with the companions they were leaving behind. No doubt some were extracting promises to send the trinket home for burial in case its owner never returned. It was a wise precaution.

After a brief conference with Ederras, Jelani was the first to leave the tower. She rode a dun mare with a black mane and tail, and black stripes along its back and lower legs. The horse shied and lowered her head as she drew near Bastiel.

The unicorn lifted his head and pretended not to notice. To him, a horse was a mere beast, no closer kin to him than an ape to a man.

"So, you and Ederras . . . ?" said the sorcerer.

I shook my head, disappointed. The men of the Mendevian Crusade were as full of gossip as any I had met in Cheliax. Many of them had joined while still barely more than boys. I had expected better from a woman.

Ignoring her question, I asked, "You know something of the demons?"

"As much as many," she said. "But I'm no demonologist. My talents lie in wind and sand."

"But you have some experience with the wardstones?"

"Yes. My first assignment was to restore a failing wardstone to prevent a breach. Is that why I was chosen for this . . . mission?"

I suspected she had stopped herself from calling it a snipe hunt.

"One of the reasons." I nodded down the hill, where Aprian led his selected crusaders and a few packhorses toward us. "What of the rest of the troops?"

"There are no rookies left in this squad, if that's what you're asking," said Jelani. "I'd say the ones Aprian chose are as good as the ones remaining with Lieuten— that is, Acting-Captain Ederras. Naia is our best archer. Erastus is the second-best tracker. All of us have been over the line more than once."

Good, I thought. I didn't want a sergeant who would leave his former commander with the least of his soldiers any more than I wanted one who would choose them for me.

Aprian presented the selected nine in two ranks. Already I had seen they were practiced riders, guiding their steeds with the economy of motion one sees in veterans. At a glance, a few stood out: a dwarf riding an improbably tall horse, a black-skinned half-elf, the Qadiran archer Jelani had called Naia, and a black-bearded Andoren with an eagle-shaped spaulder on one shoulder.

"None of you asked for this assignment," I told them. "After what you've just faced, you deserve a week's leave in Nerosyan. Unfortunately, the horde has other plans."

"These accursed demons have no plans," grumbled the dwarf. "They're all mad as a box of frogs."

"Pipe down and listen to the captain, Urno." Aprian barked like every sergeant I had ever met.

"You've just seen how they're massing along the wardstone line. Even Urno doesn't need a high horse to see they're preparing for a push."

Urno's eyes widened. The Andoren chuckled and slugged him on the shoulder with a clank of armor. The others relaxed now that I'd shown them I could make a joke, if a rather poor one.

"We have several sites to examine. I won't keep it from you: each will be worse than the previous. If Queen Galfrey's oracles are correct, in one of them we will find our target: a book containing some of the rituals used to open the Worldwound. Once we return it to court, the queen's sorcerers will unlock its secrets and close this damnable chasm forever. Let us pray we find it sooner rather than later."

The crusaders offered little reaction to that astonishing pronouncement. I had hoped for more, but I recalled Ederras's remark about snipe hunts. No doubt they had been promised grand salvation in the past, and it had never proven true.

"What's the first site, Captain?" asked a young Ustalav. He had the longest, darkest eyelashes I had ever seen on a man.

"What's your name, soldier?"

"Dragomir, madam," he said. Aprian caught his eye, and the young man corrected himself. "I mean, Dragomir, Captain."

"The first site we will visit is Yath."

Dragomir paled and drew the spiral of Pharasma over his heart in a distinctively Ustalavic gesture. The others made their own signs of prayer: the wings of Desna, the blaze of Iomedae, and others.

"Captain, Yath is gone," said Aprian. "I saw it fall."

"There wasn't so much as a doorknob left," said Urno.

"We have our orders," I said. "We will search whatever remains of Yath. Once we clear it, we move on to the next site."

"You said each is worse than the one before," said the man Jelani had identified as Erastus. Like Naia, he carried a bow in addition to the standard crusader sword and shield. From his dark complexion and accent, I might have taken him for a Chelaxian, but his blond hair marked him as a man of Isger. "What could be worse than Yath?"

"Let's hope we don't have to find out," said Naia. The Qadiran sat atop a black destrier, the very image of a desert ranger. Along with her bow and scimitar, she carried a war lance with a blue-and-white streamer.

A crack of thunder echoed across the hills. Heads turned in every direction until the black half-elf stood tall in his stirrups and pointed. "There!"

We saw a red flash above the city of Kenabres, followed by a rising plume of smoke and detritus. Seconds later, a sharp report reached us, followed by the dull roar of some incomprehensibly large animal. The cloud continued to rise, blossoming at its crest to form the shape of a mushroom. It was difficult to judge its height from such a distance, but I estimated it was more than a hundred feet tall.

"The wardstone!" cried Jelani.

"The people will need our help," said Dragomir.

By the watchtower stables, Ederras and his troops scrambled to finish loading and mounting their horses. He turned to us. Even at the distance I knew his eyes were fixed on me. He lifted an arm, not pointing at Kenabres but beckoning to me.

"He wants us to go with him," said Aprian.

"We can't," I said. "We have our orders."

"They're moving," said Dragomir. The demons hovering in the hills near Kenabres had indeed begun moving toward the city.

By the watchtower, Ederras shouted an order. His troops followed him toward Kenabres, their horses gaining speed with every step. Even with our help, I could not imagine how they would survive.

"You knew this would happen," Aprian said. It was not a question.

"The queen's oracles had a vision. I didn't know it would come so soon."

I drew the Ray of Lymirin and held it high. Even with the demons so far away, its holy steel flickered white. "Follow me," I cried. "For the crusade, Queen Galfrey, and Iomedae!"

A few of my troops cast longing glances at their comrades racing toward Kenabres. Despite the desire to join them, they followed me. As we rode across the changing land, I thought of Ederras and wondered which of us led the more courageous soldiers.

And which of us led the more doomed.

Chapter Two
The River

Radovan

The boss peered through his spyglass. "There."

I squinted at the Ustalav side of the river. In the distance, the Hungry Mountains had just gnawed the sun to death, smearing the sky with blood. Shadows huddled on the west bank. On account of my devil blood, I see just fine in the dark. At a distance, not so much.

"Let me see."

He handed me the glass, but the barge captain snatched it away. She put it to her eye.

Zora Gorcha was a tough old bird. She looked a good ten years older than the boss, but she couldn't have been much past half his age, which was working on a hundred. Even so, more red than gray curls spilled out of her headscarf. I didn't mind that. Even the rope of garlic around her neck didn't put me off. I like garlic almost as much as redheads and older women.

Everybody on deck was wearing garlic, including Arni. The big dog hated the stinky collar, but the boss taught him to leave it alone. Arni listened to me sometimes, but he always obeyed the boss.

Even the big bay draft horses tethered beside the Red Carriage wore loops of garlic. At first they'd eaten the bulbs off each other's necks, which Zora said was good for repelling mosquitoes, but the boss disagreed. He made the crew adjust their tethers, saying too much garlic was bad for horses. Besides, bugs weren't the bloodsuckers he was worried about.

Zora peered through the brass tube of the spyglass. "Is a different man, no?"

"A different man," said the boss. "Yes."

"You have dangerous enemies, Count Jeggare."

"I did not conceal this fact from you, Captain. I trust you are not frightened."

"Not frightened," she said, looking him up and down. "Impressed."

The boss clicked his heels and made a little bow.

"Come on," I said. "Let me see."

"Wait your turn. I am boat captain. You are only . . . What did you say?"

"Bodyguard."

"Bodyguard," she said, all dubious-like. "I wonder."

"Come on, you've had your look."

Zora slapped the spyglass into my hand. She tilted her head back to look down her hooked nose at me.

She fancied me, all right.

It took a few seconds to find the cultist. He wore the same kind of tattered cloak and leathers, but he wasn't the tall, lean guy we'd seen the night before. This one was built like a wrestler, kind of like me. Bigger, maybe.

Hard to judge without somebody standing next to him. I wanted to get my mitts on his neck and work out which one of us was stronger.

Zora gasped and stepped away.

"Radovan," said the boss. At his heel, Arni whined and put his head on his gigantic paws.

"What?"

"You . . . growled."

"I didn't."

Did I?

Zora shot me the Varisian evil eye, which looks kind of like the tines, only low and backward. I got the feeling she fancied me a little less. She shouted at her crew to keep well away from the Ustalavic shore.

We'd been hugging the eastern bank ever since we got clear of Razmiran. Even so, the first night we spent alongside Ustalav, these mooks began showing up. They just stood there watching us. They hadn't tried anything.

So far.

The boss studied my face like a page in a book.

"So what if I did growl? You hate these Anaphexis jerks as much as I do. Aren't they pretty much the evil opposite of your little club?"

"The goals of the Anaphexis are indeed the antithesis of the Society's," he said. "And please, for the thousandth time, I ask you to cease referring to the Pathfinder Society as my 'little club.'"

"Aren't you still on the outs with them? Or did that last letter change your mind?"

The boss touched his coat pocket. He had at least three different letters there, two of them from queens, all of them asking for the same favor. "I have yet to decide, but that is beside the point. The Anaphexis merely remind us of our oath."

"*Your* oath. I never promised those mooks nothing."

"The word of a count of Cheliax binds both him and his—"

"Don't say 'servant.' Don't say 'henchman.'"

"You know perfectly well I never refer to you by those terms. I was about to say 'friend.'"

"Yeah, yeah."

"In any event, you know I made that agreement for your sake as much as my own. More so, in fact."

He had me there. One look at me, most folks realize my family tree has roots in Hell. The Anaphexis, these killers of knowledge, they knew my big secret: my family tree also has roots running under the throne of Ustalav.

A light came up where we'd seen the Anaphexis twerp. He waved a torch over his head. Like his buddies on the previous nights, he wanted to make sure we saw him.

We got the message, all right. If we broke the deal and landed on the Ustalav side, it meant trouble for my people: the wolves, the witch, and the freaks.

I felt the copper coin I wore around my neck. Scratched and half-melted, the face stamped on one side did kind of resemble me if you were looking for a family resemblance. A dozen times I almost lost the coin, but somehow it always turned up. It was damned near the only thing I still had since the last time I was in Ustalav. Well, that and the starknife.

The starknife hung from my hip. Its double-edged blades shot out at compass angles from a ring around the grip. I'd learned to throw it all right, but it never seemed like something I ought to bloody. Most of the time I kept it with my pack. Since we'd gotten close to Ustalav, I'd hung it from my waist for I don't know why.

Maybe I thought I'd see the woman who gave it to me, and she'd see that I'd hung on to it. I kissed my thumb and drew the wings of Desna on my heart.

Are you there, girl? You standing there, hidden on the black shore, waiting for me? I've lugged this promise around a thousand miles. Sometimes I think it's getting heavier, but tonight it feels—

The boss coughed.

I'd been talking out loud. That was worse than growling.

"Why, Radovan," he said. "You are a poet."

My blood turned cold. "You take that back right now."

"Whatever for? I meant it only as a compliment."

"You take it back, or I will beat your ass right here in front of the gods and everybody."

He started to laugh, but then he saw my eyes. One thing we have in common, he's only half human, too. His elf blood lets him see plenty good after dusk. What he saw in my pretty yellow eyes sobered him up.

"Very well, you are nothing like a poet. Please permit me to withdraw my careless and utterly unfounded inference to the contrary. Your untarnished reputation deserves not the least such blemish, and I implore you to forgive my hasty and misinformed—"

"All right, all right! Forget it."

He raised an eyebrow to let me know he'd humored me.

Feeling like a dope, I took another peek through the spyglass. On the shore, the cultist waved the torch overhead. In the firelight, I could make out the dried-blood color of his cloak. I saw the lumps of his black mask. The boss said Anaphexis assassins made those masks out of the flayed faces of their first five victims.

As the cultist watched us watching him, a dark shape moved in the woods behind him. Its eyes reflected the torchlight.

"Hey!"

"What is it?" The boss reached for the spyglass, but I shrugged him off, careful not to give him a spur in the heart. I wasn't really going to rough him up, poet talk or not. At least, I was pretty sure I wasn't.

Out of the shadows, a black wolf jumped the Anaphexis guy. It knocked him down and tore a hunk out of his middle. He drew a blade, but another wolf ran in to clamp its jaws around his wrist. The first wolf went for his throat as another two melted out of the woods to join the feast.

A second later, we heard the scream. Just the one, and then all we could hear was the sound of waves lapping around the barge.

"Tell me what you see," said the boss.

"Looks like our enemies ain't the only ones watching us tonight. We got some friends out there."

Three wolves tore the body to pieces while the first one stepped away. It stood up on its hind legs, shifting gradually into a familiar figure.

I knew that figure.

She picked up the guy's torch and let its light show off her body. The flame turned her skin to gold. A moment later, she brushed back her long black hair to make sure I had a good view.

It was a real good view.

"That's my girl." This time I knew I was muttering out loud.

"The witch?"

"The harrower. She's sending us a message."

"Let me see."

I shrugged him off again. "She ain't decent. I wouldn't want you to be scandalized. She's got company, though. Three of them. Can't tell which ones unless they shed their skins."

"Please tell me they didn't kill the Anaphexis agent."

"Well . . ."

He sighed.

"If it makes you feel any better, it don't look like they're leaving any evidence."

"Let us pray not. Their master is not a fool, but it's possible he will attribute the loss of one agent to mishap. What is she saying?"

He must have thought she'd learned his Pathfinder hand signs or something, but her message was a lot simpler. "She misses me."

"Malena does?"

"All the girls miss me, boss. You know that."

"No doubt they, too, have been dealing with the encroachment of the horde."

That was the thing, the reason we weren't going home just yet.

The demons.

All winter, fiends kept popping up all across Elfland—which the boss insists I call Kyonin, but my way's funnier. At first we thought it was fallout from our caper in the Fierani Forest, but they weren't coming from the Witchbole. They were showing up all across the Inner Sea, and they were all coming from the one place they were supposed to be stuck: the Worldwound.

The first summons came from Telandia, Queen of Kyonin, Wearer of the Viridian Crown, High Protector something something—I forget the rest. On account of we did her a good turn, she asked us to check out why these demons were pouring out all over the world. The boss was inclined to help, seeing as she'd done him some good turns, too. Anyway, it never hurts to have the queen of the elves owe you a favor.

The elves put us on a riverboat, along with the Red Carriage and the boss's fancy new horses. They took us up the West Sellen between Razmiran and the River Kingdoms. Those guys were having their own demon troubles.

Unlike some of the river towns we'd passed, the people in a city called Tymon weren't running from the fiends. They unleashed their gladiators on them. Those demons they didn't kill they enslaved for the arena. That didn't seem like the smartest idea, but it stopped them breaking up the joint.

Tymon was also where the boss's mail caught up to him. He'd already had a few magic messages from Queen Abrogail's sorcerers back home in Cheliax, as well as from some wizard with the Decemvirate, his little club's inner circle. I half expected him to rip up their note, but the Pathfinder letter was the one that got his attention, on account of they used the magic word: "book."

While everybody around the Inner Sea wanted to know what had gone wrong at the Worldwound, the Decemvirate had an idea how to sort it out. Whoever it'd been that first opened the door to the Abyss a hundred years ago did their homework first. That included something called the *Lexicon of Paradox*.

The boss knew the title. It was some kind of famous evil book, like the *Lacuna Codex* we'd found and lost and found and lost again. Once the boss knew the Pathfinders were interested, he wanted to be the one who found it. Whether he planned to deliver it to Elfland, Cheliax, or the Pathfinders' headquarters in Absalom was anybody's guess. I had a feeling what he really wanted was to put it in his own library back at Greensteeples. That didn't seem too smart of an idea, either, but he's the boss.

The elves left us in Tymon, where we hired Zora Gorcha. Her crew included men from both Ustalav and the River Kingdoms—but no Razmirans, those lunatics who called their king a god.

I liked having the Ustalavs on the boat. Even though I was born and bred Chelish, the human part of my blood was all Ustalavic, far as I knew. It was about time I brushed up my Varisian, too. I'd been forgetting all the best curses and getting bored of the ones I remembered.

"Captain!"

One of the sailors pointed up at the southern sky. Zora yelled at her sailors to finish setting torches along the gunwales. I gave the boss the spyglass before he could ask for it. "Is it him?"

The boss fiddled with the spyglass until he got it in focus. His hand dropped to the hilt of the Shadowless Sword. A princess from the other side of the world gave that to him. No lie.

He drew it an inch out of the scabbard, letting its magic pierce any illusions. When he stood up a little straighter, I knew the answer before he said the name: "Kasiya."

"That guy don't know when to quit."

The boss snapped the spyglass shut and put it in the pocket of his long coat. Like my new leathers, it was elf-made but in the Chelish style.

The horses snapped and stirred. During the river voyage, they'd kept quiet as long as I kept my distance. With Kasiya on his way, they sensed something wickeder than me.

From the sky came the sound of barking dogs. Arni grumbled to hear it. The ruff of his neck went up.

Zora ordered her men to double-double-up. A pikeman joined each of the sailors poling the boat upriver. A third man hustled over to each pair with a covered fire pot. A fourth lowered buckets into the river and drew them back onto deck.

The little dot in the sky became a blob. I could start making out details.

A pack of long-legged dogs flew through the sky. They pulled a chariot driven by Prince Kasiya, the Osirian vampire.

I'd seen the gold-masked creep a couple times since Kyonin, and the boss knew him from way back. Kasiya's cloak floated up behind him. He shook a javelin that crackled with red lightning.

Something hung off the sides of his chariot. Whatever it was was heavy, because each time he shifted his weight the whole thing tilted one way or the other.

As they got closer, I saw the four other guys hanging off the sides. It was hard to make out details, but there was no mistaking their pale skin, clawed fingers, and red eyes.

Kasiya had been busy making little vampires.

I pointed. "Boss—"

"I saw them." He handed me his loop of garlic and drew the Shadowless Sword.

"You sure about this?"

"Let Arnisant defend the horses," he said. He sent the wolfhound toward the Red Carriage while he moved toward the side of the barge nearest the chariot. "You support the crew. Drive any boarders toward me."

"Got it." He shot me a look. I must have had a tone. "I said I got it. It's just I'm used to being the mayhem."

The boss smiled at that. We'd been a couple years in the field, and he was becoming more and more a regular guy. Or maybe he'd always been one, and it was just showing more since we'd been away from Egorian and all his fancy peers.

One of the passengers dropped from the chariot. Kasiya's vampire minion howled as he saw he was going to miss the barge by thirty yards. He plunged into the river. A moment later, he came up screaming, flesh sloughing off his arm. He went down again, water boiling where he'd been.

"Idiot," the boss spat. "Even his spawn are susceptible to running water." Then he looked at me and added, "But Kasiya is no less dangerous for his stupidity. Do not allow any of them to touch you."

"Check." I pulled the big knife from the spine of my new jacket.

He shook his head at the blade. "I wish you would learn to use a sword or a spear—anything with reach."

I shrugged. "What can I say? Old dog."

"Try the scrolls."

"Boss, you know I can't—"

"Just try one before they close with us."

I sighed. No matter how often I tried using the flippy scrolls, they never worked for me—except for the one time. But that was before I *knew* they weren't supposed to work for me.

That was the problem, the boss said. It worked when I didn't know better, so I must have had a knack. The problem was that the more I thought I couldn't use the riffle scrolls, the less chance I could make them work.

That's what you call a paradox.

Before I could dig a scroll out of my jacket, I saw a flicker of light above us. "Hey, look out!"

A tiny red flame shot down from Kasiya's javelin. It got bigger as it got closer.

The boss plucked a riffle scroll from the bandolier beneath his coat. It was a stack of paper strips the size of my thumb, one end shut with a brass brad. The boss pressed his thumb against the other end, pulling back the edges to let the pages snap free one after the next. Each page glimmered for an instant, the glow of one blending into the next to form fragments of arcane symbols. Riffled like that, the pages cast a spell.

The boss's magic shot up at Kasiya's fireball, barely visible even to my devil eyes. When the spells met, the fireball flickered and vanished with a whoosh.

The rest of Kasiya's vampire slaves flew down at us. Not "flew" flew. More like "fell screaming" flew.

"Brace yourself, boys!" I said it again in Varisian, even though all the Ustalavs spoke Taldane better than I spoke their language. Speaking Varisian made me feel more like a vampire-slayer.

One of the vamps hit the deck, rolling until its claws clung to the planks. It crouched for a second, hissing. Its eyes fixed on one of the pikemen, a fat, bearded

Ustalav. The man's jowls went slack. He pulled the ring of garlic off his neck and threw it over the side before walking toward the vampire.

I ran in, sliding to take out the fat man's legs. He fell beside me, stunned but getting mad when he realized I'd knocked him down. There was no talking to him since the vampire put the whammy on his mind. I headbutted him. It took two shots to knock him out, and was I going to regret that later. I dropped the extra garlic rope around his neck to make him bite-proof.

Kasiya's vampire slave hissed at me, lashing out now and then to keep the other sailors at bay but still unwilling to get close to the garlic. I got to my feet and shot it the tines.

That's one Chelish gesture that never needs translating. The vampire showed me its teeth.

I showed it mine.

The vampire damn near swallowed its tongue.

"All right, boys," I began. I wanted to drive this mook toward the boss, but one of the sailors had a different idea. He swung his fire pot, but the vamp leaped right over him. It landed neat as a cat on the gunwales.

From the clothes I figured the vamp had been a man of the River Kingdoms. Death grayed its face and hollowed its cheeks. Its nails had grown dark and ragged. The thing lashed out at the sailor.

I slapped my arm, filling my hand with darts from the secret pockets in my sleeves. I flung them hard. Two struck deep into the vamp's face. The third went flying past, into the river.

Snarling, the vampire plucked one out of its cheek and made a show of licking off its own half-congealed blood.

The nearest sailor broke his pole across the vampire's neck, but the monster hung on to the gunwales.

I looked to either side. The boss had just snapped another scroll at Kasiya, whose chariot was about to fly right over the barge. Two pikemen had one of the other vamps pinned to the deck. The third vamp was nowhere in sight.

The horses screamed.

Another vamp—this one a patchy-bearded dwarf— came scrambling out from beneath the Red Carriage, Arni on its heels. Maybe the garlic collar helped, but I had to think anything with half a brain would run from the big wolfhound. Arni was so big he could barely squeeze under the carriage as he chased his prey.

I tumbled forward and kicked the feet out from under the former dwarf. The creature's momentum threw it across the deck to slide toward the boss, who finished snapping another scroll straight up as the chariot passed overhead. Lightning crackled above us, but none of it touched the boat.

The dwarf vamp grabbed the boss's ankle.

I winced to see it. A vampire's touch was supposed to suck the life right out of you. The boss said that wouldn't happen to him, but I wasn't so sure.

The boss looked down like he'd stepped in something nasty. All casual, he thrust the point of his sword three times into the dwarf's head before turning his attention back to the sky, where Kasiya's chariot circled back toward the barge.

The vampire dwarf rolled away, mostly dead. Or dead again. Deaderer. There's got to be a word. I'd ask the boss later.

A couple of sailors smashed their fire pots against the thing. The bucket brigade waited for the vamp to stop struggling before dousing the flames. They timed it just right. The river water hit the burning thing just in time to turn its ashy skin to mud on the deck.

The same thing was happening with the vampire skewered by the other pikemen. Their buddies lit up the monster, and they held it out over the water until its screams became just the sound of its last fatty bits sizzling away. Then they dunked the charred remains into the river. The water boiled more from the unholy flesh than from the heat.

The rest of the sailors were still playing tag with the vampire who'd taken the darts. The garlic wasn't doing the trick anymore. The vamp had ripped the necklace off one sailor and grabbed another one by the throat. The sailor's face withered before our eyes.

I remembered the boss's warning: You don't want those things touching you.

I ran two steps, jumped, and came down with all my weight on the vamp's knee. The impact felt like kicking a pile of rocks, but it annoyed the thing enough that it let go of the sailor and came for me.

The vamp had already picked my other dart out of its face, leaving only a black sliver of a wound. You had to kill these guys fast, or they just got back up.

"Finish that one," said the boss. He ran past us, snapping off scroll after scroll as Kasiya's chariot flew by again. I kept one eye on the boss while backing away from the vamp. These things have some wicked quickness.

The boss's first scroll sent bolts of silver at Kasiya, but they splattered like raindrops against an invisible globe. The second scroll didn't seem to do anything except cover that magic shield with a web of white light before vanishing. The third was a fireball. I expected to see it fail as it hit Kasiya's magic barrier.

Instead, it exploded.

The chariot dogs fell in all directions as the chariot drew a smoking arc above the river. Kasiya and his fancy little cart made it to the Ustalav bank before crashing into the woods.

"Good job, boss!"

Just then I remembered the riffle scroll the boss told me to use.

The sailors stabbed at the vamp with their pikes, but it dodged them and came for me. It hammered a careless sailor to the deck as I got my thumb on the scroll's edge. I could smell its decaying breath as I snapped the pages free. The scroll tingled against my thumb, and a little cloud of dust blew into the vampire's face.

The vamp flinched, maybe thinking it would burst into flames or start choking on poison.

But there was nothing. I hadn't cast a spell. I'd only blown paper dust in its face.

The vamp hit me straight in the chest, hard as a mule's kick—and I know what I'm talking about when I say that.

The blow threw me back into a couple other guys. We hit the gunwales tangled together. We all moaned, but when I tried to get up I really felt it, like the vamp had put a hole right through me.

Now I can take a punch. Desna knows I've taken plenty before. This one knocked more than the wind out of me. I half expected to hear my heart splash into the river behind us.

Out of the corner of my eye, I saw the gray blur of Arni racing toward the vamp.

"No!" I tried calling him off, but he didn't listen. He don't like seeing me or the boss get hit.

"Arnisant, down!" At the sound of his master's voice, the wolfhound flattened his body on the deck.

A whooping sound cut through the air. A whirling silver flash passed through the vamp's neck. Black-red spray covered the deck between the monster and me. Its head tumbled off and slid toward me through the gore. Startled eyes looked up at me where it came to a rest between my knees. Its body collapsed a second later.

The Shadowless Sword flew back to the boss. He caught it with a casual gesture. As the hilt touched his palm, I saw a glimmer of magic. He'd done some spell I'd never seen before. Maybe he'd been doing more than "diplomacy" with Kyonin's other queen last winter, and the scaly old gal had taught him a few new tricks. Probably she'd just let him loose in the library, but I can dream, can't I?

He wiped the blood on the cloth hanging from his scabbard before putting the sword away. I saw a gleam in his eye. He was proud of his stunt. Couldn't blame him for that. It was a pretty slick move.

The crewmen were helping each other stand up. One or two were hurt pretty bad, but everybody was alive. That was something that didn't happen to us all the time. Desna smiled.

Zora Gorcha offered me a hand up. Behind her, some of her crew were waking the other guy a vamp shook by the throat. He looked thin and gray, but he was alive, with no bite marks anywhere I could see.

When she saw that all her men had survived and her boat wasn't on fire, Zora grabbed my face and planted a garlicky smooch on my lips. My knees went all weak, but not from the kiss. Not even from the garlic.

I'd taken one hell of a hit from that vamp.

"The Count Jeggare, I am thinking he saved your life." Zora laughed as she looked me up and down. "Tell me again, Radovan, which of you is bodyguard?"

Chapter Three
The Splinter

Varian

It's a foot of mud out there. The least you could do is get me a phony pony." Radovan lounged in my accustomed place on the rear bench, while I sat on the forward seat. Even inside the carriage, it was best for him to remain as far as possible from the horses while our hirelings released them from their harnesses.

"Conjure one yourself." I pushed four riffle scrolls across the polished surface of the map table.

"Come on, boss. Last time I gave myself hooves, and that just ain't right." Beneath the table, Arnisant whined. "See? Arni agrees with me."

"You will have fewer mishaps the more you focus your attention on the desired effect. And I know perfectly well that you nudged Arnisant under the table."

"Poke my little buddy to win an argument? Never!" Radovan shifted guiltily in his seat.

"Little? If you continue to overfeed him, he will soon be larger than you." Beneath the table, Arnisant settled his heavy head on my foot. Seeing the dog loom over a pair of Ustalavic wolfhounds in Tymon assured me that he was exceptionally tall even for his enormous breed, but Radovan had spoiled him while awaiting my return to Riverspire in Kyonin. If he had devoted as much energy to exercising the dog as he had to chasing elven women, Arnisant would have been slim as a whippet. "Also, this is not an argument."

"I'm no wizard."

"Indeed not. That is what makes your gift so precious. We should have begun testing far sooner." For that omission I blamed myself, but we had enjoyed precious little time for reflection since leaving Egorian two years earlier. In fact, I thought, enough time had passed that I might safely return, if not for recent diversions and obligations.

"Come on, boss. I could use a break from these tests." He pushed up the sleeve of his new dark leather jacket. I felt a pang of guilt to see the wounds on the coppery skin of his forearm.

"Very well." Important as they were, I was loath to continue the painful experiments without a better understanding of his unique condition.

Logic suggested that only the sign for the devil known as Fell Viridio would currently have an effect. From his scorpionlike attributes, I surmised poison would be his sigil, but topical applications had resulted in no atypical reaction.

The problem might have been dosage. I had begun to suspect that only a fatal application of the activating agent would release the devils who had over the course of centuries designed Radovan's bloodline to produce their portal to our world. "We shall suspend our experiments until such time as we can enlist a healer to stand ready," I said. "But you have nothing to lose from activating a riffle scroll."

"Hooves."

"A fleeting inconvenience in the pursuit of an invaluable advantage."

"I loved those boots."

"Perhaps you fail to appreciate how rare it is for someone untrained in the arcane arts to wield this ability. As you yourself might put it, you have a knack." It was almost the truth. To hear Radovan tell it, his attempts with the riffle scrolls were as likely to produce bizarre unintended effects as they were to succeed. Unless he was exaggerating—always likely when he spoke of women or his own misfortunes—he was proving every bit as unlucky as he was lucky.

"Yeah? Like your 'knack' for letting your sword fly around on its own?"

"Ah, that." I thought of how my last fencing master would have admonished me for throwing my weapon. Vencarlo Orsini was the epitome of tradition, and he had demonstrated only scorn for combining spells with swordplay. "It is a skill I learned—in theory, anyway—at the Acadamae. I assumed I could never employ it because of my . . . Well, my particular disability."

"The puking."

"Not to put too fine a point on it, but yes. Yet as you can see from my example, persistence has its rewards." Radovan's resistance to studying his own condition puzzled me. At over three times his age, I was surely the proverbial old dog, not he, yet I had never lost my appetite for knowledge. "The matter at hand is not my use of an apprentice's trick, but your knack for activating my riffle scrolls."

"I think that vampire knocked the knack right out of me." He rubbed his chest. It was unlike Radovan to complain of a physical injury, even one so profound as the enervating touch of a vampire. However, I had to allow that I had noticed a general malaise about him since his wound. "Boss, we should have gone after your old pal."

"Kasiya was never a friend, not even in life. And nothing would please me more than reducing him to ashes, but not at the cost of drawing down the full wrath of the Anaphexis."

"We could beat the hell out of those mooks."

"Do not be so certain. Besides, should they reveal the secret of your ancestry, Prince Aduard would have your head to eliminate even the remotest possibility that you could mount a challenge to his claim. In any event, this fanciful speculation is moot if we do not succeed in our present mission."

"So there's no time to waste." He pushed the scrolls back across the table, his little smile suggesting he thought he had won an argument. "You get me a pony."

"Each of these scrolls represents a chance for you to do it yourself. Are you not always saying Lady Luck smiles on you?" I pushed them back, thinking again that as often as Radovan used his favorite oath, "Desna smiles," he just as often cried—

"Desna weeps! I've tried plenty. You got to do it for me."

"No. If you cannot do it yourself, you can trudge through the mud to the Looter's Market."

Radovan picked up a scroll and held it between his fingers and palm, just as he had seen me do hundreds of times before. He leaned back on the carriage seat and eyed me skeptically. "You've got another one in your pocket, don't you? When these don't work, you'll set me up, right?"

I shook my head.

"All right, here goes nothing." He put his thumb on the edge of one of the scrolls.

"Not in here!" I lunged from my seat, hand upon the carriage door, my heart pounding at the prospect of a phantom horse suddenly appearing inside the carriage.

Radovan laughed. "You should see the look on your face."

I composed myself. "Very amusing."

"When I get to the market, you want I should go ahead and hire the ones I like?" My reaction to his prank had obviously lifted his spirits.

"As many as eight, plus a scout if you can find one."

"All right." Radovan sniffed one riffle scroll while securing the others in pockets concealed in his jacket. "Could be a while, if I have to walk."

"I expect to see you riding back before dusk."

"Yeah, yeah." Before leaving the carriage, Radovan retrieved his curved Chelish blade from the table and snapped it securely into the sheath hidden in the spine of his jacket. The grip hung down like the stub of a tail. Much as he liked to boast that he lacked the most common features of typical hellspawn—horns and a tail—Radovan took a perverse delight in drawing attention to his infernal heritage through his particular fashion sense.

After Radovan's departure, I lifted the curtain to peer out at him. He took shelter beneath the dripping eaves of the stable and squinted at the far end, where my men tended to the six enormous bay horses that had drawn the Red Carriage to the village of Gundrun. They squealed at Radovan's scent, hating him on sight as all equines do.

Radovan responded with his favorite vulgar gesture, index and least fingers extended on either side of his throat: the tines. He stuck out his long tongue for good measure, an addition that always caused me to wince in distaste.

He looked around to ensure no one else was watching him. Gritting his teeth, he pointed the scroll at an open space and thumbed the edge.

The pages snapped open, but no glamour appeared. He summoned no phantom steed.

Radovan pried open the scroll. Even through the carriage window, I could see the pages were now blank. While he had failed to summon a mount, he had expended the scroll's magic, even if obviously not in the manner intended. That much was promising.

Suddenly he turned to look directly at me, and I spied the result of his magical malfunction: his front teeth, unappealing at the best of times, had grown thick and square as a horse's.

Smothering my unbidden laughter, I dropped the curtain too late.

"I can't do it with you watching!" he shouted. His oversized horse teeth caused him a ridiculous speech impediment. As he recognized his condition, he brayed, "Desna weeps!"

Taking my satchel, I exited the other side of the Red Carriage with Arnisant at my heel.

Across from the stable stood a half-collapsed inn, the ragged remains of its upper floor shored up with crude repairs. Above the entrance hung a rack of antlers, now broken to stubs and covered in blue-gray mold. We had heard the tale of the Gilded Antlers at Clefthorn Lodge. Since demons demolished most of the upper floor decades ago, the people of Gundrun called their lone tavern the Splinter.

A loud curse from the stables suggested that Radovan's second attempt to conjure a phantom steed was no more successful than his first. I bent to peer under the carriage, only to see him glaring back at me. His teeth were back to normal, but he sucked at his fingers as the flaming ruin of the second riffle scroll sizzled on the damp ground.

"Quit watching, I told you!"

Arnisant and I retreated into the Splinter.

The tavern smelled of wood smoke, roast boar, sweet beer, spiced mead, and sweat. At our appearance, the chatter of the common room subsided except for the strains of a harp and a husky female voice trailing off in her song. The residents of the tavern looked up as we entered.

They were predominantly Kellids, a wind-burned people with dark hair and eyes the color of clear skies and old steel. They wore furs cinched with leather harnesses, although a few of the men went bare-chested to show off tattoos or war paint. Some of the women appeared equally formidable: tall, lean, and muscular. None sat more than an arm's length away from a dagger on the table or an axe leaning against the wall.

For the passage from the river to Gundrun, I had enlisted only men from the River Kingdoms, knowing the resentment Sarkorians reserved for Ustalavs, whom they still cursed for the Bloodwater Betrayals. Radovan knew not to mention his human heritage in Gundrun, although I feared his infernal features would inspire even more fear and hatred.

I need not have worried. So close to the Worldwound, one naturally expects to see a few of the demonblooded, but I was surprised to see them mingling so casually with the untainted humans. One man with insect eyes might have been fully half demon. Surreptitiously drawing the Shadowless Sword an inch from its scabbard, I confirmed that neither he nor any of the other guests lay under the guise of an illusion.

I released the sword as the one-armed proprietor emerged from behind his bar to greet me. He made a fair approximation of a Chelish bow, evoking chuckles from his regulars. "Welcome to my humble establishment, Your Excellency. My name is Whalt, and I'm at your service. One word of caution: even one-handed, I can still out-pour and outdrink any barkeep in Gundrun."

Some of the tavern patrons laughed gamely at his remark. For my benefit, the harper called out the obvious punch line: "That's because you're the *only* barkeep in Gundrun!"

Whalt grinned, exposing large yellowed teeth. His courtesy seemed sincere enough, and he had troubled himself to learn the correct manner in which to address a count of Cheliax. A wreath of gray-white hair surrounded his spotted pate, and his blue-gray eyes seemed both keen and friendly. On the wall behind the bar I noticed a sundered shield, a semicircular absence suggesting that a large fiend had bitten through its steel-reinforced wood. The bite mark matched the point at which Whalt's arm had been severed. I recognized its pattern from all-too-recent firsthand observation of a particularly loathsome fiend.

"Is it Whalt the barkeep?" I said. "Or Whalt the slayer of swamp demons?"

He grimaced in appreciation of my deduction. "That it was, a swamp demon exactly. Kala keeps promising to make me a song about it one day. For that clever guess, I'll buy your first drink myself. But no, I didn't slay the one that took my arm. For all I know, it's still swimming along the West Sellen, choking on my strong left hand."

"You fought at Drezen."

Whalt blinked. "You know your Sarkorian history, Excellency. But one free drink is all you'll have from me."

"I shall buy the drinks tonight. A round for the house." The patrons raised a hue and toasted me with tankards the size of helms. Their cheer presented as good an opportunity as I could have wished for my inquiry. "And a purse of gold to the man who can guide me into Storasta."

The cheers faltered, and the patrons turned away. The harper looked at me a moment, then plucked the strings and began chanting "The Song of Sarkoris."

I knew the mournful epic all too well. My opinion of the piece must have shown on my face, for Whalt chuckled.

"Are you still wanting to buy that round?"

"Yes, but only if Kala changes the tune." The attentive musician cocked her head. The scars on her face suggested she knew battles through more than their songs. "Play me 'The Ballad of Prince Zhakar.'"

"Everyone dies in that one, too, Your Excellency."

"But they die bravely, and it has a better melody." I tossed her a coin. She caught it neatly and changed her tune.

I indicated a vacant table near a shuttered window. "Bring a platter of that roast boar, along with a goblet of your best red wine. Also a plate of whatever wholesome vegetables you have. I shall rest here to await a message from Clanliege Martolls Clefthorn."

"Ah," said Whalt. "In that case, you might prefer to order the bottle."

I raised an eyebrow.

"Martolls never even saw a hurry from a distance. You'll be a long time waiting." He returned to his bar.

I took the seat nearest the window and opened the shutter to peek out. The drivers had finished stabling the horses. One stood guard beside the carriage while the others entered the tavern for their respite. I saw no sign of Radovan. If he had left hoofprints behind, whether from a phantom steed or a riffle-scroll mishap, the rain had already churned them away.

Arnisant sat on the floor beside me as I set out the contents of my satchel. I opened my maps of Sarkoris, both those from before the opening of the Worldwound—not coincidentally at the moment of the great god Aroden's death—and those created by crusaders and Pathfinders over the past century. Soon I would add my own observations to the ever-changing cartography of the land.

After opening my journal to resume my personal chronicle, I began to reach for my writing kit but paused. Instead I removed the four letters from my coat pocket and laid them before me in order of precedence.

The first bore the Imperial Seal of Cheliax stamped in crimson wax. To Her Infernal Majestrix, Abrogail II, I owed my ultimate allegiance. The message from her counselors commanded me to search the ruins of Lost Sarkoris for the *Lexicon of Paradox*. Since the wards confining the demons to the Worldwound had failed, the queen's sorcerers hoped the dire rituals within the *Lexicon* would prove potent against the inevitable encroachment of the Abyss on the borders of the Empire. In the meantime, the decimation of the lands between Cheliax and the Worldwound would dilute the strength of the horde and simultaneously improve the Empire's relative strength.

The message from Kyonin arrived on pale green parchment and bore the seals of both Queen Telandia and her cousin, Prince Amarandlon. No doubt she had forced him to act as her clerk as a punishment. Since few beings in the world are more subtle—or more vengeful—than an elf lord, I considered the message with the utmost skepticism.

The prince wrote that Telandia too desired the *Lexicon*, although his subtler message was that the elf queen should be satisfied with a mere facsimile of the book. Copying the *Lexicon* was a greater favor than the queen might have realized, since it was believed that even perusing the dread tome's contents could shatter a reader's sanity. I wondered whether Amarandlon had taken the liberty of adding that suggestion himself.

Despite my indeterminate status in the Pathfinder Society, the Decemvirate had also sent me a message, this one sealed with a black ribbon. The letter's arrival in Tymon suggested that the Ten chose to contact me after learning that I had already been dispatched by Queens Abrogail and Telandia. My anonymous correspondent even went so far as to address me as "venture-captain," although the tone of the "request" left no doubt that the title was an enticement rather than an assurance of reinstatement.

The most curious of the missives was the fourth letter, inscribed with silver ink on black paper, sealed with the ankh of the Silver Crusade. Venture-Captain Ollysta Zadrian had withdrawn from the Pathfinders to create a faction embracing the essential ideals of the Society with the addition of Zadrian's zealous worship of Sarenrae. Her letter was the most unexpected.

> *My Esteemed Colleague, Venture-Captain Count Varian Jeggare,*
>
> *You shall, I pray, forgive the brevity and directness of my appeal. With the rupture of the wards surrounding the Worldwound, time is more precious than ever.*
>
> *Whilst we have seldom found ourselves in a position to cooperate, I sense that you and I share a desire that our efforts should benefit not only our former Society but all the people of Avistan.*
>
> *By now you have received various requests for assistance in recovering a particular lost tome. If you should locate this* Lexicon of Paradox, *I implore you to deliver it to Crusader Queen Galfrey of Mendev. Her conjurers are best poised to employ the powers of this depraved tome against the forces of chaos.*
>
> > *By the light of the Dawnflower,*
> > *Ollystra Zadrian*

As I closed the letter, Whalt returned. He set before me a silver chalice that appeared recently polished. From beneath his injured arm he plucked a bottle of wine and displayed it as if presenting a great treasure. In truth, while its faded label designated a good Taldan house, the year had been a rather poor one, the grapes suffering from blight.

While Whalt steadied the bottle with his injured arm and drew the cork, a startlingly pretty barmaid brought the meat, along with a platter of fresh bread, cheese, and berries. Her clothes were worn but far too fine for a servant, and fit her lithe figure so perfectly that there could be no question that they had been tailored. I discerned in her curtsey, and by the simple but elegant diadem upon her brow, that she had been raised among nobility, not beneath them.

As the barmaid withdrew to the kitchen, Whalt anticipated my unspoken question.

"Shal's new," said Whalt. "A little shy. Near as I can figure, demons caught her group. She took shelter in the Riversoar ruins. Eventually she got hungry enough to come begging. As you can see, I needed an extra hand."

He looked to me for a laugh, but Shal had aroused my curiosity. "Riversoar was the Clanliege before Martolls Clefthorn, yes?"

"That's right." Whalt's cheer vanished, and he withdrew with a bow. "Enjoy the wine, Your Excellency."

Clearly he wished to avoid discussing the history of the Riversoars, whose razed clanhold we had spied in rain-dimmed silhouette upon our arrival.

I dropped a thick slice of pork to the floor. Arnisant looked to me for permission even as drool began streaming from his jaws. After a moment, I gave Arnisant the signal to eat and heard the savage sounds of his devouring the meat.

I closed my eyes to search my memory library for references to the Riversoar clan.

All I found were passing references to its fall, presumably at the hands of demons. Yet those demons had allowed Gundrun to survive. How had the Riversoars attracted their ire and not the town?

While he had received us hospitably enough, Clanliege Martolls Clefthorn had promised us nothing in return for our gifts of Druma steel and Cullerton wool. Radovan and I had spent hours within his gloomy wooden fortress, the icons of a dozen gods glowering from the walls, while Martolls recited a litany of past glories of which even his liegemen appeared skeptical. When he finally allowed me to make my request for aid, he barely pretended to entertain the notion before directing us to seek our meals at the Splinter.

Without Clefthorn's aid, we would need to recruit our own warriors. Perhaps the best we could hope was that Clefthorn would allow us to use Gundrun as a base of operations.

Arnisant made a querulous sound. Even with his haunches on the floor, his head rose higher than my shoulder. He looked up.

Above us, the ceiling that once provided a floor for the second story had been torn away. Burns and claw marks were still visible on the remaining planks. Crude repairs provided a new roof less than five feet above the naked beams. On one of those beams crouched a young woman.

She might have been fifteen or twenty-five, for the blue stripe painted across her eyes shrouded her age even more than the shadows. Her shaggy black mane blended into the wolf pelt over her shoulders, its fur still glistening from the rain.

Annoyed at the intrusion, I turned to signal Whalt. He was nowhere in sight, nor was the winsome Shal.

Arnisant woofed a warning, but I too had sensed the movement from above. No sooner had my hand touched the Shadowless Sword than the strange woman dropped from her perch into the seat before me. Radovan would have admired her nimble maneuver.

"You sent your man to the Looter's Market for a guide." The young woman's voice was girlish, but she spoke with the confidence of experience. "He won't find one there."

"But you know of one."

"You're talking to her. Alase Brinz-Widowknife. You haven't heard of me because you went to the Clefthorns. Ask anyone else in Gundrun. You'll like what you hear."

"Have you been to Storasta?"

She whistled low and drank directly from my wine bottle. I drew a deep breath to calm my irritation as she wiped her mouth with the back of her hand. Her fingers were rough and calloused. "No one has ever asked to go there."

"So you cannot do it?"

"I didn't say that. I've slipped in once or twice. The place is full of demons. And worse."

"Worse than demons?"

She peered into the empty bottle as if it were a spyglass. "Maybe you ought to get another one of these, and we'll talk about my fee."

While her insolence annoyed me, something about her jutting chin reminded me of my first encounters with Radovan. Intuition told me they would either get on well or else hate each other on sight. I wanted to see which.

"First, tell me what you know of the demon lord Deskari and the Abyssal horde."

"All there is to know."

"How?"

"Me, I'm the last of the Widowknife god callers. My uncle passed down all the stories. He had them from his mother, she from her aunt, and so on all the way back before the time of Deskari—the first time of Deskari. My ancestors fought beside Aroden when he was still a man."

I knew the self-proclaimed "god callers" of Sarkoris were actually summoners, specialists in the arcane art of drawing beings from other planes into our own world. With one particular being, known as an eidolon, a summoner formed a special bond similar to that between wizard and familiar. As the summoner grew in knowledge, so did her eidolon grow more powerful. Thus I could well imagine how a primitive culture like the Sarkorians' might mistake eidolons for gods.

It remained to be seen whether Alase Brinz-Widowknife was a knowledgeable summoner.

"One of the Three was also a god caller. What was his name?"

"Opon, but before the end he figured his mistake." She glanced at the open mouth of my satchel and saw the arcane runes on the spine of my grimoire. "Another of the Three was a wizard."

"He tried with Opon to close the gate. His name was Wivver Noclan." I replied before the impertinence of her turning the questions back on me struck home.

"That's right, Wivver had no clan before or after they opened up the first little pinprick into the Rasping Rifts. Deskari whispered through that little spot, but the men knew they'd done a mighty wrong. They tried to close the hole. They might have done it too, if not for the witch."

"Areelu Vorlesh," I said.

"I seen her, you know. Not close, but across the red river at Undarin."

"What drew you there?"

"I went to see the Widowknife Clanhold. All my life I've wanted to take it back from the demons and their cults. Now that they're spilling out into the wide world, I'm thinking they'll take new nests down south."

"An astute observation, except for one point."

"Oh?" Her tone was challenging.

"Demons are creatures of chaos. It is nigh impossible to predict their actions."

The words echoed another problem I'd been musing on. Though he was no fiend, my description was equally applicable to my self-professed nemesis, Kasiya.

In life the Osirian prince had been an indolent dullard who used his station to take from others what he could not earn himself. His unholy resurrection had granted him terrible powers, but enhanced intellect was apparently not among them. If revenge were his sole motive, then he had proven himself as inept as a sorcerous vampire as he ever did as a dilettante Pathfinder.

However, it would be folly to assume that Kasiya, however petty, harbored only revenge in his dead heart. I had to consider the likelihood that he followed me because I sought the *Lexicon of Paradox*. His recent attacks had come from what he believed to be a safe distance—it required a certain effort to suppress my own impulse to gloat in proving him wrong on that count—so it seemed likely his intention was not to kill me but rather to goad me to quicker pursuit of the *Lexicon*. It would not be the first time Kasiya had attempted to steal the fruit of my efforts.

The vampire had already obtained the *Lacuna Codex*, the compilation of fell arcana gathered to oppose the Whispering Tyrant before the martyrdom of General Arnisant imprisoned the lich beneath the foot of Gallowspire. My own brief study of the book had unlocked none of its great secrets, but I was certain of one fact: its most enigmatic rituals were capable of stripping a great being of its powers—or, I inferred, of bestowing them upon another.

The tavern door opened as it had a dozen times since my arrival. This time it was Radovan who stepped inside. His dark leathers glistened with rain. I noticed with some satisfaction that his boots were only slightly muddied. I prayed that indicated he had successfully cast the riffle scroll.

The waitress Shal brought him a rag. He winked at her as she put it in his hands, but then their fingers touched. Shal recoiled as if stung.

"It's all right, sweetheart." He smiled and reached out to reassure her, but at the touch of his hand on her hip, she yelped. His smile shrank. "Honest, I don't bite. Not right away, anyway."

She fled behind the bar, pausing briefly to look back at him. He offered her his little smile. Wide-eyed, she fled into the kitchen.

Some of the local men laughed and made jokes in Hallit. Radovan must have picked up a few words of the local tongue, for he rankled at the phrase "short southerner" and threw the tines at his abusers. The unfamiliar gesture only made the men laugh more.

"Radovan." I beckoned him over.

He eyed Alase skeptically. "Who's the kid?"

"Our new guide. Allow me to introduce Alase Brinz-Widowknife."

Alase stood to face Radovan. Even on her feet, she was closer to Arnisant's height than to Radovan's. "Don't worry," she said. "I'm bigger than I look."

"Hey! That's my—well, I used to say it."

"Did you find suitable guards?" I asked.

"Only four good ones. Guy in charge of the market says a lot of gangs are trying their luck during the— what do you call it? All the demons spilling out of the Worldwound."

The news was disappointing but not entirely unexpected. "Assuming we receive no word from Clanliege Martolls—"

"You won't," said Alase. "But hire me as your guide, and others will join us."

"You don't want to interrupt," said Radovan. "Makes him grumpy."

"As I was saying," I continued, "in the absence of aid from the clanliege, we shall set off for Storasta in the morning. Alase says she knows the place."

"You're telling me this bitty little thing snuck in there all by herself?"

"You can ask me yourself," said Alase. "And I never said I went by myself."

"Oh?" I said. "Who accompanied you?"

"Tonbarse," she said. "My god."

Chapter Four
The Ruined City

Oparal

As the river mist receded and Trathen's Gate appeared to the west, a lone horseman awaited us atop a barrow mound. At its base lay the pallid corpses of the defeated.

Among the tangled bodies lay the faded white and gold of Iomedae, the red and blue of Mendev, and the various hues of foreign banners. When I saw the gonfalon of House Celverian mud-pasted to a skeletal corpse, I wondered whether Ederras knew his kinsmen had fallen here.

Like me, the Chelish paladin had dedicated his life to the Children of Westcrown, a resistance movement opposing the diabolical House of Thrune that had seized control of Cheliax after Aroden's death. Despite our long camaraderie—we had been friends for years before the incident that he deemed my betrayal—I could not name a single member of his family.

I nodded at Sergeant Aprian. Over the weeks of our fruitless search of what had been western Sarkoris, he and I had developed a shorthand of gestures. He sent Naia and Erastus to scout our flanks while the rest of us advanced with a cautious eye toward the piled bodies. Porfirio and Aprian moved away from me, the better to spread the Inheritor's light should the dead stir.

The rider's face was white as frost, his hair and beard knotted with ice. He held a long lance from which hung the gray scrap of an ancient banner. Curtains of rotting flesh sagged from his steed's flanks, parting to reveal glistening organs inside the cage of ribs.

"Who dares approach Storasta?" The wight's voice crackled like ice on a spring pond.

"Oparal, knight of the Order of Saint Lymirin, in service to Queen Galfrey of Mendev." I felt Aprian's eyes upon me and knew that later, beyond the others' hearing, he would admonish me with great deference and courtesy. He had been at war against fiends for so long that he no longer embraced the protocols of honorable combat.

"What fool's errand brings you to lost Storasta, Oparal of Lymirin?"

"Why should I answer one who fears to reveal his name and allegiance?"

When the cold man spoke, no cloud of breath appeared before his withered lips. "Khistian Yadranko, Herald of Lalizarzadah, unrivaled potentate of Storasta."

Jelani moved her horse close and whispered, "Carrock rules Storasta."

I remembered the scouts' report, but I liked the sorcerer's implied suggestion.

"Has your mistress Carrock's leave to make such a claim?" I said.

A sound like rattling dice echoed up from Yadranko's dry throat. "The tree-lord abides in his hollow. Lalizarzadah looks down from her high tower. She is the superior."

"Stormont Isle," Jelani said, nodding toward the West Sellen River. There in the morning mist loomed the silhouette of a walled fortress high atop a rock.

The ruin of Stormont was one of the sites most likely to contain the book we sought. It was also, along with Carrock's How, one of the most dangerous locations in Storasta. I could not have taken it with ten times as many troops supported by battle wizards, inquisitors, and clerics.

Yet I had my orders.

"Khistian Yadranko, does your mistress keep a library?"

Again the hollow laugh. He tipped his lance toward me. "You must win your answer."

"Accepted." I restrained the urge to look at Aprian, who undoubtedly disapproved.

"You realize it's a trap," said Jelani.

"Stay back until I've sprung it."

"Yes, Captain. Stay warm." She drew a snowflake upon the air. Magic tingled on my skin.

I raised my hand for a lance. Tollivel tossed me his. Securing it beneath my arm, I raised my shield. It was made for melee rather than jousting, but with a thousand prayers to Lymirin invested in its steel, it would protect me from all but the direst blows.

"Now," I said.

Bastiel leaped forward, galloping by his second stride.

Yadranko waited until we had closed half the distance to the barrow. He lowered his lance and charged down the hill. My eyes remained locked on him, even as I saw the bodies of the defeated begin to stir.

"Iomedae, grant them rest." As I murmured the words, the radiance filled my heart and spread throughout my limbs. Holy warmth suffused and surrounded us.

From the ground, clammy hands reached for us and shriveled. Between hoofbeats, I heard their sighs as the radiance severed the chains of the world from their accursed souls.

Unmoved by the destruction of his minions, Yadranko met my charge. His spear shattered against my shield with a golden flash and an eagle's cry. My lance pierced his rotten shield and skewered him just beneath the breastplate, lifting him from his horrid steed.

Bastiel charged on, stopping only at the top of the mound. I lowered the wight to the ground and dismounted. Bastiel snorted, dancing and circling us, waiting for the undead who survived the Inheritor's radiance to follow.

Jelani hurled a ball of fire to engulf the plague steed and the nearest undead knights. An instant later, Aprian and Porfirio rode in to cleanse the field with holy radiance. By the time Naia and Erastus closed the flanks, none of Yadranko's fallen foes remained.

A foot upon his chest, I pulled the lance from Yadranko's body. He fell back with a sigh.

"My answer, Khistian Yadranko."

He raised a frosty hand toward my face. I slapped it away. Even through the blessed steel of my gauntlet, I felt the cold prickling at my flesh. "Honorably defeated," he rasped. "You shall have my answer. And then shall I have yours?"

I nodded.

"Lalizarzadah burned the libraries of Stormont Keep decades ago. You will find no records there. Now tell me, why have you come to lost Storasta?"

I drew the Ray of Lymirin to give him my answer.

When it was done, Aprian approached. "You can't trust the dead."

"No," I agreed, yet some vague intuition told me that Yadranko had answered truthfully. Maybe the dying wight calculated that I would disbelieve him. I chose to believe that he craved one last taste of honor before oblivion. "Still, we shall save Stormont for last."

"Captain, if I may speak freely."

"Allowed."

"In war, deceiving the enemy is not only honorable, it is compulsory."

"But it is not always necessary," I said. "I had my fill of deception in Kyonin." He could not understand just how truly I spoke. While assigned to escort a pair of visitors and report to the elven queen, I had discovered that the greatest deceivers were not the foreigners but my own people, the elves.

"You could have let Naia and Erastus take him from the flanks. You could have sent me in your stead."

"I'll keep that in mind as an option."

"Captain, we can't risk losing you on a point of honor."

"Noted," I said. "Appreciated."

Naia and Erastus returned to celebrate our morning prayer. Only the Mwangi-born Silvio abstained, taking his place as sentinel on the mound. The rest of us dismounted, drew our swords, and knelt before the crosspieces symbolizing Iomedae's radiance.

I removed *The Acts* from the silver chains securing it beside the Ray of Lymirin. As much as the sword, the accounts of the Inheritor's ancient miracles were my weapon, for they assured me of the miracles made possible by valor, honor, and justice. We praised Iomedae for her miracles, both her ancient acts and the wonders that had preserved our lives these past weeks and months.

My platoon had first visited the infected site where Yath once stood, searching for clues among the debris. Detritus we found in plenty—shattered spears, fragments of stone and wooden furnishings, a length of rusty chain with a single manacle still encircling a skeletal arm—but no books or scrolls.

Stymied by the desolation of Yath, we moved on to the next site, and the next, constantly under assault by demons and the changing land. We fought roving bands of fiends and cultists. Only a few had coherent goals, such as capturing escaped slaves or harrying the crusaders who tested the shifting battle lines.

For two weeks we sheltered in the remains of a razed longhouse, surrounded by three rival demon gangs unaware of our presence. While they quarreled, we rationed food and water. It was there I first began to know my troops.

My fellow Chelaxians had joined the crusade for prosaic reasons. After Bolivar strangled the man who had raped his neighbor's daughter, her parents spent their savings to bribe the magistrate into letting him join the crusade in lieu of hard labor. Gemma was a wanted thief who went nowhere without her prized coil of spidersilk rope and half a dozen keen knives.

The paladin Porfirio pledged himself to the Children of Westcrown until the inquisitors rooted out his identity. Despite Queen Galfrey's decree freeing slaves who reached Mendev, the half-elf Silvio took up his fallen master's hammer and fought on.

The foreigners had more romantic stories.

The Qadiran Naia swore five years' service to the crusade after a priest of Iomedae healed her mortal wound. Dragomir left Ustalav with a broken heart. Erastus defied the Widow Queen and fled Isger before her devils could capture him. The Thuvian Jelani joined to earn a cure for her wasting disease. The Andoren Eagle Knight Tollivel, cashiered for bribery, claimed his discharge was motivated by family vendetta. The dwarf Urno said he lost a bet.

Only Aprian came from a noble house. A second son, the Taldan joined the Order of the Sunrise Sword before devoting himself to the crusade, where mischance led him to demonic possession. Despite the liberation of his soul at the fall of Yath, some anonymous faction at court prevented his advancement.

Of all the crusaders, I came to trust Aprian the most. His competence aside, there was a calm about him that reassured me as much as it did the troops under his command. Thus, one night as we sat beside a feeble fire, I almost answered him when he inquired about my history with Ederras.

"Pardon me, Captain," he said when he saw my hesitation. "It's none of my business."

I nodded my thanks, intending to let the matter drop. Then, for some reason I could not understand— perhaps because Aprian did not press me—I added, "It wasn't his fault."

Aprian said nothing.

"It is possible I was too . . ."

Aprian shrugged. "Nobody's perfect."

My jaw clenched at the hateful phrase. We must all strive for perfection. That is what I had believed ever since I had been accepted into the Order of Saint Lymirin. It was not an ideal I was ready to discard, no matter how many times I fell short of it.

In the weeks that followed, Aprian did not mention the matter again.

We rose from prayer and mounted our steeds. We entered Storasta through Trathen's Gate unchallenged. The city walls had fallen to rubble many decades earlier. Skeletons both fiendish and human protruded from the churned earth.

In the center of the city crouched a great hollow, thick with greenery. According to the briefs, those trees could lift their roots and walk the land. The surrounding vines could creep along the ground to trip a man, or to drag him into the boughs and hang him.

All this ambulatory vegetation served the great tree-lord known as Carrock, once a friend to druids and protector of the city. More than any other part of Storasta, Carrock's How resembled the lair of the Queen of Thorns, where I had faced the worst horrors of my life—at least before facing the Worldwound.

Unlike the dragon queen's sanctuary against the roving demons of the Fierani Forest, Storasta had succumbed to the taint of the Worldwound, and so had Carrock. Our primary concern was to avoid him and his forces while searching the city for the *Lexicon of Paradox*.

The intelligence we had gained at the hidden Fort Amerine days earlier suggested three sites most likely to house the *Lexicon*. Of these, I reserved Stormont Isle as the last to explore, not solely because of Yadranko's words, but more because of the fort commander's warning that a terrible demon made her lair within the fortress ruins. Her description of the fiend corroborated Yadranko's claims about his mistress Lalizarzadah. We would not dare rousing her wrath unless absolutely necessary.

Of the two other likely locations of the *Lexicon*, I chose to search Riverkeep first. Leaving Erastus, Gemma, Urno, and Bastiel to guard our mounts, I led the others into the ruins of the fortress nestled between the eastern wall and the West Sellen River.

In the upper floors we found little more than dust and the debris of a century's abandonment. The prints of long, naked feet led us through the servants' quarters and into a wine cellar. There we found fresher bones and trails of blood. We followed them to a passage poorly concealed behind an empty wine tun.

Not ten feet into the cellars, Porfirio grunted in pain. Weeks earlier he had confided in me that he felt the presence of evil as a painful tightening in his guts. I extended my feelings outward. The butterflies of evil fluttered in my belly.

Aprian thrust a thumb against his temple and nodded. He felt evil as a stabbing headache.

The sensation grew stronger as we followed a damp passage to a descending stairway. Even the non-paladins began to sense the presence of vile things by the carrion stench.

"Ghouls," said Porfirio. He shrugged the shield off his shoulder and secured it to his arm.

"Worse," said Aprian. He hefted his own shield and glanced at me. "You won't be immune."

While I had not grown up among my people, I still enjoyed the benefit of pure elven blood. I secured my shield to my arm. With a thought, I activated the image of Saint Lymirin on its face. The figure of a winged and eagle-headed woman radiated white light, but less than usual. There was far more than a stench of evil about this place.

We reached the lower basement and stepped calf-deep into icy black water. The river had seeped into the basement. Moss hung thick upon the walls, its mottled surface suggesting tapestries designed by insane artists.

Across the room, more than a dozen pairs of round, white-green eyes reflected the light of my shield. I turned it slightly upward. The light revealed patches of obscene fungus hanging from the wall, but also reflected to show the creatures whose feast we had disturbed.

The fell ghouls squatted beneath a waterfall spilling through ragged cracks in the keep's foundation. Translucent webbing had grown between the creatures' blanched and scaled fingers. Gore smeared their long yellow teeth as they pressed putrescent morsels into their maws from some communal corpse beneath the water. They were all hairless, most of them naked.

The exception was their king. Upon his scrawny shoulders lay necklaces of river stones and gnawed bone strung with threads of gut. Unlike his minions, he stood at our arrival, shriveled genitals dangling between his bony thighs.

A female clutched the leader, pressing her sagging breasts against his arm and staring at us. "Too much to eat all at once," she called to us. "You may leave an offering for Ploscaru. Three, perhaps. Yes, three, but not that little one." She pointed a bony finger at Urno.

Ploscaru shook his misshapen head and held up a hand.

"No, five!" said the female, speaking for him. "The rest of you may run, for all the good it will do."

"A generous offer," I said. "I have one to make in return. Tell us where the books reside, and we will leave you here to gnaw these bones."

Ploscaru unleashed an inhumanly long tongue, red and swollen. A spectral hand appeared in the air just before his own. Behind me, Silvio shouted a warning, too late.

Black tentacles rose up to grasp our legs. Simultaneously, the watery ghouls rushed us.

I slashed at the rubbery appendages binding my legs. Beside me, Aprian ignored the tentacles, holding his sword's crosspiece before his face and half-closing his eyes in devout reverie. The light of Iomedae spread from his prayerful heart to sear the nearest ghouls. The undead shrieked as their skin blistered and burned, but they did not withdraw.

They fell upon Porfirio even as the paladin freed himself from the binding tentacles. He raised his sword, but two of the ghouls leaped upon his arm and dragged it down. Two more grasped his legs and lifted him up.

"No!" cried Dragomir. He lunged forward to aid Porfirio, but the tentacles held him back.

I started toward Porfirio, but a sixth sense caused me to pause and free Aprian first. It took only two strokes to sever the tendrils binding him, but then Ploscaru's bodiless hand reached me.

It pressed against my neck, cold as ice. In an instant, it chilled my veins and numbed every nerve in my body. My grasp slackened, and I nearly dropped the Ray of Lymirin.

The rest was a blur of rising panic.

My crusaders strove to reach Porfirio, but the ghouls dragged him under the water while their fellows gave them the cover of their own bodies.

Ploscaru's hand darted toward me again. I struck it out of the air with my sword. Across the cellar, the ghoul king cried out in pain. He cried out again as Jelani sent a ray of flame across the chamber. He drowned his screams and vanished beneath the water.

Aprian moved forward, only to plunge into a watery pit. A pair of ghouls pulled him down. I dove after him, and Bolivar joined me. As the brawny Chelaxian got his hands under Aprian's arms, I channeled the radiance. Water boiled off the seared flesh of the ghouls. One of them floated to the surface, destroyed. Its nearest fellows fled toward the waterfall.

We pursued, but Ploscaru conjured a veil of sickening colors. Just the sight of the wriggling hues forced a wave of nausea through my guts and staggered half my crusaders. Before I shook off the effect, no ghoul remained except the few we had destroyed.

Dragomir plunged into the water beneath the falls, calling Porfirio's name before diving again and again into the black depths. We joined him in the search until at last we pulled him away, exhausted.

We found the passage leading from the cellar to the river, but it was too deep to follow. I looked to Jelani, but she anticipated my question.

"Wind and sand," she said. "I have no spell to let us breathe water."

"Outside," I said. Dragomir balked. I shook his shoulders. "Quickly! They have taken him to the river."

We rushed up the stairs. Even before we left the keep, we heard the sound of melee outside.

Carrock's How had come to the Riverkeep—or so it first appeared.

Vines writhed along the overgrown streets, and a pair of fiend-touched treefolk directed a mob of wolves, satyrs, nymphs, and dryads to attack our guards and steeds.

Bastiel whinnied and reared protectively before the horses. Urno split the skull of a leaping wolf. The beast writhed in agony for an instant before its moss-stained fur thinned, its body convulsing as it transformed into the figure of a hairy man and lay still.

A trio of satyrs charged. Erastus put an arrow in one's throat. Another sprouted two of Gemma's daggers from its shoulder and chest.

We fought with all our might and courage. For every dryad or werewolf we felled, another seemed to take its place.

When we briefly gained the advantage, I ordered the crusaders to mount. Once controlled, the horses were no longer a liability but an asset. With their greater mass, they pushed back the monsters that had overwhelmed us while we were on foot. Bastiel and those horses best trained for battle crushed the skulls of werewolves and satyrs under their hooves. We wet the overgrown streets of Storasta with the blood of demon and monster alike.

And still they came.

As we fought, I looked to Dragomir. Tears streaked his face as he turned his head to look back at the West

Sellen. Like the rest of us, he must have realized all hope of recovering his comrade was lost.

As if to spite our mourning and the battle before us, loathsome creatures emerged from the river. River ogres and grindylows crawled toward us, driven by the command of a sodden hag who then withdrew, cackling, into the rushing waters.

Pinned between equally horrid foes, our choices narrowed to defending the keep, which we already knew to be indefensible, or to break free to the west.

"Follow me, escort formation."

They did not need me to tell them who we escorted. Jelani and the archers took the center. Erastus and Naia sheathed their swords in favor of their bows. Standing in their stirrups, they took turns shooting arrows into the mobs from the forest and the river.

Deadly though they proved, the archers could not match the carnage of Jelani's flame. Her searing magic destroyed the creeping vines and sent the treefolk lurching to dip their flaming crowns into the river.

We fought our way westward through the ruined streets of Storasta, pausing when we could, fleeing when we must. Aprian and I unleashed the radiance upon the shambling dead who dared close with us. Others, their faces dusted with yellow pollen, we could not turn with holy light. Instead we cut them down with blessed steel.

In the shelter of the ruined buildings of the Rushwaters, we won respite for half an hour, but our foes sought only to encircle us as we caught our breaths. Rather than let them surround us, we pressed farther westward.

Our steeds pushed through herds of plague aurochs milling along the muddy streets, but the brutes would not be shooed away. They turned on us, and we found ourselves fighting a third battle.

To escape the infected beasts, we cut through the river mob and won another brief pause until the forest horde reached us once more. We fought until our limbs became numb, fleeing for another respite whenever the opportunity presented itself. There we healed the most grievous wounds and braced ourselves for the next onslaught. We fought until the sun began to hide its face from the carnage we left in our wake.

As darkness approached, the Ray of Lymirin blazed its hatred for the wretched fiends who lumbered down from Stormont Isle while we continued to fend off werewolves, satyrs, nymphs, and river ogres. Soon we fought not for the crusade, nor for our fallen comrades, but for survival.

We needed a wall to put at our backs, a door to shut against the constant attacks from all directions.

And then we saw the sign.

Golden light blazed within the unfinished tower standing on the farthest spur of land beyond the Rushwaters. It could only be Nekrosof Tower, the second site we wished to explore. Six black pits surrounded the stark prominence, illuminated by both the last rays of the setting sun and the sudden golden radiance from within the cathedral.

That steady warm light was not cast for Pharasma, the Lady of Graves, to whom the cathedral was dedicated before Storasta's fall. Her followers preferred the flicker of candles. It was a sign from Iomedae that we should seek shelter.

"Follow me!"

I raised the Ray of Lymirin as my banner and led the crusaders toward the open doors of the cathedral, ever watchful for pursuit.

None of our foes followed. At first I thought they were wary of sanctified ground, but then I thought again about the pits surrounding the tower. They were not pools, nor were they fashioned for storage or defense. They appeared like gaps left by some great objects removed from the earth.

Inside the cathedral, the light was so bright that it took our eyes a moment to adjust. When it did, we saw the golden altar to Iomedae, and it did not stand unguarded. Robed choirboys stood in ranks to one side.

Behind the altar stood Saint Lymirin herself.

A full head taller than a tall man, the eagle-headed woman raised her golden wings in a benediction as we entered. On her left, a blonde girl dressed in raiment of gold and white greeted us. "Welcome, crusaders. Here you shall find succor from the tainted land."

On the saint's right, a girl with ginger hair said, "Welcome, champions of the glorious crusade. No evil shall follow you here."

The saint lifted a talon to indicate an open area where pews once stood before the nave. "Shelter your beasts within these walls, and no harm shall befall them."

I feared a trap, but then a sudden impulse made me cast away my doubt. "Come in," I told my troops.

In Cheliax, where I had been raised, and in Kyonin, where I had gone to rejoin my people, I had found deception and betrayal at every turn. Here in fallen Sarkoris, so near the Worldwound, I had expected even worse.

Instead we had found a miracle.

From a dark corner of my mind, suspicion continued to niggle at my thoughts. Yet no sooner did I entertain the doubt than a pang of guilt shook me from my suspicions.

The Inheritor promised solace to those who fought with courage and devotion. Did it not then follow that she should offer her greatest miracle in the heart of this wretched ruin?

To the east lay a large space where once the congregation had gathered. If nothing else, it provided ample room for the horses.

Hesitantly, doubtless sharing my initial suspicions, the others obeyed. I remained atop Bastiel, hoping my presence would calm him. He nickered and swished his tail unhappily.

"It's a trick," said Aprian.

Normally I would have agreed, but some unbidden intuition argued that we had found a sanctuary against the evil surrounding us. It was a test of our faith, surely. "Jelani?"

She had already traced a now-familiar rune upon the air. "There is no magic here, none that I can discern. That only makes sense if . . ."

I followed her gaze to what lay upon the altar before Saint Lymirin. How had I not noticed it before?

It was a Kellid man, but not one I recognized. He rose, and his eyes widened as he saw us. "Captain?" He shook his head as if awaking from a deep slumber, confused.

"I don't know you," I said. "Who are you?"

He gaped, first at me and then at himself as he looked at his hands, then his arms.

"Your courage has earned the blessing of resurrection," said Saint Lymirin.

The man continued examining his naked body, his expression of incredulity growing stronger by the second. "I'm Porfirio!" he said. "This isn't my body!"

"Liar!" shouted Dragomir. "This is a trick!"

"Faithless!" whispered one of the angels at Lymirin's side. "Would you question this miracle?"

"No!" cried the man who said he was Porfirio. He turned to Dragomir. "Don't you know me? You must."

"Impossible," I murmured. Aprian and some of the others echoed my doubt. Yet were we not paladins? Were we not the ones whose faith was mean to be tested and retested?

Dragomir stood unmoving. His eyes narrowed, anger building beneath those dark lashes even as his lips trembled. "You lie. This is all an illusion."

"No," said the blonde angel. "Such visitations as this are rare."

"Accepting them is a test of faith," said the redhead. "But if you must reject the miracle . . ."

"Dragomir, believe me! I'm Porfirio, your dark falcon."

Dragomir choked. He took a step forward but stopped himself. He looked to me for permission.

"No," I said, but without certainty. I drew the Ray of Lymirin and urged Bastiel forward, hoping the presence of the sword or unicorn would somehow reveal the truth. "We have seen such fell magic in this ruined city. You think you can deceive us?"

"If in your heart you know that to be true, strike me down," said the saint. She dismissed the girls with a gesture. They stepped aside with such grace that I could no longer deny what they truly were: angels. Their lips moved in quiet prayer.

With Bastiel's first step forward, I knew I must challenge this seeming miracle, to expose it for the falsehood it must surely be.

With his second, I saw the saint raise her hand, but only in a gesture of benediction. How could I strike a blow against my patron saint?

With his third, I lowered my sword, knowing I had made a terrible mistake. I sheathed the blade and placed my hand upon Bastiel's neck, his signal to bow. Grudgingly, he obeyed as I dismounted and dropped to one knee.

"Peerless saint, forgive my doubt. Let us receive your blessing."

"That you shall, my dear," said Saint Lymirin. She raised her hand for another benediction. I felt its power settle upon me like the weight of a thick, warm cloak.

"Oparal," whispered an unexpected yet familiar voice. "You have been enchanted. We are here to help."

Without further warning, Bastiel reared and shrieked.

Behind me, my crusaders shouted and drew their blades. I drew the Ray of Lymirin, but a moment too late. A fiend leaped over me and stabbed its wicked blade deep into the face of Saint Lymirin.

Chapter Five
The Coven

Radovan

As we came up from the bone cellar, the boss started to cast a riffle scroll on me. Instead, he handed it over. "You do it."

"Seriously?" There wasn't any time to argue. I took the little book and snapped it off. Even as I tossed the spent scroll over my shoulder, I felt the magic tingling in my legs.

"Well, what do you know? Desna smiles."

The boss cast a few more spells. He made me quick and strong as hell. One more, and he vanished from sight.

Before we poked our heads up into the cathedral, the boss made the rest of us invisible, too, telling us to stick close. Lucky thing we'd brought only four of the Kellid swordsmen, including the seven-foot giant Kronug. We'd left the rest of them with the Red Carriage across the river.

Once Alase came back to the Looter's Market with me, everybody who'd turned me down before suddenly wanted to join. She might have been little, but she had a big reputation, at least in Gundrun.

And she seemed to know everybody—which ones were drunkards, which ones cowards, and so on. She talked me into firing one of the guys I'd picked and helped me choose the new ones. At first I didn't trust her so much, but when she explained why each one made a good guard, I started to come around. We ended up hiring nine instead of eight, like the boss said. But we both knew he only told me eight because he didn't want more than ten.

Along with Kronug, we ended up with the braggart Valki, Barek and his big mustache, an axe-thrower named Selka, Roga with the punched-out teeth, Gannak with the pierced nipples, Zoresk with fists the size of quart jars, and a kid named Dolok whose scarred red face was his scariest weapon. We even ended up hiring Kala, the harper from the Splinter. She said she'd write an "epic" about our "quest."

I told her she was real cute, since we were exaggerating.

The four we'd brought to the cathedral were bright enough to do what the boss said. Arni had already learned the trick of sticking tight to the boss even when he was invisible. And Alase, she was little enough you had to squint to see her even when she was visible. They'd be all right.

None of us needed telling it was all an illusion upstairs. There hadn't been any altar to Iomedae when we'd come through a couple hours earlier. There sure as hell weren't any saints and angels and choirboys and stained glass in the windows. It didn't take a wizard to suss out that the saint was running a scam. I figured the boss was way ahead of me on that count.

On that count. Sometimes I crack myself up.

When I saw Oparal and that pointy-headed horse of hers, I got a lump in my throat. It never occurred to me I'd end up missing the elf paladin, but there it was. She looked so fine even in the fake holy light that I was going to get a second, lower lump if I didn't put my mind back on business.

The boss did some magic whispers that only those of us he picked could hear. By the way he was talking, I knew that included Oparal. When the time was right, he slapped my shoulder. I was going to be the opener.

I took a running start and jumped like I used to do back in Tian Xia. With the boss's magic running through my veins and muscles, I could jump as high now as I could when I was living in a devil's body. Desna smiled, and I didn't crack my head on the rafters.

After I flew clean over Oparal and her stupid unicorn, I figured I'd hit the saint hard enough to drive the knife clean through her bird skull.

I figured wrong.

Whatever the thing was—and it sure wasn't a saint— it had a skull plenty harder than bone. The knife scraped deep into the side of its face. It would have taken off an ear if she'd had any. Instead I just sheared off some feathers.

Saint Birdface didn't appreciate the free shave. She opened her yellow beak and let out one hell of a screech. She didn't sound half so much like an eagle as a banshee. Before jumping in, I should have asked the boss what his Shadowless Sword showed him she really was.

The crusaders didn't notice the—what's the boss's word?—the incongruity. As far as the knights knew, I'd just stabbed Iomedae's messenger in the face. They drew their swords and came at me.

"Hey, I'm not the bad guy here!" I shouted. "Come on, boss! Show them what we got."

I expected to hear his magic message again, but he was busy trying to wipe out the illusion. I heard his riffle scrolls snapping off across the room. The illusion over the room and the bad guys stayed in place, but all of a sudden I could see little Alase.

She knelt with an open hand on the floor, like she was feeling for tremors. Instead, a blue circle of light formed all around her, and the paint across her eyes blazed under her shaggy black bangs. In the days since we'd left Gundrun, she hadn't showed us anything other than the best path to get us there, despite all her big talk of being a god caller.

Now she was cooking up some big magic.

While I was distracted, the bird-saint shoved me back, strong as an ogre. I kept hold of the knife, but only barely. I planted my feet to stop from falling into the crusader's swords. They raised their blades, ready to cut me down.

"Oparal, tell your pals I'm all right!" I shouted. The unicorn reared like he was going to come straight down on my head, but he'd never been fond of me. "This whole joint is all one big illusion, sweetheart."

Oparal hesitated. Lucky for me, her men—and a few women, I'd noticed, a couple of them not too hard on the eyes—waited for her nod before cutting me to bits and gobbets. One of the guys was naked, but another of the crusaders sheltered him with his shield.

Oparal said, "Stay your hands. I know this man. He's not capable of harming a saint."

"Hey, sweetheart, I'm plenty capable. You know better than anybody, after all we've been through."

Oparal jumped down from the saddle and put herself between me and the unicorn. "You will address me as Captain."

"You got it, Captain Sweetheart." I tipped her a wink.

She shot back a look meant to turn me to stone. It worked, a little. Good thing it wasn't me that was naked.

I turned back to the fake saint just as one of her talons caught me under the chin.

Turns out even fake saints pack one hell of a wallop.

The blow sent me flying ass over teakettle all the way over the illusion of the altar. The floor hit me just as hard, shattered glass and stone tearing holes all over me and my new jacket.

It's always got to be the jacket.

I'd get mad about it later. At the moment, all I could see were green and yellow starbursts.

I blinked and rolled, trying to figure which way was up. A strong hand grabbed my arm and pulled me forward. My vision cleared in time for me to stop myself from stabbing Oparal. Mussing her pretty elf face would have been a damned shame.

It was her eyes I remembered best. The elves don't have whites—or, like the boss explained, their irises are so big that that's all you can see. Oparal's were the color of iron.

"What are they?" she said. Her head kept turning as she tried to keep an eye on me and the angels at the same time.

She looked so serious, I wanted to kiss her. But like the boss always says, now was not the time. Besides, the last thing I needed was another shot to the jaw.

I remembered real good just how hard Oparal could punch. "None of this was here when we came in. It's all a trick, and you can bet that ain't your saint."

Behind the paladin, the eagle-headed woman leaped toward us. I kicked Oparal's foot and pulled her down with me. The saint's talons swept through the space where the elf's neck had been.

The crusaders brought their shields up and tried to put themselves between the saint and their captain. The choirboys groaned and shuffled while the two little angels jumped onto the backs of a couple crusaders.

Oparal rolled up to her knees. She sneered at me, knowing perfectly well I'd jerked her away from trouble but still mad about it. She raised her shield to catch the saint's next strike.

The blow struck her shield but still beat her down into a lower crouch. I rolled to the side and kicked the saint's legs.

I might as well have kicked a couple of stone pillars.

One of the angels who'd jumped on a crusader grabbed his head in two cute little hands and twisted it right off.

I shouted, but a second later I realized it was just the guy's helmet came off. His face was all red under his beard, but he kept his cool. When he twisted around to headbutt the little angel, a flash of yellow light exploded between their skulls. She flew back and hit the floor hard. A second later she jumped to her feet again, an evil grin on her face.

The other guy with an angel on his back was a dwarf who took it personal when she started beating him with his own shield. He shook his axe. "I won't have it, angel or waif! I'll crack your wicked little noggin!"

The angel dimpled, giggled, and disappeared. The dwarf stood straight, like a weight had just come off his back.

Arni leaped to help the dwarf. He shook his head, confused by the angel's disappearance. He snuffled at the floor and whimpered at whatever he smelled.

That's when I realized the place didn't stink half so bad as it had when we first came in. Whatever illusion they'd put on the place, it masked the stink as well as the sights.

"Here, boy!" I took a swipe at the saint to keep her off me. Arni ran in to bite at her heels, keeping her spinning between me, Oparal, and the crusaders.

A bird doesn't have much personality on its face, but by the way her head kept turning, I figured she knew this wasn't going her way. Her beak opened and closed, her throat bulging. It looked like she was about to hork up a mess.

I wasn't wrong.

Gallons of spiders poured out of her mouth, spilling onto the floor all around us. I got some on my kickers and had a bad second or two trying not to scream too high.

Get it straight: I'm not afraid of spiders. I just don't like them.

Some of the crusaders didn't like spiders any better than I did. Once they started screaming, I didn't feel so bad.

Most of the swarm poured out over Arni. He threw himself on his back, rolling to get them off. A few fell away or got crushed under him, but it wasn't going to be enough.

"Arni, out!" I pointed to the wall where I hoped the boss was still standing. "Come on, boss! Show us what we got in here!"

He had a bunch of spellbreaking scrolls left. At least, I hoped he did. This fight was going to be a lot harder if we couldn't see what we were really fighting.

I couldn't see the boss or our guards, but I had a pretty good idea where they were. Nearby, Alase stood up. Her hair was damp. She was panting like she'd just run a mile, and the blue rune on her forehead glowed under her bangs.

"What'd you do, girl?" She didn't even look my way, and I figured she couldn't hear me over the shouts of the crusaders and Kellids, not to mention the groans of the choirboys who were hemming them in against the west wall.

A giant boulder fell down among the choirboys. That's how it looked, anyway. It wasn't a boulder, though. It was black and furry, and when it growled I felt the need to pee. It stood up, tall as a bear—tall as the biggest damned bear I ever saw. Only it wasn't a bear. It was a wolf with a glowing blue rune on its head. The rune and the wolf's eyes were the same color as Alase's.

Halfway back to the boss, Arni rolled once and came up in a low crouch, growling. He was born to hunt wolves, but he'd never faced one this size.

"Arni, down!"

Before whatever was going to happen happened, the boss ripped off another scroll. All the holy images in the cathedral melted away.

The first difference was that there was no shrine to Iomedae in this joint. I already knew that, but now all the crusaders could see the cathedral was dedicated to Pharasma, Lady of Graves. Even with most of the carvings of saints and martyrs gouged out, you could tell where we were just by the bones and spirals carved into the gray stone beams. Shards of stained glass littered the floor beneath arched windows, and you could still see where there'd been railings to separate the priest from the congregation.

The cathedral wasn't the only thing hiding under an illusion.

That wasn't a bird-headed saint but a hag standing in front of us. She was a big, ugly gal wearing a skirt of river weeds braided with rusty blades. A damp rat scampered through her skirt like a squirrel through vines. Her cheek and ear were ragged flaps of gray skin oozing blood. Her hair hung down in slimy hanks, and a pale green ghost of her hand hovered just over the real thing. Even hunched over, she stood almost as tall as the boss or Oparal.

There was a smaller hag where one of the angel girls had stood. Her yellowed eyes opened big as saucers as she saw the boss had blown their cover. It took her a second to recover her cool. Then she cackled and made a nasty sign with her rubbery fingers before vanishing.

The choirboys were drowned men, once crusaders and swordsmen, burglars and wizards—the kind of guys dumb enough to explore a place like Storasta for treasure. Now they were equal parts rust, rot, and river slime, dropping bits of themselves at every step. I'd fought things like them before. They stink in more ways than one.

But they weren't alone in that. With the illusion gone, the whole cathedral reeked. We'd smelled it when we first snuck in to explore the cellars.

The worst stench came from the corpse of a gigantic—well, I don't know whether it was a frog or an octopus. When we passed through here earlier, the boss had called it "the amphibian," but that didn't do it justice. He'd also told me it was still just a baby, so I knew I didn't want to meet its mama. Before moldering away against the north wall, it must have weighed five or six tons. Now it had to be less than half that, because what the rats hadn't eaten had shrunk down to a mess of rotten hide and slime.

I thanked Desna the hag had thrown me into the sharp pile instead.

That one was a different kind of mess. Something had smashed a big hole in the west wall. A bunch of people must have been huddled there when it happened, because I saw bones in the crumbled stone and shattered glass. I'd brightened a corner of it with my own blood.

Speaking of which, I was starting to feel the pain from the shot to the chin. I touched the wet bib forming beneath my neck, and my hand came away not just wet but pooling with blood.

"Desna weeps!"

"Here," said Oparal. As her crusaders covered her from the hag and the unicorn stamped on spiders, the paladin sheathed her sword and took me by the throat.

"It's not too late to take back the Captain Sweetheart thing, is it?"

She squeezed a little harder than she had to, but I felt the tingle of holy light beginning to close my wounds.

"No you don't!" shrieked the hag. She cackled out a spell of her own. Her ghost hand leaped out to tear the paladin's healing glow off of me and onto her own mutilated face. She put her ear back in place with a gesture like a lady adjusting her hair, and it stayed. The cut I'd given her sealed up neat as stitches.

"Oparal," the boss's voice whispered in my head, too, "move your crusaders back that I may incinerate the river dead. Radovan, an invisible hag is creeping up on your left."

"Got it."

Oparal shouted a command and her crusaders formed a wedge-shaped shield wall and backed up to the west. They covered us while the drowned men covered their hag, who was busy with another spell. Before she could finish it, four golden bolts of force caught her in the chest. They'd come from one of the crusaders, a pretty southern gal who I noticed was the only one not wearing armor.

The hag shot her an evil look but kept jabbering her spell. Then five silver-gray bolts shot out from the south, hitting her all over. The hag screamed as she lost her place and her own spell fizzled.

The magic crusader looked over to the south, but the boss was still invisible. What we all did see was the four Kellids standing guard around Alase, who glowed for a second like she was wearing armor made of blue light before it faded out of sight. I could barely see her behind the big swordsman, but she was shaking one fist over her head while pointing her open hand at the big black wolf.

So that's what she meant by her "god."

Behind me and to the left, I heard the squish of a bare foot on the floor. One more step, and she'd be close enough.

"Could use a hand, Sweet—er, Captain."

Oparal dropped her shield and raised her sword above her head, taking the hilt in two hands. I'd seen her take that stance before, and things hadn't gone well for the critter under the blade.

The invisible hag took another step toward me. The hard part was not flinching before she made her move. The hairs on the back of my neck turned to needles. I tried to look like I was focused on the drowned men, but the bleeding from my neck made me anxious. I ducked low and threw an elbow back.

I caught her low in the belly. An instant later, the hag's claws swept past me, visible again. Oparal's bright sword came down, missing the hag's neck by inches. Still, she cut a deep wedge into her shoulder.

Shrieking, the hag spun away. Oparal took a step toward her but stopped before chasing her.

The boss shouted, "Oparal! Alase! Pull back your beasts." I could see him then, standing with Arnisant at his side against the west wall, the Shadowless Sword in one hand, a riffle scroll in the other. With half the pouches on his bandolier hanging open from all the spells he'd already cast, he looked like some kind of swashbuckler. I bet he'd get a kick out of a painting like that. Maybe I'd get him one for his next birthday, if we both lived that long.

"Bastiel!" shouted Oparal.

So the big fellow had a name. The unicorn pranced back, stomping spiders as it retreated.

"Tonbarse!" called Alase. The giant wolf leaped away from the drowned men.

With the critters clear, the boss let loose another riffle scroll. A little flame flew across the cathedral, growing bigger with every foot. When it reached the main entrance, it exploded into a huge ball of fire. Flames sizzled on the wet bodies of the drowned men, drying them off more than it burned them. Still, a few of them went wobbly and fell to the cathedral floor.

Across the room I saw the boss raise his chin, proud of himself. He hardly ever got to use his favorite spell in the land of demons, where the fiends shrugged off most of his best stuff.

The crusader wizard cocked her head at the boss and threw a fireball of her own. Hers exploded a few feet closer to the undead mob. Since they were already half baked by the boss, hers seared most of the survivors to crisps.

"Go!" said the boss. Arnisant dashed out first, tripping the first walking dead man and sinking his fangs into the second.

Sometimes I think that dog will eat anything.

The Kellids leaped in, howling their clan names and chopping the undead with their giant swords.

At a word from Oparal, the crusaders moved in from the other side. One shouted, "Iomedae!" Otherwise, they fought without talking, paying as much mind to their shields as their swords.

I heard the sound of tumbling rocks. It grew louder as I looked up. Nothing was falling on us. Instead, the rubble of the broken west wall was rising up all around me.

Skeletons stood up from the wreckage. Shards of glass in their bones threw beams of green, blue, and gold through the clouds of dust rising from the rubble.

The hags were nowhere in sight, but a dozen voices cackled through the cathedral. I was beginning not to like our chances so much. I kissed my thumb and drew the wings of Desna over my heart.

"Radiance!" shouted Oparal.

She stepped back, leaving me to fight off the skeletons. I gave the first one a swift kick to the breastbone. It fell back into a couple more, which helped it stand back up. They came on, bony fingers reaching for my eyes.

Behind me, golden light flared from three different spots. The skeletons' bones burned and cracked. Here and there an arm fell away. Ribs crumbled to ash. Blackened skulls fell to the floor and shattered.

I turned around, squinting into the light. Oparal and two of her men—including the bearded guy who'd lost his hat to a hag—held their swords with the crosspieces before their faces. Their eyes half closed, their lips moving, they called down the wrath of their goddess.

It was pretty good wrath. Seconds later, the skeletons settled down with the dust. The hags' cackling laughter turned into crazy screeching.

One of the Kellids screamed, too—Zoresk. Everybody looked at him at the same time. A hag rode on his back, one claw in his mouth, the other with a claw stuck deep in his eye. The big man thrashed, dropped his sword, and tried to grab her neck in his big hands, but her nail reached his brain first.

Gannak and Roga leaped for her at the same time, each one trying to be the hero. They got in each other's way. The hag vanished, and Zoresk died before they reached him.

The crusaders moved in at the same time, the bearded paladin ordering them forward with shields up, all cautious. When one bumped against the invisible hag, she shouted a warning. All the swords near her slashed down at the space in front of her shield. A hag screamed and reappeared for a second before throwing the woman who found her up against the wall. The crusaders on either side moved in to fill the gap she'd left.

"The door!" shouted Alase.

Tonbarse was already bounding toward the cathedral door, where another mob of drowned men was pouring inside. This bunch was still wet from the river, half with limbs or faces nibbled away. One of them was some kind of ogre or half-fiend with a spiral horn curling across its cheek just under a red eye.

Arni ran so close behind Tonbarse that for a second I thought he was going to try to drag the big wolf down. Instead, a hag's voice cried out. Right before my eyes, Arni shrank, his floppy ears growing long, his curly gray coat turning brown and soft.

In the middle of the ash pile that the boss and the crusader wizard had made of the first undead mob, the hag who'd been the saint laughed and patted her bulging belly while she pointed at what she'd done to Arni.

That witch turned my dog into a bunny!

"Boss!"

I didn't wait to see what he did. I ran at the hag.

She waved at me, a creepy gesture all by itself, but with the added nasty of green slime glistening on her palm.

I didn't want any of that on me, so I veered off to grab Arni. Confused, the poor little guy—and now he really was a little guy—hopped between the legs of the soggy dead.

I stuck the big knife back in its sheath and dove after him, hands open to scoop him into my arms. Just before I could touch him, stinking black whips shot across the room and snatched him away.

Rolling back to my feet, I kicked one of the drowned men away. I must have lost more blood than I realized, because even that much effort nearly put me on the floor.

Turning, I looked back at the witch. It was her hair that had snatched up Arni. She cradled him in her arms, holding him tight while stroking the spot between his ears with a knuckle. All she had to do to rub that slime on him was turn her hand.

"What a plump treasure you are," she crooned to Arni before looking up at me. "How fat and succulent for the roasting spit!"

"You let go of my dog, hag!"

She fixed her eye on me and shot a quick glance at Oparal. The paladin had grabbed one of the other hags by the hair, while the hag held onto her sword arm to keep the holy sword out of her guts.

I saw a nasty gleam in the eye of the hag holding Arni, and I knew without the boss telling me there was magic in it. She was trying to tell me something without everybody else hearing what she had to say. She made a V with her fingers and waggled 'em.

I got it all right. Elf ears for bunny ears. Arni for Oparal. The hag grinned when she saw I understood the message.

"I got a better idea," I said, taking the big knife in hand and throwing her the big smile.

That got her attention. When I ran for her, she dropped Bunny Arni and reached for me with a slimy hand.

The nasty stuff was enough to make me flinch. At the last second I went low instead of high, but she still saw it coming. As I brought up the big knife to gut her, she beat away my hand and grabbed me by the face.

Even with the boss's magic in me, she was stronger. I hollered as the slime burned into my pretty mug. She lifted me up as if I were the one light as a bunny.

I dropped the knife, screaming and scratching at her hand, trying to tear through it to scrape away the slime.

She spun me around and threw me across the room. I clawed at my eyes, but it was too late. They'd already turned to slime. Where my fingers sank into them, they started dissolving, too.

I could barely hear the boss shouting my name over the sound of my own screaming. Then I fell into something cold and wet and rancid. My stomach turned inside out, filling my throat with vomit.

There was something else moving inside whatever I'd fallen into. A thousand little legs crawling down my collar and up my sleeves.

Then they began eating me alive.

Chapter Six
The Cathedral

Varian

For an appalling instant, I feared Radovan was dead before he plunged into the rotting hulk. When his screams grew louder than the din of battle, I felt a fierce mixture of relief that he lived and pity for his agony. Dozens of red-and-black centipedes, each the length of my forearm, poured out of the amphibian's corpse.

For an insane instant, I imagined they fled from Radovan's screams. No natural insects, they had been tainted by the foul energies of the Worldwound. Their myriad hooked legs left trails of sizzling venom across the carcass.

For a hopeful instant, I prayed my earlier hypothesis proved correct and that Desna had guided the hag's aim when she flung Radovan into the ugsome pile.

"Your friend!" Alase shouted beside me. Pity replaced the usually tough tenor of her voice. Her fingers traced arcane gestures I recognized as a spell to enhance our alacrity. "Tonbarse, defend us!"

The great wolf loped forward, but some invisible force turned him aside. He yelped at the impact, then growled and snapped blindly at his attacker.

Alase's call to Tonbarse reminded me of Arnisant's plight. The hare he had become hopped miserably across the cathedral floor, balking each time it encountered the trampling feet of the drowned men, their hags, the crusaders, or my remaining Kellid guards. Arnisant wanted to go to Radovan, but he could barely control the unfamiliar legs of his transformed body. He could do no good in his present form. "Arnisant, come!"

Alase exclaimed again as something dark flew out of the amphibian's flank. The ragged object fell wetly to the floor. Fiendish vermin scattered from it, fleeing the howling prisoner that thrashed within the gigantic carcass.

The discarded thing first appeared to be a great hank of flayed flesh, and I shared Alase's horror. But then I recognized it as the latest of Radovan's perpetually doomed jackets.

A stream of Chelish curses followed the garment out of the putrid heap, transforming midstream into even fouler words in the tongue of Hell. The amphibian's carcass swelled and shuddered.

Before I could shout a warning, the remains exploded, showering friend and foe alike with malodorous gore. The stench had been disgusting before, but now it became truly noxious. Throughout the room, all the living creatures—even the hags—gagged and choked. The combatants staggered away, retching uncontrollably.

I covered my mouth and pinched shut my nose. Once I felt I would not regurgitate at the slightest motion, I tugged the scented handkerchief from my sleeve and wiped the tears from my eyes.

An infernal figure uncoiled from the shredded remains of the amphibian's carcass, dripping like a child from the womb of an unwholesome mother.

In their nook against the eastern wall, the horses screamed and threw themselves against the walls in a futile effort to escape. Even the dead men balked in their attacks, and everyone present looked toward the new arrival.

The devil was far larger than I had remembered, standing nearly twice my stature as it rose to its full height, and with even more mass than the mighty Tonbarse. I wondered whether the enclosed space emphasized its true size or it had grown since I first saw it in Kyonin.

It resembled an emaciated devil with a humanoid frame and a scorpion's tail arching from the base of its spine to hang over its head. Unlike the drawings of its kind I had studied, this fiend had the triangular build of a wrestler and a dark, iridescent carapace over rufescent limbs. Its visage was a dreadful conjunction of arachnid and flayed human skull.

I knew it by the name it had told Radovan: Fell Viridio.

Viridio first entered Golarion when Radovan selected him to step through the gate—or rather, to step through Radovan himself. Through a centuries-old scheme, Radovan had been born a gate to other worlds.

Terrible worlds.

From the last prince of Ustalav down to Radovan, a coterie of devils had sired or borne all the remaining descendants of the Virholt line. Their goal: to breed their personal passage from Hell to Golarion. But all did not go according to their plan. At some point demons had insinuated themselves into the bloodline, causing Radovan to be born a flawed portal not only to Hell but also to the Abyss.

This imperfection proved fortunate for Radovan in one respect. While both Viridio and a devil named Norge had previously transposed their bodies onto his, neither could dominate his personality. Once Radovan had endured the devil's sigil—in Viridio's case, apparently venom—the fiend could project its body into the world, but its psyche remained an observer.

Encouraged by his survival of the hag's grievous attack, I called out to him. "Radovan!"

The devil turned to me, its mandibles twitching on either side of a toothy maw. "Radovan's not here, you conceited little cripple. You know my name. Speak it!"

The room went silent but for the moaning of the drowned men and the restless clatter of horses' hooves. Oparal's crusaders, uncertain where the greater danger stood, shifted away from Viridio while continuing to hack down the undead. My men retreated to stand by me, I suspected more to receive the protection of my magic than to grant me the safety of their swords.

Full well did I know, contrary to popular belief, that speaking a devil's true name does not always grant one power over the fiend. Under certain circumstances it can seal one's doom by granting it power over the speaker. I recalled that Viridio had required Radovan to utter his name to bring him through the gate, while Norge had never done so.

"Go on, say it," insisted the devil.

I dared not.

The standoff continued as Oparal regrouped with her crusaders. They stood back to back, defending each other with shield and blade against foes both seen and unseen. The drowned men staggered back into the cathedral entrance and stood wavering, halted by some unheard command from their mistress. Tonbarse returned to Alase, and the rather large brown hare that Arnisant had become leaned heavily upon my shin, trembling.

A shrieking laugh broke the silence. With the Shadowless Sword in hand, I saw through all illusions, including invisibility. One of the hags stood not far from the devil. Hers was the only head thrown back, but I heard the laughter of at least four voices. While my sword revealed only visual illusions, it required no great feat of deduction to realize the hags had multiplied their voices to give the impression of greater numbers.

Viridio was no more fooled than I. His monstrous hand lashed out, grabbing the nearby hag around the waist and hoisting her up before his face. She shrieked and raised her hands to weave a spell, but the devil shook her hard, spoiling the effort.

Viridio scanned the room. He glowered at the crusaders, with a brief, sinister smile at Oparal's unicorn. He barely seemed to notice me or Alase, but his eyes lingered on Arnisant and Tonbarse before he turned to the hag who had presented herself as Saint Lymirin.

"You there, fake saint. I see you just fine." The leader of the hags had begun tracing a spell in the air, but the sound of the devil's voice halted her gestures. "What's your name, witch?"

It occurred to me that Viridio had not been present for the illusion of Saint Lymirin. I perceived a shift in his speech pattern.

The hag froze, perhaps uncertain whether Viridio was bluffing about seeing her. His gaze so perfectly followed the motion of her face that she relented and revealed herself to all.

"You can call me Briktawite, dearie. I can see you aren't like these other trespassers. Perhaps—"

"You were really going to eat that bunny?"

Again she hesitated, sensing as I did that a penalty would accompany the wrong answer. "No," she said slowly. "The truth is that we prefer horseflesh, and manflesh when we can find it. You can see we have plenty to share. The bunny was just my little joke."

"Huh," said Viridio. His deep laughter vibrated through the stone floor. He stretched his neck in a familiar gesture, first left, then right. Radovan's mind was at least partially present, if not struggling for control. "Funny joke."

"Yes!" said the hag, cackling with laughter. "Did you see their faces?"

"I see yours." Viridio opened his fiendish jaws and bit off the head of his captive, his segmented eyes never leaving Briktawite's sagging face.

The captive had no time to scream, but Briktawite and her surviving sister shrieked for her.

Among the shattered pews, the horses panicked again. With no path of escape that did not lead to undead, hags, a devil, or a gigantic wolf, they lunged against each other and the stony walls. Unchecked, they would soon kill themselves.

"Blech." Viridio chewed a few times and spat out the pulverized remains of the hag's skull. "Bitter. I want something fresh. Is that a rat in your skirt?"

"What?" screeched Briktawite. She reached down to touch the rodent, which clung tightly to the strands of her skirt. "Not my precious Wriggletooth!"

Tossing aside the remains of his snack, Viridio pounced.

Briktawite's hair flew up like sodden whips, catching a rafter and pulling her upward. Viridio's claws caught in her skirt, tearing away river weeds and rusty blades—but not the rat—before he crashed to the floor. Marble tiles crumbled under his weight. Nearby, the unicorn reared and shrieked, its body twisting side to side as it struggled with the opposing instincts to fight or flee.

"Come to me, Bastiel!" called Oparal. Still skittish, the unicorn obeyed, treading a wide detour around Viridio to reach his mistress.

From above, Briktawite cried, "Heaven and Hell! The coven is broken. Muslera, flee for your life! Every witch for herself!" She leaped off the rafter and flew through the gap in the sundered western wall.

Still invisible to all but me and Viridio, Muslera flew after Briktawite. I saw no benefit to pursuit, but I watched Viridio's black eyes follow the witches as they fled toward the setting sun. He muttered, seemingly to himself.

Then he answered himself in a different tone.

Radovan was negotiating with his devil.

I heard a sound above me. The enormous Tonbarse had moved close. He looked down, licking his chops as he stared at the hare huddling against my foot.

"Mind your wolf," I told Alase.

"Tonbarse is not a wolf. He is a god."

"Mind him anyway." I drew a riffle scroll from my bandolier and discharged it at the hare. In a matter of seconds, the creature grew larger and more hound-like until Arnisant sprawled on the floor beside me, surprised by his changing center of balance. Recovering himself, he sat proudly at my side, gazing defiantly up at the far larger Tonbarse.

"What about your god?" said Alase.

"What?"

"It's still Radovan, isn't it? You called him Radovan."

"It's . . . It's complicated," I told her. The truth was that I did not know the answer, though I hoped for the best. "Radovan? Are you with us?"

The devil—Radovan, Viridio, or both of them together—had made no aggressive moves since the hags' departure, but he continued to stare out the broken wall. I moved to give myself a view of his face, but he turned away. I glimpsed only his multifaceted eyes and the slight motion of his jaws, as if he were mouthing words to himself.

"Captain?" asked Oparal's bearded sergeant. "Your orders?"

"Aprian, you're with me," she said. "Bastiel, stand fast. The rest of you calm the horses. Count Jeggare, I trust you have the fiend under control."

"Of course." The lie came easily, and I regretted the need for it. I told myself I had spoken hastily, surprised by Oparal's commanding tone. In Kyonin, the paladin had been assigned to serve me at the behest of Queen Telandia. Here, she commanded her own squad of crusaders. Her assertive manner was both unfamiliar and strangely appealing.

Oparal drew her sword. Its blade blazed white, but not as brightly as I had seen it shine in the presence of demons. If it grew brighter, we would have warning that more of them approached.

Oparal and Aprian strode toward the drowned men massed by the doorway. They held their blades point-downward as they advanced, prayers upon their lips.

At the approach of the living, the now-masterless dead lurched forward. Before they could lay their loathsome hands upon the crusaders, golden light radiated from the hilts of the paladins' swords. The damp faces of the dead parched and withered. Their bodies fell to the ground, inanimate.

That was one problem solved. I turned to address the next great danger in the room.

"Radovan?"

"Stay away, boss." Despite the *basso profundo* voice, the speech patterns were more Radovan's own. He continued to face west, away from us, murmuring to himself.

Arnisant looked at me for permission. In the past, his intervention had calmed Radovan in his struggles with an infernal presence. I gave Arnisant the gesture to go.

The hound padded over to sit beside the fiend, in which I hoped my friend's mind had regained dominance. Radovan raised a massive claw. My breath caught in my throat, but he brought it down gently to stroke Arnisant's head. The big hound seemed tiny beside the enormous devil.

"Count," said one of the surviving sellswords. It was Gannak, he of the regrettable nipple rings. When I turned to him, he indicated the line of crusaders standing at attention behind their impatient-looking commander. One of them removed his cape and gave it to the naked man they had defended during the fray.

It was time to address the last great danger in the room.

"Well met, Captain Oparal." I bowed in the fashion of the Mendevian court, hoping she would not consider the gesture too calculated. My smile, while tempered by our continued peril, was quite sincere.

"Count Jeggare." She returned my bow with a military salute. She did not return my smile, but she did nod. "I suppose I must thank you for your timely intervention."

"Not at all," I said. "I thank Desna for the concinnity of our meeting."

Her eyes narrowed as she worked out the meaning of the term by context. "You should thank Iomedae for the opportunity to mete justice against those who would profane the images of her servants."

"Praise Iomedae," murmured her crusaders. The response might have seemed rehearsed in other circumstances, but I saw true devotion in their weary eyes.

Oparal's strained dogma stole from Desna in her aspect of Lady Luck, but I nodded polite agreement. The faithful of Iomedae often attributed the aspects of other deities to their goddess. Crusader logic, while often twisted by the inquisitors of Mendev, often sounded both simplistic and sincere.

"Speaking of concinnity," I said, "do I surmise correctly that you have come in search of a book?"

Oparal's dark eyes narrow in suspicion. I sympathized with her distrust, especially after the hags' elaborate ruse, but it pained me to see her skepticism directed at me. After the events in Kyonin, I hoped we had earned some measure of mutual trust. She said, "I am here in service to Crusader Queen Galfrey."

"As am I."

Her expression of disbelief could not have been more insulting, or more sincere.

While not the simple truth, neither was my claim false. Still, I thought it best to clarify. "That is to say, I am acting indirectly in her service. I have come at the behest of Ollystra Zadrian of the Silver Crusade." Oparal's expression remained nonplussed, but some quality of the dusky light in her gray eyes prompted me to add, "And also at the behest of other parties."

"Abrogail." She spat the queen's name, reinforcing my suspicion that her allegiance in Cheliax lay with the Wiscrani rebels who sought to overthrow the House of Thrune. That would explain her distrust of me, her distaste for the intrigues of the elven court, and her subsequent admission to the Mendevian Crusade.

"Her Infernal Majestrix, yes. And also at the request of Queen Telandia Edasseril."

Behind Oparal, the other crusaders exchanged glances but remained silent. Their commander was less reticent to voice their concern.

"You are a man of many loyalties," said Oparal.

"I prefer to think of myself as a man of many friends," I said. "You among them."

"I aided you at the time because I was in service to Queen Telandia."

"As you are now in service to Queen Galfrey. Perhaps you are becoming a woman of many friends."

She did not miss the implication of my verbal riposte. Her brow furrowed, and for a moment I feared she might treat me as she had Radovan on their first meeting, with a brutal slap. Instead, a rueful smile crossed her dark lips. "Fair enough, Count."

"Please, Oparal. Let me remind you that, in the field, you may address me as 'Varian.'"

"In the field, you may address me as 'Captain.'"

Her insolence stung. I felt my cheek flush as though she had indeed slapped me this time. "Must I remind you of my station?"

"We are not in Cheliax Jeggare."

"Nor are we in Mendev, Captain Oparal. We are in a land of chaos, surrounded by dreadful foes. To survive, we must aid each other, but to succeed we must do more than that. We must cooperate. How is it that you cannot—?" As her face hardened, I realized my mistake.

In my ire, I had failed to consider her position and that of her followers. We had come to their aid unbidden, and despite their prowess against the hags' undead forces, the crusaders might well have suffered disaster had we not intervened.

In short, we had humiliated them. For all their virtues, the Mendevian crusaders were also known for an abundance of pride.

Lowering my voice, I opted for a delaying tactic. "Perhaps you and I might discuss the particulars in private, later. Until then, I would welcome your assistance in the ossuary."

"The crypts?" Oparal appeared surprised.

"It would not be the first time we have explored a tomb together." I smiled in what I hoped was a disarming manner. Her continued expression of perplexity confused me for a moment until I realized the truth. "You did not expect to find the *Lexicon* here, did you?"

"No. We sought shelter from a battle. The hags' illusion— You think the book is here?"

"Throughout Storasta, the clergy were instrumental in preserving ancient knowledge. In many cases their libraries far exceeded those of the sages and scholars who in the south are better known for such deeds. Furthermore, my information on these ruins—" I nodded toward Alase, our guide "—indicates that the other likely sites have been thoroughly pillaged or taken over by hostile forces, demonic and otherwise."

As Oparal considered what I had said, she glanced over my shoulder and did a double take. I looked back to see Viridio had risen and walked back toward the mutilated husk of the amphibian. His chitinous feet crushed a few of the remaining fiendish centipedes.

Oparal had beheld Viridio before. The fiend made a terrible sight, especially when the battle-lust was upon him—not to mention the rotting flesh of a giant amphibian.

As Viridio passed too near him, the unicorn whinnied and reared.

"Bastiel, stop it!"

Despite Oparal's command, the unicorn moved forward, horn lowered to strike. He stopped when Arnisant interposed himself. The hound and unicorn had squared off before.

Viridio—or rather, Radovan in Viridio's body— appeared not to notice the exchange. With every step he shrank a few inches. His scorpionlike features melted away as his skin returned to its natural coppery hue. Lanky blond hair fell to his shoulders. Where the hag's slime had previously destroyed his face, Radovan's golden eyes appeared unmarred. The physical restoration was a wondrous side effect of his unique transformations.

For that phenomenon and others, I sometimes thought that Radovan's condition could prove more blessing than curse, if only it could be controlled. Since torturous pain accompanied the transformations, Radovan naturally did not share my opinion.

Radovan stopped beside the damp leather of his elf-crafted jacket. In the dim light, its leather appeared black rather than green. He held it up, noting a few holes and tears but no egregious damage. He shook off the worst of the nauseating mess covering the garment and shrugged it on.

The short jacket did nothing to protect his modesty.

"Radovan," I said. "There is a lady present."

"She's seen it all before." He pointed at the naked crusader, whose half-cape also failed to lend him decent privacy. "Besides, that guy's got no pants neither."

The other crusaders turned to their captain, apparently intrigued by the implications of Radovan's remark. Oparal's cheeks darkened. Her jaw clenched, but she refused to dignify their curiosity with a response.

Radovan stepped barefoot into the carcass of the abomination and picked through the remains. With a low whistle of relief, he retrieved the starknife he seldom used but always kept on his hip. A moment later he found the Ustalavic copper he had carried since our first visit to Caliphas. After a few more moments, he lifted the shreds of his leather pants. They were beyond repair.

"Dammit!" he grumbled, tossing aside the remnants of the garment. "Any of you mooks got a spare pair of britches?" Before anyone could answer, he resumed his search of the carcass.

The crusaders exchanged reluctant looks. No one wanted to lend clothes to a man who not only transformed into an enormous fiend but also thought nothing of stepping barefoot into a huge rotting corpse.

"I implore you," I said to the company at large. "I have money."

"Desna smiles!" Radovan turned, grinning as he held up his boots, intact if irredeemably besmirched. "I wasn't sure I got them off in time."

"Here." Oparal's bearded second offered me a worn pair of leather trousers from his horse's saddlebags.

"I believe I speak for all present when I offer you my heartfelt gratitude, Sergeant."

Aprian smiled, but only for a second. After handing off the trousers, he returned to stand two feet behind and to the right of his captain.

As Radovan made himself decent, Oparal and I took turns introducing our companies while they lit torches against the increasing gloom.

I memorized the names and deduced the nationalities, social rank, and in most cases the soldiers' individual motivations for joining the crusade. Silvio was obviously a former slave, perhaps freed on the battlefield. By his grim demeanor and the corner of a lace handkerchief protruding from his breastplate, I imagined the former Eagle Knight, Tolliver, had fled a failed romance.

The others impressed me to various degrees and in different manners, but none stood out so much as the pragmatic Sergeant Aprian and the Thuvian sorceress, Jelani. Alone among Oparal's company, Jelani offered no outward clues as to why she had joined the crusaders.

After reciting the names of our surviving Kellid swordsmen—Roga, Gannak, and the giant Kronug—I introduced our guide to Oparal. "This young woman is—"

Alase stepped in front of me and offered the paladin her hand. "Alase Brinz-Widowknife, guide and god caller."

"Ah, yes," I said. "And apparently her own herald."

"All part of the service, boss."

"Hey!" said Radovan. He sat on the floor, folding cuffs at the end of Aprian's pants to keep from treading on them.

"What?" said Alase.

"Never mind. Forget it. What's a god caller, anyway?"

"How can you not know that?" Alase spread her hands. "Maybe you got some different name for it. When I call Tonbarse, he fights beside me."

"More often before you," replied the giant wolf. Everyone but Alase startled at the human tones of his deep voice. More disturbing by far was the unnatural manner in which his lupine lips stretched to form the syllables.

The diminutive god caller ignored her eidolon and walked a circle around Radovan, examining him from every angle. She seemed disappointed that he had put on his clothes. "I've heard tell of callers like you, who wear the god's body like armor."

"You don't know him like I know him." Radovan scoffed. "Viridio definitely ain't a god."

"Radovan! Let us avoid uttering that name."

"How come, boss? We've said it plenty since Kyonin."

"Yes, but . . . humor me."

"You got it, boss." From the floor, he smiled up at Alase, not too widely, but enough to assure me he had once more recovered from his trauma with astonishing alacrity. "See? That's what I call him."

"He pays me, too. Why are you the only one to call him 'boss'?"

"Forget it. Tell me more about how I'm a god." He looked past Alase to wink at Oparal. "Turns out my body really is a temple. Maybe I need some paladins of my own, keep the place shipshape."

"Not a god," said Alase. "A god caller." She looked at him again, reconsidering.

"See, boss? You and the captain sizing each other up, it don't matter. I'd outrank you both, even if I wasn't already the Prince—"

"Radovan."

He blinked, realizing he had gone too far. "—of Eel Street. You know, royalty among the street gangs. That's what I meant."

Oparal shook her head and turned her back to Radovan. "Why were you here? We withdrew from a mob of wicked fey, including treefolk like those we saw at the Century Root, only tainted by the Worldwound."

"That doesn't sound like something you'd want to take on," said Radovan. "Not without the dragon, anyway."

Alase's mouth fell open. "You had a dragon?"

"Not 'had' had." Radovan cast a skeptical eye at me and added, "Not me, anyway. The boss, on the other hand, dropped in on her last winter, and I can't vouch for anything he may or may not—"

"Radovan!" I choked.

He shrugged. I saw mischief dancing in his golden eyes. It was a relief to see him in good humor after the trauma of Viridio's return, but not at the cost of my dignity.

Oparal cleared her throat. "What is it you found downstairs?"

I bowed my thanks for her returning us to the more pressing matter. "Come with me, Captain. There is something I wish to show you."

Chapter Seven
The Ossuary

Oparal

Bastiel blew and struck his hooves upon the stone floor.

The unicorn wanted to accompany me everywhere, but he was simply too large to enter the crypt stairway. When I reached up to soothe him, he tossed his head to avoid my touch. He danced aside and pushed once more toward Radovan.

"Take it easy, big fella." The hellspawn raised his empty hands and stepped behind a granite pillar. The muscles of his neck tensed. The torchlight reflecting in his yellow eyes gave him a wolfish cast, and I feared as much for Bastiel's safety as for his if they should fight.

Again I felt a fluttering against the ceiling of my stomach. The sense of surrounding evil had persisted ever since we set foot in the accursed city, so strong that it made me second-guess my gut reactions.

From our first meeting, I had detected an aura of intense wickedness from the hellspawn. Count Jeggare later persuaded me that what I sensed was not Radovan himself but the result of his ancestral connection to Hell. That revelation did little to reassure me, but later events in the City of Thorns persuaded me that these Chelaxians were both foes to demons and allies to elves. And when the veil of deception was finally lifted on our expedition, I found it was not the Chelaxians but the elves who had most deceived me.

Perhaps Radovan was not truly evil, but the butterflies didn't know.

"Bastiel," I called. Ignoring me, the unicorn positioned himself for a clear charge at Radovan. A glance at the count and his hirelings told me he would remain patient a little longer while I gained control of my unruly steed. "Bastiel, come to me now!"

Before Bastiel could obey, the count's wolfhound rushed to Radovan's defense, barking furiously at the much larger unicorn. While I could not fully trust the count or his hellspawn henchman, that hound had always seemed to be a paragon of courage and loyalty. If only Bastiel could have demonstrated a fraction of the hound's obedience.

"Bastiel!"

At last he withdrew, but he did not come to me. Arnisant herded him like a shepherd, cutting him off each time Bastiel took a step in Radovan's direction. They ended up beside the horses who stirred, still frightened, in the eastern wing.

"Jealous old thing," Alase clucked at Bastiel.

"You don't know what you're talking about," I said, bristling.

"Right." Alase looked at the hellspawn and back to me. She rolled her eyes.

While I sensed no evil in her, nor from the night-black wolf she summoned, Alase struck me as reckless, even dangerous. From the writings of Pastor Bromon Shy, which were popular among the crusaders, I knew that these self-professed "god callers" of lost Sarkoris were simply arcane summoners who thought of their eidolons as gods. Therein lay their true danger: Superstition blinded them to the truth. They could not distinguish good from evil.

Jelani smiled at Alase before glancing back at me to see whether I'd noticed. She saw that I had and tried to smother her smile.

After all these weeks of forging squadron unity, we would soon be undone by gossip and misfortune. I had hoped for better from Jelani. A woman can be a perfectly rational being. Put her with another woman and remove the bonds of discipline, however, and suddenly their collective maturity drops to the level of goblins, small children, or men.

I glanced at Count Jeggare as I went to calm Bastiel. Whatever else one might say about the count, he was almost as clever as he believed himself to be. With a gesture, he called off his hound, while I spoke quietly to the unicorn who had graced me with his service.

"You've nothing to fear, Bastiel." He allowed me to stroke his nose as I murmured words meant only for his ears.

Some mistake them for beasts, but unicorns understand elven and human speech perfectly. According to song, they can even speak, but I had never encountered another unicorn, and I had never heard Bastiel utter a word. Before we met, Bastiel had suffered grievous wounds at the hands of the fiends of

Kyonin. Perhaps the trauma had taken away the power of speech. "I won't be going alone, and I need you here to guard our backs."

Bastiel nosed my hand. I removed the gauntlet and let him nuzzle my palm. His body bore the faded scars of a hundred battles, but his pink lips remained perfectly unblemished. "You're the one I trust," I said. "You know I'll always come back to you."

He raised his head to look down on me. His eyes were the perfection of blue, halfway between the color of the sky and that of the deep sea. After one last instant of fear, Bastiel's gaze dissolved into one of uncomplicated acceptance.

Count Jeggare ordered his swordsmen to remain on watch beside my troops. The Kellids seemed reluctant to remain behind, except for the enormous Kronug, whom I'd seen rubbing a bruised lump on his shaved skull. The crypt ceilings must have been too low for the towering warrior. Despite their celebrated courage, after witnessing the magic of their employers, the Kellids must have wondered whether they were the guards or the guarded.

Jeggare activated the light on one of his rings, but rather than lead the way he passed the light to Radovan. The hellspawn and the wolfhound descended while Jeggare waited for me to join them.

Alase whispered to her enormous wolf and pressed her suddenly glowing hands upon its flank. "Wait here, Tonbarse."

The gigantic beast regarded her with a paternal attitude before nodding like a human. Alase gripped his midnight fur, which glimmered here and there with a light not of our torches, but of the unseen stars. "I'll be right back," said Alase. She followed Radovan down the crypt stairs.

To see her bid the animal farewell gave me an unwanted pang of sympathy. Wolf, hound, and unicorn, I thought. Was the presence of our inhuman companions a sign that we were meant to work together?

Wolf, hound, unicorn, and fiend, I reminded myself. Perhaps Radovan's devil was the real sign. One of these inhuman companions could not be more unlike the others.

Dragomir exchanged a glance with the man who claimed to be the reincarnated Porfirio, who stood awkwardly in the ill-fitting clothes taken from his own saddlebags. I did not recognize his body, but the way he held the borrowed sword and shield were familiar. Neither the butterflies nor Jelani's spells revealed deception.

I beckoned my sergeant over and quietly asked, "What do you think? Is he really Porfirio?"

Aprian shrugged. "It seems incredible that the hags would actually reincarnate him only to return him to us."

Lingering by the crypt stairs, the count raised an eyebrow, reminding me not to underestimate his half-elven hearing. I sighed, exasperated as much by my mistake as by his eavesdropping. I beckoned him over, and he readily obliged.

"I presume you have an opinion on the matter."

"The cruelty of hags rivals that of the most depraved devils," he said. "I would not be surprised in the least to learn they did in fact slay and reincarnate him. Beyond using him to reinforce their illusion, murdering him a second time before his lover's eyes is exactly the sort of sport a coven of hags would relish."

"His lover?"

"Pardon me," said the count. "I thought it was obvious."

I looked again at Porfirio and Dragomir, who remained standing close, speaking quietly. They had always seemed close, but I had taken their bond for the camaraderie of soldiers. I looked at Aprian, who nodded confirmation without any indication that I was the last to understand.

"Oh." I recalled his words to Dragomir and felt embarrassed to have been oblivious to their unusually strong bond. I had no sense for such things, as I had proven in my last friendly hours with Ederras. Whether between men, women, or a man and a woman, the mysteries of romance held no allure for me. Beneath the shadows of love lay only deception, pain, and the sundering of genuine friendship.

"Aprian, take command here."

He nodded acknowledgment.

I considered leaving both Porfirio and Dragomir with Aprian. Keeping them together would give them an opportunity to recover from their shock, yet I wanted another paladin with me before exploring the crypt. In Cheliax, it was considered bad for morale to put paired couples in the same unit, yet the Kyonin rangers would never separate lovers in the field. The choice was infuriating, yet in the end I chose to leave Dragomir. "Porfirio, Jelani, Urno, you're with me."

With a borrowed sword at his side and a spare helm upon his head, Porfirio responded without hesitation. Despite his larger size and strange face, he moved more or less like the crusader I had seen dragged away by ghouls only hours earlier. He followed me down the stairs.

Jelani illuminated her dagger with a touch and held it up as a torch. We descended the stairs, following the light of the count's magic ring. Within ten steps, the walls changed from polished granite to rough-hewn stone.

As the count moved forward to meet Radovan and Alase, Porfirio came close and whispered, "Excuse me, Captain?"

I nodded.

"Is this Count Jeggare the one known as Abrogail's rat-catcher?"

The question shocked me because I should have known the answer. At Porfirio's prompting, I remembered the name Jeggare from the Children of Westcrown's caution list. At the time I gave it little mind since the Jeggare in question operated in Egorian, not Westcrown.

Now I realized I might have allied myself with one of the wicked empire's most notorious servants.

In the weeks we had spent in the Fierani Forest, Count Jeggare had more often defied than confirmed my expectations of a Thrune loyalist. Furthermore, he had surprised me more than once with his knowledge of the Inheritor's teachings. At the time I thought he was revealing a secret, but I considered that he was also well versed in Abyssal and infernal lore. Perhaps his familiarity with *The Acts of Iomedae* was the result of his studying the enemy.

"We will discuss it later," I whispered close to his ear. "Keep in mind that a half-elf's hearing is better than yours, and sound carries far in narrow passages."

His eyes widened. He nodded. Again, despite his strange features, I knew those expressions for Porfirio's own.

Jeggare's party awaited us at the base of the stairs. We joined them in a roughly circular antechamber. Despite the late summer warmth above, frost rimed the rough stone walls, and our breath formed fleeting spectres in the air. I suppressed a shudder.

In the center of the floor was graven a cluster of bones winding out into the outer passage, which also appeared to spiral outward. I glanced up at the vaulted ceiling. Its architecture shared the stately grace of the cathedral above us, with the addition of a chandelier composed entirely of yellowed bones.

Jelani transferred the light from her dagger to the chandelier, but could not suppress a shudder. "Is this a Sarkorian or Ustalavic crypt?"

"An astute question," said Count Jeggare. "The founding clergy came from Odranto after an Ustalavic priestess received an unexpected inheritance when her entire family was killed. She sold the estate and used the resulting wealth to lure the most celebrated architect of Kavapesta here to build Nekrasof Tower. Unfortunately, neither the priestess's largess nor the architect endured long enough to see the cathedral to completion."

"The stone of the walls looks like the same used in the wardstones." I traced a silvered rune upon the wall. "And these sigils appear Sarkorian."

"Once Storasta was a melting pot of Sarkorian and foreign architecture." Jeggare indicated a prominent carving on a rose-colored stone set into the wall. "This marble marks the founding of the cathedral in 3851. When Adyson Stormont came to Storasta six years earlier, he brought civilization with him."

Alase snorted.

"Perhaps I should say he brought southern culture with him, and those who joined him here brought more. Before the Pharasmins erected the tower above us, this site was already dedicated to the gods. Perhaps you saw the pits outside."

I nodded.

"They were once standing stones."

"That's so," said Alase. "They stood in a ring around this tower till mighty Carrock pulled them out to decorate his how."

"His what?" said Radovan.

"An old word for 'hollow,'" said Jeggare. He fixed his eyes on Radovan, as if expecting a retort. When none came, Jeggare seemed both relieved and disappointed. Since his transformation, Radovan had remained distracted, even after he ceased muttering to himself.

"Carrock? The fiend who chased us here?" said Jelani.

"He was the hero of Storasta, once." Alase chanted, "'Carrock enduring, valorous.'"

Jeggare nodded agreement. "The final passages of 'The Song of Sarkoris' describe his fall and corruption as the fiends fell upon the city."

"With respect, Count Jeggare, while I enjoy your illuminations of history—"

"Yes, time is a factor. Allow me to show you what we discovered before you arrived."

He led the way down the outward-spiraling passage. To either side, the keepers of the dead had crammed bones into alcoves four ranks high. The nooks were not home to individual skeletons but instead to collections of similar bones: shins in one, thighs in another.

"Ghastly," remarked Porfirio. This time, I did not mind his sharing the sentiment with the others, but I was surprised when Alase was the first to agree.

"This is not right," she said. "The people of Storasta would not gather the dead in such a manner. Our shamans released the bodies of our dead into the river."

"For the Sarkorian dead, so did the Pharasmins. The clerics of the Lady of Graves respect local customs." Jeggare pointed to rows of names engraved between the catacomb cells. "These are southern and Ustalavic names. No doubt these are their bones."

Jelani gasped as she peered into the shadows before us.

"Ah," said Jeggare, shining the light of his ring down the corridor. "The first tableau."

Cemented into the wall were the skeletons of half a dozen figures, including a rearing warhorse. Their bones had been tinted to suggest clothes, armor, hair, and even blood streaming from their wounds.

Atop the horse rode a man as tall as Kronug. Beneath his steed's hooves, a skeleton decorated in shamanic designs lay fallen on the ground, a shattered headpiece beneath his cracked skull.

"Uloric Dziergas," Jeggare translated from the legend carved beneath the scene. "After the shamans of Storasta burned the city's bridges to protest southern trade treaties, the warlord gathered the witch-wardens of Sarkoris's other cities and overthrew them."

"That is so," agreed Alase. "He conquered, but he did not rule. He left Taare Trathen in charge of Storasta."

"Trathen's Gate," said Jelani.

The count rewarded her with a bow, bringing a smile to Jelani's lips. I would have preferred to see her brush off such a courtesy with a military demeanor. "After he rebuilt the bridges, Trathen put up that wall and spent the rest of his life expanding the city's trade with southern nations."

"Half of the rest of his life," said Alase. When Jeggare raised an eyebrow, she said, "He spent the other half in the brothels on the strip of land just west of Carrock's How. And so the Storastans called it 'Trathen's Finger.'" She wiggled her smallest finger in front of her crotch, in case we did not understand her inference.

At first, only Radovan chuckled. Infected by his laughter, Jelani joined in.

Radovan and Alase were threatening to become bad influences on my sorcerer.

"But this makes no sense," said Alase. "Ulori Dziergas didn't die here. He didn't even remain after the battle. How can these be his bones?"

"They are not his, nor are the bones in the other tableaux those of the figures they depict. The Pharasmin sects who create such monuments believe that, after death, an individual's bones lose all spiritual association with the departed soul. Like wood, feathers, precious stones, or other beautiful materials, they are natural material to be used in holy art."

"And southerners think us strange," complained Alase. "You're the strange ones."

"Sweetheart, you got no idea how right you are." Radovan gave her that crude grin he thinks is so irresistible.

Alase grinned back at him. "Maybe I'll find out."

"Maybe you will."

"Let's move along," I said.

Jeggare appeared ready to express a similar sentiment, but I noticed Jelani's gaze kept returning to Alase and Radovan. In her eyes I saw a mixture of amusement and longing. Maybe the unrestrained banter of the summoner and the scoundrel provided her a welcome release from the regimen of the past few months. Yet it was that very discipline that helped us survive the perils we faced.

No matter, I decided. Alase and Radovan were definitely bad influences.

We followed the spiraling catacombs outward. Between long ranks of bone depositories, we encountered several more tableaux, each more garish than the last. Without pausing, the count explained that the dyes were fresher than those we observed at the beginning, where the images were hundreds of years old. We were moving forward in time the farther we traveled along the spiral passage. At last we came to a place barely a century old. Farther along the passage, empty crypts gaped like mouths to either side. Farther still, the stone supports gave way to rotting timber frames and walls of dark clay.

"Here," said Jeggare. He stopped before a tableau of a ceremonial procession beneath a great tower whose parapets disappeared into the clouds. Three skeletal figures walked arm-in-arm, each adorned in symbols of witchery and arcana. One bore a cudgel, one held a pointed knife, and the third walked with a staff with an elaborate, bejeweled head. Behind the trio, a pair of bearers carried away a litter. The first held his bony finger to his lips, as if slipping away from the scene of a burglary. Rather than a human occupant, the litter held stacks of books, scrolls, bundled sticks, pots, and urns—all carved of stone and dyed in startlingly bright colors. On each item I noticed a Sarkorian pictogram.

With his long index finger, the count indicated a line of engraved text. "This tableau was created only a few years after the first opening of the Worldwound. Unfortunately, the legend was never completed. However, if you are familiar with Storastan history, it seems apparent that—"

"That's God Caller Opon with the cudgel," said Alase. She seemed oblivious to the count's annoyance at the interruption. "And in the middle is Areelu Vorlesh. You can tell by the knife and the beads trailing off her pelvis like the tail of a dress."

"Thank you, Alase. As I was explaining—"

"And this is Wivver Noclan with his wizard's staff. He was the first to realize their mistake, for all the good it did him. Like the count said, these can't be their bones. Opon and Wivver went straight into the portal when Areelu gave herself to Deskari. She's not dead. She's not even mortal anymore. She learned the trick to turn herself into a fiend, or partly, anyway."

"If you will permit me to finish . . ."

"Go on, you. You're the boss."

Radovan sneezed into the corner of his elbow to cover a laugh. Despite his mirth, I saw deep lines on his face I hadn't noticed before. His transformation had left its mark on him.

Jeggare straightened his posture and continued. "The gist of the image is that these skeletons represent the three prisoners responsible for opening the rift to the Abyss."

"Prisoners?" said Porfirio. "I thought the Three were powerful witches."

"One was a witch. The others were a wizard and a summoner—what Alase would call a god caller."

"I call Tonbarse. He's a god." She spoke with deliberate patience, as if addressing a group of children. "I'm a god caller."

To camouflage my scorn, I signaled to Porfirio to cover the path behind us, to Urno to watch the dark passage before us.

"The ancient Sarkorian clergy—priests, shamans, and druids, among others—distrusted wielders of the arcane, whose powers often led the ignorant to consider them heralds of the gods, or even gods themselves. Rather than destroy them, however, the priests of Sarkoris strove to contain and control their powers."

"They locked them up," said Alase. "They put them in the tallest tower ever built, on the highest hill of the High Cairns."

"A fortress-tower known rather prophetically as the Threshold," said Jeggare. "Its keepers called it a place of learning, where arcanists could employ their talents in the service of the priests."

"Their slave masters," said Jelani.

"Just so. If we had lived in that time, Alase, you and I would surely have found ourselves among their 'guests.' Naturally, those confined within the Threshold saw it as a prison. Opon, Areelu Vorlesh, and Wivver Noclan joined forces to escape. Their plan was to create a number of portals to various destinations. Thus, when the prisoners escaped en masse, their keepers wouldn't know where to begin searching."

"That's not the truth of it," said Alase. "The way it was handed down to me, it was that they wanted to open the doors to all the worlds, show the people the true faces of all the gods."

"Whatever their intention, the Three succeeded in opening portals—thousands of them—but none led to any place they wished to travel."

"I know," said Jelani. "Every one of those little gates led to the Rasping Rifts, the Abyssal domain of the demon lord Deskari." It was a relief to hear my sorcerer contribute to the conversation. I had no wish to depend entirely on Count Jeggare and his summoner for historical intelligence.

"The same demon that Aroden, while he was still a mortal man, once drove into the Lake of Mists and Veils," I added. It was important that the count understand we crusaders were not ignorant of Sarkoris's history. Still, Jeggare provided more detail and a different perspective from the sermons I had heard in the temples of Nerosyan.

"Once the portals had opened even a crack, Areelu heard the whispers of Deskari," said Jeggare. "Seduced by the promises of power, she cast her collaborators into the rift, trapping them between this world and the Abyss."

"Poor devils," said Radovan. "I know exactly how they felt."

Alase cocked her head at him. "They've been imprisoned for over a hundred years."

Radovan shrugged. "So I know kind of how they felt."

"What does this have to do with our current mission?" I said.

"Compared with the other details of the tableau, these carvings are highly distinctive." He tapped a stack of books carved into the wall. Then he removed a notebook from his satchel and opened it to a sketch of a closed book. "Look at this."

I recognized his work. During our journey through the Fierani Forest, he had often stopped to record drawings of the ruins and natural monuments we encountered. The sketch before me seemed less authentic than those, as though he had drawn it not from life but from a description.

It was a thick volume, its pages ragged rather than cut straight. Dark metal reinforced its corners in a distinctive scalloped pattern. Its cover was composed of some thick hide on which Jeggare's sketch suggested a fine, irregular pattern. Upon the book's face were foreign ancient characters.

The count saw me frowning at the letters and said, "Ancient Thassilonian. This is entitled *The Lexicon of Paradox*."

"Yes? And what does it have to do with the tableau?"

"Look here." Once more he tapped the carving of the book.

Once he pointed it out, I recognized the scalloped corners of the volume.

"Surely it doesn't mean they're the same book." Even as I expressed my skepticism, I dared to hope that we had at last discovered a useful clue. Would we have seen it without Jeggare's help? I wished to believe so, but I had my doubts.

"We know from the letters of Pastor Shy that Wivver Noclan had some knowledge of the *Lexicon*," said the count. "This tableau suggests that some party or parties stole away with the materials he and his colleagues used to open the portals at the Threshold."

I mulled over that information. "But what good is that to us? Where is the book now?"

The count tapped the pictogram inscribed on the book's spine. There was no such mark on his sketch of the book. "What does this symbol mean, Alase?"

"Widowknife Clanhold," she said. "That's in Undarin, where Areelu Vorlesh bloodies the river with her sacrifices to the dread lord Deskari."

"Those who did not follow Vorlesh in giving themselves over to Deskari were soon slain," said the count. "But a few escaped, taking with them the arcane instruments of the apocalypse. These they spread throughout the land to keep them from Vorlesh and the Lord of the Locust Host."

"Which ones went to Storasta?"

He tapped another pictogram, a spiral at the base of a great tree. "This means Storasta."

"All right. But where in the city? Do we search Stormont Isle? Iomedae preserve us, do we need to fight our way back into Basseri Green?"

"*The Bones Fall in a Spiral*," said the count.

"What?"

"Pharasma's holy text," he said. "Radovan? If you would."

"Stand back, ladies," said the hellspawn. As he manipulated a few elements of the tableau, that portion of the wall swung inward to reveal a secret chamber. A gust of stale wind escaped the compartment, causing Porfirio's torch to flicker. I looked back to see him standing sentinel behind us, then looked ahead of our group to check on Urno.

The dwarf was nowhere to be seen. His dwarven sight required no torchlight, yet I did not expect him to wander so far.

"Urno?"

He didn't reply. I moved down the passage.

"What's wrong?" asked Jeggare.

Before I could answer, I spied Urno just beyond the terminal curve of the passage. His axe and shield lay on the ground. He stood oddly erect, his head thrown back, one hand grasping some unseen yoke just beneath his throat.

"Wait," said the count. He drew his sword a few inches from its scabbard. His lips whitened as he peered into the darkness. "Show yourself, Kasiya."

"Vampire," Radovan whispered. He repeated the warning to Alase and Jelani, although everyone heard him the first time.

A languid chuckle emanated from the darkness. "You will regret not addressing me by my rightful title." I detected an Osirian accent.

"No, I thought not," said the count. "If my appearance were as loathsome as yours, I too would hide myself in shadows. You were a prince only in life, Kasiya. Now all shall address you as 'Your Lowness.'"

With an angry hiss, Urno's captor appeared behind him, one bandaged arm looped around his neck.

He was of average height, with a lean, muscular build, but every inch of him was concealed in linen wraps and royal finery. He wore a sort of doublet of peacock feathers and a pleated scarlet kilt. From his hip hung one of those curved Osirian swords, a pair of books suspended on chains, and what looked like a toy chariot with a blackened shield and tongue.

A golden mask concealed Kasiya's face, its impassive features painted in enamel. Something dark crawled beneath the openings at his eyes and lips. I thought of worms.

I drew the Ray of Lymirin. Unlike the count's sword, it revealed no illusions. Its powers were far less subtle.

As I moved, the count cupped his hand and shone the light of his ring down the corridor. Urno struggled listlessly in the vampire's grip, his mind as much a captive as his body.

I turned the Ray point-downward. "Iomedae, hear my—"

"Now now," oozed Kasiya's voice. "Can your crusader maiden answer before I tear out your little friend's throat?"

Beside me, the others moved.

Kasiya yanked Urno's head back, exposing his neck. The dwarf shouted in pain.

"I'm beginning to think you don't like this fellow very much."

"Release him."

"Perhaps I shall," said the monstrosity. "First, all of you withdraw into the cathedral."

Valor demanded I refuse, yet I had come too far through too many mortal perils to let one of my troops die before my eyes. I hesitated.

"Kill him," the count said to me.

"But he'll bite Urno."

"With what?"

"Well, his fangs—" Feeling foolish, I realized the flaw in Kasiya's plan. He couldn't bite anyone's throat out until he removed that heavy mask.

The vampire cocked his head as he began to understand. I was already charging.

Behind me, the count triggered one of his rifle scrolls while Jelani uttered an arcane word. A handful of darts and stars whizzed past my shoulder. One glanced off

Kasiya's golden mask, but another stuck in the middle of his golden forehead.

Kasiya shoved Urno forward, forcing me to shift my attack away lest I impale my own man.

"You," said the vampire as he backed away. Silver and red bolts of arcane energy shot into his body, arms, and face. He went down to one knee, all the while keeping his golden gaze locked upon mine.

I raised the Ray above my head, took the grip in both hands, and swept the blade downward. It sizzled as it passed through a greasy miasma where his body had crouched an instant earlier. The foul cloud persisted, rising up to disappear into the earthen ceiling of the passage.

Glancing back, I saw Porfirio already tending to Urno. He lay his hands upon the dwarf's upper chest, light spilling from his palms as he prayed Iomedae's mercy. Urno coughed and muttered thanks.

"How can somebody that stupid keep finding us?" said Radovan.

"It is a mystery to me," said the count. His mocking tone gave way to frustration. "But what he lacks in intellect, he certainly makes up with persistence. We must not delay. What have we found in the hidden cache?"

Jelani peered into the hidden vault. It was no larger than a bookshelf, less than half filled with carved sticks and tiny glass containers. She cast a spell I had seen her use many times in the past. "There's magic here, but nothing powerful."

"Take it all," said the count. I wanted to remind him that I remained in command of my people, but I felt the urgent need to return to the others. We had no way of knowing whether the vampire had arrived alone or in force.

Reading my expression, Jeggare added, "If you agree, Captain Oparal?"

"Yes, I agree. For now," I added. "But I want to know a great deal more about this Prince Kasiya and why he is here."

"I am at your service."

Chapter Eight
The Looter's Market

Radovan

By the time Jelani and I reached the Looter's Market, every mook in Gundrun was staring at us. We'd made a quick stop at the Splinter to warn Whalt he had big business coming in a little while later. He lit up at the chance to line his coin box with the visit of a big company.

Nobody was going to miss me and Jelani for a couple more hours, when the others finally caught up. There was only so fast they could go without leaving the wagon and carriage behind, but the two of us ran ahead to get things ready.

"Are we in danger?" asked Jelani. Her hand strayed to the rune sticks we found back in the bone cellar. The boss had divvied them up with her. I'd half expected him to offer her some riffle scrolls, too. For some reason, I was glad he hadn't.

I didn't answer right away. She'd been asking me questions nonstop ever since we passed the great big rune stones surrounding the town. Some had symbols of gods I recognized: Gorum, Gozreh, Torag, even Urgathoa. That last one seemed like a damned bad idea if you don't want to call down a plague.

Oparal had Jelani tag along with me when the boss sent me ahead to make things ready in Gundrun. At first I figured Jelani knew the place, but it ended up being me leading the way through the burned-out, tumbled-down houses. I reckoned she was here to keep an eye on me.

She wasn't the only one. The boss kept bugging me about my little chat with Viridio in the cathedral. The big demon put on a good front, but was scared enough to let go of me right away. I'd caught his fear like a cold. Now all I wanted was to get the hell away from the Worldwound.

So, yeah. We were in danger all right. Just not from anything in Gundrun.

I leaned back in the saddle and winked at Jelani. "Don't worry, sweetheart. We're just making an impression. Little town like this, people seldom see a man of my good looks."

She laughed the way I like to hear.

When I first saw Jelani, she seemed as hard as the rest of Oparal's legion of virtue. But she brightened up a little every time I looked her way, like spring was finally working its way in. Didn't hurt a bit that she wore snug furs instead of steel plate and chain.

It wasn't me that drew all the attention. Wasn't Jelani, either. What caused the stir was my phony pony. I felt big and proud. Maybe it took two scrolls, but I made it myself.

After my first "incident," as the boss called it, the phantom steed he summoned me looked all smoky.

We figured that was on account of fire was the sigil for Norge, my first devil. Later, when Norge was dead, or sleeping, or whatever, the next steed the boss got me was all green with a mane like sea foam. Back then, we didn't know what that meant.

After Viridio came through me the first time, my phony pony changed again. This one had great brown blisters all over its body, hard ones like the shell of a bug. Its orange mane was soft and wet, like an overcooked squash. I hated the feel of it. I hated looking at its swimming yellow eyes.

Still, it made one hell of an impression.

We got off our horses. Jelani tethered hers to a hitch. I just left mine standing. Because it was all magical, it went nowhere I didn't tell it to go.

Jelani took a scrap of parchment out of her glove. Our shopping list.

First we bought all the traveling food we could find, mostly dried beans and salted meat. I paid for the stuff from the boss's purse and told the sellers to deliver it to the wagon they'd find outside the Splinter around dusk.

For insurance, I gave each merchant the look that said *it'd better be there, or I'll find you*. In Gundrun, even the grocers were big, tough guys. The ones that didn't seem impressed, I gave the big smile.

That sealed the deal.

Second stop was for stuff the crusaders needed replaced: boots, laces, pouches, packs, waterskins, buckles, stuff like that. Jelani paid with crusader gold, all fresh minted with the stamp of Nerosyan. Seeing Queen Galfrey's profile on the coins made me want to tell Jelani about the coin on the string around my neck. The one with my face on it.

Not actually my face, you know. But there was a strong family resemblance.

I resisted the urge. It's good practice.

From a fat leatherworker I bought new pants for Aprian. There was nothing wrong with the ones I'd borrowed, but some guys are fussy about other guys going around bare-assed in their trousers. When I shucked them off for the guy to chalk up the size on a new pair, I caught Jelani checking me out. I guess she hadn't seen enough back at the cathedral.

"Are you cold?" she said.

"No." Feeling small, I said, "How come?"

"Gooseflesh." She ran a finger across my hip.

Suddenly I was resisting another urge. Any day, I was going to be an urge-resisting expert.

The tailor threw back Aprian's trousers. He'd already chalked up two new pairs, one for Aprian, a shorter pair for me.

"Are you sure one pair is enough?" said Jelani.

"Good point." I showed the leatherworker four fingers. No matter how much Viridio didn't want to come back so close to the Worldwound, it was a smart idea to be prepared.

While the guy worked on the pants, I checked out the other goods on display. I thought about having him make me a bandolier, like the boss's, but decided against it. Somehow I couldn't see myself throwing around wind, fire, all that kind of thing. Maybe I was having better luck with the riffle scrolls, but I didn't see myself doing it all the time. I just liked having a phony pony.

Over a sawhorse hung a pair of saddlebags decorated with demon faces. I liked the look of it, asked the price. The guy said a big number.

"For that much, these demons better jump out and make me breakfast, dinner, and supper."

He shrugged and kept working. I ignored him and picked over the cheaper stuff. He said a different price.

"Throw in some of these," I said, holding up a handful of buckled leather straps. They'd be good for securing luggage on top of the carriage.

We made our deal. I hoisted the leering saddlebags, and Jelani and I wandered through the rest of the market while he worked.

While the town smelled plenty rotten, I didn't see much in the way of fish in the market. When I got a better look at the river, I saw why. It was just a weed-choked runnel, barely wide enough for two fish to swim side by side. So much for the Silverscale River.

"What's that?" Jelani pointed at a hill that used to be an island in the dead river. On top were the burned-out ruins of an old fortress.

I hadn't had a good look before, but I remembered what they were. "Riversoar Clanhold. They were the family in charge before somebody gutted their chief in the streets."

"Rough town."

"I told you, sweetheart, don't be scared. I'll protect you."

She squinted at me, but out of the corner of my eye I saw her smiling while I pretended to look at a table full of dolls. Along with other carved tools and toys, I spied a little wooden box, a little bigger than a deck of cards. Along each side were carved a hammer, star, key, crown, book, and shield. I knew what that meant.

"Do my eyes deceive me?" A mouse-faced character in a velvet coat jumped up behind the table. He popped up so quick, I nearly popped him one. "Or does a countryman stand before me?"

I saw Ustalav in his face, too, but I knew better than to say so around here.

When the demons came out to play, way back when, lots of Sarkorians tried to cross the border. Afraid they were infected, or maybe just not wanting to share their land, the princess of Ustalav had her armies push them back across the river. These days, when the locals thought of Ustalavs, they spat.

"I'm from Cheliax."

"But you look just like—"

"Yeah, yeah," I said. "I get that a lot."

"Golin Imbrenhol, at your service." He stuck out a hand.

I didn't take it. I didn't like the way he sank his teeth into his esses. Instead, I slid open the top of the box and saw what I'd expected: harrow cards.

"How much for these?" I cut the deck and flipped one card over. Jelani leaned over my shoulder for a look. Her hand was warm on my arm. I could smell her breath.

Looking down at the card, I saw a pair of slaves, one raising his shackled wrists up to the sun as the chains shattered. It was one of my favorite cards: The Big Sky. I thought about that for a second before admitting I didn't know what the hell it meant. Not without a harrower to explain it to me, anyway.

"Ah, you have a discerning eye, my Chelish friend. Those once belonged to Baba Narcisa, matriarch of one of the oldest Sczarni clans. The Sczarni are among the oldest people of Avistan, roaming the northern lands from Varisia—"

"I know about Sczarni." Fortune-tellers, con artists, robbers, thieves. Sometimes werewolves, as it turns out. They weren't just my kind of people. They were my actual people.

"Of course you do. The Sczarni travel far and wide, even in your great southern empire." The way Golin said the words made me feel greasy. I didn't mind he didn't give a damn about Cheliax as long as he didn't mind my not giving a damn about his pitch. That didn't stop him. "Baba Narcisa passed down that very deck to her granddaughter, who also had the gift. She passed it to her daughter, Luminita, who fell afoul of a vengeful witch. Hard on his luck, Luminita's brother sold her deck to a traveling merchant, who later sold it to me."

"How much?" I counted the cards. Fifty-four, none short, no extras. Considering what happened last time I found an extra card in a harrow deck, that was good luck. I kissed my thumb, drew the wings.

"As you can see, the box alone is worth—"

"How damn much?"

"Two hundred—"

"Desna weeps." I snapped the box shut and put it back on the table. "What do I look like, the Prince of Ustalav?"

Sometimes I amuse myself. That's not always smart. Now it was Golin squinting at me.

"Are you sure you don't have family in Ustalav? For a countryman, I could go as low as one hundred and—"

"You know what? Forget it. I'm hungry. Let's go, sweetheart."

I took Jelani by the elbow and moved away, all offended-like. We didn't hustle, but we didn't linger neither. I figured even odds we'd get out of sight before

Golin picked up his fancy box and felt it light one harrow deck.

"You really shouldn't call me sweetheart," said Jelani.

"You don't like it?"

"The captain warned us against fraternizing."

"She calls it 'fraternizing,' huh? It's a wonder she and the boss don't get along any better than they do."

Jelani looked a question at me.

"They both like big words. Anyway, the captains ain't around, not yours, not mine. Maybe we could take a walk, find a nice grassy spot with nobody else around."

"I thought you were hungry," she said. "For supper."

"Oh, we got plenty of time." I reached my arm around her waist. Something pricked me in the back.

Starknife.

Maybe I'm not Sarkorian superstitious, seeing a god in every tree and wolfhound, but you don't ignore a sign like that. Anyway, I couldn't. Maybe it was just on account of we were so close to Ustalav. Maybe it was the harrow deck in my pocket.

Or maybe this close to Ustalav, Azra could see me.

I lost my appetite and let go of Jelani.

I took the starknife off my hip and put it in one of the demon saddlebags. When I closed the flap, I felt less like somebody was watching me.

But only a little.

"Let's fetch the pants and make sure everything's ready at the inn."

Jelani shot me a look. "Sometimes you're very difficult to read."

"It's all the big words I get from the boss."

She had to think about that one for a second, but then she laughed again. It's the kind of joke that'd be funnier if she knew me better. Maybe there'd be time for that later, farther away from the Ustalavic border.

We got back to the Splinter around sunset. Jelani stabled her horse and brushed him down. I let mine turn to mist and blow away. The saddle and bridle went with him, but the saddlebags fell to the ground. I reminded myself to take them off first, next time.

Inside the Splinter, Whalt had already put a tankard upside down on each of the tables he'd set aside for us. That curvy little vixen Shal was helping him. She tensed up when she saw me, just like last time.

That was a new one on me. Seeing how she smiled at the other fellows, I wouldn't have figured her for so shy. Maybe she was intimidated by my masculine charms, not that she'd had a chance to see the best ones.

She relaxed and gave me a smile, which was more like it. The light caught her eye and gleamed off the silver band she wore around her head. I liked to think her smile was more for my winning personality than the gold in my pocket, but I knew better.

I knew better, and I didn't care.

I sidled up all casual. It's one of my many knacks.

"Happy to see me, Shal?"

"You remember my name?" She dimpled. If the girl wasn't a professional, she had a knack of her own. "I was afraid I'd offended you the way I behaved before. It's just you remind me of someone from my past."

"Forget about it," I said, giving her a squeeze.

Now that I was so near to her face, I felt a little weird about her, too. It wasn't that she looked like anybody I knew. I was pretty sure about that. But there was something familiar about her. The smell of her hair really drove it in hard.

I stepped back, trying not to let on that she gave me a gitchy feeling.

She blinked at me. I blinked back.

"Shal," said Whalt. He sounded more puzzled than angry. "Fetch the man a drink."

She looked at me, and I felt confused for a moment. Then I realized what she was waiting for. "Beer," I said. "Make it two."

"Right away." She gave me another dimple, a real naughty one. I watched her hustle behind the bar. She had a lot of bustle in her hustle, let me tell you. Still, there was something wrong.

"Shal's been a real help to me," said Whalt. "I wouldn't want anything to hurt her."

The way he warned me, he sounded more like a concerned uncle than a territorial boyfriend. I was all right with that.

"You don't even got to worry, Whalt." He kept his eye on me, and I realized what he was thinking. "That second beer ain't for her."

Jelani rescued me by coming through the door. When she smiled at me, Whalt relaxed and gave me a nod.

Jelani and I took the seat the boss had last time we were there. The beers came out. Shal looked annoyed as she put one in front of Jelani. They turned their necks to look at each other and smiled knives.

I watched Shal go back to the kitchen. Jelani switched her beer for mine.

"What?"

"I don't fancy barmaid spit."

I hoisted the tankard. I didn't see anything wrong. "She didn't have time."

"I like to be sure."

"Here's mud in your eye." The beer was cellar-cold and honey-sweet. I liked the stuff Zora Gorcha had on her river barge, bitter and black. I didn't used to drink so much beer, but lately I'd gotten fond of a couple pints at the end of the day.

Jelani took a long drink and gave herself a mustache. I enjoyed watching her lick it off, but it was time to stop dancing and start talking.

"Did I give you anything good for your captain?"

She shrugged. "I think she already knows you better than I could after one afternoon."

"I was surprised she didn't sic you on the boss instead. You could talk magic stuff."

"Too obvious," she said. "Besides, I got a whiff of the inside of the carriage the other day."

"Oh, it's better now. He tries to be careful, but sometimes he goes too fast and loses his supper."

"Oparal told me a little about his unorthodox method."

I nodded. "When he puts the spell in his head, it puts butterflies in his stomach. With the riffle scrolls, he's putting down only a little bit of the spell at one time. He's all right if he doesn't go too fast. After he's cast a lot of them, though, sometimes he goes too far. If you watch early in the morning, you can catch him emptying that little silver bucket."

"I've never heard of such a thing. Was he cursed?"

"I don't think so. Not as far as I know, anyway. Until he figured out the secret of the riffle scrolls, he knew all kinds of things about magic but couldn't cast any spells without wrecking himself."

"Fascinating." She sipped her beer and I sipped mine. "Did you get anything useful to tell *your* boss?"

"He's not too worried about you. Or your captain. He thinks a lot of Oparal." When Jelani raised an eyebrow, I added, "I know! Surprised me, too. He's more curious about your sergeant."

"Aprian?"

"Something about the body language of some of your other guys, like they're scared of him."

"Ah."

"Don't tell me 'ah.' I bought you a beer."

She smiled. It looked real enough, but it was different from the flirting in the market. We'd both known from the start that the other one was supposed to suss us out, and it wasn't personal. In fact, it was kind of a great first date.

"Two years ago, Aprian was possessed by a demon."

"Poor bastard. How'd that happen?"

"He put on a magical ring without having a sorcerer examine it first."

"Rookie mistake."

"Not the way I hear it. His squad was under attack, and they were looking for any edge against the demons. It was a mistake of desperation, not inexperience."

"Anyway, the important thing is that he got unpossessed." Now there was a thought. "How'd he do that anyway?"

Jelani shrugged. "The fall of Yath freed him."

"Yath? That was some demon stronghold, wasn't it? The boss told me a little."

"Right. But the tower itself was a demon. The magic released when it fell—or died, or was banished, depending on how you look at it—"

We heard the sound of approaching horses at the same time.

Jelani raised her tankard. "Alas, Radovan. It appears the fates have conspired against our tryst."

"Yeah?" I bonked her tankard with mine, and we drained them. Shal hovered at the next table, pretending to wipe it down while we pretended she wasn't eavesdropping. "Not this afternoon, anyway. Some other time?"

"If you play your cards right."

"Another round?" said Shal. She stood beside us, one fist on her hip. And what a hip it was.

"Sure thing, sweetheart." I patted her on the bottom. She flipped her hair in Jelani's direction but still didn't leave.

"So now that one's your sweetheart?"

"You're all my sweethearts. Say, speaking of cards, look what I—"

The door slammed open. Oparal stepped in. Her holy sword was in her hand, lit up bright as a Tian rocket.

"What the hell, Oparal?" I stood up and stepped away from the table. Shal froze in place. I grabbed her wrist and pulled her back to the wall, out of any trouble that was going to break loose.

"Captain?" Jelani did the same as me but in the other direction. One hand went to a pouch at her waist. Maybe she didn't act like the other crusaders, but she was ready for action.

"It's in here somewhere," Oparal shouted. "Evil."

The boss came in close behind her. He also had his sword drawn, a riffle scroll in his other hand. Behind him, I saw the crusaders and our guards all standing around the red carriage, looking like they were ready for an attack at any second.

The boss looked right at me. "Radovan, get away from her."

"What?" I had a bad thought. If someone poisoned my drink, was that the same as venom? Would it let Viridio come out and ride me around? I looked at my hand, but it was the same as ever. "It's all right. I'm fine. How many times I got to tell you I'm not evil? It's just—"

"Down, you fool!" The boss snapped off his riffle scroll. Oparal came charging straight at me.

"Protect me!" Shal breathed into my ear.

That seemed like the right thing to do.

I feinted right but moved left, gathering Shal up in my arms as I rolled us both out of the way. Oparal changed course to follow us. This time I heard the growl coming up inside me.

"Boss! Call her off! There's nothing wrong with— Oh, hell no."

It took a second to realize the growling was coming from Shal, not me. By the time I decided to let her go, she had her hooks in me.

And by hooks I mean claws.

She still looked good, but she sure looked different. Her face wasn't so sweet, and her body wasn't as curvy, but she was the kind of girl who'd never go home hungry from Trick Alley—especially considering what she was wearing, which was not a stitch.

The bad news was the claws, the tail, and the deep red wings opening above her like the canopy of a fancy bed. In a flash, one of the wings was gone, and a rain of hot blood splashed down all over me.

"Dammit, Oparal!"

Shal jumped up to crouch above me, screeching like a possum. She jumped, her remaining wing flailing uselessly without its twin. She crashed against a table with a cry.

Four arcane bolts sizzled past my face to drill black holes between her shoulder blades. I didn't have to look to know they'd come from Jelani.

"No!" Shal cried. "Whalt! Help me!"

Whalt was standing at the bar, his mouth hanging open. He didn't move an inch toward her, but he didn't raise a hand, either.

Five more magic bolts shot into the succubus. She slumped over the table. Her screams dimmed to sobs.

Oparal moved forward, sword raised.

Succubus or not, that didn't seem right. I got in Oparal's way. "Back off, Captain."

With her free hand, she slapped me hard across the face. Braced, I soaked it up. "Snap out of it. You're glamoured. You don't know what she is."

I shoved Oparal. She wasn't braced, so she fell back a step. Oparal reached for me again. I slapped her hand away. I climbed onto the table with Shal and cradled her head.

"I know exactly what she is." I lifted Shal's face to look at mine. She smiled at me, weak and hopeful. I pulled the big knife out of its sheath in my jacket. "She's my problem."

I put it in under her chin, nice and quick, straight into the brain. That'll do for demons just what it does for people.

"No!" shouted Whalt. His good hand reached out, but he pulled it back without coming for me. He looked me in the eye, his face trembling between rage, horror, and sorrow. He was going to feel that for a while.

I got up, trailing blood. Oparal went to the bar and threw me a rag. I caught it. She met my gaze and nodded like she was giving me her approval, not that I wanted it.

The boss came over to check me for hickeys. Seeing none, he looked down at the dead demon and frowned.

"Curious," he said. Snapping off a riffle scroll, he peered at the circlet on her head and nodded like he'd confirmed something he'd been suspecting. He took the circlet and slipped it into his pocket.

I looked around to see whether anybody minded, but nobody said boo.

Jelani put her hand on my arm. "Are you—?"

"I'm fine," I said. For a second I wondered where all the light had gone, then realized we'd stayed long enough for nightfall. "What do we do now? Sit down and eat? Or get the hell out of here?"

"You aren't going anywhere," said a big voice by the back door. I recognized him from our visit to Martolls' lodge. He was one of Martolls Clefthorn's sons or nephews.

"Has your father considered my request at last?" said the boss.

Before the words were out of his mouth, another Clefthorn man shut the front door and dropped the bar. A third dropped down from the shattered upper floor. A couple more skittered down the wall like spiders. It wasn't light from the fireplace I saw dancing red in their eyes.

The head guy grinned, showing off his fangs. "Prince Kasiya sends his regards."

Chapter Nine
The Changing Land

Varian

Despite the improvements the Kyonin druids had made to the suspension of the Red Carriage, the jolting ride from Gundrun made inscribing new scrolls impossible.

The drivers were not to blame. The men had done an admirable job directing the team across the scrub plain, avoiding herds and predators when necessary.

The trouble was the inconstant terrain.

A century earlier, the land between the Shudderwood and the Forest of Soldiers was known as the Sarkorian Plain. The chronicles Kala sang for us at night described an idyllic land of plentiful game and breathtaking vistas. Many of the most enduring Sarkorian songs had been composed by hunters inspired by the landscape alone.

A century of Abyssal corruption had transformed the once-beautiful land into a living nightmare.

The volcanic sky glowered down through brown and yellow clouds. Sporadic eruptions of thunder echoed across the plain. Where pure sunlight shone upon the land, it exposed patches of russet slime drowning the early summer grass. Stagnant water pooled in ravines and sinkholes. Lonely trees reached out with too-human limbs, fingers blossoming with cankers.

As I gazed upon the strange flora, revulsion wrestled with curiosity. I yearned to collect samples for later study. Perhaps through means alchemical or arcane, I might discover a method to purge the land of its demonic plague.

Yet that was not my present errand.

Setting aside my pen, I took up a pencil. I removed the most current map of southern Sarkoris from my journal and covered it with a sheet of paper no thicker than an onion's skin. Through the carriage windows, I saw the vast and changing land to either side, where my Kellid guards rode on my left, Oparal's crusaders on my right.

Beyond the crusaders to the north, where the dense Forest of Soldiers once stood, only sparse stands of blighted trees remained. Elsewhere, mounds of shrieking fungus had overtaken the woods.

Past the Kellids on the south, the withered remains of the Shudderwood concealed the Moutray River, whose winding course formed a natural division between Sarkoris and Ustalav. Blackened trails through the forest marked the wake of great demons leading their slaves into the land of mists and restless graves.

I mused that the arrival of the horde should precipitate recrimination among the counts serving Prince Aduard, whose ancestor had turned away the Kellid refugees. The descendants of those hearty folk might otherwise have bolstered the defense of Ustalav.

The plains fared no better than the woods. Herds of plague aurochs roamed the grassland, unchallenged by unafflicted fauna. Most of the other surviving creatures had also grown tainted by proximity to the mouth of the Abyss. Giant scabrous hares chased flightless birds and tore them to pieces. Fiendish carrion birds wheeled in the sky, descending not to devour but to taunt the dying before feeding on their carcasses.

A few hours earlier, we had spied cultists leading chains of captives north toward the Sarkora River. When I asked Captain Oparal whether she wished to pursue the slavers, she hesitated but ultimately declined. A shadow of regret darkened her steel-colored eyes, but she was resolved to pursue her mission over all else.

Oparal was the first to offer me consolation after the fight at the Splinter, the aftermath of which troubled me as much as the prospect of abandoning slaves to demons troubled her.

Once Oparal had cut a path to the door and removed the bar, Sergeant Aprian and another paladin joined the fray. I felt more grateful than ever for their company. Without the garlic we had left on the river barge, my people had no protection from the fledgling vampires. Yet paladins, like priests, could fend off the undead with the power of their own faith.

Rather than withdraw to the paladin's protection, however, Radovan leaped to the attack—despite my repeated warnings to avoid the vampires' touch.

Still enraged by his own killing of the succubus Shal, Radovan plunged the big knife into one vampire spawn's heart, stabbing another with one of the sharp elbow spurs that were the second-most-distinctive feature of his Hell-crossed ancestry. After his savage attack, he frowned, disappointed at the result. Contrary to popular myth, the strike to the heart was not sufficient to reduce his foe to dust.

Fortunately for Radovan, as I snapped off a riffle scroll and blasted out the still-fresh brains of one of his assailants, Jelani did the same to the other. The Thuvian sorceress favored me with an appreciative nod as she noted the relative power of our spells. She was no apprentice, but as the paladins destroyed the remaining spawn with the radiance of their goddess, I took a certain pride in Jelani's acknowledgment.

With the vampire's spawn died our last hope of establishing a base of operations in Gundrun. Rather than remain to explain why we were obliged to slay Martolls Clefthorn's kin, I deemed it best to depart at once.

Oparal and I brought our forces back to the carriage, the wagons, and the horses. We could not rest in Gundrun that night, nor anywhere close enough for a vengeful Martolls Clefthorn to spy us. While a tear-faced Whalt dragged the body of his demonic barmaid into the street for burning, I had Radovan fetch him a heavy purse from the carriage. It was more than enough to repair the physical damage to his establishment, even to rebuild the ruined upper floor. As restitution for the deeper harm we had inflicted on him, it was a paltry gesture.

The only meaningful reparation I could make to Whalt or the people of Gundrun was to recover the *Lexicon of Paradox*. I consoled myself with a silent promise to do everything in my power to return Sarkoris to its rightful people.

Finding the book was not our ultimate goal. It was also necessary that we deliver the tome to those who could turn its powers against the demonic horde, to drive them back through the Abyssal rift and seal it forever.

My strengthened resolve raised two perturbing questions.

The first was whether I remained, as Radovan might put it, "up to the job." Since my miraculous resurrection in Tian Xia, I felt haler than I had in decades. Furthermore, I apparently had gained a vital resistance to the enervating touch of the undead, as Kasiya proved while failing to destroy me in Absalom.

Despite my regained vigor, I felt the weight of age upon my mind. Radovan's surprise at my use of a trick every apprentice learns was a painful reminder that I had forgotten the essentials of wizardry. Despite circumventing my disability, I had much to relearn.

Worse, for two years I had labored under the assumption that I could prepare only so many riffle scrolls as I could inscribe in a single day. After discovering a scroll wedged between the cushions of the carriage seat, I realized I could exceed that number simply by accumulating riffle scrolls on a daily basis. The only limiting factor was financial, which is of course no limitation to any Jeggare, much less to me.

Frustrated by my mistaken assumptions, I told myself I was trying too hard to discover exceptions that did not exist, to create new formulae for my unique condition when the old ones still applied. But gradually I accepted the truth: My problem was not that I was thinking too hard; it was that I was thinking too sloppily. My mind, my one true and private possession, had begun the inevitable spiral into entropy.

Chaos.

The very thought was too terrifying to contemplate. With an act of will—or perhaps of cowardice—I turned my mind to the second question.

It should not have been a question at all, but there it was: to whom should I deliver the *Lexicon* once I found it?

My sworn loyalty lay with Queen Abrogail. Throughout my long life I had surrendered so much to the ambition and authority of House Thrune that it was all but inconceivable I should deliver the *Lexicon of Paradox* to anyone else. And yet I knew in my heart, both the new half and the old, that Abrogail would reserve that power, watching as the demons burned nations and eradicated peoples, until the horde threatened the Empire. More than most living Chelaxians, I knew what the monarchs of House Thrune were capable of sacrificing in the service of their own glory and that of Cheliax.

Telandia of Kyonin, beauteous and serene, could be trusted little more than Abrogail to extend her aegis beyond those closest to her throne. Surely she would bend all her might and all the powers of her wizards against the horde. But would she do so before exorcising her own land of the fiend Treerazer? Would she, whose people constrained their half-breeds to isolated communities, fight as fiercely on behalf of humans as she would for the pure-blooded elves?

Ollysta Zadrian and her Silver Crusade, and by extension Queen Galfrey and her Mendevian Crusade, seemed at first blush the more altruistic patrons of my quest. And yet I was not ignorant of the pogroms launched by Galfrey's inquisitors, no less horrific for their official temple sanction. Would Galfrey have the courage and the will to hold back her servants from adding to the fiends' atrocities rather than end them?

Without certainty, I dared not defy Queen Abrogail.

Such thoughts did nothing to improve my hasty cartography. I put away the pencil and my journal. Slipping off my boots, I drew my legs up into the lotus position and rested my wrists upon my knees. I envisioned Irori's trigram of body, spirit, and mind. Mine were out of balance.

Allowing my body to follow the rocking motion of the carriage, I refused my mind entrance to both my memory library and my vault of dreams. Once banished from knowledge and desire, my thoughts lay on the shore of the void, and my spirit felt some echo of tranquility. Soon, I would feel the serene embrace of—

Bang bang bang bang bang!

The harsh clatter on the carriage window arrested me from my meditation. There was Radovan, his conjured steed pacing the carriage while he rapped his knuckles on the glass.

"Hey, boss, check it out! First try!"

Wincing at the painful intrusion, I waved him off. He rolled his eyes and shouted for Arnisant. "Come on, boy. Let's race!"

For a moment I wondered at my friend's resilience. Immediately after the attack at the Splinter, he seemed touched by Whalt's mourning over the death of the succubus.

Recrimination sprung its ambush: Would I have spared Radovan the painful task of killing Shal if I had the Shadowless Sword in hand when first I laid eyes upon the disguised succubus? Perhaps if I had indulged Radovan in his common gossip about women, we might have compared notes and suspected her deception. Only now did I realize that the Shal he saw differed so greatly from the illusion the fiend presented to me, likely as a function of the magical circlet I had taken from her corpse.

Such speculation reminded me that I had not asked Radovan just what he was communicating with the devil Viridio in Nekrasof Tower. It was apparent that they had reached some sort of understanding. On the previous occasion Viridio had "ridden" Radovan's soul, the devil remained incarnate and ferociously active for a much longer period.

I feared Radovan had struck a bargain without benefit of my counsel. Although I often assured him that he was smarter than he appeared, Radovan was by no means prepared for the scale and precision of intellectual subterfuge required to negotiate an infernal compact.

Until we found the opportunity to speak privately, there was no profit in uninformed speculation. Enough of such fruitless meanderings, I decided. Letting my eyelids sag, I relaxed my shoulders, and—

Bang bang bang bang bang!

Captain Oparal looked in through the other window. While keeping pace with my team of six Kyonin draft horses, Bastiel turned his head to gaze at me with a keen intelligence. Of course I understood that unicorns were sentient creatures, but I had also read they had the power of speech, which Bastiel seemed to lack.

"May I join you, Count?" shouted Oparal.

I nodded assent and reached for my boots, intending to call out for the driver to stop. Before I had donned the first boot, the carriage door opened, and Oparal swept through the door and into the opposite seat with the agility of a circus acrobat.

"My dear— Captain." I caught myself before saying "lady," since I did not know the station of Oparal's parents. Considering that she was born and raised outside of Kyonin, I could only assume they were of common rank. "You have become a swashbuckler."

She stared, perhaps wondering whether I had complimented or insulted her.

"Forgive my disarray," I said, tugging on my second boot while trying to maintain a modicum of decorum. "I was not prepared for such a swift arrival."

"Please pardon my impatience. I have questions."

"Certainly. May I offer you—"

"Nothing, thanks."

It was one thing to endure interruptions from Radovan and this Alase Brinz-Widowknife. I expected better manners from an officer of the crusade. Since she showed me so little courtesy, I felt free to pour myself a goblet of wine. After nosing the bouquet, I secured it to one of the clever latches built into the edges of the map table. For a brief moment, I mused on the genius of the creator of the Red Carriage.

"This Prince Kasiya," said Oparal. "What can you tell me of him?"

"Brother to Khemet II, the pharaoh known as the Crocodile King. He never had reason to believe he would ascend the throne of Osirion. Unwilling to live in his brother's shadow, he traveled the world. Near the end of his life, he fancied himself a Pathfinder."

"The story goes that you killed him in some personal feud."

"Kasiya blames me for his demise, but he died of his own greed and stupidity."

"Is that some clever way of saying you killed him without admitting it?"

I bristled. "It is not."

"One hears rumors."

"What you need to know about Kasiya is that, despite his intellectual limitations, he remains dangerous. Somehow he acquired the *Lacuna Codex*, another fell volume of arcana. No, not from me. I had delivered it safely to the Grand Lodge in Absalom." I did not share my suspicion that some party within the Decemvirate must have aided Kasiya in the theft—to what end, I could not yet imagine without further evidence.

"And now he's after the *Lexicon*. Why?"

"It's difficult to say. Kasiya is a creature of impulse, not design. In that sense, he is not unlike the demons of the Worldwound."

"Did he come here only to pursue his vendetta against you?" Oparal's gazed hardened. For a moment I felt the urge to explain myself. Then I reminded myself of my station. A count of Cheliax has no need to explain himself to a captain of the Mendevian Crusade.

Still, we were allies, and not for the first time.

"Possibly. But it would be unwise to assume that is his only reason. Besides, even should he acquire the book, Kasiya is more apt to destroy himself with it than to imperil anyone else."

"Because he's not as clever as you?"

"You may be surprised to learn that I do not include myself among those who could wield the high rituals within the *Lexicon of Paradox*," I said. "Besides, even those who browse its pages risk madness, or so it is said."

"Please." Oparal's smile surprised me. For the first time since our reunion, she seemed to lower her guard. "Wizards say that about all their books to keep the apprentices from smudging the pages."

She knew more than I realized about the mundane tricks with which wizards exaggerate their true powers. I returned her smile. "That is often so, but not in this case. The name of the book itself reveals its nature: it is a sort of dictionary of impossibilities, detailing arcane reactions that cannot exist in our world but which somehow do in the chaotic realm of the Abyss."

"Hm." She seemed unconvinced.

"Remember, the Three who first opened the Worldwound did so with the knowledge in this book, among others. The spells and rituals within the *Lexicon* are capable of disrupting the very fabric of reality."

"Isn't that what magic does anyway?"

"Certainly not!"

Her slender eyebrows leaped at my unintended volume.

"Although magic may seem mysterious to those who do not wield it, there are rules to the arcane. One must first understand the formulae before evoking the elemental forces or conjuring beings from another plane of existence. It is a highly rational pursuit."

"I'm not disputing you, Count. It's just that Jelani describes her magic quite differently."

"Of course she does." I concealed my disdain, or hoped I did. "Many sorcerers confuse their hereditary affinity for the arcane with the fantasy that their talent is unbound by logic. But make no mistake: sorcerers, for all their romantic interpretations of the formulae, are as bound by the Laws of Arcana as any wizard."

"While this is very interesting, I didn't mean to change the subject. What I really—" She leaned toward the carriage window. "Oh, not again."

Drawing aside the curtain, I saw Radovan kicking the flanks of his phantom steed as it galloped through the screen of Kellid defenders. Hot on his heels, Bastiel charged after them, horn lowered.

"He won't actually harm Radovan, will he?"

"No," said Oparal. She frowned in consideration. "I don't think so."

The Kellids laughed and pointed. Astride the mighty Tonbarse, Alase whooped and cried out to the giant wolf to join the chase.

Before I could decide whether to intervene, Arnisant ran to intercept the unicorn. His ferocious barking startled the Kellids' horses and shied Bastiel off course.

"That dog is a marvel," said Oparal.

"He is," I said with some pride. Recalling my grandfather's advice, I had given the hound not just a good name but a great one. General Arnisant sacrificed his life to imprison the Whispering Tyrant. My hound had also proven unshakably brave and selfless.

A sharp whistle interrupted the commotion. The crusaders reined in their horses and repeated the signal, each whistling and holding up a fist. Ahead of us, I saw the outrider Naia atop her steed, standing stock-still with one fist raised and her lance pointing westward.

A sound of thunder echoed across the plains.

The carriage slowed as the drivers recognized the signal. The front window opened, and the driver peered in. "Orders?"

"Slow the carriage."

Watching us, the Kellid riders also slowed their mounts. What they lacked in the formal discipline of the crusaders, they compensated for with a keen instinct for danger.

Oparal was already out the left door as I opened the one on the right. Desiring a higher vantage, I jumped up, placing a foot on the lamp fixture to climb onto the roof. The carriage rocked, and I lost my grip.

Already standing atop the carriage roof, Oparal reached down to grasp my shoulder. She pulled me up with the barest of efforts. I murmured thanks but turned my face away to conceal my chagrin.

The thunder sounded again, this time not so distant. Oparal and I surveyed the western terrain, following the direction Naia indicated.

Perhaps half a mile distant, a herd of tainted aurochs stirred within a cloud of plague flies. I heard their deep, unsettled lowing beneath the rumble of thunder.

We were not so close that our presence should have caused them such distress. And yet I saw no other threats nearby, not even after drawing the Shadowless Sword a few inches from its scabbard. I had removed the spyglass from my coat and begun to scan the sky when Oparal reached out an arm to indicate a point midway between our position and the herd. "Look."

Furrows deformed the earth, their wakes collapsing to form the erratic ravines I had seen earlier. Something burrowed through the ground.

Or rather, some*things*. I counted four individual trails of disturbance, a larger one leading three others.

"Stop!" I shouted. "Stop moving at once, everyone! Stand absolutely still!"

The crusaders obeyed at once, although they looked to Oparal, who nodded in support of my order. The Kellids did the same. Alase and Tonbarse slowed to a halt.

Bastiel continued to chase Radovan.

"Stop this instant!" I shouted.

Radovan grimaced at me before looking back wide-eyed at the pursuing unicorn. "Can't, boss. He'll skewer me!"

"Bastiel, stop!" shouted Oparal.

The unicorn screamed and tossed his mane, but he obeyed. A moment later, Radovan halted his steed and signed to Arnisant to sit. The hound obeyed instantly.

"What is it?" Oparal lowered her voice to a whisper.

"The Shoanti of the Storval Plateau call them—well, an approximate translation would mean something like 'earth-feaster,' or 'thunder under the— Ah, my apologies, but there are some terms with no Taldane equivalent."

"What do the Varisians call them?"

"Landsharks."

"They're turning toward us."

I raised the spyglass to confirm what her keen elven eyes had already perceived.

"Captain," called Aprian. "What do we do?"

When Oparal hesitated, I reached for a riffle scroll. "Remain perfectly still," I said. "I will create a diversion some distance from us."

"What's she doing?" Oparal pointed down at Alase, who had dropped to the ground beside Tonbarse. Her hands glowed that particular blue of her eyes and rune as she pressed them deep into his night-black fur.

She said something to the enormous eidolon, and he dashed away.

"Alase, no!" I shouted. "They are attracted to vibrations. His steps will draw them to us!"

She turned and cocked her head at me, spreading her hands in an exasperated gesture before raising a shushing finger to her lips.

Tonbarse loped toward the approaching furrows, moving far faster than his earlier pursuit of Radovan and Bastiel. I realized then that Alase must have imbued him with greater speed before she sent him on this suicidal mission.

As much as Arnisant, the eidolon seemed utterly fearless as he charged toward the danger. Perhaps his courage came from the knowledge that death on this plane of existence would not destroy him but simply return him home. Even so, I knew that summoned creatures still felt pain and fear.

Even without the spyglass, I could see a sharp ridge protruding from the earth at the head of the first, large furrow. Grass and soil parted to either side like waves beneath a galley's prow.

When the great wolf came within a hundred yards of the furrows, he veered away. The furrows turned, rising briefly to expose a glimpse of hardened flanks shining with copper, silver, and flakes of quartz.

Tonbarse led them away, but I feared the effort would prove futile. The moment he perished or escaped, the burrowing predators would return to us. At least his sacrifice would give us time to prepare. I selected a riffle scroll and considered our options.

"Look," said Oparal.

Tonbarse continued to turn, and I understood his plan. He did not intend simply to draw the landsharks away from us. He meant to lead them directly into the herd of aurochs.

Pausing twice to allow the pursuers to hope, Tonbarse ran directly toward the herd and leaped among the aurochs. Despite their Abyssal afflictions, the horned beasts were huge and powerful creatures. Nonetheless, Tonbarse shouldered like a shepherd dog before leaping away, frisky as a pup.

The aurochs' bleating rose to bullish roars. They thrashed their curved horns both at the intruder and against each other. Stamping their hooves, the injured shrieked, while the rest bellowed in anger.

"Where did they go?" asked Oparal.

I saw that the furrows of earth marking the path of the landsharks had vanished and understood what it meant. "They dove deeper into the earth."

"Why? Are they coming back to us?"

"On the contrary. Observe."

At the edge of the herd, the earth erupted, expelling what at first glance appeared to be a gigantic marquise-cut stone. As it reached its apogee above the herd, the creature extended its four limbs, each barbed with long talons. It fell upon the aurochs as its three offspring, each the size of Tonbarse, burst up from the ground beneath the beasts' hooves.

The bloodbath that followed was horrifying, even witnessed at such a distance.

"Inheritor preserve us," said Oparal.

I looked down to see Radovan shaking his head, lips pursed in a whistle as he sat astride his peculiar phantom steed. From those lips I read the words he spoke. *Desna weeps.*

On the ground, Alase stood tall and waved cheerfully in the general direction of the carnage. Puzzled at first, I understood her gesture when I saw that Tonbarse had broken free of the slaughter. He sat back on his haunches in a posture strikingly similar to the one Arnisant assumed after he had laid a fallen partridge at my feet. The eidolon raised his snout in a human gesture of farewell. The blue rune upon his brow faded. So too did the wolf, disappearing from our world as he presumably reappeared on his home plane.

"Captain?" asked Aprian.

"Is it safe to move?" Oparal said.

I nodded. "The creatures should remain occupied for some hours to come. Still, we should shift north for the next few miles."

While she gave Aprian his orders, I signed to Radovan that we would resume our journey. With a wary eye on the unicorn, Radovan yelled, "Show's over, gang. Let's get a move on."

"Bastiel!" Oparal called. With a last baleful glance at his enemy, the unicorn trotted over to the carriage.

Alase reached her arms out to Radovan. He pulled her up and settled her on the saddle before him. From what I understood of summoners, there was nothing preventing Alase from summoning Tonbarse to her side once more.

Noticing my puzzled expression, Oparal guessed my own question. "What is it with him?" she said. "He's not even that good-looking."

As discretion is the better part of valor, I declined to comment on the manner in which she framed her opinion of Radovan's appearance.

Chapter Ten
The Last Bastion

Oparal

A hundred feet above us, the breeze ruffled the fringe high upon the plateau's edge. We rode along the base of a great cliff, the hoofbeats of our steeds echoing off the stony wall.

A riverbed meandered nearby, parched but for a runnel of murky water. Strange wildflowers sprang up on either side of the damp channel. Their blossoms looked beautiful until they lunged down to snap at frogs splaying through the puddles. The prey appeared no more natural than the predators. The frogs' bright-colored skin and fringed tails attested to their fiendish taint.

Bastiel veered away from the flowers without a word from me. Trusting the unicorn's instinct, I allowed it.

Without looking up from his sketch of the queer animals, Count Jeggare remarked that the stream had once been a branch of the great Sarkora River, whose main course lay on the other side of the plateau, beside

Undarin. More than his geography lesson, I admired his ability to hold his journal steady and draw a coherent figure while mounted on his phantom steed.

Farther from the wall, our caravan moved west. My crusaders mingled more and more often with the count's hirelings. They needed no warning from me to avoid attachments with mercenaries, but I could see it was a relief for them to interact with new faces after so long in the field.

The boastful Valki was especially amusing. No one took his stories seriously, but one had to admire his talent for hyperbole. At times I thought the skald, Kala, was silently memorizing his most outrageous stories to turn them into songs.

Among the Kellids, Alase Brinz-Widowknife was the most intriguing and, as both scout and a repository of clan lore, the most useful to our mission. Yet the giant Kronug was as physically gifted a warrior as I had ever seen, and I had never seen a more accurate axe-thrower than Selka. In small packs, the Kellids had proved themselves extraordinary hunters. I doubted my crusaders could have stalked and slain the giant elk that supplemented our rations in recent days.

"First scout returns," called Aprian.

Erastus rode back from the west. Sweat poured down his face, but his breathing remained steady as he drew rein and saluted before us. "A walled town, Captain. A few hundred residents, all human as far as I could see. Farmers."

I turned to Count Jeggare. He replaced his journal in the satchel hanging from his conjured mount's saddle. Bastiel remained stoic at its presence, but he obviously disliked the unnatural thing. The unicorn grew restless only when Radovan and Alase rode up on their own strange steeds.

"Valahuv," said Jeggare, flipping to the maps in his journal. "It must be Valahuv."

"Dangerous people," said Alase. The summoner—I refused to think of her as a "god caller"—sat comfortably on her giant wolf's shoulders without benefit of saddle or reins. The breeze blew back her bangs to reveal the glowing rune on her forehead, identical to the one on her wolf's brow.

"Were you seen?" asked Aprian.

Erastus shook his head, and I believed him. Both he and Naia could vanish like phantoms into the night, or like snakes through the grassy steppes. "They don't appear dangerous. They look half-starved."

"One of their gods was Ommors," said Alase, "Dweller in the Delvegate."

"What does that mean?"

"According to Pastor Shy's *Witch-Cults of Northern Avistan*," said Jeggare, "Ommors demands blood."

"Desna weeps," said Radovan. "We got another vampire?"

"More likely a fiend posing as a deity," said Jeggare.

Alase stroked her giant wolf behind its ears. "Forgive the outlander, Tonbarse. He is ignorant of our ways."

"I am well aware of your beliefs," said the count. "You will pardon me if I speak directly when speculating on the nature of the beings we encounter."

"I might maybe pardon you," said Alase. "But I can't promise Tonbarse will."

The lupine eidolon sat on his haunches, somehow without dislodging his summoner. His face remained unreadable.

"We need water," I said. "And it would be good to have a fortified base in case we must retreat in haste from Undarin."

"We're still at least two days away," said Jeggare. I had thought us closer, but Jeggare's maps had proven more accurate than ours. "Yet I concur. These people might provide critical intelligence."

"Or they might sacrifice us to their blood god," said Aprian. When we all looked at him, he shrugged. "I'm just pointing out the obvious."

Radovan alone found the remark amusing. No one else smiled.

"We will approach in force, but I'll lead a smaller group to parlay," I said. "Aprian, you're with me. Jelani also."

Aprian saluted and went to fetch the sorcerer.

"I do have some experience in diplomatic matters," said Jeggare.

"Your courtly talents would be wasted on these people, Count."

He began to reply, but Alase cut in. "I'll go with you," she said. "Widowknife people come from Undarin. My ancestors knew the god callers of Valahuv."

"But you said you've never been here before."

"That doesn't matter. They'll know Tonbarse."

"They will remember." The huge wolf nodded like a man. His deep voice and the human motion of his bestial lips still unnerved me.

"Very well," said Count Jeggare. "The rest of us shall stand ready in case you require assistance."

"Thank you, Count."

Tolliver's shout alerted us to Naia's return. She reported no exceptional sightings to the east, nor any substantial source of fresh water.

I took the lead with Aprian and Jelani riding their warhorses on my right, Alase on Tonbarse on my left. Count Jeggare and Radovan followed a short distance behind, their phantom steeds leading the Red Carriage, the supply wagon, and the rest of my crusaders and their sellswords. I could almost imagine myself at the head of an army.

Within the hour, we reached the western terminus of the plateau, and Valahuv came into view.

The village walls were made of stone taken from the cliff. If not for a few peaked roofs and plumes of smoke rising above the walls, one might have looked directly at the site without realizing it harbored a village.

Before us lay half a dozen plots of tilled earth. Villagers knelt along the furrows, pulling weeds. A few unarmored sentries leaned on crude spears. When one saw us, he sent up a hue that leaped from voice to voice. The others dropped their tools to scurry back into the village. The heavy wooden gates closed, and a clamor arose within the walls.

With no road to follow, we approached on the untilled border between two fields. Green sprouts had begun to poke through the gray surface of the soil. Their shapes were unfamiliar to my inexpert eye, and I wondered how wholesome food grown so near the heart of the Worldwound could be.

Behind the village, a grand stair wound up the cliff face toward a small castle. A single watchtower rose above its curtain wall. At first I saw no sign of habitation. Then a bell sounded inside the village. A bird rose from the tower roof.

The shape of a hawk, it was no natural creature. Even at a distance, its wings refracted the sunlight as though they were made of rose-colored crystal.

A hundred yards off either flank, Erastus and Naia had their bows in hand. They wouldn't shoot until they received a signal from me or Aprian.

"Hello!" I called out as we neared the wall. It was barely more than twelve feet tall, but the defenders had cemented sharp stones and shards of glass to its top. Such a fortification might deter bandits or rival tribes, but it was useless against demons. I wondered how Valahuv had survived.

The hawk descended, flying a loop around the carriage and the supply cart. When Selka hefted a throwing axe, the bird veered away.

"What the hell is wrong with you?" Radovan snapped. "Put those away!"

The woman had muscles like a dwarven miner, but she pouted and slumped her shoulders. I would never understand what it was about Radovan that elicited such fawning behavior among otherwise capable women.

"Tammerri," said Tonbarse. "I remember her."

"You know that creature?"

"We met before the world's wounding," he said.

Only then did I appreciate just how ancient Tonbarse might be. Among the shorter-lived peoples, we elves are known for our longevity. If I understood correctly, even the half-human Count Jeggare was approaching a century of age. No wonder the primitive Sarkorians mistook their eidolons for gods.

Tammerri rose in a spiral. As it banked, the sun reflected gold upon its wings, then crimson, then—for only an instant—blinding white.

"People of Valahuv!" I hailed the wall a few more times before signaling Aprian to take over.

"Captain," said Count Jeggare. I whirled around, for a moment believing he had crept up on his silent steed to whisper in my ear. He remained some fifty yards behind us, Radovan at his side. He cupped a palm beside his mouth, using the same spell with which he had alerted us to the deception at Nekrosof. With his other hand, he pointed his spyglass toward the castle on the cliff.

A man descended the stair. He appeared tall and lean, and he carried a long stick with a T-shaped head. Tammerri flew to him, perching atop his staff. Either the man was very small or the bird was very large.

I wanted a look through Jeggare's spyglass. Aprian could fetch it for me, but sending him for such a trifle would be insulting. Fetching it for myself was no better.

I cupped my hand to my mouth and whispered, "Would you be so kind as to join me, Count?"

His ghostly steed carried him silently to my side. Anticipating my need, Jeggare handed me the spyglass. I put it to my eye for a better look at the man descending the cliff stair.

His lined face suggested he had lived some fifty or sixty years, despite the thick yellow hair that fell upon his shoulders. He wore a dun-colored gown ornamented with crimson thread and copper wire. The symbols on his raiment appeared related to the vivid mark upon his brow. An identical rune appeared on the head of the bird.

Magnified by the spyglass, Tammerri appeared even less like a mortal avian and more like a stylized drawing brought to life.

The man disappeared behind the walls of the village, and a clamor followed him to the village gate, which opened. The man emerged alone but for the eidolon perched upon his rune-carved stick.

"Wait here," I said. "Alase, you and Tonbarse come with me. If you have no objection, Count."

"Of course not," he said. His voice was perfectly civil, but I sensed it was difficult for him to watch me take the lead.

We approached on foot, Tonbarse falling in without a word from Alase. He behaved more like a protective uncle than a pet or guardian beast.

The man from Valahuv went barefoot, and even unshod he was as tall as I. As he came within fifty feet of us, I silently focused my intuition on him. His aura betrayed no wicked intent. I doubted he had performed any recent blood sacrifices.

"I am Oparal of Iomedae, Captain of the Mendevian Crusade. This is my guide—"

"Alase Brinz-Widowknife." She touched the glowing rune on her brow and spoke again in her native tongue. I regretted not bringing my own translator. It occurred to me that the count spoke fluent Hallit.

It was probably occurring to him, as well. Despite the certainty that I had been right to leave him behind lest he assume command, I felt a little foolish.

"Feinroh Balemoon," said the man, touching his rune. Upon his hands I saw bandages stained black and yellow. By the tender motions of his hands, I knew the affliction caused him pain.

The hawk spoke in a woman's voice. "Tonbarse."

The great wolf nodded. "Tammerri."

"What do you seek here?" said Feinroh Balemoon.

"Fresh water," I said. "And any report you can offer on the demons of the area."

"No fiends dare approach Valahuv. Our gods protect us."

"Let us speak to your scouts to learn the lay of the land. We have supplies to trade."

"There are no scouts among us. No one strays from the village. Everything we need is here."

"What of medicine?" I asked. "Have you no healer who searches the land for herbs?"

Feinroh lowered his arms, letting his sleeve conceal his afflicted hands.

I offered him my own. "Here," I said. "Let me share the radiance of Iomedae. Hers is the light that heals."

Uncertain, Feinroh looked at Alase. She nodded. Behind her, Tonbarse nodded at Tammerri.

Feinroh held out a hand. I clasped it between both of mine and prayed. "Bright Goddess, Inheritor of Aroden, cleanse this man's affliction."

Feinroh startled as the warmth penetrated his diseased limb. For an instant we both saw the bones beneath his flesh. As the light faded, he gazed in wonder at his hand. Peeling away the wrappings, he saw that the skin beneath was healed and whole.

"Can you do this for others?"

"For a few, yes," I said. "I can do so again after my morning prayers. So can my sergeant."

"Heal my people, and you may have all the water you can carry."

"And you'll tell us what you know of the surrounding land?"

Feinroh looked to his eidolon.

Tammerri turned her hawk-like head to me and said, "I have ranged as far as Domora to the west and Undarin to the east."

"May I bring my people inside the village?"

"Yes," said Feinroh, "so long as you swear not to climb the Thunderstair."

"There is evil here," said Porfirio. I had become accustomed to his reincarnated face and body, but not the new voice. It was deep and resonant, rather more commanding than the one he had before.

Aprian nodded.

I had felt the butterflies stirring ever since we entered the village, but I sensed no malice from its people. The sensation was worst when I gazed toward the castle and the cliff beneath it. Some dire thing dwelt beneath this Thunderstair.

"We might have brought the evil with us," said Porfirio. His gaze fell upon Radovan, who sat near the fire in the camp we had made between the count's carriage and supply cart. There our people mingled with the few villagers bold enough to speak with us after Aprian and I had healed the most severely injured and afflicted.

Several of the women of Valahuv seemed intrigued by Radovan, who told outlandish stories of his travels in Kyonin and distant Tian Xia. Yet none of them could penetrate the barrier formed by Gemma, Alase, Jelani, Selka, and Kala, who vied for his attention in a fashion I had never before observed in grown women.

Their fascination with Radovan had begun almost the moment we met him and the count in Nekrosof Tower. At first I hoped the summoner had claimed his full attentions, but I had glimpsed him flirting with both Alase and Jelani on different occasions, and the other women seemed only too eager for a turn.

The only other gander among the clustered geese was Dragomir. He offered Radovan a drink from his own cup. Radovan toasted him with a Varisian phrase before draining the leather tankard. For a moment I feared the sound of the native tongue of Ustalav would anger the Sarkorians. Fortunately, none of the inhabitants appeared to notice that Radovan and Dragomir were Ustalavs.

"It doesn't make any sense," said Aprian.

"I know."

"He's not even that good-looking," said Porfirio, scowling at Radovan.

Hearing him echo my earlier words gave me pause. I prayed I had not sounded so unconvincing.

"You said he's not using magic," said Aprian.

"So Jelani assured me." I wondered whether I could depend upon her judgment. She seemed smitten with the hellspawn ever since accompanying him to the Looter's Market. I wondered just how complete her report to me had been.

"You have to admire the lad's courage," said Urno. "That's too many pins for any juggler. He'll be lucky if it ends only in tears, not blood."

"At least Naia has better taste," I observed.

The others stared at me, bemused. It took me a moment to realize why they smiled at me. "Don't tell me . . ."

"He's not her type," said Porfirio. "No more than she is mine."

I smacked my forehead. "I really have no sense for these things."

"Of course not," said Urno. "One look at your unicorn, and we all realized—"

Aprian coughed to silence the dwarf. Urno looked blankly for an instant before shutting his mouth.

My embarrassment at my own foolish assumptions about Naia, Dragomir, and Porfirio tempered my irritation with the men. We are fools to think we understand the hearts of others, every one of us.

Porfirio huffed. "I'm not going to stand here another minute while Dragomir embarrasses himself in front of everyone."

"Don't start any trouble," said Aprian. "It's a wonder we've gotten along with these mercenaries as well as we have."

"Don't worry, Sergeant. I'm just going for a walk." Porfirio paused to look back ruefully at the attention Dragomir and the women lavished on Radovan before vanishing into the dark.

"Well, my watch is up, and he can't warm them all tonight, can he? Someone ought to be ready to console the runners-up." Urno rubbed his palms together and went to sit by the fire, nestling in between a startled pair of village women.

"You wouldn't think so to look at him," Aprian said, "but Urno is the company heartbreaker."

"You're right," I said. "I wouldn't think that."

"I think his record stood until the day you arrived near Kenabres and had all the boys throwing themselves at your feet."

"Please, don't remind me."

Aprian chuckled, an easy, friendly sound. From the start, he had treated me with both the respect due my rank and a camaraderie unhindered by the hope of sex. I tried and failed not to wonder whether I was simply not his type as well, but I put that thought aside.

I was reminded of our previous conversation about such matters. Perhaps because he hadn't raised the question of my past relationship with Ederras again, I felt a curious need to tell him.

"Ederras was never my lover," I said. "He was my best friend."

Aprian turned to me, nodding as if the shift in topic were completely natural. He said nothing and listened.

"He had a lover, though. Everyone found her charming and worldly. But I knew." I patted the space just above my stomach, where the butterflies of evil dwelled. "I felt it in here."

Aprian nodded again. "At the time, Ederras was still in grace with Iomedae?"

"Yes, or at least I assumed so. It was my own feelings I doubted. I was confused, uncertain."

"Because you were afraid you might be in love with Ederras?"

"No," I said. "That's not what frightened me. I think—I want to think, anyway—that if I had loved him as something more than a friend, I could have told him. What frightened me was the idea that I was capable of jealousy."

"We're all capable of jealousy."

"But we shouldn't be," I snapped. "We must strive to be better than that. I want to be better than that."

"You want to be perfect."

"No—I mean, yes, of course. Don't you?"

The miracle of his smile was that it contained not a trace of condescension. "It could be easier for me, since I put on that damned ring and let a demon take control of my body. More than most, I know I've never been perfect and never will be. But I guess it must be harder for you because of how you look and what you've accomplished so early in life. Others can't see the flaws that trouble you so much. They treat you differently because they can't tell just how imperfect you feel."

I tried to speak, but my voice caught in my throat. I coughed and said, "That's right."

Aprian turned to look back at the fire, but he remained by my side. "I guess you told Ederras about his lover."

"Yes. I was the one who presented him with the proof that she wasn't who she claimed to be. She was a diabolist, a spy. She was using him to infiltrate the Children of Westcrown."

"What did he do?"

"He insisted on confronting her alone. I almost followed him, afraid he would kill her. Instead, he let her go. Then he left the Children."

"And ended up in the crusade."

I nodded.

"The way you talked with him back near Kenabres, I got the impression you'd forgiven him."

"Yes, of course."

"But he still hasn't forgiven you."

I shook my head.

"One day he will," said Aprian. "Or maybe he won't. It doesn't matter."

"Why not?"

"The only forgiveness you need is your own."

I was ready to scoff at him for offering me a platitude, but laughter erupted from the campfire. Radovan's stories were only marginally less preposterous than Valki's, but I had witnessed some of the events he described. He exaggerated relatively little, although they were certainly colored by his particular point of view.

Radovan reached another punch line, causing another roar of laughter.

Count Jeggare opened the window of the nearby Red Carriage and stuck his head out. "If you would kindly lower your voices while I work . . ."

"Sorry, boss," said Radovan. "All right, ladies. Lean in close. I'll whisper the next one in your ears. You see, I once met this temple prostitute . . ."

"Shall I break it up?" said Aprian.

"Let him finish this one," I said. "Then make sure all of our troops who aren't on watch are in their beds. Alone."

"Yes, Captain."

As they departed, I went to the Red Carriage for a word with Count Jeggare. Bastiel joined me, turning his head in an equine approximation of a sidelong glance. I knew he understood everything I said, but sometimes I wished he could speak like Tonbarse or Tammerri.

As if conjured by my thought, Feinroh Balemoon approached our camp. He smiled, as he had done with increasing frequency since we cured his people. "I was just talking to your god, thinking he wished to visit the unicorns of the northern forest. I am afraid that Tammerri reports they have all but vanished."

It seemed both peculiar and refreshing to meet someone who treated Bastiel as the intelligent being he was. Apart from Radovan, who seldom had anything pleasant to say to Bastiel, everyone treated him as if he were an unusual horse. Just because he could not speak did not mean he did not understand every word he heard.

"Where is Tammerri?" I asked, slightly suspicious at the eidolon's absence.

"I summoned elementals to fetch your water," he said. "To do so, I had to release Tammerri."

"Your summoned creatures cannot exist in this world at the same time?"

"Not through me," said Feinroh. "The relationship between god and caller is unique. Only a fool would offend a god by devoting less than his full attention to drawing it into this world and tending its needs."

"I see," I said, though I didn't, not truly.

"You say you have come to drive the demons from our land."

"That is our hope."

"And then you will claim Sarkoris for your own?"

"No," I said with emphasis. For myself, I meant it. I also believed Queen Galfrey's motives were pure, but I was not so naive as to believe the matter would be resolved by the queen of Mendev alone. "Naturally, I cannot speak for all parties who have sent forces to the crusade."

Feinroh studied my face as I answered. He did not seem satisfied, but neither did he accuse me of dissembling. "Perhaps I should ask the man in the wheel-house."

"Count Jeggare has no authority over me or my troops."

"Some of these swordsmen work for him, not you. Is that not so?"

He had learned a surprising amount about us during the hours of our visit. "Yes, but we are cooperating on this mission."

"To rid our land of demons?"

"We hope that will be the eventual result. But if—when—we succeed, we shall have a powerful weapon against the Abyss. We will—" I stopped myself. My impulse to explain myself to this refugee in his own country was trivial compared with the need for some measure of secrecy. Already the count's mercenaries knew too much for my peace of mind, and I could not be certain that the demons had no spies within the village.

We continued to speak as my troops and Count Jeggare's settled in to sleep. Radovan retired to the Red Carriage with the hound. The interior lights dimmed, but one persisted on the count's side. He had stayed up late each night inscribing more and more of his unusual scrolls. Either the process took much longer than I realized, or he was creating enough to supply an army of wizards.

Soon it became clear that Feinroh held out little faith that the crusade would prevail against the horde. He told me stories of the first three Mendevian Crusades, tales passed down by his ancestors. Through Sarkorian eyes, the crusades were a series of tragic failures led by foreigners hoping to claim the land of Sarkoris for themselves. All the while, the people he served had found shelter at the foot of the cliffs, where the demons never came.

Feinroh remained unmoved by my assurances that Queen Galfrey, at least, had only the purest of motives in coming to the aid of his people. "In my youth, I met others who called themselves crusaders," he said. "The horde took them all, bodies and souls."

Before I could frame a response, Aprian approached. By his expression, I knew he had words for my ears alone. Excusing myself, I led him away as Feinroh went to patrol the streets of Valahuv. Just as we set our sentries, so did he watch over his people while strangers resided among them.

"Captain, Porfirio is missing."

"Are you certain?" I found it difficult to imagine the young paladin sulking over the slight of Dragomir's attention to Radovan, but he had endured an extraordinary trauma at Storasta.

"He was meant to relieve Naia at her watch, but he never arrived. He is not here at camp. Erastus and Silvio just completed a sweep of the village. No one has passed through the gate. Unless he is hiding from us . . ."

Anticipating his conclusion, I looked up at the Thunderstair. The moon remained hidden on the other side of the high plateau, but starlight limned the stone stairs. It occurred to me that Aprian's human eyes could not see even that much in the darkness. I needed others who could see as I did.

Feinroh had forbidden us only one thing. If I were to alert him to my suspicions, I doubted he would permit us to search his castle. Worse, he may have been complicit in Porfirio's disappearance.

"Bring me Silvio," I said. "And wake Urno. I shall fetch the count and Radovan. You remain here. If Feinroh attempts to follow us, delay him."

"Captain." Aprian nodded and moved away. Either he understood I chose those who could see without light, or else he was simply that obedient. Either way, I understood why Ederras hated to part with him.

A rap on the carriage door and a few whispered words was all it took to enlist the aid of Jeggare, who immediately set aside his pen, and Radovan, who appeared fully alert after rising from his slumber. They understood the need for stealth in this matter, for we were about to break the one promise Feinroh had demanded of us.

Bastiel wished to accompany me. It took me strong whispered words to ensure he remained at the camp. Once assured that he would not disobey, I led the others to the Thunderstair, resisting the temptation to draw the Ray of Lymirin. If it sensed the presence of demons, its light would alert all Valahuv to our transgression.

Radovan slipped past me on the stairs. Before I could protest, he whispered, "They can hear you clanking in Lastwall. Let me go ahead."

I didn't like it, but I allowed it. Moments later, I heard a distant cry echoing as through a long, winding passage. I abandoned the last pretense of stealth and whispered, "Hurry!"

We reached the top, warm and breathing heavily. Moonlight lit the western half of a semicircular courtyard. A lone tower stood on the west, near the plateau's edge. In the east, still shrouded in darkness, crouched a low arch set at an angle to ground, like the doors of a storm cellar. But there was no door, only a rune-carved frame of weathered stone surrounding an iron portcullis left wide open. Radovan crouched beside it, his face close to the ground.

"Somebody just went this way," he said.

"This must be the Delvegate," said Jeggare. "Below us is the lair of the 'god' called Ommors."

As if responding to his words, the distant cry we heard earlier came again. This time there was no mistaking its source.

"Follow me." I stepped inside. The passage descended not in stairs but in a gradual ramp reminding me of an elven tomb I had once explored with Jeggare and Radovan. There the resemblance ended, for instead of the delicate elven architecture, this subterranean passage contained crude niches carved into its walls. Ancient Sarkorian runes and pictograms marked each site, perhaps naming those interred there.

I counted two hundred steps before drawing the Ray. Its bright steel glowed dully, confirming what the butterflies already told me. There was evil in these passages, but no demon.

The passage widened into a larger chamber. Jeggare activated the light on his ring. Dried blood flaked upon the walls. Bloodstained cocoons hung from the ceiling. The limbs of desiccated corpses protruded from the fraying crimson sacs. As I took another step, my feet touched something sticky on the floor.

"Aw, hell no," said Radovan, looking down at the blood. "Fresh."

Urno grumbled and hefted his axe. I shared his urge to strike, if only we could find the foe.

Count Jeggare discharged a riffle scroll. Radovan flexed an arm and said, "Thanks, boss."

"Porfirio!" I called. "Where are you?"

No one answered. If anything, the silence seemed to grow heavier.

We hurried on, ignoring the crypts and carvings in the walls. Now and then, Jeggare cast another spell. Sometimes I felt the magic touch me. Under other circumstances, I would have protested that he did not ask my consent. I allowed it.

When the passage branched, we always took the path of fresher blood, gleaming bright red against the dark stickiness of the rest of the passage.

In a cool, damp grotto, we found Porfirio.

His tangled limbs lay beneath a monstrous arachnid. It stood as tall as Urno, but each of its translucent wings was longer than I. The creature's body appeared to be composed almost entirely of freshly let blood. Only its black mandibles appeared solid.

Willing sacrifices?

I perceived the greeting—not the words, but their meaning—as a voiceless message in my mind.

Jeggare spoke to it in the language of Hell. The creature answered in kind. I could not understand what they said, but the count's haughty demeanor for once encouraged me. In their heated exchange, I recognized only the name "Ommors."

"What does it want, Count?"

He responded to something else the creature said before replying to me. "Blood and souls."

"It can have escape if Porfirio lives," I said. "Or it can have death."

"I will tell it you are deciding who will be its sacrifice. The moment it responds, we attack."

I nodded.

Jeggare spoke again. When he paused, I could wait no longer.

I was the first to strike. The Ray of Lymirin sizzled as it plunged into the creature's gelatinous body. An instant later, Radovan appeared to materialize from the shadows behind the beast. His big knife plunged again and again into the thing's abdomen.

The count's magic bolts drilled into the monster. Urno's axe crashed down upon its head, creasing its skull without reaching its brain.

Squealing, the monster rose from the floor, its wings a crimson blur. It clutched Porfirio's mangled body in its eight limbs. His fingers moved. He was alive!

I wanted to pour Iomedae's radiance into its infernal body, but the day's healing had sapped my god-granted strength.

We struck again and again until the creature sped past us. We pursued it up the spiraling passages and out the Delvegate, where it rose into the night sky, beyond our reach.

The count emerged beside me. He drew a scroll from his bandolier and cast it on himself. He crouched and leaped into the sky, pursuing the creature.

"Careful, boss!" cried Radovan.

No! cried the hateful voice that was not a voice. *I have protected you feeble cattle far too long. Let the horde take you!*

Jeggare threw another volley of magic bolts at the monster and soared toward it, his Shadowless Sword held out like the tip of a lance.

The monster drew Porfirio to its maw and bit deep. Its body swelled, glowing red in the moonlight. Porfirio howled in utter desolation, revived just long enough to endure the agony of the creature devouring his soul. The monster dropped him.

Jeggare hesitated only an instant before veering off to catch Porfirio's lifeless corpse while Ommors flew off into the northern sky.

Chapter Eleven
The Tower of Zura

Radovan

My hackles pricked up. It wasn't the cool night air that had my blood running cold. It was the waiting. Days after everything had gone to hell in the refugee village, we were sneaking into another wicked town. Only instead of one fiend waiting under the Thunderstair, there were thousands of the damned things waiting for us in Undarin.

It was enough to make a guy tense is what I'm saying.

The demonblooded sentry rounded the corner and saw Gemma crumpled on the walk. He was smart enough not to touch her, just not quick enough to check his back before I moved in. I got my fingers in his mouth and pulled back his head. The rest was quick and wet.

Gemma rolled up to her hands and knees. She was already crawling to the next corner while I shoved the body against the corner parapet. With his horns and long chin, the demonblooded didn't look much different from some hellspawn I knew back in Egorian. No wonder people get us mixed up with them.

I crawled after Gemma, pausing now and then to peek down at Undarin.

Below us a bridge connected the Widowknife Clanhold to the other side of a wide ravine that had been a river before the Worldwound. As Gemma and I snuck in, we saw a torrent of bloody waste gurgling out of the clanhold subbasements. The nasty stream trickled south before falling into the Sarkora River, way below.

On the other side of the bridge, the city of Undarin sprawled across the edge of the plateau before tumbling off the cliff. It crept across a few little islands in the river—rocks Alase had called Gorum's Chain—before crawling back onto dry land.

The Cliffside District echoed with screams and cracking whips. The bigger buildings had been turned into temples to demons, which the nutty Kellids took for gods. The biggest temple was for Deskari, demon lord of locusts, worst of the bad lot that came through the Worldwound when the Three first opened the door. That's where all the action was tonight. When the boss spied a procession headed down there, we knew we'd never have a better shot at sneaking into the Widowknife Clanhold.

Most of the hubbub came from the temple of Deskari, but there were other hot spots. A circle of cultists danced around a blood-caked statue of a muscle-bound demon, armored, horned, winged, clutching a lash of lightning. Just looking at it made me feel like something was uncoiling in my belly.

Viridio? I thought. *Is that you in there?*

Whatever it was—my devil, my own fear, or that salt pork that had gone off—it clenched and loosened, slinking away somewhere.

Another demon statue stood just on the other side of the bridge to Cliffside. The succubus spread its wings as if welcoming visitors to the fortress. I didn't like it, even from behind. It made me think of Shal and the harm it'd done Whalt when I got rid of her.

Down below, the Sarkora River split the city in half. Half a dozen little islands carried streets on their backs, connecting Cliffside to the southern bank. The demons had smashed most of the bridges, but one still connected Cliffside to the Steppeside.

Across the river I heard the aurochs lowing in their pens, and the slaves weeping in theirs. I kind of wanted to slip down there on the way out, pick a few locks, but that didn't seem like a smart idea. I didn't want to die in Undarin.

The sky was lousy with what looked like giant moths and locusts. They were really demons, most of them bigger than me, some as big as the stupid unicorn. The demons didn't fly like sentries. At least, I couldn't suss any pattern to their rounds.

That's the thing about demons. Even the smart ones got no pattern, no rules, no code. You can't predict them. You can't deal with them. If you're real lucky, you can hide from them. If you're less lucky, you can kill them.

You don't want to be unlucky with demons.

Case in point: The second sentry showed up early. One glance across the corner, and he spotted me crawling across the wall. A big Kellid, he called out in Hallit, "Hey!"

I rolled to my back and moaned like I was drunk.

The sentry lowered his voice, talking more Hallit words I didn't know. I understood the tone all right. He bought my act.

When he came around the corner, Gemma caught his ankle. He fell facedown over his spear. Gemma locked her legs around his neck and choked off his shout. He struggled to get his weight on top of her. He almost managed it before I cut his throat and pulled him off.

Gemma touched her chin. It was the sign criminals threw each other back in Egorian. I'd had a feeling she was a hometown girl. I returned the gesture.

Keeping low, we checked for any sign we'd been spotted. The bailey was empty except for a drowsy guard and some Arni-sized toad demon snoring at his feet.

Gemma looped a spider-silk rope around an inner parapet right above the guard. She made a harness from the other end and tapped her chest to say, *My turn*.

I lowered her, all smooth and quiet. She guided the rope with her ankles, like a spider. When she got close enough, it looked like all she did was stroke the guard's neck. She held his head in place while he slapped his hands against the wound and bled out.

The toad coughed mid-snore. Its bulging eyes opened, each the size and color of an orange.

Gemma signaled, *Down*. As she flipped herself right-side-up, the toad-dog belched. Its sticky tongue shot out, trapping Gemma's legs, trying to pull her close.

It was farther than I like to go when I'm not full fiend, but Alase and the boss both whammied me good before we went in. Knife in hand, I rolled over the edge.

I hit the demon dead center, knees on its back. Stuff a lot bigger and nastier than its tongue surged out of its mouth. To make sure, I drove the big knife into its flat skull.

The impact knocked the wind out of me, and I'd cut myself pretty bad on its back spines, but nothing felt broke.

Caught between rope and tongue, Gemma gagged at the stench of the demon, or maybe at the sight of its guts all turned inside out. It took me a few slices to sever the tough muscle, but then she was free.

All right? I signed.

She shrugged and nodded.

Burglar signs weren't too different from Pathfinder hand-signals. Considering the kinds of jobs the boss did for his little club, that was no surprise. Pathfinders were all a bunch of burglars, when you got down to it.

We moved to the gate and peered between the bars.

Across a barren riverbed, an arching bridge connected the Widowknife Clanhold to the rest of Undarin. I thought "barren," but earlier we'd seen shapeless things oozing and seeping around in the gully.

Across the bridge, the succubus statue showed us her rear assets.

Just the other side of the gate stood a couple of guards. Light from the torches behind them threw long shadows over the bridge. One of the bruisers was all demon, a red-skinned brute with plates of armor bolted right through his skin and into the bone. The way he growled and shifted all the time, I figured it hurt. The other was a Kellid, tall as Kronug and twice as wide. Judging by his mane of spines, I guessed there was more than a whiff of demon in him.

I took a pebble from the ground and tossed it at Big Red, who didn't notice. Gemma did the same for Porcupine, who did. He looked behind him, didn't see us, and cursed his partner in demontongue. I grinned to think how things could have played out if we weren't in a hurry.

A ball of darkness covered up the guards and their torches. We heard their quizzical voices and then a familiar hum. The point of Oparal's holy sword swept out of the darkness once, but she had sense enough to sheath the thing before stepping out of the boss's conjured gloom. By the time they finished, Gemma and I had the gate open.

Naia and Erastus dumped the corpses into the gully. The moment the bodies stopped tumbling, a sloshing sound began moving toward them. I had a feeling the bodies wouldn't be there come morning.

The boss dispelled the dark, revealing himself and Alase, without Tonbarse. The big black wolf was too conspicuous for this kind of caper.

The boss took out one of the spell sticks we'd found in the Nekrosof catacombs. He broke it in half. After an instant of glamour, exact duplicates replaced the dead guards. There was nothing to them but looks and a bit of sound, but they'd fool anybody who didn't need a conversation.

The boss smiled in relief. He clapped me on the shoulder and whispered, "That was a spell quite beyond my ability. Now I understand how you must feel."

Things were going real smooth. That should have made me happy, but instead it made me nervous. From the start I said seven was too many for a sneak job. Nobody wanted advice from, you know, an actual burglar.

If it had to be seven of us, at least we got the right seven. Gemma was a devil with a knife and knew how to stay hid. Naia and Erastus were great shots and plenty stealthy, too. Neither Oparal nor the boss trusted the other enough to stay behind, and Alase talked herself in on account of it was her ancestral house.

The Kellids were only too glad to guard the Red Carriage. The crusaders would have followed Oparal into the Abyss, but most of them weren't made for the sneaky stuff.

The big problem was the stupid unicorn. It pitched such a fit that the boss suggested casting a spell to put him to sleep. Oparal said no, but it was too late. The unicorn heard what they were saying and came after me. Me! Arnisant reminded the pointy-headed horse who was boss, shying him off until Oparal cooled him down. In the end, both the unicorn and Arni stayed back.

After we got everybody inside the gate, the boss blew another couple scrolls to make Naia and Erastus invisible. They'd be our lookouts and cover any hasty retreats.

"Which way?" said Oparal. She looked up at the south tower.

The resident demon cult had been redecorating. After scratching their demonic symbols over Kellid carvings, they'd built a couple iron frames on the sides of the tower. The frames squealed as the wind tugged at them. They looked like a windmill's sails, but the shape was wrong. It took me a second to realize they were bat wings, or maybe dragon wings . . . or maybe succubus wings.

I realized it wasn't wind-shredded canvas hanging from the rusty frames. It was human skin. The sight made my own skin crawl. I'd seen plenty of bad stuff in my time, just not so big and out in the open.

"The Tower of Zura." Alase pointed to the roof of the tower. Above the wings stood a sigil wrought of iron. It looked something like a moon-horned helm with jagged sides and a hook curling down for a nose. I'd seen it before.

"Have we come to the wrong place?" said the boss.

"No, this is the Widowknife Clanhold. Over there is the Tower of Dawn, and this was the Tower of Twilight. The Cult of Zura has stolen it from the Widowknife clan."

"What is Zura?" said Oparal.

"Demon lord," the boss and I said together.

"Maybe we should take this conversation inside," I said.

That time, nobody disagreed with the actual burglar.

Alase pointed at a little door at the base of the south tower, well away from the big entrance. By its rusted iron frame and the lack of a path leading to it, I figured it hadn't been used in a while. "We need to find stairs. The library is on a high floor. It looks down upon the plateau."

Alase knew that much because of a poem she'd memorized. She'd learned it from her uncle, who'd had it from his mother, and so on like that. The boss would have preferred it if somebody had written it down, but it was better than nothing.

Opening the tower door was a piece of cake. Once I caught its pins, I realized I could have raked it open. If the whole place was that loose, I could go wherever I wanted.

Slipping the picks back into their secret pocket in my sleeve, I felt the bulge of one of the riffle scrolls the boss made me carry. I didn't like having them.

For one thing, they spoiled the line of my jacket. For another, just the other morning I'd conjured a surprised-looking phantom pig that disappeared in a cloud of farts.

Having a knack for scrolls was all very good, but I didn't want to rely on one in a tight spot.

I peeked inside to make sure it was clear. The others joined me, and I shut the heavy door real quiet. The boss twisted his light ring. A row of furnaces ran along one wall, rusty iron vats set in the wall above them.

I had a listen at the inside door. When it checked out, I raked open the lock. Every bit as easy as I'd figured. Before we left, I wanted a look inside those furnaces. They reminded me of something I'd seen before. They were rusted shut pretty good, but I got one open enough for a look inside. A big hole had rusted through the tank set above the furnace.

"What do we need to know about Zura?" asked Oparal, trying to look over my shoulder. She could see just fine in starlight, but here in the pitch black, it was all me. I saw that the furnaces heated the vats, which were connected to big vents on top.

"She was the first vampire," said the boss. "Once an Azlanti queen, she discovered the secret of longevity through hemotaphagy."

"What does that mean?" said Alase.

"Blood-drinking," I said. My voice echoed in the iron chamber, real spooky. Also, I liked showing off I knew the big word.

"Some say Zura's fall heralded the Age of Darkness in ancient Azlant. As a vampire, her sins were numberless.

Upon her death her soul fell into the Abyss, but rather than suffer she throve, becoming both vampire and succubus. In the Sodden Lands, the Koboto people worship her as one of the Three Feasters. Both the Bekyar tribes of the Mwangi Expanse and the halflings of the Kaava Lands—"

Oparal cut in. "How much of this information do we need, Count?"

"Those who would dedicate a tower to Zura either worship vampires and succubi—"

"Or else they *are* vampires and succubuses," I said, trying to be helpful and lighten the mood at the same time. The way everybody looked at me, I knew it was no use.

I climbed inside the furnace—it was roomy—and poked my head through the hole in the tank above. Six big vents rose up from the tank. They were narrower, but I figured I could slip inside. Plus, now I knew what the furnaces were for.

"You see what we got here, boss?"

"Hypocaust."

"Bless you."

Oparal shot me a dirty look, but I saw the ghost of a smile haunt the corner of her mouth. She thought I was funny. She just didn't want to let on. What she needed was a good laugh, a few pints, or maybe just one hell of a straight-up fight. Anything to take her mind off the crusader she'd lost.

If losing Porfirio was hard on Oparal, it was worse for his buddy Dragomir. The Ustalav had been all grins and laughs early on the night we spent in Valahuv, but he looked like he'd lost ten pounds overnight. His pretty eyelashes, which for a while made me worry I'd have some competition with the ladies, now made his half-closed eyes look sewn shut. He was starting to give me the creeps. I was glad they'd left him back with the carriage.

The reincarnated paladin was the first of the crusaders to die on this mission, which to me seemed like some kind of miracle by itself.

Of course, he'd been the second to die, too, which was a whole different kind of miracle, and not the kind even I could laugh about. None of us pointed out that Porfirio had brought it on himself by poking his nose in. That Feinroh Balemoon guy did that for us while he was running us out of his village, screaming that we'd turned their god away from them.

At least Feinroh still had the bird. The way the crusaders were looking at him, he was lucky they didn't pluck and roast that god, too. Instead, they collected Porfirio's body, and we left with our fresh water.

"I don't understand," said Alase. "What does 'hypocaust' mean?"

"It's a means of heating a building by channeling hot air or steam through narrow passages beneath the floors," said the boss. "Such a system requires regular maintenance. It seems entirely likely that the new occupants of the tower never learned to use it."

"Can we reach the upper floors this way?" asked Oparal. She was no dummy.

"Perhaps," said the boss. "But we could not expect to find access from the hypocaust chambers to the rooms we need to explore."

"I'll go," I said. "Have a listen here and there, catch up with you afterward."

"I'll go with you," said Gemma.

"No," said Oparal.

"Then I'll come," said Alase.

"No way," I said. The last time I'd let a pretty little bit help me in a tight space, I'd wound up down in a pit. "You can't see in the dark, and we don't want a flame in there with all the dust. Besides, you got to help the boss find the library."

The boss gave me the nod. I looked to Oparal, not that I needed her permission. She nodded at me, and I tipped her a wink.

"I'll meet you upstairs." I started to climb inside the furnace, but then I realized they might need more doors opened. I handed over my rake pick to Gemma. I had a feeling she knew how to use it.

I climbed into the furnace. That was no favor to my kickers, but the ashes had disintegrated to a fine powder. I tried not to stir it up too much as I pulled myself up into the water tank.

A narrow channel on the side connected it to the tanks on either side. It was the vents on top that I wanted. They angled up only a couple of feet before leveling off.

My jacket got a couple of scrapes, but nothing too serious. Time was, that would have bothered me a lot more. These days, I was getting used to the idea that I wouldn't have any jacket for long. Something always ruined it for me.

Usually something from Hell.

The space beneath the upper floor was only a couple of feet tall. In a few places there was a square stone rectangle filling up the space, probably a stairwell. The rest was full of little pillars set about three and a half feet apart, all across a space that must have covered a third of the tower. The other steam tanks must have fed the other two-thirds of the floor.

Crawling quiet as a snake, I got partway across the space before hearing sounds above me: screams, the crack of lashes, the sizzle of flesh, and inhuman laughter. Under other circumstances, I'd have guessed it was a torture chamber. In a place like this, it could have been a party.

Across the room I found another set of vents rising to the third floor. When the hypocaust was working, the second floor must have been the hottest, with each of the ones above a little colder.

Going up to the third floor was just a little trickier, since the passage went about ten feet almost straight up. Once I got under the floor, I heard the scrape of furniture and chains above me. A little farther along, I heard something boiling. On the other side of the tower—right above the place we'd broken in—I heard quiet footsteps and figured I'd caught up to the others. I listened hard but picked up no whispers.

Maybe it was a mistake, but letting the boss know where I was became a temptation. I can resist anything else.

Hoping anyone else would think it was just rats, I scratched out a simple pattern the boss and I had worked out years ago. After a pause, he scratched back the answer.

So far, so good.

I went up another floor. Nothing to hear, so I went up another.

That's when things got interesting.

First I heard a metal squealing. It took me a second to figure it out, but then I recognized the sound of the big metal frames hanging off the tower outside. As I moved closer to the center of the tower, I heard voices.

One was definitely a woman, the second one a man. The third, I don't know what it was. Its voice felt like fingernails on slate. Hearing it made my teeth hurt.

Worse than the sound of that voice was the language they were speaking. I recognized it as demontongue. I could even say a few nasty things a demon could understand, but I couldn't follow a conversation.

The man's voice sounded familiar, but I couldn't place it. That was frustrating, but I couldn't say I regretted never learning the language. Chaos talk was one of the few languages even the boss wouldn't speak, although he understood it well enough. He told me speaking it too much could mess with your mind, change the way you think. Make you crazy.

More like a demon.

Still, that man's voice was killing me. I knew I'd heard it somewhere before. If only he were speaking Taldane or . . .

I felt along my arm until I found the riffle scroll I needed. The boss had scratched a word into the leather cover: *comprehend*.

That was one I hadn't tried before, but I figured there was nothing to it but what he'd already told me. I thought about what I expected the magic to do. Then I thumbed the edge.

The pages tickled past my thumb. I didn't see any magic happening, but I got a snoot full of dust. I managed not to sneeze, but I choked a bit.

"What was that?" said the woman's voice.

"I heard only the sails," said the man. He sounded distracted, like he was busy with some chore, but now

I knew his voice. It was Prince Kasiya, the boss's old nemesis.

That third voice scraped across my ears. "Why are you nervous? You said your mistress would depart from the temple."

"That's what she told me," said the woman. I could hear the shudder in her voice. "But she doesn't trust me—she doesn't trust any of us. I wouldn't be surprised if she returned here before heeding the summons to Iz, just to catch me at schemes."

Kasiya snickered. I'd heard that mocking sound from a lot of noble types in past. It made me want to slap it right out of him. "Schemes are exactly what we're hatching, Yavalliska. Can you blame her?"

After a moment of icy silence, the woman laughed with him. "Of course not," she said. "There are no sisters among succubi. We were not made to serve each other or to work in concert. It is agony simply to suffer her close presence. But Areelu Vorlesh never learned the lessons taught in the cradle of the Abyss. She was born a human and thinks that makes her superior to me. Soon she will learn otherwise."

"Do not underestimate Areelu Vorlesh," said the third, monster voice. "She was the first among the Three. You cannot overthrow her rule alone."

"Then it is good that you came to me, Ommors."

Ommors, I thought. Desna weeps! That was the name of the spider-thing we chased out of the Delvegate.

"Do not forget that I have precedence, both by rank and by virtue of first arrival," said Kasiya. "You will open the library to me the moment Vorlesh leaves Undarin. Once the secrets of the *Lexicon of Paradox* are mine, no one will stand before you."

"I am grateful for your generosity, Your Highness."

Even from under the floor, I could hear the sarcasm. Kasiya obviously missed it. "It is well that you understand."

"What is in this *Lexicon*?" said Ommors.

"That's none of your concern, demon."

"Daemon," screeched Ommors. The sound itched in my teeth. "If I had not already sated my thirst, I would drain the last ounce of your blood, vampire. My kind have hunted your kind for ages."

"You will dare no such impertinence when I am the god of vampires!"

"Now, now, Prince Kasiya," said Yavalliska. "The distinction between demons and daemons is more important than you may understand. Unlike my kind, daemons—"

"Don't lecture me, fiend. Your obsession with such trivia reminds me of that . . . *Pathfinder*." He spat. "I am a prince. It is I who decides. It is I who commands. I do not crab my hand on notes or dull my eyes in candlelight over monographs on the varieties of fiends."

"But weren't you once a Pathfinder?"

"I will not be mocked."

"Then it is best you do not speak."

Kasiya gasped. The guy would have been a hit as a court fool, except he wasn't in on his own joke. Still, when he spoke I could almost feel the ice forming on the floor above me. "One word to Areelu Vorlesh, and I could have you destroyed."

"Perhaps," cooed Yavalliska. "But she needs nothing from you. Your success depends on my assistance."

Ommors said, "Why do I have to wait? For centuries the people of Valahuv worshiped me as a god. All I crave is blood and suffering. Undarin has ample supplies of both."

"Areelu Vorlesh will not suffer your presence in her city. You must serve me before I grant you sanctuary when the city is mine."

Ommors made a chittering sound but didn't say anything I could understand, even with the spell. I heard a window open. Somebody left, but I still heard two of them moving around above me.

Glass clinked. Someone settled into a chair. I wondered whether I should go back to find the boss or stick around and listen some more. It hadn't been so long since I left, so I crawled toward the sound of the clinking glass. Before I got there, Kasiya spoke again.

"Are you well?"

"I felt . . ." Yavalliska got up and moved to where I'd heard the window open. "No, she is still at the Temple of Deskari. Her escorts are assembling, but she has not emerged."

"Once I have used the *Lexicon* to take Zura's place as the god of vampires, you will have a place at my side." A pause. "What? Does that thought repel you?"

The window closed. "No, my prince. It is not that. I simply feel her presence, even at this distance."

I heard Kasiya rise from his seat. He walked right over me as he went to her. "You need never fear her again, once the *Lexicon* is mine. But you must learn to hold that insolent tongue of yours."

"So long as that daemon is among us, I must present an image of strength and independence," purred Yavalliska. "Surely you understand."

Kasiya hesitated a moment before saying, "Yes, of course."

What a sucker, I thought—in more ways than one.

Sometimes I crack myself up. I stifled a chuckle.

"Ommors will serve us both. The daemon is more powerful than you realize, easily seduced by the blood it craves."

"I know something of that impulse."

"As do I, my prince. But there is no shortage of worship and sacrifice here in Undarin. And once we see Areelu Vorlesh depart for Iz, we shall slip into her tower and search every inch of her arcane library. Then you can use this *Lexicon of Paradox* to assume your rightful place as god of vampires."

They might have had more to say after that, but it was time for me to go. I'd heard enough: the boss was searching the wrong tower.

Chapter Twelve
The Widowknife Chronicle

Varian

Any misgivings I had about letting Radovan scout through the hypocaust vanished when we reached the first guard station. With a scroll I rendered Gemma invisible. The effects would not long endure, but the spell would persist even after she did her work.

Gemma crept around the corner. We heard a muffled grunt, and a moment later the body of a demonblooded sentry came sliding back, dragged by the invisible woman. We concealed the corpse in the furnace chamber and crept along the ground-floor hallway.

Pausing only to allow Gemma to listen at closed doors, we encountered nothing more dreadful than snoring from the guards' bunkroom. We proceeded up the stairs on the far side of the corridor.

There I heard Radovan scratching a signal from within the walls. If Desna smiled upon us, he would find egress above. Otherwise he would have to retrace his path all the way to the entrance.

Traversing the second floor proved more challenging. Rather than a single straight corridor, a circular passage separated an inner sanctum from a number of outer chambers. Semicircular braziers set into the stone walls glowered with banked coals. Red and yellow light spilled from the outer chambers, some with their doors wide open, others sealed with prison bars.

In more favorable circumstances, I should have liked to search them all. Yet we could tell by the sounds alone that most of the chambers were occupied.

Reluctant though I was to expend one of my last remaining invisibility scrolls, I placed a hand upon Oparal's shoulders. The others knew the sign; Gemma placed her hand on my shoulder, Alase on hers. I discharged the scroll and we vanished from sight.

Oparal led the way past orgies and tortures, experiments vile and cruel. Nothing I had seen even in the laboratories of the Acadamae could compare. The obscenities we saw perpetrated in those alcoves made the Acadamae's necromancers and diabolists seem no more malign than boys plucking the wings from insects or incinerating ants with a beam of sunlight focused through a lens. Despite the surgical nature of some of the proceedings, the leering faces of the vivisectionists, human and fiendish, left no question that they took far more pleasure than learning from their experiments. The blood resulting from their violations of their subjects pooled on the floor until it gurgled into drains that carried the effluvium through the basements to run off the falls and pollute the Sarkora River.

Few of the demon cults I had uncovered in Egorian had been half so abominable.

Once the paladin paused before me, and I imagined I could feel her holy blade trembling in its scabbard. For a dreadful instant I feared it might be one of those fabled sentient weapons that could overcome its mistress's caution and send her berserking into a futile attack.

Whatever the cause of her hesitation, Oparal resumed our course. On the other side of the tower, we ascended an unguarded stair to the third floor. It, too, presented us with a circular path around a central chamber and six more rooms on the outer perimeter.

I felt a hand upon my back. It moved to touch my arm. "If the library is on this floor," whispered Alase, "it must be through one of the first two doors to our left."

"I'll check," whispered Gemma. Her hand left my shoulder.

A moment later, I saw the nearest door handle move. The door opened a fraction of an inch before closing again silently. The same occurred on the next door. Moments later, Gemma whispered, "Definitely not libraries."

I heard the horror in her voice and was content not to have seen the occupants of the room myself.

We hastened past the third-floor chambers before the invisibility expired. I prepared to extend it with my last such scroll, but Desna smiled upon us. The stairs and the landing on the fourth floor were uninhabited.

The fourth floor was little more than half the circumference of the first. Surrounding a small circular landing were only four doors. We went to the westernmost. Gemma reappeared as she knelt before the lock, removing Radovan's rake pick with a grim smile.

"I should buy one of these," she whispered. When she saw Oparal's concerned frown, she added, "You can see it's useful."

Oparal made a grudging nod and a hurry-up gesture. Gemma opened the door just wide enough to peer inside. She continued to peer as she opened it further and further, until eventually she stepped inside and beckoned the rest of us to follow. Once we did, she closed it in near silence.

Moonlight streamed in through a tall window to the west. Mismatched tapestries hung from a heavy rod above the window. Without prompting, Oparal closed them. Once they were covered, I activated the light on my ring, cupping it to direct the light toward the floor.

Mammoth-wool rugs covered the floor. Their faded colors told me they were original to the tower when it was dedicated not to Zura but to the myriad Sarkorian "gods" associated with twilight and sunset. Three-legged stools, the lacquer long since worn off the seats, surrounded a pine table perched on giant elk antlers. A row of half-melted candles ran down the table's spine, their dusty heads indicating long disuse.

High upon the walls, the painted skulls of beasts and men glowered down at us. A few empty spaces showed where the old had made way. Gory remains of several demon skulls were relatively new additions. I speculated they were fallen rivals of Undarin's mistress, the half-demon Areelu Vorlesh.

Beneath the grim skulls hung boxes of bone and wood, woven baskets, their bellies burst or sagging.

In some of them I spied scroll-sticks similar to those we discovered in the ossuary beneath Nekrosof tower. These had either been expended or never completed.

In the base of some of the hanging boxes we found circular stains in colors I recognized from the tinctures we had found beside the scroll-sticks in Storasta. A few drops in a draught of water, and the concentrated liquid became a potion. The ancient Sarkorians may have been known for their unorthodox worship, but they were no strangers to the arcane.

Between them, withered parchment draped over long pegs like wool through a loom. At first glance, I speculated that someone had made an effort to restore old manuscripts, but blowing lightly across the parchment produced a cloud of dust. If there had been any efforts toward restoring or preserving these documents, they had been abandoned decades earlier. My hopes of finding the *Lexicon of Paradox* in this chamber plunged.

Gemma listened at the door while Oparal stood by the window tapestries. One was made of coarse aurochs yarn, braided and dyed to form images of enormous animals with tiny human hunters at their feet. The other was a rude quilt stitched of foreign military banners: Ustalav, Isger, Mendev, and others. The blood of the fallen stained every patch.

Oparal parted the tapestries, shielding the gap with her body as she peered outside. Without turning, she said, "You must see this, Count."

I gave Alase my ring, demonstrating how to direct its light with a cupped hand. While she removed the scrolls from their racks and set them on the table, I joined Oparal at the window.

Rather than step aside, Oparal beckoned me close. With two fingers, she once more divided the tapestries, raising her shield to prevent the light from betraying our presence. Our faces close, we peered through the careful gap.

Our high vantage gave us a new perspective on Undarin.

The southern bank remained relatively dark, with occasional bands of demons or cultists roving the avenues between slave and animal pens. A few hovels remained, but most had been left in ruins after the capture of the city nearly a century earlier.

There was little traffic on the bridges that leapfrogged the Sarkora River, only a few sentries marked by the light of their torches. As we watched, a lone traveler crossed one of the bridges, avoiding the ogre-sized guard. Perhaps offended by the cringing pedestrian, the gigantic figure reached him in two great strides, grasped him by the head, and hurled him into the river. The victim's scream reached us even over the clamor of the nearer Cliffside.

If not for the demons flying over its roofs, creeping along its alleys, and crouching on the corners of its buildings, Cliffside might have appeared like any other bustling city. Many of the structures fallen in its conquest had been restored, others redecorated in haphazard fashion, much like the Tower of Zura in which we stood. The centers of attraction all appeared to be converted to temples, the largest of them clearly dedicated to the demon lord Deskari.

From that great hall emerged a procession escorted by a hundred torchbearers. In its center walked a figure striking not only for the batlike wings arching from her back but also for her regal bearing. Even at such a distance, I knew she could only be Areelu Vorlesh. I withdrew my spyglass and put it to my eye.

It was difficult to judge her height because her bodyguard consisted entirely of hulking demons, yet even dwarfed among the brutes she gave the impression of being tall. Horns curved from the sides of her head in stark contrast to the sumptuous black hair she allowed to cascade over one fair shoulder. At her hands and feet, the seemingly soft flesh gave way to a necrotic hue that highlighted her green-gray veins. Demonic sigils marred her otherwise beauteous thighs and belly. Her eyes were red as hot coals.

Vorlesh's entourage turned eastward, toward the Widowknife Clanhold. Even at their stately pace, they would arrive within half an hour, far sooner than we had hoped. Before panic could seize me, I saw that another procession moved to intercept her.

A score of men approached, representatives of various foreign nations. Among their banners I spied the thorny tower of Ustalav, the alabaster mask of Razmir, various ensigns of the River Kingdoms and crude tribal emblems of the Mammoth Lords, among others.

"Abrogail sent envoys." Oparal's lip curled in a sneer. Her elven eyes had no need of my spyglass to recognize the crest of Cheliax among the embassy.

I offered it to her anyway. "Note the man beside the Ustalavic ambassador."

She saw what I had noticed: a man in the blue-and-red checks of Mendev. Her sneer melted into a despairing gape.

"It's only reasonable to make a pretense of diplomacy," I said. "His presence here does not mean Queen Galfrey is ready to capitulate."

Oparal would not be reassured.

Areelu Vorlesh received the delegates one by one. Some offered gifts. Others knelt and raised their arms in gestures of supplication.

"Tell us when she moves again. We must depart before she returns."

Oparal responded with a grim nod. I left her to her vigil and returned to the table, where Alase had arranged the parchments in three groups.

She placed a hand above the first stack. "Songs and chronicles," she said. "The lives of the Widowknife clanlieges, their feuds and treaties. These are mine."

Even without her personal stake in the chronicles, I shared Alase's desire to liberate such treasures from the enemy. It was certain our intrusion would be noted, and the theft of such documents would hardly compromise our mission. I nodded assent.

Alase moved her hand to the second stack. Upon the first page I recognize the names of demon lords and infamous spirits of the First World. "The gods and their priests, the druids and the Green. I will take these, too."

I nodded again, not without reluctance. Much as I would love to add such knowledge to my own library, Alase had the better claim.

She moved her hand to the third stack, consisting of the few volumes written on paper or vellum, often bound as books rather than scrolls or loose pages. "Foreign stuff."

They were the holy texts of the gods of civilized people: Pharasma's *The Bones Fall in a Spiral*; *The Eight Scrolls* of Desna; and Torag's *Hammer and Tongs*, the latter consisting of lacquered pages in an iron binding.

How curious, I thought, that the fiendish occupants of the tower had not destroyed these scrolls and books. Demons revel in destruction and the ignorance of their slaves. Why should they preserve such history and theology? Perhaps the answer lay in the person whose approach limited our time in the Tower of Zura.

Alone of the three who opened the Worldwound portals, Areelu Vorlesh dedicated herself to the demon lord Deskari. She alone embraced the Abyss so completely that she studied the secret paths of corruption and transformed herself into a half-fiend. Unlike Radovan, whose fiendish ancestors seduced his human forebears in an insidious scheme to create their own gate to the material world, Vorlesh had begun life as a human being and chosen corruption; it had not been forced upon her.

My stomach churned as I considered the psyche capable of choosing such a path. It was difficult enough to understand the desperation of my sovereign's great-grandmother, Abrogail I, who signed the compact binding our nation to Hell. Yet she had bargained with the Prince of Law, and in return the devils serving Cheliax preserved the empire—and universal order— all across the Inner Sea. To willingly surrender oneself to chaos was incogitable.

"There is no time to read all of this for some clue as to where the *Lexicon* might be," I said.

Alase nodded. Her sympathetic grimace was little consolation.

"Are you certain this is the only library?"

"No," she said, and I realized the question was foolish. While this stronghold was her home by birthright, she had never before set foot inside the Widowknife

Clanhold. I wondered how I had let such a basic fact of her history slip my mind.

Recently I needed to remind myself of the most obvious facts. I shuddered to think that the proximity of the Worldwound was somehow affecting my emotions or, worse, my thoughts. I had seen its effects on the others, from the tightening stoicism among the crusaders to Radovan's increasingly frequent jokes. Everyone dealt with the fear in a different manner.

"Oparal?" I whispered. When she turned, I signaled for her to close the tapestries. Retrieving my ring from Alase, I shone it about the room once more, signaling the others to join in my search.

Apart from the door and window, there was no other apparent egress. Arching supports at the pillars helped hold up the flat ceiling. If an attic lay above this topmost floor, I saw no access to it from this room.

"Vorlesh must have removed it to her tower," I said.

"If this book is as powerful as you say, then Areelu Vorlesh would have used its powers long ago," said Alase. She motioned for my lighted ring, which I relinquished. "Or she would have delivered it to her master, Deskari."

"If so, then it is well beyond our reach."

"I will not give up so easily," said Oparal. "Not after all we've endured already."

"Do we have time to break into the other tower?" said Gemma.

"We must."

"No," I said. "Not without time to replenish the scrolls I expended. We must withdraw before we are discovered."

Alase shone the light of my ring upon the ceiling and once more over the walls. She was careful to avoid the tapestries covering the window, so I saw no reason to caution her further.

"Once they discover the sentries we've slain, the cultists will double their guard," said Oparal.

Even considering the undisciplined nature of demonic forces, I could hardly dispute that possibility. I had, however, some experience with demons, and thought another reaction more likely. "In their wrath, they will first send out patrols to find us. Vengeance runs stronger than caution in demons. We must take pains to conceal our vehicles. When we return, it must be in greater force. Perhaps after a period of days—"

Alase stood atop the table and peered at the ceiling, moving the light of my ring back and forth. Only then did I perceive the faint tracing in the stone. The marks were so shallow and, upon the walls, so frequently obscured by baskets, shelves, and parchment racks, that I couldn't perceive a pattern. "What is it?"

"The course of the stars," said Alase. "There's the sun and the moon. On the walls, there are forests and hills. There, that looks like a mountain of ice. Look—there's more all across the floor."

In an instant, Oparal pulled away one of the mammoth-wool rugs. Beneath it lay a film of blue-black mold. Freed from the layer of rugs, its spores stung my eyes and nose. I plucked the handkerchief from my sleeve and dabbed my eyes before covering my nose and mouth. It was some comfort, but I wished I had perfumed the cloth more recently.

The others choked and wiped their eyes before pulling away the rest of the rugs. The mold obscured only a fraction of the covered area. With the toe of her boot, Gemma scraped away a patch. Underneath, we saw the continuation of the patterns Alase had found on the ceiling.

Alase dropped to her knees and cut off a swatch of untainted rug with her knife. Using both hands, she began to scrub the moldy floor clean. Gemma followed her example, handing Oparal a hank of rug. Next she handed one to me. I balked for only an instant before joining the effort. She cut off another and knelt beside me.

Disturbing the mold brought a flood of tears to our eyes. We stepped away when necessary, stifling sneezes and wiping our noses. At last I extinguished the light and opened the tower window a few inches, trusting that no one would notice such a small motion. Afterward, we took turns breathing the fresh air while the others continued the excavation.

At last, Gemma voiced the doubt that gnawed on my mind. "Is there any point to this?" she said. "Or are we just wasting time we should be spending getting away?"

Oparal hesitated before answering. "Radovan may be awaiting us in the furnace room," she said. "Or else—" She shrugged, unwilling to voice the other doubt we shared. Probably we would have heard an alarm had he been discovered, but it was equally possible he had become trapped in the hypocaust or cut off by the unexpected arrival of more guards or visitors to the tower.

As everyone paused in the scrubbing, I heard a scratch upon the wall. Oparal turned her head, her elven ears locating it before I could. She indicated one of the support pillars against the northern wall.

I scratched back our recognition signal.

"I'm right here, boss." The stone wall muffled Radovan's voice. "It's pretty tight, but I think I can—"

One of the "pillar" stones shifted. The scrape of stone was much louder than our whispers and shrugging. Without a word, Gemma returned to the door and put her ear against the keyhole. She looked up and nodded at me.

"Here," said Oparal, pulling me aside with a bruising grip. I rubbed my arm but made no protest under the circumstances.

With a tug on each of her leather gloves, she gripped the stone that Radovan had moved and pulled it away as easily as one might remove a slice of cake.

I had known she was strong—often had I witnessed the effect of her sword on fiends and other monsters—but I had assumed much of that strength was granted by her holy sword. There was some other magic at work, for her power was far greater than that of any elf I had met.

I retrieved my ring from Alase and shone it through the gap. One of Radovan's elbow spurs vanished as he wriggled around and downward. Soon his face appeared, dusty and laced with cobwebs. He winked at us and smiled. "Maybe we can move a couple more? It's a little tight in the shoulders."

The rest of us stood back while Oparal took care of the rest. As she removed the stones, I saw the "pillar" was not at all a load-bearing structure but simply a passage upward. Next time we needed to open a door, I thought, she could do the honors without benefit of a lockpick.

Soon Radovan emerged from the wall. He slapped dust from his jacket and reported what he had heard on the floor below.

"Kasiya," I seethed. For all his spoiled incompetence, the vampire had a talent for interfering in my affairs.

"He heard us talking about Undarin," said Alase. "He came here for the *Lexicon*."

I had considered that probability before we left Storasta. Knowing Kasiya as I did, I was simply surprised he had found the city and ingratiated himself with this Yavalliska. It was far for him to travel without the comfort of his chariot, whose undead hounds I had incinerated. Imagining his humiliation at transporting himself under his own power was meager solace, but it was some. "Let us pray he has not found it."

"He hasn't," said Radovan. "Not yet, anyway. From what I heard, I don't even think this Yavalliska ever saw the book. Something about the way she was talking to him made me think she wasn't convinced it was even here."

"Unless the tableau at Nekrosof was intentionally misleading, or the book never reached Undarin, or it was later removed . . ." The possibilities were too many to anticipate.

"No," said Alase. "You were right before. Now you're thinking so clever that you're becoming stupid. My people wouldn't spend so much time on the image in the temple of the death goddess unless it had meaning."

Ignoring her insulting compliment, I focused on the truth in it. Alase was correct: the ancient Sarkorians would not have gone to the trouble of creating a work of art revealing the location of the *Lexicon* if it had not already been delivered—and secured.

"The drawings on the walls of this room. They're another clue, like the tableau of bones in Nekrosof. The key is to understand what they mean."

"It's Sarkoris," said Alase.

I bit my tongue rather than snap that I had already deduced as much. The stars above and the horizon on the walls left the floor to be a map of the rivers and cities of ancient Sarkoris. I shone the light on the floor near the center of the room. "Where is Undarin on this map?"

Oparal scraped away more mold with the heel of her boot. Scratched into the floor was the image of an aurochs standing on one side of the river, a pair of towers on the other. Wrinkling his nose at the smell, Radovan knelt and rapped on the stone floor with the butt of his big knife. "Feels solid enough," he said. He poked at the seams of the stone with the tip of the blade before glancing at the spot where he had entered the room and considering their relative positions. He gestured with both hands, indicating lines to either side of the area. "The support pillars ran like this. There's nothing under here."

"Where is Storasta?"

Scraping away more mold, we uncovered the sinuous lines of the Sarkora River and its tributaries. There were marks suggestive of the plateau we had seen to the south, and to the northeast the lands devoured by the gaping mouth of the Worldwound. A crown of stag's antlers marked a spot that had to indicate the city of Iz.

Far to the south, the Sarkora ran into the southeastern wall of the library. Where a mark should have indicated the city of Storasta stood only another pillar-like protrusion resembling the one through which Radovan had entered the room.

"It just ends," said Oparal.

"Were there hypocaust vents—?"

Radovan was already shaking his head. "The only one going up was the one I came through, and that one dead-ended a few feet up. Besides . . ." Once more he looked back at his point of entrance and imagined the pillars beneath us. He indicated parallel rows to either side of the pillar. "There's nothing down there, either. This pillar ain't standing on anything.

Oparal moved to the pillar, but both Radovan and Gemma hissed, "Wait!"

Together they examined the wall while I shone the light for them. Impatient, Oparal returned to peer out the covered window. "Count!"

I left Alase once more holding the ring and went to see what had alarmed Oparal.

The meeting outside the Temple of Deskari had concluded. Perhaps a third of the visiting emissaries withdrew across Gorum's Chain to the winding stairs, escorted by fiends. What remained of the others lay on the street or slathered across the faces of Areelu Vorlesh's honor guard.

At first I couldn't see the half-succubus, but then I glimpsed her flying off to the northeast, surrounded by locust and moth demons. From her trajectory, I knew she wasn't returning to the stronghold. Considering the map of Sarkoris at our feet, I surmised she was heading in the direction of Iz at the northernmost margin of the Worldwound.

"Desna smiles," said Radovan. He had succeeded in triggering the concealed panel in the false pillar. It swung open to reveal a package wrapped in soft leather. He lifted it carefully from its niche and brought it to the table, then stepped back to allow me the honors.

Care gave way to urgency as I opened the leather wrapping and removed the woolen batting underneath. Inside was indeed a book, but its binding was unexpected. Rather than the skin—fiendish or human—one might expect from a tome of dread arcana, a strangely supple bark covered it. Branded into its surface were Sarkorian pictograms, an anomaly among the many dialects of Hallit with no written counterparts. I recognized the signs for witchcraft, reality, the Green, and high arcana.

"Is it the *Lexicon*?" said Oparal.

The book collected pages of different materials, various parchments, strips of bark, even leaves of hammered copper. On some were scrawled rituals in ancient Thassilonian, on others incantations in antiquated Hallit. Still others contained geometric designs and unfamiliar maths suggestive of portals between disparate planes of existence. The contents were far too disparate and obscure to comprehend, but there could be no mistake: we had found the *Lexicon of Paradox*.

"Count?"

I smiled, lifting the book from its wrapping to show the others the fruit of our success. As I did so, I felt naked pages on the bottom. Turning the book over, I saw the stack of pages was barely more than half as thick as the book's spine, and there was no back cover.

"Looks like I spoke too soon," said Radovan. "Desna weeps."

We had recovered but half of the *Lexicon of Paradox*.

Chapter Thirteen
The Falls

Oparal

Radovan and Gemma searched for another secret compartment. Of course, they found none.

"What advantage in dividing the book in halves only to hide both in the same room?" said the count. The fatigue in his voice blunted his usually pedantic tone.

I felt some sympathy for his disappointment, but that was nothing compared to our need to depart this wretched lair. "There's nothing else for us here. Let's go."

The count returned the book to its wrapping and secured it in his satchel.

Gemma listened at the door, nodded, and opened it. We slipped into the corridor and made it halfway to the stairs before we heard the first alarm. The count translated the word most often repeated: "Intruders!"

"Count, Alase: if you have any more bolstering spells, now is the time. We must fight our way through."

"We could go out the window," said Gemma. Once again she had found an opportunity to use her spidersilk rope.

"They'll spot us before anybody reaches the ground," said Radovan. "I've got a better idea." Rather than explain, he went back into the library. By the time Alase closed the door behind us, he was already pulling at stones to widen the hypocaust vent.

"Stand back," I said. He was slow to obey, so I moved him.

"Careful, sweet—"

I struck the corner of the stone wall with the heel of my palm. With a cloud of mortar, the stone yielded.

"I see you got this," said Radovan, stepping back.

The pain to my hand was considerable. While the tough leather of my gloves spared me cuts, my magic belt gave me strength, not invulnerability.

"All right," said Radovan when I opened the hole all the way to the floor. "That should be plenty. Follow me."

He stepped through the hole and dropped, folding his knees so quickly that he appeared to vanish into a deep chasm rather than a mere two-foot passage.

Alase followed him.

"It's pitch black," Gemma said, prompting Jeggare to go next. With the light of his ring illuminating the hypocaust passage, Gemma waited for me to go next.

"I'll bring up the rear," I said.

"You're going to need help." She nodded at my shield, too wide to fit through the opening.

I set the shield aside and kicked at the corner of the stone protrusion, loosening another block. Gemma tugged at the strap beneath my pauldron. Instinctually I drew back, but I saw the need. I allowed it.

Demonic voices shouted from the hall.

"There's no time," said Gemma. "Go!"

I plunged headfirst into the hypocaust passage. The faulds around my hips caught in the opening. They stuck fast, preventing me from moving forward or going back.

Gemma pushed on my legs. I struck my faulds with the heel of my fist, denting the steel only slightly. Behind us, the doors of the library burst open. A fiendish voice uttered hateful, unintelligible words.

Count Jeggare's light dazzled my eyes for an instant. "Help her," said Alase. She crawled out of the way to let Radovan move toward me. He braced his feet against the little pillars supporting the floor above us and offered me his hands. I gave him one and continued to beat at my faulds with the other.

As he pulled, Gemma let go of my legs. A demon screamed. A moment later, so did Gemma.

With one last smash of my fist, the faulds slipped through the opening. The instant I was free, I twisted around to reach back.

Gemma reached for me as fiendish talons closed around her face. One plunged into her eye, another widening her mouth to her ear.

"Cap—!" She flew away, out of my sight.

"Come on," Radovan hissed in my ear. When I didn't comply, he tugged at my arm. I resisted, then relented.

We crawled on elbows and knees, dragging our bodies through the hypocaust chamber and into an angled shaft leading to the floor below. Count Jeggare awaited us, letting us pass him before breaking one of the rune-sticks from the cache in Nekrosof Tower to fill the level above with a mass of thick, sticky webs.

The cries of fiends grew muted behind us as we descended to the third floor, and then the second. At each pause, I glanced back but saw and heard no sign of pursuit through the hidden passages.

Fiery blasts and shouts greeted me as I awaited my turn to emerge from the vents. By the time I stepped into the furnace room, the battle was over.

Erastus and Naia stood over the bodies of three guards, two men and a half-fiend. I saw from the dropped shovel and torches that they had meant to fire the furnaces beneath us, roasting us in the hypocaust.

The count dropped an expended riffle scroll into his coat pocket even as he kept the point of his Shadowless Sword trained on the body of another fallen half-fiend.

"Hurry," said Naia. "Guards approach the first bridge."

We burst out of the furnace room and ran across the courtyard. No one barred our path, but a rough voice cried out a warning above us. Erastus turned and shot. Naia's arrow flew an instant later. The wall sentry toppled, both shafts jutting from his chest.

"Wait!" said the count. "Stay near me." He discharged another of his peculiar little scrolls. Those nearest him vanished. I moved toward the spot where I had last seen Erastus and bumped into him. I put his hand on my arm and reached blindly until I touched Naia.

"Ready."

We ran past the count's illusory gate guards. The lifeless images ignored us as we rushed across the bridge leading back into Undarin. We turned left at the statue of Areelu Vorlesh, its upper body cloaked in darkness, and ran south toward the bridge leading out of Undarin and into the eastern fields.

An unseen force shoved me down to one knee before I caught myself from falling. I lost contact with Naia and felt Erastus's hand leave my shoulder. An instant later, I saw Erastus appear, tumbling away from the statue we had just passed. He looked up at the monument, eyes wide.

The shadows fell away from the statue, revealing not only the image of Areelu Vorlesh but a pair of demons.

The two were of a kind, winged and lanky with oversized claws and tusks jutting from the jaws of their batlike faces.

Each of them pointed a long finger at Erastus.

Two crooked black rays leaped out to strike the Isgeri in the chest. Ever stoic in battle, Erastus wailed in agony as the dark energies drew flickering radiance from his body and dispersed it. The fiends were devouring his soul.

"Go now," I said. "Stay close to the count. I'll follow."

"But Captain—" said Naia, who remained invisible.

"It's an order. Go."

I drew the Ray of Lymirin.

Its light leaped up toward heaven, a beacon every fiend in Undarin could see. On the statue, the death demons opened their mouths to shriek.

But I heard only the choir.

I ran toward them, leaping onto the statue's base to slash at the taloned feet of the nearest demon. It leaped away, its wings blasting me with an infernal stench.

The other demon glared not at me but at Erastus, who backed away, reluctant to obey my last command. "Go, I said!"

His eyes met the demon's. They widened and sank down into his skull, the last reflection of life dying as the fiend drew out the final ounces of his soul through his eyes. His face withered and grayed. He fell.

Grasping the statue's arm, I pulled myself up to strike the fiend that slew Erastus. The Ray sang vengeance as it cut deep into the abomination's scaly thigh. I struck again as it leaped away, severing the talons of its trailing foot.

Darkness enveloped me as a heavy body drove me off the statue and onto the ground. Talons scraped across the back of my cuirass. Sharp nails dug through the chainmail where my missing pauldron left a gap in my defense. A heavy body fell upon me, strong limbs encircling my chest.

I twisted, but the fiend remained atop me, its knees digging into the pits of my arms. Its unholy halo dimmed even the divine light of the Ray. I stabbed blindly over my shoulder.

The demon clutched my wrist, holding the sword at bay with one hand. Its strength was terrible even before it added the second hand and pushed my own blade down toward my neck. Even the magic of my belt wasn't enough for me to resist.

"Iomedae," I whispered. "Grant me strength."

At my prayer, the radiance suffused my body, strengthening my muscles. I pushed back, forcing the blade away from my throat.

The demon's jaws opened in an expression of surprise. I shoved with all my magic- and deity-granted might, pushing it off of me. For all the power of Iomedae, I knew I had not hurt the fiend in our struggle.

Behind the demon, Radovan raised his big knife to stab again from behind. The fiend twisted around to fend off the surprise attack. When it released my arm, I raised the Ray in both hands and struck off its wing and arm together.

It reeled, and Radovan stepped around to strike it again from the side. Harried from both sides, the fiend lashed out, but Radovan had already withdrawn. I struck again, spilling the fiend's viscera in a steaming pile. The demon fell.

"I told you to go."

"You ain't the boss of me. Besides, if I went back without you, that stupid unicorn would kill— Get down!"

We hit the ground just in time to avoid the swooping attack of the other death demon. It flew past us to land beside Erastus.

The fallen ranger stood, his head turned at an unnatural angle. He cast away his bow and glared at us with undead hatred.

I knew that stare. I warned Radovan, "Don't let him touch you."

He crouched, sidestepping to flank the demon. "Got it. Also, company's on the way."

I had already seen the emaciated figures of assassin demons stalking toward us. Radovan and I had faced their kind before, in the Fierani Forest.

But not alone.

We had to move fast before we were overwhelmed. When I saw the demon's eyes flick toward Radovan, I charged. As the fiend moved to defend itself against the Ray, I turned and thrust instead at Erastus. The sword pierced his armor and split his heart. It was the only mercy I could offer.

"Find peace in the light, crusader."

Above the radiant choir, I heard a bone-crunching impact. Radovan cried out in pain. I turned in time to see him hit the ground at the base of the statue. The death demon coughed its mockery as it stalked toward him. Ichor streamed from its wounded thigh and foot as it locked its eyes on Radovan.

"Don't look!" I shouted, but too late. Radovan gawped at the demon's face. Multicolored soul essence rose from his body to stream toward the fiend's gluttonous eyes.

A prayer to the Inheritor on my lips, I gathered all my faith into a single blow. When the Ray came down upon the demon's spine, it came with all the weight of Iomedae's wrath. The sword blazed and sang, combining its own righteous fury with my own. The death demon fell in uneven halves at Radovan's feet.

He shook his head, stunned as much by the blow that threw him to the foot of the statue as by the fiend's gaze. The assassin demons moved to cut off our escape left and right.

I pulled Radovan to his feet. "Go now, and no argument."

"I'm not going to let you—"

"You're no use to me here, not without your devil upon you." He flinched. My words stung, but he needed to hear it. "Go now, before—"

"Viridio!" he shouted. "Come on, I'm inviting you through!"

"Stop it! What are you doing?"

"We need the big fellow. Come on, Viridio!" Radovan beat his chest. "Get in here!"

A shadow fell toward him. I pushed Radovan aside and struck upward with the Ray. The death demon screamed as it rose once more, retreating from my holy blade.

Radovan rolled back to his feet. He appeared less startled by the sudden attack than by the absence of any physical transformation. "It's no good," he said. "I don't think it's enough to call on him. What I need is his sigil, venom, and plenty of it."

"I need you to tell the count to look for me in the river."

He frowned, but his eyes widened with understanding. He nodded. "Will do."

"Now get out of here. I can't fight and watch out for you at the same time."

He didn't like hearing the truth, but he accepted it. "Give 'em hell, sweetheart."

I disliked the familiarity, but I allowed it.

He ran, raggedly at first, and then with arms and legs pumping. I went with him as far as the second bridge. To the south, a befouled stream from the cellars of the Widowknife Clanhold fell into the Sarkora River.

Radovan paused once to look back. I waved him off and turned to face the chaos alone.

The remaining death demons flew up, out of reach of the Ray. I felt the absence of my shield as they pointed down at me and shrieked. Yet they did not attack. They waited as the mob approached.

Far more of them were human than I had expected, the rest orcs and half-breeds. They wore garments in the colors of filth and violence. The boldest ran to the front clutching curved daggers that reminded me of Radovan's big knife.

I braced for the rush.

And still they did not come. Instead, they stood well back from me as a buzz of insects rose behind the mob. As it grew louder, the crowd parted to allow their champion to approach.

A head taller than I, the man wore mismatched armor: one pauldron decorated with a demon's face, the other with the Andoren eagle. Upon his shield was welded an iron locust, its wings sharpened to blades. Bloodied with paint and scratched with Abyssal runes, the sword of the Inheritor lay embossed upon on his breastplate. Considering his size, it had to have been made specifically for him.

The man had once been a paladin.

I reached out with the radiance. Even surrounded by demons and cultists, his presence stood out as the most evil.

"Where did you fall, crusader?"

He unsheathed a heavy blade. A cloud of darkness streamed out of the scabbard after it, each tiny mote growing within instants to form a locust the size of a man's thumb. A few perched on his armor, one upon his cheek. The rest formed a dark halo around his head. He came toward me.

His blade flew high, but I was not deceived. The first attack came from the razor wings of the locust on his shield. I retreated and stepped aside, swinging the Ray in both hands to deflect the shield. Once more I lamented the loss of my own shield.

The fallen paladin rushed me. This time I stepped to his right, calling on the radiance as I struck his blade. Blinding light seared the hovering locusts as our swords clashed. With both hands, I should have struck the weapon from any lesser foe. This dark crusader was as strong as I, even with my magic belt.

I hooked my ankle behind his, but he stood fast. Breaking our blade lock, I stepped past him. Borrowing a trick from Radovan, I shot an elbow into his back. Even a spur of steel would not have penetrated my foe's back plate.

He whirled, but not following me as I had expected. His shield slammed into my sword arm. The locust wings caught my cowter, their razor edges tearing at the steel.

I kicked backward, this time catching his calf. He fell into a half-kneeling position. I turned hard to the right, sweeping my blade across his neck. The Ray's edge sparked on his heavy steel collar.

He swung his sword low. I leaped, but not high enough. The back of his hand caught my heel. I tripped, rolling away as I came down.

He also retreated, panting less from the exertion than from his close call with decapitation. He motioned to the mob of cultists as he stepped back. At his unspoken command, they surrounded me.

Brandishing the Ray sent those nearest me scurrying away. One lingered a moment too long. My blade licked out. The cultist fell, pushing himself away with his feet as he clutched his bleeding throat.

The dark paladin uttered a demonic phrase. He pointed at a cultist whose face wept with blisters. "Kill her!"

The chosen cultist gaped, eyes wide for an instant before narrowing with malicious intent. He raised his wicked dagger and leaped for me.

Even as I turned to sweep the Ray across his undefended belly, I knew the fallen paladin was ready to strike. As I eviscerated the cultist, I continued to turn, dropping to the bridge and rolling as the dark paladin's sword smashed the stones inches behind me.

He struck again with his shield. I continued to roll, barely avoiding the crushing blow. When he struck again with the sword, I surprised him by rolling backward, parrying with the Ray. I kicked up with both legs. The surprise blow knocked his shield aside. I released his sword and thrust the Ray beneath his shield arm.

He wore no besagew beneath his spaulders. The tip of the blade thrust deep into his armpit.

He roared in pain as I rolled back to my knees and scrambled away. His shield slumped at his side.

I stood and asked again, "Crusader, where did you fall?"

His only answer was to spit a curse.

Crying out the Inheritor's name, I flew at her betrayer. My first strike beat aside his swarming blade. The second he caught in a last, desperate raise of his shield. I struck the steel locust from its face in a shower of sparks. His shield arm fell dead at his side.

"Deskariiiii!" he screamed.

A miasma of dark insect wings intensified around him. Motes of corruption burned my eyes and filled my nostrils. A million infinitesimal mandibles gnawed my flesh, striving to burrow into my heart.

He struck and struck again. Dazed by the power of his demon lord, I slashed wildly. The Ray deflected his sword once, twice, but not the third time. It cut through my pauldron and deep into my breastplate. An instant of ultimate cold, and then I felt the wet wound trickling down my shoulder.

I stepped back, both hands steadying the Ray in a defensive posture.

"Iomedae!"

She answered, the radiance surging through my body. It did nothing for my sundered armor, but it seared the corruption from my wound before closing it.

My foe uttered a profanity to the lord of locusts. The insects swirled around the fallen paladin's body to form another suit of armor.

Thus healed and fortified, we threw ourselves back at each other.

As he flung the dark powers of the Abyss at me, so did I hurl the might of Heaven at him. His was the stronger arm, mine the fiercer blade. His servitude to Deskari was absolute, but so was my devotion to Iomedae. He would fail, because he fought to destroy me, while I fought for time.

As I retreated, parrying a furious sequence of head strikes, I glanced over the bridge. The ravine lay much farther below us than I had realized, or perhaps it only seemed so now. The polluted stream from the cellars of the Widowknife Clanhold looked far shallower than I had hoped. The sluggish waters barely dampened the channel before pouring down into the Sarkora River below.

I kicked my foe's knee. As he lowered his guard, I struck at his head. He raised his blade again, but it was too late. I shifted my aim and swept the Ray in a downward arc. Its blinding white edge cut through his tasset. A gout of blood and severed chains from his chausses followed as I withdrew the blade.

Daring a glance upward, I saw the circling death demons—and above them, a human figure rapidly descending.

At last, Varian had come for me!

I feigned a parry of my foe's next attack, instead stepping aside to throw a short punch into his already-battered face. The way was clear for me to leap, but a lingering qualm held me back. Escape was not enough.

Raising the Ray once more, I gazed into my opponent's eyes. "Crusader, this is where you fall."

"Destroy her!" he shouted. "All of you, do it n—!"

I thrust the point of the Ray through the symbol of Iomedae upon his breastplate. His final word dribbled crimson over his chin.

The sight of his demise made the mob hesitate. That brief pause was all I needed to vault the rail and fall.

I splashed into the foul runoff, both shins cracking as I had feared. Gripping my legs, I prayed twice: once for the blessing to heal my injuries, second for forgiveness for asking so much of the Inheritor. Merciful Iomedae healed my legs.

Staggering to my feet, I ran for the lip of the falls. Behind me, the mob of demons and cultists poured into the riverbed, clamoring for my death.

A grave-cold bolt struck me on the shoulder, another on my hip. My soul shuddered at the touch of the essence-shriveling spell. The wings of the death demons beat close behind me. I could not allow them to slow me.

I ran to the edge and leaped into open space, turning to slash the flying demons. The Ray cut through the face of the first. The second demon clutched the blade and tried to wrest it away, but the sword's holy light seared its taloned hands. Despite its agony, the fiend held onto the sword, tearing it from my grip and flinging it away.

My heart sank as I saw it flying through the air, falling in its own arc toward the befouled waters below us. Without the Ray, I could never defend myself against such fiends and villains as I had faced in Undarin. I was lost.

Except for my ally, whose flying body dove toward me. I opened my arms to welcome the rescue. "Count!"

But even as I spoke, I saw that my rescuer was not Varian Jeggare. Hands as strong as my own closed on my arms, denting my armor even as they arrested my fall. They pulled me close enough to smell my savior's breath, its rotting stench barely covered by the scent of cloves.

Behind a mask of hammered gold, Prince Kasiya's withered lips parted to reveal his long, sharp fangs. He smiled.

Chapter Fourteen
The Mourning

Radovan

More than the demons of Undarin, it was the storm that chased us up the river. Ahead to the west, the sky was gray above a swamp that spread as far as I could see past the southern plateau. Behind us, the sun peered at us through a black eye. Yellow lightning licked around the purple clouds. I counted to seven before the thunder rolled up behind us. The horses screamed.

The storm was getting closer. Either that or I'd been hanging out the carriage window too long and spooked 'em.

I ducked back inside and settled down on the front seat. What I saw across the map table wasn't any more encouraging than the sky.

The boss had a half-full wineglass clipped to the corner of the table. In front of him lay the *Lexicon of Paradox*, its pages opened to the point near the end, where somebody had torn it in half.

Beside the *Lexicon* was the boss's open journal, or the latest volume anyway. He'd started one fresh for this project. A pen, a quill, and a brush danced over its pages.

While he waggled a finger and stared at the pages, the pen wrote out letters in a foreign language. Even though I couldn't understand the words, I could see they were exactly the same as the ones on the *Lexicon*, right down to the handwriting.

The quill and brush worked on the drawings, sketching out scenes of sacrifice and vivisection.

Vivisection. That was one my least favorite words I'd learned from the boss over the years. It was a word that came up a lot in our line of work.

The carriage wheels hit a rut, scattering the riffle scrolls and spell sticks across the table. Wine bottles clinked beneath the table. By the sound I could tell at least some of them were empty.

The bottles hadn't been down there before we went into Undarin. The boss had killed a few since coming back from failing to rescue Oparal.

That was bad. Usually a new book, even an evil one like the *Lexicon*, kept the boss's mind so busy that he didn't want a drink. This time it wasn't enough. He was obsessed and drunk at the same time. Something told me that made it a bigger problem than usual.

The carriage hit another rut, a bigger one. Wine splashed onto the boss's shirt cuff and stained the corner of the journal. I grabbed the glass like to set it aside while he tugged a handkerchief out of his sleeve to mop up the spill. While he wasn't looking, I tossed back the rest of his wine, figuring if it was in me, it couldn't make him any drunker.

The boss kept his attention on his spell. I thought about helping to straighten up, but he didn't like anybody touching his papers.

The table wasn't the only thing that was a mess. The boss couldn't stop running his free hand through his hair, leaving him looking like a mad hermit instead of a count. I still couldn't see the gray he'd started developing a few years back. Ever since we left Tian Xia, he'd lost the gray he'd started growing a few years back. One day, I knew I'd catch him dying it.

Come to think about it, he'd been mighty spry lately, especially during our tour of Kyonin. It was like he'd been to Thuvia for the famous sun orchid elixir, which guys as rich as the boss bid on to stay young forever. But he hadn't been out of my sight lately, except for a few weeks in the winter, when he went off to visit the Queen of Thorns.

He waved the pen, quill, and brush away, letting them fall on the table. He'd finished copying what he had left of the *Lexicon*. The rest was missing, torn away a long time ago by the looks of its bark-like cover.

"What do you say, boss? Time for a break?"

He gnawed on a knuckle while comparing the original to the copy. Lowering his head to peer at the tiny print, he let his tangled hair fall over the *Lexicon*. The handwriting changed from page to page, sometimes right in the middle of a bloodstain. It was like nobody wrote much in that book before something bad happened to them and somebody else had to take over.

The boss flipped back a few pages, mumbling while he compared the original to his copy. I couldn't understand a word he was saying. The more he put his nose into the *Lexicon of Paradox*, the crazier he got.

"You've got to sleep, boss," I said. "Come on, you've been awake way too long."

"Not yet. First I have to understand this. The implications of the oscillating spirit-vessels alone . . ." He raised his head and tilted it to the side. For a second, he seemed to see me. "That made no sense, did it?"

"That magic stuff never makes sense to me. You're tired. Go to sleep."

He stared straight ahead. "No. They're still after us. She wasn't there. I searched all along the bloody river, but my spells last only so long. There were more demons pouring out of the city every minute."

"Come on, boss. Gimme the book." I reached for it.

"No!" He snatched it back. "I have to learn where the other half is hidden. I need to copy it again, this time in my own hand. Only then can I consign it to my memory library. Perhaps then I will be able—"

"Boss. You're no good to anybody like this. The book, it's making you twitchy." I reached for it.

"No! You cannot take it from me."

Don't touch that!

I pulled back my hand. I knew that voice, but I hadn't expected to hear it again—not in this world, anyway.

That book will mess you up!

"What do you care, you little turd?"

"Pardon me?" said the boss.

Hey, I care! The others may have given up on you, but I'm still your pal.

"Quang?"

"Quang? Quang? What is Quang?" said the boss. He checked the windows and under the table.

He was in worse shape than I'd thought.

The first time I'd heard the imp's voice was after the demons of the Witchbole cut me open to make a gate to the Abyss. That's when I met Quang and all the rest of my devil ancestors, the twisted sicks who'd pruned and spliced my family tree all the way down to me. Their idea was to turn me into their own personal gate from Hell. Unluckily for them, the demons got to me first. Luckily for me—depending on how you look at it—I made a deal with the devils.

"I'm not talking to you." I pointed at the boss. "Quang, how come you can talk to me? I thought only Viridio could do that now."

"Where is this Quang?" snapped the boss.

I held up a hand.

I don't have a lot of time, Spikes. Just take my word for it. You got to get clear of that book. And then you got to get away from the Worldwound. What were you thinking coming here, anyway? We're smarter than that, you and me.

"Speak for yourself, you little twerp." I blinked and realized I'd insulted myself. "Anyway, don't call me Spikes. I always hated that."

"To whom are you speaking?" said the boss. He shook his head and sat up straight, his voice clearer than it had been. He was a little more like his usual self.

"It's Quang. You know, my imp."

That got his attention. He shut up and listened. A second later, he put his head down on the table, as if he were listening to the wood.

Just go. Get as far away from the Worldwound as you can. And leave that book behind.

"You sound scared."

You should be scared, too! Don't forget, you're connected to the Abyss as well as to Hell. Since what went down in Kyonin, there are plenty of demons who know what you are.

"What's Viridio think of this? How come I can't hear him? Where are the others?"

They know better than to be anywhere near when you're so close to the . . . Uh-oh. We're going to have to . . . Oh, angel balls! Quang's voice faded, like he was moving away.

I thought about the little hell my devils gathered in to look through me, its slick walls, half stone and half flesh. When I'd met them, their eerie voices echoed through a passage I couldn't see. Now I wondered where that passage went.

"Quang, where'd you go?"

The imp didn't answer.

"Listen, boss, this book might be more wrong than we realize. Let's put it away for a while."

"I must finish studying it."

"No, you got to sleep." I snagged the original and the copy he'd made in his journal.

"Give that back this instant."

"Nope, it's mine now. You can have it back after you sleep."

He glared at me. I glared back. We had a little standoff.

"Listen, boss, I'll put it right here." I took his satchel from beneath the table and pushed all the scrolls and sticks inside, then the books. I lifted the seat and stuffed the whole shebang inside. "Satisfied?"

"Do not flatter yourself that you could keep that from me if I wished to take it."

"Yeah, I know. Don't hurt me."

He started to turn away but then whipped back to glare at me. "Are you patronizing me?"

I didn't know which answer would set him off worse, so I said, "Maybe."

He glared some more before a yawn spoiled the effect. He folded his coat for a pillow and lay down on the seat. Since Variel had refurbished the carriage, it was almost the size of a bed. "Wake me in an hour."

I reached for the carriage door and stopped myself.

If Quang wanted me away from the book, maybe that meant there was something in it I wanted to see. Maybe something bad for him.

Maybe a way for me to get rid of those devils once and for all.

All quiet-like, I opened the seat lid and snuck out the boss's journal, leaving the original book inside the satchel. If there was a magic reason the book was bad news, maybe it was safe to take a peek at the copy. Besides, if there was something about the book making the boss peculiar, maybe Jelani would have some idea what to do about it.

I waited until I heard the boss snoring. He always says he doesn't snore, but that's only true when he hasn't been drinking. I tucked the journal under my jacket, opened the carriage door, and swung out onto the runner.

There was my phony pony, keeping pace alongside the carriage, right where I'd left it. I jumped right into the saddle, and it didn't even squeal. A real horse would have bit me rather than let me jump onto the saddle. Phony ponies are the best.

After twisting around to put the journal in the saddlebag, I stood up to check the sky. Still nothing coming after us but the storm.

A nasty idea crept into my brain. What if the storm was full of demons, and they'd been chasing us the whole time?

Sometimes I give myself the shudders.

Seeing me peer around made Kala suddenly look over her shoulder. Then Kronug and Gannak did the same, and they all caught my creepy feeling.

That was fine. We needed to be jumpy, ready to hide or fight at the first sign of incoming demons. It was only a matter of time before a patrol spotted us.

Since losing four of their own, the crusaders had gone back to keeping their own company. Nobody had it as bad as Dragomir, who'd been snippy even with his own people. I never heard Aprian raise his voice to the guy, but the first time we stopped to rest the horses, he'd taken Dragomir aside and had a quiet chat. That calmed Dragomir, but there was a darker storm in his eyes than there was above our heads.

Maybe they didn't feel safe unless they outnumbered the Kellids. Maybe they blamed the boss for not finding Oparal, or maybe they blamed me for leaving her. The only good thing was that the stupid unicorn stuck with them, riding between Naia and Jelani.

I wanted to chat with Jelani, but not if it meant tangling with the unicorn. I decided to wait until we made camp.

Over on our side, Arni ran between me and Alase. He and Tonbarse were getting along the way he and the unicorn never did, which was kind of weird since Arni was bred to hunt wolves. Alase shot me a sympathetic look. Or maybe it was a different kind of look. It didn't matter. Even before our bad night in Undarin, I was feeling pretty damn far from frisky. Maybe later I'd show her a good time.

Even thinking that, I felt a pang of guilt for no good reason. We weren't in Ustalav, I told myself. I could never go back there anyway. I hadn't promised that witch a damned thing.

Besides, she wasn't even that good-looking.

That last thought made me feel guiltier and meaner than ever. I kicked the pony, even though it did whatever I wanted just by thinking it, and rode up with the Kellids.

They'd taken our loss in stride, maybe because now we'd lost fewer Kellids than crusaders. Valki had stopped bragging about how he would have killed every demon in the tower, stolen the book, and razed the town behind him. Only Kronug looked like he was about to cry, which was surprising. I'd taken him for a tough guy. Maybe he just had a stomachache.

I rode ahead to get out of the dust of the carriage wheels. I felt bad for the wagon drivers. They wanted to move side by side, but the boss had made it clear he didn't want two sets of wheel tracks for the demons to follow.

Aprian rode around the other side of the Red Carriage and came up beside me. "How is the count?"

"Tired." I figured that's all he needed to know.

"Everyone will need to rest soon, especially the horses."

He was right about that. "Let's get some cover first."

"Agreed." He said it like it was the two of us who were in charge.

Come to think of it, I guessed we were, as long as the boss was asleep. That idea didn't bother me as much as it might have done a few years back. In Ustalav, I'd been kind of in charge of some Sczarni, and the boss was letting me hire the guards these days. So far, none of them had turned on us, so I figured I was doing a good job.

"On behalf of the troops, I want to thank you."

"What?"

"Naia told me you stayed back to fight beside the captain."

I shrugged. He was trying to say something nice, but it only made me feel bad. "For all the good it did."

"After we met in Storasta, Oparal told me about you and the count."

"Well, you got to understand she's got a particular point of view. We're not as bad as all that."

"She said you saved her once before, in a city of thorns and demons."

"She told you that?"

He nodded.

"What do you know? Maybe she had a soft spot for me. Back in Kyonin, even though it was hard to tell sometimes, we were on the same side all along."

"I hope the same is true this time," he said.

"I figure it is."

He rode beside me without talking for a while. Then he said, "A man like you could distinguish himself in the crusade."

I almost laughed. I should have seen that one coming. "Forget the recruitment pitch, Sarge. I like the job I got."

"I know," he said, almost but not quite smiling. "Still, we count quite a few Chelaxians among our ranks."

"Many of them hellspawn?"

He shook his head. "No. Not many who have been demon-bound, either."

I remembered what Jelani told me about Aprian's demon possession. Of course I'd told the boss, who explained to me how it was different from what I'd gone through. "Yeah, but you got better. I was born the way I am, and that won't ever change."

"I sympathize. There are those among my superiors who will never forget that I was once the vessel for a fiend. But the way Oparal saw it, you and I are not so different. Neither one of us chose what happened. We're men, not fiends."

"I get what you're saying, but it's not the same. What you had was like a fever. Now you're cured. Me, I got Hell bred into my bones. Even when Viridio ain't home, I've still got the blood of devils in my veins."

"When I was possessed, my body remained as it is, but the demon took control."

"For me, it's the other way around. The devil wants to tell me what to do, but he can't make me." That was mostly true. When my devils came through, I got mad real easy. Sometimes I got confused. Once I bit off a hag's head, but I'm not sure that wasn't my idea. Anyway, so far I always ended up on top.

So far.

Aprian sat back in his saddle. "Your situation is certainly unusual."

"The boss calls me an 'aberrant paradigm.'"

"I don't know what that means."

"That's because you're all right."

He had to look at me a second to tell I was giving him a compliment. After that, we talked a while about other stuff, like who to put on watch first, who'd do the night's cooking, boring stuff.

Every now and then, Aprian said something that reminded me he was from a noble house—a high-class phrase, or a word I'd learned from the boss. Maybe his family wasn't so rich and powerful as the Jeggares, but being born noble was still a big deal. Even so, he never rubbed my nose in it. To listen to him talk to me, you might think he grew up on Eel Street.

After a while, we smelled sulfur in the air. Brown and yellow plumes stained the mist of the swamp. That must have been from the hot springs the boss told me about the last time we looked at the map.

Me and Aprian, we led the carriage and wagon behind a wild mass of blackthorn shrubs. Once we got the horses unhitched, unsaddled, and watered, Dolok made a beeline for some three-foot-tall mushrooms. Alase yelled at him, but it was too late. Thin tendrils shot out of the cap to stick in his arm. They turned red as we ran to him. Dolok was on the ground by the time the Andoren Tollivel hacked at the "tongues" while Kronug pulled Dolok away.

Lucky for Dolok, we still had a paladin on hand. Aprian put his hands on the wounds and prayed. I'd say Desna smiled on the idiot, but it was Iomedae's power that healed him. Pity Aprian couldn't do anything for the poor guy's face rash. He looked like somebody had beat him with a cheese grater.

We made sure none of the other plants and rocks were going to kill us before settling in to camp. I looked in on the boss. I half-expected he'd be back up with his nose in the book, but he was sawing logs, so I let him alone.

By the time it was getting dark, we settled down to some grub, which Urno and Gannak had been arguing over until the dwarf threatened to pull off the Kellid's nipple rings. Gannak was no dummy. He gave in and let the dwarf finish cooking alone.

Nobody talked much. Kala didn't play or sing. Nobody was telling jokes. Even I knew better than to try and lighten the mood.

Jelani sat alone near the fire, shivering. It got plenty cold after the sun set, especially close to the swamps. Something told me it wasn't the temperature bothered her, though.

"Hey." I pulled the boss's journal from my saddlebags. "You want to take a look at this?"

She frowned, curious until she opened the book. Then she winced. "Is this a copy of the *Lexicon*?"

I nodded.

She flipped the pages, closing her eyes a few times at the ugliest drawings.

"I know," I said. "Nasty stuff. Can you read any of the text?"

"Some of it," she said. "Here, this is Thassilonian. I'm not fluent, but I can understand some. This here I think is a form of Hallit. I can speak it, but you rarely find it written."

"Before you read any more, I got to warn you: I think it's making the boss peculiar."

She looked a question at me.

"It's not just the wine. It's not just that he's upset about Oparal."

"We all are."

"There's something more going on. I got a feeling it's something to do with this book."

"I've heard of tomes whose contents threaten the reader's sanity."

"Yeah, we bumped into stuff like that a few times. This one time, the boss cut out the pages and divvied them up among a few other scholarly types. They read their parts and compared notes."

"So that no one of them suffered the full brunt of the effect."

"Just like that."

"Thanks for the warning. I'll glance through this and consult with the count."

"Actually, maybe just get back to me. He doesn't know I took it."

"Oh."

I grimaced. "Yeah, it's like that. Or maybe after I put it back in his satchel, you can mention you're curious, all casual-like."

"I understand."

"Thanks," I said. "You're a doll. I owe you one."

She rolled her eyes, but as I got up to leave, she added, "I'll collect later."

I turned away, grinning until I saw Alase staring at me from across the fire. She raised an eyebrow and gave me The Look.

She'd been full of cuddles on the way from Gundrun to Valahuv, but nothing had happened. Most of the time it was just on account of we were on a job with lots of others around us. Still and all, we'd had our chances. Instead of slipping away, like I'd have done any other time, I got an itch on my neck when I looked south.

It shouldn't have bothered me. It just did.

"I'll take first watch," I said to nobody in particular. With the boss out of commission and Oparal out of the picture, it was just me and Silvio who could see any good at night, so I checked he'd heard me. He had.

Throwing the saddlebags over my shoulder, I slipped out of camp.

I moved out far enough that I wouldn't get caught between the banked fire and anything that was looking in that direction. Pretty soon I couldn't see it, either. I didn't get lost, but all of a sudden I was in a colder, darker spot. Trees reached up on either side of me, leaves rustling.

A hoarse voice called out, "Hellspawn!"

For a second I thought it was one of my devils, but my ears heard the voice—it wasn't just in my head. I turned and saw the unicorn.

In the dark, he looked like a charcoal sketch, not that he looked much different in daylight. Except for his blue eyes, the big fellow was all shades of gray from the wounds he suffered from the demons of the Fierani Forest.

I looked around for Jelani or Alase. Somebody was doing a magic trick, and this wasn't the boss's kind of gag. "Very funny. Knock it off."

"Nothing is funny," croaked the unicorn. This time I saw his horse lips move all unnatural, like how Tonbarse's wolf jaws formed human words. The way his lips peeled back at every word, it looked painful for him to talk.

I reached back and tugged the big knife from its sheath. Maybe demons could possess unicorns the same way they did humans. "Whoever the hell you are, get out of the stupid unicorn now. We got wizards. We got paladins. We'll exorcise your ass right out of there."

"Idiot! I am not possessed." He lunged a step forward. I was starting to believe this was the actual unicorn.

Even demons don't hate me that much.

"How come you never talked before?"

"You hear my ruined voice and still ask such a question?"

He did sound pretty bad, but it wasn't like I couldn't understand him. "What does that mean? You don't talk because you're vain?"

He charged me that time. I jumped out of the way and got a roll in some stinging brambles for my trouble.

"Hey, truce! You got something to say, spit it out."

"It's your fault she's gone."

He was talking about Oparal, of course. Maybe it should have made me mad, but I'd been telling myself the same thing ever since the boss came back without her.

"Listen, I'm sorry." I said. "Turns out I'm not so tough without a devil riding me. I couldn't stay any longer."

"I would have died beside her. Gladly!"

"Yeah, I get that."

With no warning, he reared, screaming. "But she stood beside you!"

Of course she had. It wasn't like we could sneak a unicorn into the Tower of Zura. But maybe that wasn't what he was driving at. "Hold on, are you saying you're jealous because Oparal was sweet on me?"

He reared and screamed again, coming down hard just inches from my face as I threw myself back. "You conceited hellspawn! You and your half-breed master, you dirtied her thoughts with talk of compromise and complications. You dimmed her purest light! You inhuman . . . thing!"

"Inhuman? I don't got to take that kind of crap from a defective unicorn."

"Oparal saw past my injuries to see my true heart. She chose me, not you."

"I'd say she took some time to warm to both of us."

"You aren't even a man, you're—"

"Hey! Without that horn, you'd be pulling a plough. You're the one who's not a man."

That tore it. The big fellow came at me again. Much as he deserved it, I didn't want to stick him with the big knife. Instead I threw myself back into briars, rolled through and started running. Maybe I could make it back to camp before he caught me.

Maybe I could hide behind Aprian.

As it turned out, I didn't have to. The unicorn ran off into the darkness. His hoofbeats faded as I listened.

I should have been glad about it. Instead I was worried the big jerk would run into more trouble than he could handle on his own.

Jelani intercepted me on the way back to camp.

"Are you all right? I heard Bastiel whinny."

"It's all right," I said. "I didn't hurt him."

"But what did he do to you?"

I looked down at my dirty jacket. Hundreds of little stickers poked out of the leather. I was a mess. "Damned stupid unicorn! Mostly we just had words."

She looked at me funny.

"What?" I said.

"You make it sound like you were talking with him."

"I was. Turns out he could talk this whole time."

She frowned.

"It's true!"

"Surely one of us would have heard him communicating with the captain before this. Maybe you also need a rest. How much of this notebook did you read?"

"None! Come on, I'm telling the truth about the talking unicorn."

"Whatever you say." She held up the journal in both hands. "You were right about this book, in any event. I'm no expert, but I'm certain it's having an effect on the count. I could read barely more than a page before the confused and contradicting statements began to give me a headache. And that's not even mentioning the horrors in its illustrations."

"The boss spent the whole day with his nose in that *Lexicon*." I took it from her and stuffed it back into the saddlebags. "That was before he used a spell to make a copy. That must have been even worse than reading it."

"I can only presume that would intensify the effect."

"Maybe I ought to look in on him."

She said something else as I walked away, but between her and Bastiel, I'd had enough. It wasn't time to wake up the next shift, so I did another couple rounds of the camp. By the time my head cooled, I felt the weight of the day and the night before. Sleep sounded like a good idea.

When I got back, I heard the carriage door open and close. I waited, figuring the boss was taking care of business on the other side.

Gannak was sitting watch in the middle of camp, Arni snoozing on the Kellid's feet. Gannak had been my last hire back in Gundrun. At first I was going to skip him because what the hell kind of idiot thinks nipple rings are a good idea in a fight? But once Alase signed on, she vouched for him. When I saw him giving Arni the fat of his meat, I was glad to have him along.

When he saw me, Gannak got up to wake Barek. Arni whuffed as the swordsman's feet slipped from beneath him. The hound nosed the air and whined.

I agreed. "The whole place stinks."

But Arni wasn't done. He stood up. A low growl rumbled from his chest.

Staying low, I crept around the carriage, knife in hand. There was nothing on the other side, but I saw someone had pushed through the nearby bushes. I started to follow, but the carriage jostled behind me.

Standing to the side, I reached over and opened the door. Inside, the boss lay sprawled over the map table, his face a bloody mess. I checked him. He was breathing.

"Aprian!" I opened the opposite door and yelled again. "Everybody, wake up! Boss, snap out of it." I slapped his face.

He moaned and blinked. Blood poured out of his nose and ran down his chin. He reached for his satchel, but it wasn't under the table. "The *Lexicon* . . . gone!" He crouched under the map table. "My satchel. My spellbooks!"

"Who took it?"

His mouth opened. His lips moved, but he couldn't— or wouldn't—say it.

Outside the carriage, someone shouted, "Look!"

I stuck my head out just in time to see Kasiya's chariot flying up toward the east. Instead of the lean dogs the boss had incinerated over the West Sellen River— salukis, the boss had called them—something like a swarm of bats pulled the thing through the sky. The vampire prince held onto the chariot with one hand. In the other he clutched a book against his chest.

Kasiya wasn't alone. A tall woman stood behind him, holding the boss's satchel in one hand. The other hugged Kasiya around the waist. I couldn't see her face, but her outline sure looked familiar.

"Who is that?" I said. "Boss, who took your stuff?"

He cradled his head and moaned, "Oparal."

Chapter Fifteen
The Betrayal

Varian

I don't believe it," said Aprian.

"What possible reason would I have to tell such an appalling lie?" Under other circumstances I might have been outraged by the crusader's doubt, but I could hardly believe the evidence of my own eyes—not to mention my bruised face. My head still rang from the impact of Oparal's fist.

When she first entered the Red Carriage, face pale and eyes bloodshot, I imagined myself in the throes of nightmare. I struggled to distinguish between the real horrors of the past day and those I had seen in the pages of the *Lexicon of Paradox*.

By the time Radovan revived me, Oparal had vanished along with my satchel and its contents: my journals, my grimoires, and the *Lexicon*.

"You must be mistaken," said Aprian. "The captain would never do such a thing."

"Because she's a crusader?" I suspected more than half of Oparal's crusaders had left behind unsavory pasts. Considering the fate of the street thief Gemma, I thought it best not to raise the point.

"No, Count," said Aprian. "Because she's a paladin."

A motion at the edge of camp caught my eye. Well behind Aprian, Bastiel approached. Even in the cloud-dimmed moonlight, I saw his coat was flecked with lather, tangled with thorns and swamp muck. The unicorn regarded me in a manner most disconcerting. I could not meet his gaze.

The loss of Oparal at Undarin haunted no one more than me. Her perverse return tortured my imagination even as it threatened my alliance with her crusaders. Nevertheless, it was imperative that the others understood what I had witnessed, and what I was beginning—however reluctantly—to understand. "We saw Oparal on the chariot beside Kasiya. Tell them, Radovan."

"I definitely saw someone," he said. I fixed him with a glare. "Yeah, I think it was Oparal."

"I saw her," said Roga. With his missing front teeth, the Kellid was unpleasant to regard, yet I was glad of his corroboration. Barek and Gannak also nodded.

"It was the crusader captain," said Selka. "I am sure of it."

"Did anyone not employed by Count Jeggare see this woman?" said Tollivel. Of all the crusaders, he was the most belligerent. The animosity between our homelands only exacerbated his hostility.

"I dislike your insinuation, Andoren."

He mimicked my noble's dialect. "I dislike Chelish lies."

Before I could reach for my blade, Aprian put himself between me and Tollivel.

"It makes no sense," said Urno. "I won't believe she came all the way back from Undarin only to steal the *Lexicon*."

The crusader's laudable devotion to their leader blinded them to the obvious explanation. Again it fell to me to illustrate it. "Among the vampire's many dread powers is the ability to bend mortal minds to its will."

"Not the captain's will," said Aprian. "We have all of us—every one of us—watched her stare down the most terrifying foes. She's fearless."

"I do not dispute you, Sergeant. In Kyonin, Radovan and I both witnessed her incredible strength and courage. Yet she was in combat with fiends. Who can say how much they had already weakened her body and soul?"

"You were fooled somehow. You said this Osirian vampire is a sorcerer. Maybe he cast a spell to make himself or one of his minions look like the captain."

"Yes," said Naia, "just as you set those illusory guards before the gate in Undarin."

I drew my weapon. Tolliver's hand went to his blade, but Aprian stayed him as I held the Tian sword for all to see. "The Shadowless Sword is so named both for its swiftness and for its power to cut through illusions. When Oparal entered the carriage, I touched its hilt—not to strike her, but to confirm her identity. Alas, it was indeed she who assaulted me, not Prince Kasiya cloaked in a disguise. Loath as we all are to accept the fact, all evidence indicates he has bent her to his will, through the power of his mesmerizing gaze . . . or worse."

"What do you mean by 'worse'?"

"You will recall the men we fought in Gundrun," I said. "They were the spawn of Kasiya. Fledgling vampires."

"No," said the man called Silvio. In his accent I heard both his Mwangi origin and his Chelish enslavement. "No vampire could turn the captain."

"Believe me, Kamau, we all share your faith in Captain Oparal's virtue, but she is as mortal as the rest of us."

Kamau had confided his birth name to me a week earlier, as we exchanged stories of his homeland. By using it I meant to show him respect and remind him that we shared some experience of both lands. Yet I had miscalculated. His eyes narrowed as his comrades looked between him and me, wondering what mischief I intended.

"The count is right," said Jelani. "Even a paladin as virtuous as Oparal is not immune to such a transformation, especially if she were weakened."

"Those demons that killed Erastus, they sucked the life out of us," said Radovan. "It felt like when that vampire hit me back on the barge. Oparal was definitely weakened when I . . ." He trailed off.

"When you abandoned her," said Tollivel.

"I didn't want to go," said Radovan. "If I . . ." Once more, he left something unsaid.

"How convenient for Jeggare that the only ones left behind at Undarin were crusaders," said Tollivel.

All the heat of my anger turned to ice. I prepared to issue a formal challenge, but Radovan spoke first, thrusting a finger at the Andoren's face. "I was there and you weren't. You got a problem with what I saw? We can work it out right now."

"Of course he would back up Jeggare's claim." Tollivel turned, addressing his fellows but not quite turning his back on Radovan. "The hellspawn is the rat-catcher's creature."

Radovan took a step toward Tollivel, but Aprian put a hand on his shoulder. I expected Radovan to shove it away, but instead he stopped.

"Leave him to me," said Aprian. "Naia was there also. You heard what she had to say."

All eyes turned to the Qadiran ranger. "It was the captain who told us to flee. We obeyed her. Radovan was the only one to stay."

Jelani stepped forward. "Count, I know that you believe what you're telling us. But is it not possible you are confused? Radovan said that reading the *Lexicon* was having an effect on you."

I turned to Radovan for an explanation.

He shrugged. "I was worried about you, boss. If that book was messing with your mind, I figured Jelani was the one who'd know how to fix it."

Tolliver groused, "It doesn't take an evil book to cloud that man's senses. I can smell the wine on his breath from here."

"It is my custom to drink a glass or two while at study."

The clink of glass sounded behind me. The Chelaxian Bolivar held up a pair of empty bottles he had pulled from the floor of the carriage. "Big glasses."

I could not help but feel betrayed by my fellow countryman.

"Listen up, everybody," said Radovan. "We can work out all this stuff later. For now, we've got to move. They found us once to steal the book. That means they can find us again, this time with more than just a thief."

"He's right," said Naia. She scanned the night sky.

"I concur," said Aprian. "Where do we go?"

"Well, we were headed back to Valahuv."

"We're no longer welcome there," said Urno.

"Right," said Radovan. "So we don't go into the village. But we ought to take a look. Let's say Kasiya's got his thumb on Oparal. She's as tough as anybody I ever met, so my money's on she breaks free. When she does, Valahuv's the closest place where she knows to look for us."

Irritated that Radovan had taken it upon himself to take charge, I pointed out the danger. "Yet if Oparal is in Kasiya's thrall—as all evidence suggests—then it is also where he will know to look for us."

"We stick to the swamp, keep ourselves hid. Meanwhile, you and Jelani maybe want to take a look at this." He picked up his saddlebags and withdrew a familiar volume.

"My last journal!"

"Yeah," he grinned.

I could hardly believe the evidence of my eyes. "You took it!"

"I borrowed it is all. What are you complaining about? Maybe the bad guys got the *Lexicon*, but you still have a copy."

"That's not the point!" I snatched it away from him. My pulse pounded in my temples. "You had no right to remove my belongings without—" Anger whirled in my head, not only at Radovan's presumption in taking my journal from the carriage but also at—I knew not what. The formlessness of my rage and despair terrified me. It was as if I could not control my own behavior. I—

"Boss?" said Radovan. "You all right?"

Everyone stared at me. I realized I had been clutching my face. As I withdrew my hands, I saw blood on my fingernails and felt the sting of air upon my scratched cheeks.

"It doesn't matter, anyway," I said. "The powers of a tome like the *Lexicon* are not limited to the information conveyed in its text. Its pages are infused with arcane materials, the bindings blessed—or cursed, as the case may be—with hundreds of incantations. Possessing a copy does not ensure the ability to perform the rituals inside."

Jelani approached. She reached for the journal. I held it away from her.

"Your Excellency," she said, "with your permission, I would like to aid in your study of the book."

With reluctance, I surrendered the volume to her hands.

"If I may, I'll study it with you in the carriage."

"I will come also," said Alase.

"Why?"

"The last people to use this book were the Three: a wizard, a druid, and a witch."

"And you think a wizard, a sorcerer, and a sum—a god caller—can better unravel its mysteries than one who has studied the arcane longer than your great-grandmother lived?"

She bobbed her head in the affirmative.

"I—" Her logic was not at fault, but I disliked it all the same.

Jelani said, "Differing perspectives could be of some help, even to a learned scholar."

"Very well. Radovan, you and Sergeant Aprian make the arrangements to move on."

"You got it, boss." Radovan went to supervise breaking camp and hitching the vehicles. He shouted at the unicorn, "You coming, big fella?"

Bastiel tossed his mane, but remained at the edge of camp.

"Yes or no?" said Radovan. "Just answer the question."

"Maybe I should deal with him." Aprian gave Radovan a quizzical look before approaching the unicorn. As the paladin neared, the unicorn shied but did not flee.

"Don't let him fool you, Sarge," said Radovan. "He can talk just fine. He's just pretending."

Aprian narrowed his eyes. "How much of the *Lexicon* did *you* read?"

Radovan shot him the tines, but Aprian just shrugged.

Their banter piqued my feeling of isolation. I was losing control of the expedition. If I could not regain my authority, the entire venture would fall to shambles. Yet all I could think to say was, "Arnisant, heel."

The wolfhound came instantly to my side. I had at least one faithful ally.

The company broke camp in a matter of minutes. The drivers had my magnificent Kyonin horses hitched to the carriage soon after. Once all was prepared, I stepped aboard, pausing only to empty the silver bucket and dispose of the empty wine bottles.

Jelani and Alase followed, taking places across the map table. Arnisant leaped in, turned thrice, and settled on my feet, warmer than the finest slippers— although I would need to move periodically lest his ever-increasing mass numb my toes.

As I closed the door behind the hound, Jelani winced and opened the window. She glanced at Alase, who did the same on the other side. While the need to air my sanctum mortified my pride, I nodded my thanks.

Jelani laid my journal on the table. "Would you describe the effect you feel when reading the *Lexicon*?"

"What? Am I to be examined like a patient visiting a physician?"

"Please, Count."

I drew a deep breath. I was aware that my temper had grown short, but that in itself was a reasonable response to the unreasonable events of the past day. Still, I had no wish to alienate well-intentioned allies, no matter how clumsily they pressed their assistance upon me.

"Very well," I said. "As you have seen, the text consists of five distinct languages and two different sets of Hallit pictograms. Fortunately, I have some facility with all of the represented scripts."

Jelani failed to conceal a smirk at my simple statement of fact. It was not a boast!

"I have perused the book twice," I continued, "the second time while inscribing its contents into this journal. How much have you read?"

"Far less," she admitted. "I lack your expertise with languages, but the truth is that I stopped reading after only a few passages that I could understand. Even apart from the troubling subject matter, the arcane expressions seem contradictory—maddeningly so, if you will pardon the expression. I cannot help but point to the name of the book: the *Lexicon of Paradox*."

"Yes!" A great wave of relief broke over me as I realized that at least one among our company could understand what I had seen. I opened the journal to an especially interesting passage. "The contradictions are most apparent when one compares the passages in Thassilonian to the pictograms of the Kellid wizard."

"Druid," said Alase.

"Pardon me?"

"Those are druids' runes, not wizards'."

"And you know this because—?"

"I had it from the stories I learned from my uncle, who had it from his—"

"Mother, who had it from her aunt, and so on. Yes, so I recall."

"Alase makes an important point," said Jelani. "Those who first opened the portals combined the powers of three different disciplines to do so."

Of course, I had already considered that fact, but apparently it would appear pompous to say so. Instead, I said, "The *Lexicon* is indeed well named. The rituals it contains not only combine disparate philosophies and energies, but also appear to be complete oxymorons."

"I don't understand," said Alase.

"That's because the count is demonstrating his vast vocabulary," said Jelani. Her sidelong glance assured me that her provocation was intentional, but her smile disarmed me before I could grow angry. "It's not so difficult to understand, actually. These contradictions in the text are the key. Not despite their logical flaws, but because of them, they invoke the most primal elements of arcane, elemental, and demonic energies."

"No, no," I said. "It may appear that way, but I assure you these seeming incongruities disguise comprehensible formulae that we can use to duplicate or reverse the process that first opened the Worldwound."

Jelani fixed her gaze to mine. At first I took it for insolence, but as her expression softened I realized it was a look of genuine concern. "Do you have a soft cloth, Count?"

Momentarily perplexed, I reached for my handkerchief but realized the bloodstained cloth was entirely inappropriate to hand a woman. Lifting up the seat compartment beside me, I found a clean chamois and passed it to her.

Jelani took it without a word of thanks. She unfolded and refolded the cloth before covering her finger and uttering a word of magic. A blue-white radiance pulsed beneath the cloth and subsided. She handed the cloth back to me. It felt as cool as if it had been stored for hours in an icebox.

I wondered whether her gesture was some secret suggestion pertaining to the *Lexicon*. Surely she could not think the book could overhear our conversation! Surely not, for before us lay only a copy, and my duplication of its text could not possibly have transferred the *Lexicon*'s innate arcane qualities.

Or could it? Had the bark upon the *Lexicon*'s cover been thick and irregular enough to conceal an auditory organ? If so—

"Count," said Jelani. She pressed her palm gently upon her cheek. "For your bruise."

Perplexity held me a moment longer before I understood what she meant. "Oh! Of course. How silly of me."

I held the cool cloth against my cheek. In the turmoil of my imagination, I had quite forgotten the pain. Now that I thought of it, both my face and my head throbbed.

In its way, the pain was welcome. It focused my thoughts on injury. Reluctantly, I began to accept the likelihood that reading the *Lexicon* had injured me far more deeply than Oparal's punch had done. It had wounded not my body but my sole and sacred possession: my mind.

I pulled my copy of the *Lexicon* close but stopped myself before opening the cover.

Jelani and Alase watched me from across the table. The Thuvian's expression alternated between concern and curiosity. The Kellid's face was a study in pity.

I pushed the *Lexicon* back to the center of the map table.

"I am injured," I said. Gesturing to my brain, I added, "In here."

Jelani nodded. "Good. I mean, it is good that you recognize the danger."

"Yet the greater danger is that Kasiya now has the original, as well as the *Lacuna Codex*. The rituals within the *Lexicon* are not limited to opening portals. Without a better understanding of its contents, we can't know what he is capable of doing."

Alase slid the journal close to her and opened it with two fingers. Frowning, she skimmed the pages, seeming to focus on the illustrations. She did not react to their horrific subjects, but at last she closed the cover and pushed the book away. She looked at Jelani, then me, and shrugged. "He will call a god."

Jelani smiled indulgence. "You said the same of Radovan's transformation. Is that how you see all acts of magic?"

Alase jutted her jaw. "Wizards think everything is complicated. Sorcerers think magic comes from inside them. My people understand that the world is much simpler, and we are much less important."

Jelani began to protest, but instead she turned to me. "What do you think, Count?"

"There is something to what Alase says." It was more than courtesy that prompted me to say so, but I couldn't put my finger on why her words touched me. "The rituals appear complex, and all of them concern the transfer of energies and material across different planes of existence. To be perfectly honest, the subtleties of this incomplete text escape me."

"Because they so often contradict themselves?"

"Exactly."

"I think Alase is right about wizards," she said. "Your approach to channeling the arcane is so strict and ornate, perhaps it makes you expect too much consistency."

"That's easy for you to say. Not all of us are born to a sorcerous bloodline. What comes naturally to you requires a great deal of thought and effort from a practitioner of wizardry."

"There's no need to feel defensive, Count." She smiled, and again I could see no malice in it, although part of me wished to. "But I wonder, how well do you understand the differences between sorcery and wizardry?"

"Quite well, I assure you. I studied all seven schools of magic at the Acadamae in Korvosa, not to mention several other prestigious institutions. As a Pathfinder I have traveled the world, everywhere studying the local arcana in addition to virtually every other field of knowledge, from natural history to religious customs—"

"Yes, I understand you are a well-traveled scholar. But did you never study sorcery?"

I would never grow accustomed to such constant interruption, especially with such an insipid question. "Of course not."

"Curious." Jelani looked at Alase, but the summoner shrugged. Like me, she did not follow the course of Jelani's questions, or did not care. "If you will indulge me, Count, may I ask why you rely solely on these riffle scrolls to cast spells?"

Her question caught me off guard. I had assumed that, during their flirtations, Radovan had informed her of my difficulty casting spells as a traditional wizard. Comprehending the arcane formulae was no obstacle. Before practical exercises, I found myself far ahead of my fellow students in matters of history, arcane equations, and magical theory.

Yet the moment I attempted to cast the lowliest cantrip, my body rebelled. I could extend an invisible grasp to fetch a book from across my library if I did not care to dine for the rest of the day. To set any more powerful spell in memory caused me the most debilitating of cramps and humiliating eructation.

With no other option, I described my condition in the sparsest of detail, but at every turn Jelani asked me more exacting questions. At one point, as I described my process for retaining new knowledge, she asked, "Memory library?"

"Yes," I explained. "It is an eidetic device by which I—"

Jelani cleared her throat. Her gaze flicked toward Alase, whose eyes had glazed over.

"Ah, forgive me. It is a way of visualizing new information to extend the time in which it remains in memory. In my case, I imagine everything I wish to remember—whether it is a song, an image, or an actual book—as a volume that I store in an imaginary space I think of as my memory library."

"Which resides in your head?" said Jelani.

"A whole library in your head?" said Alase. "It doesn't look big enough for even one book."

I cleared my throat. "Indeed."

Alase turned to Jelani. After a moment's silence, both broke into laughter.

After that, Alase joined the interrogation. Over the next few hours I unfolded my history of arcane study—and decades of failure as a wizard—to the sorcerer and the summoner. At every turn, they explained their own experiences of channeling elemental forces or beckoning extraplanar creatures into our world. They spoke of the arcane not as a science but as an art or a religion.

It was all very poetic, but hardly useful to my circumstances.

They drew from me the story of the riffle scrolls, a long-lost secret I had discovered in the library of an Ustalavic peer. Later I added the anecdote of the flying scrolls I had found at Dragon Temple in Tian Xia.

Jelani held up a few of the Kellid sticks we had recovered from Nekrosof Tower. "Traditional scrolls, your riffle scrolls, the Tian flying scrolls, and these carved sticks—they all perform the same function, but they take different forms."

I nodded my agreement.

She went on. "Are not wizards, sorcerers, and summoners—pardon me, Alase—god callers also three different forms of the same function?"

"Well, surely, in the broadest possible sense. Yet neither you nor I can summon an eidolon, and you do not depend on a grimoire to prepare your spells, while I can, with study, learn any spell whose formula I discover."

"Hm." She tapped a finger on her lower lip, considering. Alase and I waited for her to elaborate. Instead, she said, "In your reading of the *Lexicon*, have you discovered any clues as to where the other half was hidden?"

"None," I said. "Yet that is not surprising. There are no signs that the book was amended after it was taken from the Threshold. If those who concealed it in the Widowknife Clanhold had left a clue, I would expect it lay in the map carved into the library. Apart from the false hypocaust vent, I noticed no other anomalies in the room's architecture. Since the tableau at Nekrosof suggested the entire book traveled west from Storasta, perhaps the other half went on to another city. Dyinglight is the nearest past Undarin, is it not?"

Alase nodded. "You will not find books there," she said. "The demons who rule the place burned the temples long ago. They make their slaves work the fields and fight in the Pit of Blood."

"Charming," I said. "I hate to risk an incursion without better intelligence of the site. Are there no other sites in western Sarkoris known as repositories for knowledge?"

"In Sarkoris of old, the druids were the keepers of lore. Long before the priests came with their cathedrals and bone cellars, the druids met at standing stones and among the forests, but they carried their wisdom as you do." She tapped her temple. "In their memory libraries."

The god caller's mention of forests reminded me of the *Lexicon*'s binding. "The pages of the *Lexicon* were of different materials, but the cover was of a strange bark."

Alase nodded. "The druids shared their knowledge with the trees in the north."

"You mean they carved upon them?"

"So it is said and sung," she said.

I reached for my absent satchel before realizing I had to rely upon my memory library once more. Closing my eyes, I envisioned the room, a far larger and more complex version of my library at Greensteeples. There I went to the shelves upon which I stored my personal chronicles of the journeys I undertook on behalf of the Society, and lately on my own. Selecting the most recent volume, I lay it upon the reading stand and opened it to my amalgamated version of the map of Sarkoris.

"Here," I said, pointing to a map the others could not see. "This forest across the northern border of Sarkoris. Its eastern side is known as the Living Library. How literal is that name?"

Alase considered the question, nodding slowly, then more affirmatively. "It was a place of knowledge," she said. "There the druids shared their learning with the stones and the trees."

"Is it possible we've been approaching this problem backward?" I said.

"The *Lexicon* is a collection of knowledge from different sources," said Jelani. "Perhaps this Living Library was one of them."

"It is a long way to travel on such a slender hope," I said.

"It's at least a hope."

Alase spoke up. "Will this vampire prince not also guess about the Living Library?"

"Not likely," I said. "He lacks the benefit of a local guide as knowledgeable as you. Also, he is profoundly stupid."

Jelani laughed.

"In life he enjoyed all the wealth and privilege of his station without bending his own efforts toward study. His death was a direct result of his stealing what I had gained through my own efforts—and those of my local guide. Because he did not earn the knowledge himself, he could not recognize his own doom as it approached."

As we talked, Alase drowsed and eventually curled up to sleep beside the Thuvian sorceress. Jelani and I continued our conversation throughout the night and into the small hours. Sometime before dawn, our conversation halted as we felt the carriage slow and stop. Outside, our escorts did the same.

I leaned out the window to call for Radovan, but the hush that had fallen over our company gave me pause. Soon my bodyguard returned on foot, breathless.

"What is it?" I asked.

"Valahuv," said Radovan. "The joint is crawling with demons."

We had already lost the town as a haven, but the thought that our actions at Undarin had brought the horde to the previously inviolate sanctuary struck me like a blow from a cold iron fist. By chasing off its guardian fiend, I feared we had exposed it to the entire horde.

"Is there any way we can—?" I began.

He was already shaking his head. "The demons got scouts flying all around. We've got to be out of here before dawn."

Behind Radovan, Aprian had already quietly given the order to withdraw. His crusaders passed the word along, while the Kellids looked toward the carriage, uncertain. "Let us go with all haste," I said.

"Which way?"

Thinking back to the map of Sarkoris, I said, "Northwest. We shall at least have a look at Dyinglight before continuing."

Radovan nodded and withdrew. After a word with Aprian, he climbed onto the roof of the carriage and gave the drivers their instructions.

Alase slept through the dreadful news, and I saw no reason to wake her.

After a long, uncomfortable silence during which I weighed our culpability in the destruction of Valahuv, Jelani offered to return the rune-carved sticks I had shared with her.

My first impulse was to refuse her kind offer, but without them I was of little use as a wizard. By the grace of Desna, Oparal had not discovered all of my riffle scrolls. I transferred those in the compartment beneath my seat to my coat pockets and my bandolier. Noting Jelani's curious eye, I displayed my inventory on the table.

"Far too few subtle spells," I confessed. "But I can at least contribute to a battle or two before I must rely solely on my blade."

"Don't be so sure," she said. "I have a feeling you don't need those scrolls."

"What do you mean?"

"Have you never considered the possibility that you're not a wizard after all?"

Of course I had often questioned my abilities, but I found it insulting for her to state the obvious. "I admit mine is an unusual case, but I have learned to circumvent the issue. I have only to endure a short period of discomfort while consigning my spells to scrolls."

"But why endure even that much struggle to obey a process that comes so unnaturally to you?"

Her question left me speechless. I couldn't comprehend what she was suggesting.

"Isn't it obvious by now, Count Jeggare? You aren't a wizard. You're a sorcerer."

Chapter Sixteen
The Spear-Bearer

Oparal

Vescavors swarmed the Tower of Zura. Their caustic stench blasted my face as I bound my latest captive to the rail.

The tiny demons' eyeless heads were barely larger than my fist, composed mostly of a maw full of chisel-shaped teeth. I had seen the damage those jaws could wreak, on flesh, stone, and even steel. Noxious fumes leaked from their mouths as they jabbered nonsense. Their bodies were no longer than my forearm, their wings forming a wedge. They flew in an unpredictable series of turns and stalls, never a coherent path. Watching them dizzied me. I grasped the rail to keep from falling.

Commotion surrounded my body. My brain buzzed like a hundred vescavors caught in a barrel. My thoughts fought, killed, and devoured each other. Strange new ideas emerged like larvae from the bodies of the fallen. No sooner did I focus on one idea than another swooped down to tear it to pieces.

I clutched the railing with both hands, the iron bending under my grip. From the tower's highest balcony, I peered east. Even the bright starlight could not gentle the ravages of the land between Undarin and the nearest fissures of the Worldwound.

As I watched, a distant ridge sank back down into the salt flat from which it had erupted only hours earlier. Its dying gasps sent sulfurous clouds into the sky. Malicious stars peered through the dark veil.

A scream rose above the dozens of others emanating from the experiment chambers below. The voice sounded familiar, but I struggled to remember who it was who suffered beneath me. The shrieks of the vescavors kept dislodging my thoughts.

An apocalypse of vescavors. That's what my master had called the swarms. He had explained it to me with pride, demonstrating his knowledge of taxonomy.

I heard the familiar scream again.

An overwhelming impulse made me turn to go to the voice, but before I could take a step away from the balcony, I forgot what had drawn my attention. The gibbering of the vescavors confused all thoughts but one: the prince had given me a task.

I took another bolt from the dozens left on the table. Each was barely longer than my index finger, its tip sharp and barbed. With great care, I affixed another tether to the bolt. Checking to ensure the other end was bound to the iron railing, I loaded it into the little crossbow.

I raised the weapon and sighted along the top. The previous few hours had taught me the folly of leading the shot ahead of such unpredictable targets. Instead, I aimed for the thickest cluster of vescavors and fired.

A fiend squealed as the barb pierced its wing. Setting the crossbow aside, I pulled in the captive, careful not to tear through the membranous wing and let it escape. When it was close, I grabbed it just behind the jaw, holding fast as it wriggled around to bite me. I had not yet lost a finger to the little fiends, and I didn't intend to.

The danger reminded me of some other creature known for severing fingers. A dog, I thought. An exceptionally large hound. Before I could think of the animal's name, the clamor of vescavors turned the tide of my thoughts in another direction, and everything was lost in the haze.

Almost everything. I still had to complete this task for the prince.

My master.

First I removed the tiny harpoon from my captive, widening the wound in its wing as little as possible. The tiny abominations healed quickly, but there was no telling how soon the prince would wish to fly.

The last time he used the vescavors to draw his chariot, there had been too few. Constrained by their tethers, the little fiends turned on each other, slowing our journey, even endangering our lives. That would not happen again, not while it was my charge to amend the failing.

Pinning the vescavor to the table, I thrust the barbed hook deep into its body, careful to avoid the spine and to ensure the barb emerged inside its mouth—yet not so close to the teeth that it could bite off the hook. After paralyzing a few vescavors and losing a few barbs, I had acquired the knack. I tugged the tether to ensure a firm connection. Then I flung the vescavor into a cloud of its fellow prisoners.

They stirred like wind-buffeted balloons strung to the balcony railing. Once tethered, none of them tried to enter the tower or attack me. I didn't know why, unless there were some repelling enchantment on the tower interior. Prince Kasiya had explained only why the trapped demons couldn't gnaw through their tethers: the strands were made from the gut of a demon known as a shemhazian, famed for its toughness.

The vescavors shrieked in unison, parting in a rare coordinated motion as a large crimson figure plunged through them to land inside the chamber.

Blood splashed on the floor as the fiend landed to crouch on eight bloody legs, turning as it peered about the room. Its eyes fixed on me.

I gazed back, chin held high in defiance. Prince Kasiya had claimed this room for his own. As his spear-bearer, I had every right to be present. The daemon was an unwelcome visitor, and I would not let it see my fear, however terrible its appearance. No matter what destruction it had wreaked on my—

On my what? I had seen the daemon slay and devour someone, but I couldn't remember his name.

Ommors remembered me, however. We had chased it from . . . from some place called the Delvegate. That was where the daemon had taken someone from me, someone for whom I was responsible.

If only I could think of his name.

The winged spider-daemon chattered as it folded its red gossamer wings along the back of its bulbous body. "Where is your master now, thing? Will he return before I bind you up tight and suck the sweet blood from your corpse?"

"I serve Prince Kasiya," I warned the fiend. My hand moved toward a sword I no longer wore. "Interfere with me at your peril."

On its spindly, blood-soaked legs, the daemon moved crablike to the side, considering me from another angle. It positioned itself between me and the door, beside the desk where my master had been studying earlier. Above it hung a candelabra of mingled human and demon bones. Beside it stood an iron brazier in which smoked both coals and a queer purple substance more pungent than brimstone. "You appear to have gathered plenty of those pests to draw his chariot. I doubt he will miss you."

"I am his spear-bearer," I said. "And when I tell him you have threatened me, doubtless I will have the honor of handing him the weapon that destroys you."

"A vampire, destroy me?" Ommors's mandibles quivered. "It has been long since I found one, but in my youth I devoured vampires as a delicacy. It was a vampire, you see, that first set my fledgling soul upon the path of hunger."

"How fitting, then, that a vampire be the one to end your journey." Somewhere in my swimming thoughts, I felt a pang of fear. It slipped beneath the waves, devoured by anger. If I had my sword, were I not prevented from using it—

But no. I could not act without the prince's leave.

"I have heard quite enough." The prince's voice came from a point behind the reading table, where a pair of red candles slowly melted over demon skulls.

On one side of the table lay stacked Count Jeggare's stolen journals, atop them his thick grimoire of spells. Seeing them brought me a faint pang of emotion.

I remembered Count Jeggare. He was my ally, although I had not always thought so. Yet he had failed to save me when I fell. He did not come to my aid.

The prince did.

What was this feeling that probed my guts? Was it guilt?

The count was no friend to my master, and yet we had once cooperated. I struggled to resolve the paradox, but the squealing and jabbering of the vescavors scattered my thoughts before they could gather into a coherent shape.

In the center of the table lay the prince's most precious treasures, the *Lacuna Codex* and the *Lexicon of Paradox*. The prince himself appeared in a chair of ligament-wrapped bones, his bandaged hand raised in a gesture dispelling the illusion that had concealed his presence.

Ommors rose up on its eight legs in a posture of feline displeasure. Ripples of blood formed on its back, like the surface of a lake disturbed by a sudden breeze.

The prince gazed at the daemon through his golden mask, his mesmerizing eyes calm even in his anger. "Do not forget, Ommors, you remain here only at my sufferance."

"You are not master of this place," said Ommors.

"I shall be," said Kasiya. "Once I unlock the powers of these dread tomes, all shall fear me—fiend and mortal, living and dead. You may benefit from my ascension, or you may be among the first sacrificed to the new god of blood."

The blood daemon leaned back, stretching its forelegs in an arachnid bow. "As you say, Prince Kasiya."

The sight of them, daemon and vampire, revolted some buried portion of me. Their bickering might have been pitiable in less dangerous creatures, but in them it was horrifying.

I struggled to tamp down the disloyal thought.

The chattering of the vescavors. The stench of the brazier. I couldn't focus on any one thing for long.

"Why have you stopped?" said Prince Kasiya. He turned his cold, dread gaze upon me.

"Forgive me, Your Highness." I threaded another tether through a harpoon and reloaded the crossbow. As I took aim at another vescavor, I tried not to think about the screams from the chambers below—especially that one familiar voice.

Gemma. Her name was Gemma, and I was responsible for her.

While I continued gathering vescavors, Ommors moved to join Prince Kasiya at the reading table. I watched them out of the corners of my eyes.

"What is this other book?" said the daemon.

"The *Lacuna Codex*," said Prince Kasiya. "Centuries ago, the rebel prince of Ustalav gathered the most fell rituals and spells of his domain to oppose the Whispering Tyrant. Yet when the Shining Crusade defeated the lich, the prince hid the book rather than use its great powers."

"What sort of powers?"

"Great powers," said Kasiya. "Far too many to waste my time cataloging them to sate your idle curiosity."

Ommors shuddered, its gelatinous body rippling again.

"Do you laugh at me, daemon?"

"Oh, no, Great Prince. I do but tremble to imagine the great powers."

I disliked hearing the prince mocked, especially by such a monster as Ommors. The daemon had killed one of my men.

Porfirio! That had been his name. And I was as responsible for him as for Gemma.

My heart ached for justice, but even that pure thought felt like treachery.

Kasiya lifted the *Lacuna Codex* in one linen-wrapped hand. Unlike the *Lexicon*, it appeared relatively new, its pages uniform and white. I recalled something Count Jeggare had told me about it, that the *Codex* was not an original, but rather the magically stolen contents of that original. In its way, it too was a paradox.

With that thought in mind, I shot the crossbow. The barb flew into empty space, but an errant vescavor flew directly into its path. The less I focused on aiming, it seemed, the more likely I was to strike one of the creatures.

Ommors continued pestering the prince with questions as I reeled in my prey. Kasiya answered in vagaries, insisting that the key to unlocking the mysteries of both the *Codex* and the *Lexicon* was not understanding but intuition. "That is why these books are useless in the hands of a glorified clerk like the Chelaxian," he said. "They were not written for dabblers in arcana but for born sorcerers."

"What's the point of opening another channel to the Abyss?" said Ommors. "The Worldwound yawns before us."

"And so it does, my inquisitive insect, but without direction," said Prince Kasiya. "Without focus. All these gates do is allow passage. Combining the powers of both books, I can direct the power of the Abyss into myself."

"And into others?"

"Yes," said Kasiya. He looked toward me. I felt his gaze upon my neck. "Into those who prove their loyalty to me."

The chamber door opened as of its own accord. A moment later, Yavalliska entered.

Scarlet horns curved upon her brow. The succubus held her dark wings folded upon her back, their scarlet hooks hanging above either shoulder, bobbing as she walked. Her sinuous tail twitched behind her as the long fringe of her corset trailed upon the floor. Barefoot, she strode to the reading table and slammed a pair of bloody hearts upon its surface, spattering the open pages of the *Codex*. "It is done."

Prince Kasiya scowled at the bloodstains upon the page he was reading. He blotted them with a bandaged thumb. "What is this?"

"The hearts of my last remaining rivals." Yavalliska sucked blood off her own thumb. "Enjoy them in celebration of the first success of our cabal."

Ommors fell upon the nearest heart, sinking its black mandibles deep into the bleeding flesh. "So warm," murmured the daemon.

"That was Synfonia, Areelu's favorite. She volunteered her blood to allow Areelu to complete her own transformation from mortal to half-succubus. How I detested that fawning sycophant."

"I have never tasted succubus heart before," said Ommors, draining the organ to a pulpy husk. "It is more bitter than I had expected, but no less delectable."

"Don't become accustomed to the taste," warned Yavalliska. "With my rivals slain, the other succubi have fled. I now rule Undarin with a free hand."

"Until the return of Areelu Vorlesh," said Prince Kasiya. "She shall surely flay you for this treachery."

"Just so, Your Highness," she said. "But by the time she returns from Iz, you and I shall be gods among demons."

"And I," said Ommors, still gnawing at the desiccated flesh. It slurred its words ever so slightly. "I also want to be a god."

"Do you not thirst, Your Highness?" Yavalliska sat upon the edge of the reading table and curled her tail around Kasiya's leg. "The blood of Wyrlassa grows cool."

Even through the cacophony of the vescavors, I heard the malice under Yavalliska's honeyed voice. Something fluttered in my stomach like the wings of the vescavors.

The butterflies of evil.

But I am surrounded by evil, I thought. Even so, I knew Yavalliska for a deceiver. She was placing a lure before the prince.

Kasiya appeared oblivious to her ruse. "Please help yourself," he said. "I'm quite engaged in these rituals."

"Perhaps you would prefer to drink from a chalice?" said Yavalliska. "I will have your cup-bearer fetch one and wring the blood out of the heart for you."

I opened my mouth to protest, but the succubus turned her dark eyes upon me. I pretended not to notice as I tied another tether to a barb.

"No," said my prince. "Yester eve I gorged myself on slaves. I do not yet hunger."

As I pointed the crossbow once more at the vescavors, I snuck a glance at Yavalliska. Apart from her demonic features, she looked exactly like the image most men have of a brothel trollop, at least until they actually enter the brothel. She pouted and bit her lip, the very portrait of a thwarted child.

"Please, my prince," she said. "Do not insult me. Drink it as a toast to our impending triumph."

Kasiya sighed. Even under the golden mask, I could see the resignation in his eyes. "Very well, since you put it that—"

I could bear no more. "My prince, do not taste the heart. It is a ruse."

The golden mask turned, the bloodshot eyes gazing upon me.

Yavalliska spoke quickly. She lifted the heart toward me. "Perhaps your pet should drink the toast—a tribute to her new master and his grand design."

"Don't waste such a choice morsel on a thrall," said Ommors. The daemon snatched the heart from Yavalliska. Its black fangs sank deep, its mandibles trembling with desire.

"Well," said Yavalliska. Her arched brows sank in defeat as the daemon sucked the blood out of the blanching flesh. She cast a narrow glance at me. "There it is. Perhaps another time."

"Delicious," murmured Ommors. The daemon's voice grew dreamy as it drained the succubus heart. "How generous, Yavalliska. I never expected a demon to be such a considerate host. If there is any way I can repay the favor—"

Kasiya looked from Ommors to Yavalliska, then back to me.

"Ommors, leave us."

"But I was just—"

"Now."

Clutching the remains of the heart in its mandibles, the daemon took flight. Its buzzing wings threw a light spray across the balcony as it scattered the vescavors on its way out into the night.

"You sought to enchant me," said Kasiya. He stood up and slammed his palms against the table, knocking the skull-candle to the floor. "In my distraction, I might have fallen for your trick, if my spear-bearer had not warned me."

"Don't be absurd," said Yavalliska. "You can't seriously trust a paladin to protect a vampire."

"She is my thrall!"

"She is a liability," said Yavalliska. "It's only a matter of time before she throws off your spell."

"It is no mere spell that binds us," said Kasiya. "I am a prince of Osirion, transfigured by the power of my own undying—"

"Yes, yes," said Yavalliska. "I understand all that. But do you understand how foolish it is to keep a paladin of Iomedae by your side?"

As if by some unintended charm, the words of the succubus pulled a weight from me. The jabbering of the vescavors seemed like a distant noise, though they flew just outside the open window.

I am a paladin of Iomedae, I thought.

I remembered Gemma, captured and tortured below. I remembered Porfirio and his bereaved lover, Dragomir, whom I prayed still lived, along with the rest of the crusaders whose company I had joined to Count Jeggare's expedition.

I glanced at the masked vampire and felt bile rise in my throat.

I had been a thrall of this wicked creature, but no more. My mind was free of the tumultuous voices of the vescavors, as well as whatever poison Kasiya poured from his eyes into mine.

As I returned his gaze, his eyes narrowed in suspicion. Did he know I had broken free of his control? Surely he must have felt the change as I had.

To the vampire prince, I bowed my head, not in obeisance but to conceal the truth I feared my eyes would reveal. Without the Ray of Lymirin, I could not defeat the prince and Yavalliska together. I could not cut my way through the Tower of Zura to rescue Gemma from whatever horrors they inflicted on her in the experiment chambers below us. I could do nothing but conceal my freedom and bide my time.

"It is precisely because of her affiliation that she makes such a perfect spear-bearer," said the wretched bloodsucker. His tone of voice had changed. He suspected me, but did not yet know.

"You should at least embrace her."

"Hm," he thought. "That notion is not entirely disagreeable."

I kept my gaze upon the floor as he approached, his steps so smooth and silent that he appeared to glide toward me. When I felt his bandaged fingers on my chin, I raised my head.

"Look at me, my spear-bearer," he said.

I obeyed. As our gazes locked, I felt a calm settle over me. Not the cold certainty of death, but the warm faith of the Inheritor. At that moment, I knew how much my life was worth. It was worth one more vampire.

I raised my chin, offering him my throat, silently praying he would not bite me, but knowing with increasing certainty that he would.

If Kasiya embraced me, I would embrace him back. In my final second of life, I would drag him to the window and throw us both over the edge. He could fly, but while he did I would tear his head from his body if I could.

If nothing else, I would deprive him of myself, my soul. I would die trying to destroy him.

Kasiya studied my eyes. From his own bloodshot orbs I could perceive little of his thoughts, but his wormlike lips twitched.

He glanced at Yavalliska as if she had spoken, but I heard nothing from her. Kasiya's head turned from the succubus to me and back again, his uncertainty increasing.

He rounded on Yavalliska. "You would like that, wouldn't you? How stupid do you think I am? I will not be vulnerable to your machinations during the daylight hours. My spear-bearer stands guard above me as I rest."

"Perhaps you're right, Your Highness," purred Yavalliska. "For one so grand as you, I can see now that a paladin makes the perfect spear-bearer."

"I think her presence frightens you," said Kasiya.

"Hardly," said Yavalliska. "I simply find your choice garish. Slaves are cheap and obvious. I prefer devotion to obedience. It is not enough simply to be obeyed. I want to be adored."

"You mew like a harlot," scoffed Kasiya. "Adoration is fragile, subject to jealousy and neglect. Look at my spear-bearer, demon. She once commanded crusaders for the queen of Mendev. Now she captures vermin to draw my carriage. Yet do you see the slightest fear or disgust upon her face? There is nothing but obedience in her heart. She is the perfect subject for a prince."

"I would prefer a fallen paladin, one who would cast away the bonds of obedience and embrace me with desire."

"What an apt expression, 'fallen paladin.'" Kasiya turned his golden face toward me. "My spear-bearer felled one of those before I claimed her as mine."

I am not yours, I thought, you disgusting refuse of a once-living man.

"Are you not concerned she will turn on you?" Before I realized she had moved, the succubus stood beside me. The top of her head rose barely higher than my shoulder. She craned her neck to study my face. "After all, if your pet could slay the peerless Xagren . . ."

"Do not mistake me for some mere failed crusader. I am a prince born and reborn! Besides, without her sword, she depends on me for protection."

"Still, her presence is a dangerous indulgence. Perhaps it is better you keep only her head as a trophy. Among my minions is a talented taxidermist." Yavalliska reached up to touch my chin.

At her silken touch, I felt the muscles in my hand tighten and willed myself not to make a fist, not to strike her down before the prince. Even without my sword, my enchanted belt lent me more than enough power to tear off her wings, perhaps even her head.

As if reading my thoughts, the succubus slipped her fingers through my belt. She tugged at it, gazing pensively into my face. The barest smile dimpled her red lips. "Although I suppose without her sword, she poses little enough threat to you."

"How can you look upon her dumb face and doubt her loyalty to me?" said Kasiya. "But of course—you just returned from murdering your rivals so that you can betray your mistress. You common fiends know nothing of loyalty. You cannot imagine the strength of the bond between master and servant."

"No," laughed Yavalliska. "I daresay we of the boundless Abyss have no love of shackles, upon the wrist or in the mind. We love nothing so much as our own freedom."

"Do you not serve Areelu Vorlesh when she is here?"

"When she is here, of course I *appear* to serve her," said the succubus. "What do you think 'our own freedom' means?"

Prince Kasiya's mask wavered. Through the narrow slot over his mouth, I glimpsed thin lips twisting again. Gone was the awe his eyes had inspired in me only moments earlier. Now I felt only revulsion. Even thinking such thoughts felt like a weight of tangled chains falling from my mind.

"Now you're spouting nonsense," he said. "Freedom is an illusion for all but the gods." He sat once more before his books and returned to his studies.

Yavalliska shook her head, smiling. Abandoning me with one coy glance over her shoulder, she glided back to Kasiya.

"I've changed my mind about your spear-bearer," she whispered in his ear. When he looked up, she added, "She is perfect."

Kasiya looked at her and then at me. "Of course she is."

Yavalliska insinuated herself onto the arm of his chair, reading over his shoulder. "Are those druidic runes?"

"Yes," said Kasiya. "I suppose they are."

"You can't read them?"

"I don't need to understand these barbaric scribblings," he said. "A prince has no time to waste learning the tongues of lesser races. A simple spell allows me to comprehend any writing."

"How much of the ritual can you reconstruct from this portion of the *Lexicon*?"

"Not enough," said Kasiya. "I require the missing pages."

Yavalliska reached past the prince to close the *Lexicon*. She stroked a finger along the rough bark cover. "You should have captured this Count Jeggare and had him fetch it for you. He seems clever and resourceful."

Kasiya hissed. "I don't need the Chelaxian's help. When next he looks upon me, it will be as a mortal worshiping at the foot of a god."

"I thought you said you required only obedience, not adoration?"

"He dares to look down on me. Me, a prince of Osirion! And what is he but a glorified landlord bending his knee to an upstart house of Cheliax? The Thrunes have ruled for less than a century. They're not even a dynasty, but a mote of ash in the eye of history."

"I see I've touched a nerve. Is it for his origins or his station that you hate him most? Or is it something to do with your fraternity of grave robbers?"

Prince Kasiya fell very still. "What do you know of our rivalry?"

"Rivalry?" laughed Yavalliska. "I didn't mean to suggest a mere count of Cheliax could rival a prince of Osirion. No, I simply inquired about his name after you told it to me. It seems Varian Jeggare is known among the horde, both as a count of Hell's ally, Cheliax, and as a Pathfinder. Is it true you died while trying to steal his notebooks so you could present them as your own?"

"How dare you suggest—" Kasiya stood so quickly that he knocked over his chair. He swept up Jeggare's journals and grimoires in both arms and carried them to the brazier. "I have no need to follow in Jeggare's footsteps. This is what I think of his notes."

He cast the books onto the coals. In seconds, flames crackled at the edges of the pages.

A surprising pang of sympathy for Varian Jeggare struck me like a blow to the stomach. Clenching my jaw, I resisted the urge to rescue the books. Jeggare had invested years if not decades in those journals, and all his arcane power was inscribed within that grimoire. Its absence surely endangered him, but its fiery destruction felt to me as though Kasiya had burned him in effigy.

Yavalliska leaned close to the fire, inhaling the smoke and grinning. "Oh, Great Prince Kasiya. What a glorious display of indifference."

"You vex me, Yavalliska. Continue to do so at your peril."

"I but tease you, my prince," she cooed. "You will be more pleased with me, I think, when I tell you I know where to find the missing information."

"Is it not in the other tower?"

"My minions are searching even as we speak, but I do not think they'll find it there. Those who hid the treasures of the Threshold did so with great care and cunning. Why divide this *Lexicon* only to keep its halves close? No, I think the missing fragment is far from here, or perhaps destroyed."

"No!"

"Do not fret, my prince. As you have no doubt already seen, the secrets in these pages came from many sources, but the binding is the important clue. The keepers of Sarkorian lore were not sorcerers or wizards or witches. They were druids."

"Then where is their stronghold? Where did they keep their most secret lore?"

"I know the place," said Yavalliska. "We've been destroying it for a century."

Chapter Seventeen
The Frostmire

Radovan

Stop make chase," yelled a loud, deep, mush-mouthed voice. Even without the boss handy to say so, I could tell Taldane wasn't its native language.

"Everything worse downriver," said another big voice, this one with a rubbery wheeze at the end of every breath. "Take chance Pit of Blood, like big man."

Alase looked at me, eyes wide. She shook her head to tell me she didn't know what it was we were hearing. I could tell she didn't want to be the first one to look.

Peeking over the hollow log, I saw two giants lumbering out of the mists.

Even crouching, the gray-green things were a head taller than Kronug and massive as a draft horse. Their fishy mouths gaped beneath fiendish eyes. Four-fingered hands clutched heavy fishing gaffs.

One of them slapped the net slung around its shoulders. Stunned by the blow, the woman trapped inside stopped struggling. Her dirty fingers clutched the netting as she stared blankly at the marshy ground.

Alase put her hand on my arm before I realized I'd pulled the big knife and stood up. She pulled me back down. "We're no match for them."

"Call your wolf."

"Even with Tonbarse . . ." She shook her head.

Much as I wanted to argue, I couldn't. Without a devil riding me, and without the boss and the others at my back, I wasn't exactly giant-slayer material.

One of the giants slugged the other on the shoulder and pointed with its gaff at a footprint in the mud.

The other growled and rubbed his shoulder. Together, they waddled after the tracks. From their own prints, yellow steam rose from the ground.

The captured woman shouted something in Hallit. All I caught was "Run, Jokum!"

The giant slapped her again. She went limp, her eyes rolling back in her head before closing.

"That tears it," I said, standing up.

"Don't," said Alase. But she knew I wasn't listening. With a sigh, she put her palm to the ground and began the chant to summon Tonbarse. I caught a glimpse of the blue glow that connected them as I hustled off.

Keeping low, I ran through the swamp, parallel to the giants. Lucky for me, the ground wasn't too wet this close to Dyinglight.

We'd already had our peek at the city. Smaller than Undarin and surrounded by willows and wetlands, it was lousy with demons. I figured the Pit of Blood the big fellow mentioned had to be the arena beside the headwaters of the Sarkora River. We'd seen more activity in the nearby fields, where giant and demon overseers lashed the human and demonblooded slaves weeding the crops.

These fiendish marsh giants didn't act like they were in a hurry to catch this Jokum character. It wasn't exactly like they didn't want to catch him. It seemed more like this job was a lot better than whatever they had waiting for them back in town. Or maybe they just liked chasing slaves.

They took turns shouting threats and arguments explaining why it was better to give himself up than to risk the greater dangers downriver. Having seen Undarin and Valahuv, I had to admit they had a point.

It didn't take me long to get ahead of the big lummoxes. Then it was just a question of finding Jokum before they did. I heard him plunging through the brush a second before I heard his ragged panting. I sprinted after the sound and caught up half a minute later.

He was barely more than a kid, lean and muscular but without so much as a hint of a beard. His shaggy black hair reminded me of Alase. I hissed at him. "This way, kid!"

He took one look at my pretty mug and ran in the opposite direction.

"Dammit, boy, I'm here to help!" Under the circumstances, it was hard to blame him. Still, he wasn't making my job any easier.

He didn't make it thirty steps before something caught him. He rose up a foot or two off the ground. Only after I got close to him could I see why: he'd run into a gigantic spider web.

The thought of leaving him here did more than cross my mind. It set up camp.

It's not that I'm more scared of spiders than the next guy. I just don't like the damned things, with all the legs, and all the eyes, and just— They're nasty. That's all.

Still, it was kind of my fault Jokum was stuck there.

"Desna weeps." As I moved in to cut him free, the damned fool started screaming.

"Shut it, kid. I'm getting you out of here."

I severed a few tough strands. They weren't even as thick as my little finger, but they were strong as ship rigging. The kid screamed again. I had half a mind to belt him one, but I saw his eyes weren't on me. He was staring upward.

One big spider wouldn't have bothered me so much, but that's not what we had. Instead, it was a swarm that made the bugs back at Nekrosof look like garden centipedes.

There were thousands of the things, none much bigger than my hand, and every one of them touched by the Abyss. A blood-colored hook curled out from each joint of their legs. Their many eyes glowed in different colors: yellow, black, red, green, purple.

I kept cutting. Jokum tried to free himself, but his thrashing only wound him up more. "Seriously, kid, quit moving or I leave you here."

It occurred to me the kid might speak only Hallit, so I repeated the message best I could, which wasn't great. I ended up with something like, "Stop, stupid, or you alone."

Something about my voice got through to him. He tried to stay still, except when one of the spiders dropped onto his face. He slapped it away, but not before its bite left a sizzling wound on his cheek. He screamed again, louder.

With most of the web strands cut, I grabbed him around the waist and pulled. He came down on top of me as I wrenched him free.

"Lesit!" he yelled.

The giants stomped toward us. The woman in the net reached out a hand again. "Jokum!"

"Go, Jokum," I told him. "I'll keep these jerks busy."

Despite my tough words, I prayed Alase and Tonbarse would show up soon. Even if they did, I didn't like our chances. Alase was right. It would have been a lot smarter to leave Jokum and Lesit to their own problems. Without help from the others, who hung back more than a mile away, we couldn't take these giants on our own.

But I knew someone who could.

The giant holding Lesit moved toward Jokum. I gave the kid a kick to encourage him. Tears mingling with the blood on his face, he took one last look at Lesit and ran.

I threw a handful of darts at the giant, careful not to perforate his captive. He slapped at the wounds on his gray-green chest like he'd been nipped by gnats.

"Hey, fatty." I showed him the big knife. "Come get me."

He came after me, all right. His heavy footsteps shook the trees.

I closed my eyes and tried to keep my mouth shut as green buds and spiders rained down on me. Only then did I realize my mistake. A thousand fangs sank into my flesh as I shucked off the jacket and threw it aside. I had to drop the big knife to get my arm out of the sleeve.

I focused all my pain into a name: "Viridio!"

It feels like falling backward, only instead of coming down on my head, I come all the way around, like I'm one of those tall mirrors in a frame, and somebody's flipped me around. When I come back up the other side, it isn't me you see inside. It's nine feet of demon, claws, carapace, and fangs.

The change swirls my thoughts and takes my brain up to a full boil. The part that's still me has to struggle to stay on top. I think about who I want to hurt the most. I try not to blame Lesit, even though it's kind of her fault. With any luck, I'll have forgotten all about her by the time I'm finished with the giants.

The one holding her pauses for a second when it sees what I've become. With barely a thought, I see I've put my scorpion stinger in his eye. Much as I hate the idea of having a tail, it tickles me to see the jelly spilling out of his eye socket. I hit him again in the other eye as he shrieks and bawls. For a second I think about tearing out his throat, but I like the way he's crying. I'd like him to go on crying while I deal with his pal.

The other one brings his gaff hook down toward me. I slap it away with the back of an armored wrist. My claws are longer than the big knife, almost as long as swords. I rake them across the giant's blubbery belly and watch his blue-black guts ooze out. They smell like rotten fish and brimstone.

I hear a shout behind me and turn. The big black wolf has showed up at last. He smashes the other giant's legs out from under him, turns and lunges not for the throat but for the net hanging from his shoulders. The wolf tears off the net with the woman still inside, dragging it away. When the wolf's bright blue eyes meet mine, I see it's really me he's saving her from.

I want to teach him a lesson. As I move forward, the blind giant reaches out to grab my leg. He's still strong. His grip hurts. He pulls me down. I let him.

Once we're lying together, I wriggle around until I'm close enough to bite his throat. My venom melts his fishy skin. I get my fingers under his arms. My claws push in between his ribs. I find the pulsing heart inside. I want it. I take it. I shove it in my mouth. I feast on its bitter flesh.

When I'm done, I look around for Alase, but she's nowhere to be seen. She's taken the girl with her. That wasn't very nice. I decide to find them and tell them that I think it wasn't very nice.

The swamp is thick with trees and brush, thicker than it was before. I stop and tear down the ones I don't want to walk around. Despite the effort, the moist air cools me off. I start breathing slower. Inside, part of me is angry. Part of me is scared. The two parts both want to talk. The angry part speaks first, but not in words.

Radovan Virholt, you weakling, you imbecile! I told you never to summon me so close to the Worldwound!

My thoughts were still jumbled, but I could feel mine separating from Viridio's. It wasn't even his thoughts I felt in my head. It was more just his emotions, or maybe his instincts. Whether he was more like a man or an animal, I couldn't say. Probably a devil like him wasn't much like a man or an animal, anyway. "Hey," I said. "We're a lot farther away than we were before."

I can still feel the chaos eating away at the edges of my perceptions.

"That's probably just the swamp gas," I said. "Besides, you love killing demons. You said so in Kyonin."

I don't like sitting on the edge of the Abyss. If I were to perish here, there's no telling what would become of me. I might be banished from the chamber. I might even be destroyed along with you.

That idea sobered me up a little. "Yeah, well, I wouldn't have done it if it weren't an emergency. Besides, it all worked out. You can go any time you like. Say hello to Quang for me. The little jerk ran out on our last talk."

Quang spoke to you?

"Uh, yeah? Maybe." I realized I'd just spilled the beans. "I don't remember. What's it to you?"

Viridio made a sound halfway between a hiss and a coughing fit. I felt his thoughts hovering just above mine, like a scorpion's stinger over an ant. It hung there a while, deciding what to do with me, before I realized I was once again standing naked in my own skin.

I checked my arms and chest for bites, but there were hardly any marks left. I went back for my stuff. I fetched my jacket and the big knife, which were both in pretty good shape. Nearby I found my ruined kickers and the shreds of my pants. I cursed myself for forgetting to buy extra boots along with the spare pants back in my saddlebags. Then I walked back to catch up with the expedition.

Before I found them, I found Bastiel. The unicorn stood in a haze of mosquitoes. It took me a second to realize he wasn't switching his tail back and forth like a regular horse. It took me another second to realize that was because none of them were touching him.

"You're too late to help with the fight," I said. "You want to give me a ride back?"

"Don't test me, hellspawn. The only reason I'm not trampling you into a puddle is that I don't wish to sully my hooves with your tainted blood."

"I think it's because you don't want my big knife up your ass." The unicorn stamped and snorted, but it didn't matter. After my little workout, I still felt all the mean coursing through my blood. I was ready to take on anybody or anything that rubbed me the wrong way. "What the hell are you doing out here anyway?"

"The others were worried about you," said Bastiel.

"Yeah? And that matters to you why?"

"Because you can help them," he said. "Oparal wanted them to succeed, so I—" He huffed and snorted again.

"Yeah, yeah, I get it. So let's go back and help them." I walked up to the big fellow, but he shied away. "Calm down, you big baby. I'm not planning to ride you, bare-assed or otherwise."

"Stay away."

"Is that it?" I said. "Just like all the other horses, you're scared of me?"

"I am not a horse," he said. "And I am not afraid of you."

"You may not be a horse," I said as we headed back to the caravan. "But I've never seen a bigger chicken."

Everybody eyed me when I got back, and not just because of the pants thing. Anyway, nobody stopped to talk. They started moving the moment I showed up.

Alase must have told them what we'd seen at Dyinglight, and they decided to keep going past it. The way the boss talked about it, he expected to find what he was looking for somewhere up north, by some standing stones in the forest, or where a forest used to be, or something like that.

There was no sign of Lesit or Jokum. When I asked Aprian, he said the boss talked with them for a little while before offering to let them join the company. They'd refused, so he let them go with supplies and a couple of spare weapons. Considering how things had worked out for the other Kellids we'd met, I couldn't say I blamed them for setting off on their own.

Alase was sitting on the carriage roof with the luggage. She already had my spare trousers. She held them up, beckoning me to join her.

I ran to catch up with the carriage and jumped onto the footman's ladder. Up top, I put on the pants. I dropped the shreds of my boots on the roof.

Most of the others walked their horses through the swamp, including the wagon and carriage drivers. Even after I got my pants on, they stole peeks at me when they thought I wasn't looking.

"I guess you told them what happened."

"I said you rescued the slaves."

"What about the . . . Grawr!?" I made claws with my hands.

"They could see that for themselves." She looked at my boots. "Barek could bind those up for you. He makes boots and armor."

I nodded, figuring maybe later, when I wasn't feeling so weird around anybody.

"Your god is very difficult to call. I never met a caller who had to take poison for his god to hear him."

"I told you, it's not the same as you and Tonbarse." I looked over to see the big wolf talking as he padded through the swamp, Arnisant on one side, Bastiel on the other. I never saw the unicorn answer. Still, I could tell he was listening. "For one thing, there's five of them waiting on the other side of the gate—me—in this little hell. For another thing, they're devils, not gods."

She shrugged. "The only difference is that you have not learned to support your god when it heeds your summons."

"Yeah, because supporting the bastard is the first thing I want to do when a devil comes over to ride my body."

"Not your body," she said. "Your spirit. It is the god's body that comes across. It rides your spirit in this world."

She went on like that for a while. Most of it was stuff the boss had already figured out—or, as he put it, "hypothesized." An awful lot of Alase's version sounded like the kind of pitch I'd heard from fortune-tellers and hedge witches from here to Cheliax. Sure, Alase was the real thing, a summoner with real power, but I knew from the boss that it was all a matter of magic formulas that made spells like hers work. Sorcerers and witches and summoners, they all explained it in different ways, but it all came down to arithmetic.

"I can show you how I first called to Tonbarse," said Alase.

"I'm pretty sure it don't work the same for me. For Viridio, I need to be dying of venom before he shows up."

"What about the god who rode you before him?"

"Devil. I had to die in a fire."

"Maybe we should call to the poison devil."

"Yeah, that's better. Still, I don't want any of those mooks coming through right now."

"What I will show you won't bring your god into the world. It will only let you call to him."

"Yeah?" It occurred to me that I had some more questions for Quang. Last time we talked, he'd left in a hurry. Now that we were farther from the Worldwound, maybe he'd have more to say. "All right. Show me."

"Let's sit low."

We rearranged the luggage around the edges of the carriage roof. All pushed up against the low rail that kept it from sliding off, the trunks and bags formed a wall around us. Soon we couldn't hardly see the others riding around the carriage. Once we sat cross-legged on the roof, we could barely hear them, either.

After all our shifting around, I expected the boss to poke his head out to give me an earful about making a racket, but nothing happened. Ever since Valahuv, the boss had stepped out only to take his turn behind the bushes. Jelani did the same. When I asked, the boss just said they were studying the *Lexicon*, taking turns to make sure it didn't make either one of them too peculiar.

You ask me, that plan wasn't working out too good. They both seemed a little skittish when I brought their meals inside. When Aprian asked me what was going on in there, I joked that maybe they'd hit it off. Neither of us believed that. One look at either of them when they poked their noses out, you could tell they'd been losing sleep the hard way.

Alase scooted forward until her knees touched my shins. When she took my hands, it reminded me just how little she was. She didn't act little, though. Even though Tonbarse seemed to do all her fighting for her, I could see by the way she cut her food that she knew how to use her knife for more than eating.

"Close your eyes," she said. Her finger traced patterns on my palm. "Imagine the place where your gods live."

I didn't have to imagine it. I'd seen the joint, first when the demons of Kyonin opened me up and later in a hundred nightmares. It was a little cave, its scabby walls glistening red with blood and yellow with puss. The golden light came from me, or at least that puddle on the wall that was the point where Hell connected to Golarion and the Abyss.

"All right, I got it."

She let go of my right hand and grabbed my left. She traced more runes on it. "Now envision your gods."

"Which one?"

"The one you want to speak to."

That would be Quang. I'd seen a few imps in my time, but I wouldn't forget his barbed chin, his bat wings, the agate-green eyes, the black claws and curved barb on his tail. With all that in mind, I still couldn't see him in the little hell. Even so, something else started coming into view.

In a fleshy niche in the wall, the bulky figure of Norge melted into view. Big as a grizzly, he was one big mass of red muscle bristling with black spines and teeth. As I saw him in my mind, I started to hear his steady snoring. I could even smell the sulfur from the yellow puddles on the floor.

I started to think maybe Alase's plan was working *too* good.

"Listen—"

"Don't speak to me," she said. "Speak to the god. Call his name, and he will answer."

There was no point talking to Norge. He was half dead, or mostly asleep, or something. Besides, I didn't think I'd get anything out of him even if he woke up. So instead I called out, "Quang? You in there somewhere, you little jerk?"

My voice echoed off the walls of passages I couldn't see. I knew the devils had a way in and out of the little cavern, but I'd never seen it.

"Quang? Come over here, let's finish our chat."

"As you call to him, imagine how this place appears through his eyes."

"What do I know about how Hell looks to an imp?"

"Just try."

All right, I thought. He's a little guy, so everything looks bigger. I imagined the cavern was four times bigger, looming above me like cathedral. It started to work. I felt real small.

Then it occurred to me that Quang had never acted like he thought he was small. In fact, he flew above the heads of the other devils. I thought about what the little hell looked like from high on the ceiling. Sure enough, in my mind's eye, I was looking down on Norge and all the disgusting pools on the floor. Soon I heard a popping sound and the quick beat of little bat wings.

Where . . . ? What have I . . . ? Unholy crap! Who summoned me here?

"Who'd you think?" Not only could I hear him, but with my eyes closed I could see the little imp hovering in the little hell.

Radovan? When did you become a sorcerer?

If I could conjure a phony pony with a riffle scroll, who's to say I couldn't conjure a crappy little imp like Quang? "Turns out I got hidden depths."

You aren't using the Lexicon *now, are you?*

"What if I am?"

Don't you realize what it does?

"I'm the one asking the questions." I probably should have thought of some before calling him. "So, uh, what do you think the *Lexicon* does?"

Seriously? He cackled. *You had me going there! You don't have a clue what it does!*

"You mean besides opening portals to different worlds, yeah?"

Oh. Quang sobered up. *So you have a little more than a clue.*

"So it bothers you for the same reason Viridio can't stand being near the Worldwound. Is that it?"

You've been talking with Viridio.

"Sure. I told him to say hello."

So that's why he chased me halfway around Mammon's Bier. You squealed on me!

"What were you up to that it was squealing?"

Listen, Radovan. What we got here is a big misunderstanding. If I'm in trouble with Viridio, it's only because I'm trying to help you out.

"Help me?"

I'm not saying there's nothing in it for me, just that I've got a great deal for you.

"I notice you're the only one there, aside from Norge."

Yeah, nobody wanted to carry him out. Besides, the place has kind of grown on him.

"Tell me about this deal."

All right, here's what I got: you already know about fire and venom being the sigils for Norge and Viridio.

"Yeah?"

I can tell you everybody's sigil.

"Including yours?"

Including mine.

"Interesting." Now that I'd finally been in a tight spot and knew how to call on Viridio on purpose, I could see the use in that. "What do you want in return?"

Hardly anything. Just promise that when your boss does use the Lexicon, *the first thing you do is call me through.*

"I thought you were afraid of the *Lexicon*."

I am! And you should be, too.

"What's the catch?"

Because you're a smart guy, I know better than to try to trick you. The catch is this: when you're up close and personal with the Worldwound, there's a fair chance the first of us you call through can come all the way through. I want what we've all wanted from the start: I want out of Hell.

"And why should I want to let you out?"

You're from Egorian! You've seen dozens of imps flying around. What harm can one more little guy like me cause in your world? On the other hand, a big fellow like Viridio comes through, or worse yet one of the schemers like Dokange or Eriakne, and you have a big problem on your hands. If it makes you feel any better, think of me as the lesser evil.

Living almost all my life in Cheliax, I was used to weighing bad against more bad. From Eel Street all the way to the royal palace, you don't see a lot of choices between good and evil. "All right," I said. "Tell me what you know."

So we have a bargain? In my mind's eye, or through whatever magic let me see him, the little imp stuck out a clawed hand.

"Yeah," I said, imagining I was reaching for him. In my vision of the little hell, I saw a gold light reach out to cover his hand. "Deal."

Chapter Eighteen
The Shroud of Unicorns

Varian

When at last we emerged from the Frostmire, I saw through the carriage windows that the drooping foliage of the swamp had given way to a pine forest.

The corrupting touch of the Worldwound's fiends had not spared even this distant territory. While the nearest woods were lush with new growth, the spectres of razed trees stared in silent accusation as we rode past. Even in these earliest days of summer, a thin mist emerged from the ground to swaddle the saplings cradled in the ashes of their parents.

Our destination lay to the east, but I called out the window to order the expedition farther north, into the forest, before turning in that direction. The open expanse between us and the Sarkorian plateau made me feel as though the eyes of Deskari and his vast plague of minions were upon us.

Across the map table, Jelani lay sleeping on the opposite seat. For all of her enthusiasm, the sorceress had not persuaded me of her hypothesis. Her efforts to coach me in casting spells with intuition rather than reason had successfully tested only my patience. While I had no doubt of her benign intentions, her encouragements smacked of mysticism and wish-fulfillment, not learning and research.

Still, perhaps because of some lingering romanticism in my own imagination, I could not dismiss the notion that sorcery ran in my blood. While I knew of no direct human ancestor possessed of such talent, I had only recently encountered the elven side of my family. The Morgethais counted a number of sorcerers among their kin, some of them quite notorious. If only I had wintered in Riverspire, I might have learned more of my family history.

Yet I had given my word to visit the Queen of Thorns, and so I kept it.

At least the changing landscape refreshed my troubled thoughts. Once I could no longer see the distant cliffs through the burned and regenerating firs, I called a halt to the expedition. Aprian balked before relaying the order to his crusaders. Although I appreciated his concern about the effect the *Lexicon of Paradox* had on my state of mind, I could not overlook his hesitation. Whether or not he blamed me for the loss of Oparal, he had to acknowledge my authority or else he would imperil our success.

I emerged from the carriage with the sheathed Shadowless Sword in hand. I secured it to my waist and tucked the left side of my long coat behind the hilt. The swiftest enchanted blade in the world was no use if I could not draw it in an instant.

Radovan leaped down from the carriage roof, startling me. It had once been his custom to ride atop the carriage or on the footman's perch, the better to spy trouble ahead. Since I began conjuring phantom steeds for his use—and now he could do so himself—he had enjoyed riding freely among the others.

Lately, he and Alase had taken to nesting above our heads while Jelani and I studied my notes and maps within the carriage. Considering the attention the summoner had paid him since we left Gundrun, I kept expecting to hear sounds of improper conduct from their perch. Yet they had remained so silent that even I could forget their presence on the roof.

With a nod toward me and another toward Aprian, Radovan took command of the routine chores. The drivers released the horses, watered and brushed them. The journey had taken its toll on the beasts, even the Kyonin draft horses that had previously seemed tireless. I made them a silent promise of a summer's freedom in the pastures of my western holdings. Indeed, they were such splendid specimens that I would do myself as well as them a favor by breeding them with the finest mares I could find.

While the drivers inspected the wheels and undercarriage, I took the opportunity to stretch my legs. Arnisant accompanied me through the firs. The sweet scent of pine needles was a welcome respite from the decay of Frostmire Fen.

Arnisant froze, pointing. I followed his gaze and caught a glimpse of a brown pelt darting through the trees. The hound trembled, hoping for the command to chase. He wanted exercise after remaining confined in the carriage, but before I could release him, another movement caught my eye.

Bastiel ran through the pines, his mane flowing like silk behind his supple neck. The sun caught on his spiral horn, glinting both gold and alabaster in some fey trick of the eye.

The sight of the unicorn caught up my breath. Oparal had healed him many times since first encountering the battered creature in the Fierani Forest, yet still he bore scars from his endless war against the demons of that land. Yet none of his imperfections diminished his glorious appearance. Beside him, even my peerless draft horses seemed only common beasts.

Bastiel stopped, his noble head rising as if hearing some distant call. I cupped my ear to listen but heard nothing. At my side, Arnisant grew still, tensed to pounce. Without knowing what beckoned to the unicorn, I dared not release him. I showed him the sign to sit. He obeyed, his eyes locked on me, awaiting his next command.

"Bastiel," I said. A twitch of the unicorn's ears told me he had heard my voice, but he did not turn his head to me. His head rose again at some signal I could not perceive.

Without warning, he ran.

"Go," I told Arnisant. I ran after hound and unicorn.

My hand strayed to one of the few remaining scrolls I carried in my bandolier. One of them would allow me to alert Radovan to my pursuit. It seemed wise to summon him, yet without my grimoire my scrolls had become a finite resource. As a compromise with myself, I removed the scroll to my coat pocket, ready to cast it if necessary.

Soon I lost sight of the unicorn in the thickening fog. "Arnisant!" I called.

The hound responded with a hearty *woof!* I corrected course to follow him.

The sudden increase of fog triggered my suspicion. It was not impossible that it was a natural phenomenon, but neither was it probable. I removed the scroll from my pocket, but before I could put my thumb upon its edge, I noticed I was no longer alone.

Muted by the mist, the sound of a hundred hoofbeats surrounded me. I spied a blue eye not twenty feet away, then another on the other side of me. Arnisant returned, a querulous growl rising from his chest, neither entirely fearful nor confidently angry.

The eyes came closer on all sides. White muzzles nosed out of the mist, blue eyes on either side of delicate equine heads, spiral horns upon their brows.

Hesitant to provoke the creatures, I barely drew my sword and focused my thoughts on perceiving the real, dispelling any glamour meant to deceive my senses. We remained surrounded by unicorns.

Dozens of the creatures encircled us, and beyond them came even more—perhaps hundreds of unicorns, all in the same place. I blinked again, half hoping it was some illusion, half hoping it was not. The awesome sight swelled my heart with wonder. I understood as never before why a group of unicorns is referred to as "a blessing."

Most were slim, delicate creatures, barely larger than a deer. Others had more equine frames, sturdy creatures more than able to carry a rider. I could smell those nearest us, feel the warmth of their bodies, yet those beyond the inner circle might have been phantoms.

Whether they appeared so because of some trick of the mists, I could not say. Yet I could see none that bore the mark of saddle, bit, or shoe. They were free, even among the outer edges of the Worldwound where the demons sought to destroy or imprison every beautiful thing.

With a startled whinny, Bastiel emerged from the crowd to circle and then stand beside me. By his wide eyes and sudden movement, I sensed the others had herded him toward the center before enclosing us inside a corral of their bodies.

Bastiel stamped the ground and snorted. The unicorns surrounding us slowed their circling movements to stand facing us, horns lowered in an unmistakable warning.

Shaking off the spell of their enthralling appearance, I cast my scroll, cupped my hand to my mouth, and whispered, "Radovan, come here. I need you."

Two exceptionally beautiful unicorns pushed through the crowd to stand before us. One stood nearly as tall as the enormous Bastiel, while the other stood but a hand shorter.

"Why have you come here?" said the shorter unicorn. Her lips moved like Tonbarse's, the inhuman mouth somehow shaping words in the common tongue and a voice undeniably feminine.

"I meant no trespass," I said with a courtly bow. "My expedition seeks only to pass through this land on our way east."

The unicorn and her companion—a male, I noticed— both turned their heads as if noticing me for the first time. He said, "My sister was not addressing you."

"He speaks the truth," said Bastiel. His hoarse voice startled. He struggled with every word, as though each utterance were an agony. I felt a pang of sympathy, and understood at once why he had not spoken in my presence before.

"I am Alunelsheas," said the female. "This is my brother, Caedaynenlo. We and our cousins whom you see before you are all that remains of our people."

"I am Bastiel."

The other unicorns stirred at the sound of his name.

"We feel the pain of your loss," said Alunelsheas. "Was it your sire or dam who named you?"

Bastiel tossed his head, unwilling to answer.

"Here we are all orphans," said Caedaynenlo. His voice was warm and slow as a deep river in summer.

"And is this your companion?" asked Alunelsheas, dipping her horn toward me.

Bastiel reared and whinnied, clearly offended by the suggestion.

"My apologies," said Alunelsheas.

"My companion is . . . lost." He pronounced the word with such grief that no further explanation was necessary.

"Then stay here with us."

"Stay here? To perish under the flames of demons?"

"The fiends dare not come into the heart of the Shroud," said Caedaynenlo. "Here we are the guardians of our ancestors' spirits. We guard the land so that one day it may heal itself."

"But we too must heal," said Alunelsheas. She dipped her head. "We must replenish our numbers. We must make more sires and dams to grant our offspring names full of both strength and love. Join us."

A unicorn's scream presaged the sound of galloping hooves. Radovan's voice called out a startling profanity.

Alase shouted some unintelligible response, and I heard the deep thunder of Tonbarse's voice.

"Radovan, I'm here! Don't hurt them. They are friends." The latter lines were meant for both him and the unicorns.

The unicorns parted to allow Radovan on his dreadful phantom steed and Alase on the mighty Tonbarse to enter the circle. With them came Aprian, eyes wide as he looked around from the back of his horse.

Caedaynenlo reared at the sight of Radovan and Tonbarse. "These *fiends* are your friends?"

Bastiel said nothing. He tossed his mane again and shied from Radovan as he approached.

The unicorns lowered their horns and closed in on us.

"Don't be a jackass, Bastiel," said Radovan. "Don't listen to him, unicorns. He's just the jealous type."

"I am not!" Bastiel's hoarse voice cracked, his protest unconvincing.

"Please," I said. "Alunelsheas, Caedaynenlo, we came to Sarkoris as foes of the Abyss. We seek only to close the mouth of the Worldwound."

"Tell us, Bastiel," said Alunelsheas. "Is this true? Is this the reason you came?"

Bastiel shifted.

"Think of the captain," said Aprian. "Oparal wanted to fulfill her mission."

"Oparal," said Alunelsheas. "Is that the name of your companion? Where is she?"

The unicorn reared and screamed, his wide eyes full of agony. "Gone!"

"Then stay with us, Bastiel," said Alunelsheas. "Stay with us, and we will let these friends of Oparal pass to pursue her mission."

Trapped, Bastiel bucked and kicked, stamped and snorted, ran short circles around us until both Arnisant and Tonbarse growled. Radovan dispelled his phantom steed to make room for us to crowd together, back to back. We waited for Bastiel's tantrum to subside.

It ended suddenly. Bastiel pushed his way past Alunelsheas and her brother, vanishing into the mists and unicorns.

"So many," murmured Alase. "Dead gods and living gods."

While I did not share her views, I had to suppress a shudder at her words. After a thunder of hooves and a swirl of mists and dust, the unicorns vanished. The mists thinned, and we began to make our way back to the Red Carriage.

No one spoke until Radovan broke the silence. "Now does everybody believe me when I say that unicorn talks?"

In the days that followed, we pressed east through the ravaged forests. The northern mists rose from the ground to greet us each morning, evaporating as the sun rose. It would have been a mercy had it remained to conceal the ravages of northern Sarkoris.

Where once a vast forest had stood, only ravaged timbers and hills of ash remained. Here and there a brave young wood rose from the ashes, but the new growth halted at the margins of despoiled patches earth. We rode past the bones of goliaths, the tumbles of long granite stones that once formed druid's rings, and vast sulfurous flats.

"The Forest of Stones," said Alase. She clung to Tonbarse's thick mane.

"Aptly named." I rode beside them on Gemma's rouncey. The horse was skittish so close to the wolflike eidolon, and it required no small fraction of my attention to keep her moving in a straight path.

In ideal circumstances, I would have conjured a steed of my own. Since the loss of my grimoire made it necessary to conserve my riffle scrolls, I had given Radovan the remaining phantom steed scrolls. He had never been able to approach a natural horse without provoking mortal combat.

He also saved the scrolls against future necessity, riding atop the empty Red Carriage to survey the Forest of Stones through the lenses of my spyglass. Since his summoning of Viridio in the Frostmire, he had spent more and more time alone or with Alase, meditating in an effort to commune with his devils. Of course, I had inquired about his progress, but he seemed reluctant to discuss the matter with anyone but Alase. In other circumstances, I might have pressed him, but Jelani's hypothesis about the nature of my arcane disability continued to trouble and intrigue me, despite my certainty that she was mistaken.

Beleaguered by hope and fear, I mistook Gannak's shout for a cry of discovery. When the Kellid called out a second time, I heard the terror in his voice.

His countrymen reached him first, raising their own voices in shock and loathing. I kicked the rouncey into a gallop, commanding the others to follow even as the crusaders charged past me toward the commotion.

Calf-deep in a mire of inexplicably soft earth, the Kellids formed a rough circle around an oozing mass of flesh. Among its rippling folds gaped mouths and eyes—human, fiendish, and bestial. Here and there another mammalian ornament marred its skin: a mole, a hairy patch, a weeping nipple. Through tusks, fangs, or toothless lips, its thousand mouths gibbered a nonsense litany. My thoughts spun to hear the maddening non-words.

Gannak stood trapped in the middle of the abomination, swallowed up to his knees in the monster's roiling flesh. His supine horse thrashed beside him, already torn half to pieces. The Kellid raised the greatsword with which I had secured his service and hacked at the monster. Everywhere he struck, he opened another bloody wound. His fellows did the same all around the edges of the horrid thing.

Jelani circled on her steed, one hand dancing above her head. Blue-white bolts of arcane force shot into the jabbering mass. Its body recoiled where struck, but only for an instant before it resumed its feast.

The remaining crusaders leaped from their saddles and moved in to fight beside the Kellids. Bolivar dropped his own greatsword and clutched his head at the maddening cacophony. Others hesitated or lashed out blindly. Selka hurled an axe across the monster's fluid body and struck Valki in the thigh.

Gannak screamed in rage and pain.

"Stand back," I shouted to the nearest combatants. As they gave me room, I snapped the edge of a riffle scroll and poured a beam of flame upon the monster. Its flesh burned, the scorched eyes melting, the gibbering lips withering.

My mount reared and whinnied at the flames. I wasted a moment trying to calm her before slipping off the saddle and letting her go.

Tonbarse ran in to tear at the thing. No sooner had he wet his muzzle than the great wolf yelped and ran out, whining and pawing at his eyes. Globs of yellow spittle ran down either side of his head.

Befuddled by the chaos of the battle, I pulled two useless rifle scrolls from my bandolier before realizing I could not remember where I had secured my battle spells. In my momentary derangement, I raised my hands to form the esoteric gestures to evoke a beam of fire. I uttered the evocation.

And stood there, foolish, as nothing resulted.

Some sorcerer, indeed!

"Look out, above us!" shouted Aprian.

A cloud of flapping terrors descended on us. Previously I had seen them only from a distance. Jelani had named them vescavors—jabbering fiends about the size of a bat, which flew even more erratically than those airborne vermin. As the vescavors closed, they added their own insane song to the madness of the monster flowing across the ground.

Unable to move, I stared in horror as chaos closed in. The vescavors swarmed over Dolok and his greatsword. He tried to shake them off, but when they flew away they left behind only the hilt of his weapon and an arm devoured to the bone.

Men and women screamed, fire blossomed, and fiends cried out in joy all around me. And there I stood, indecisive, until a sharp blow across the face jolted me back to reason.

"Snap out of it, boss!" Radovan slapped me again, this time lightly, before turning to fire another bolt at the vescavors. It shot harmlessly through their swirling bodies. "Can't you light 'em up or something?"

"Yes," I said, reaching for a scroll. "Yes, of course. No, wait—"

Taking my fingers off the fire scroll, I reached instead for one more efficacious against fiends. Holding it tight, I moved back, seeking the best vantage point. I found it atop a blackened tree stump.

There I unleashed a blast of frigid energy. Where it shot through the swarm of vescavors, the little fiends froze and fell to the ground. A few flapped once or twice before a sword swept down to end their struggles. Others fell upon the writhing aberration, which snapped them up as greedily as it had devoured Gannak and his horse.

Seeing the devastation wrought by cold, Jelani began picking off the remaining vescavors with frosty rays. Aprian stepped back from the amorphous fiend to call upon Iomedae. Her radiance spread from the crosspiece of his sword, scorching even more of the tiny demons.

By the time the few surviving vescavors flapped away, our sellswords and crusaders were finishing off the many-mouthed monster. Radovan joined them, plunging his big knife again and again into the thing's remaining eyes. Tonbarse, his eyes healed by Alase's arcane connection, came back to savage the last trembling flanks of the dying monster.

Two of the Kellids were beyond saving. Gannak was devoured to the waist, and Dolok died of blood loss from his devoured arm before Aprian could lay his healing hands upon the terrible wound. The paladin spent much of his remaining radiance sealing the deep wound Selka's axe had made in Valki's leg, doling out the rest of his succor to those whose injuries were too great for mere binding.

Radovan moved near me and pointed at some imaginary discovery on the ground. "Don't look now," he murmured. "We got a visitor. Seventeen or eighteen feet behind your left shoulder. On the dead tree, just a few feet off the ground."

I knelt and pretended to look at something on the ground. While miming a conversation with Radovan, I surreptitiously raised my eyes to glimpse a great leathery wing curling around the trunk of a burned tree, its dark skin almost indistinguishable from the charred bark. Around the other side curled a long, clawed hand. Like an enormous dried leaf, a batlike ear protruded from behind its hiding place. I whispered to Radovan, "Do you recognize it?"

"Death demon," said Radovan. "Like the ones that killed Erastus back in Undarin."

"Go for the eyes," I said. "At my signal."

I rose, turning my back toward the fiend. "Aprian, Jelani, come look at this."

Jelani arrived more quickly, one inquisitive eyebrow raised. The paladin rose with a sigh, exhausted from healing the others. When they both came near, I pointed to the empty spot on the ground and whispered, "Death demon on the tree to the left. Destroy its eyes and take it alive."

To their credit, both nodded as they looked down at our feigned discovery.

Taking the last of my arcane bolt spells in hand, I nodded at Jelani as I rose, turning. "Now!"

Radovan threw his big knife. The heavy blade pierced the demon's exposed wing and pinned it to the tree. The demon screamed and peered around the scorched tree trunk to see the source of its pain. Jelani's bolts drove into one of its deep-set eyes. I snapped off the scroll and sent my own hissing missiles into its other eye.

The demon shrieked, its long purple tongue lolling out of a mouth that by comparison made Radovan's teeth seem dainty. It flapped its free wing, tearing with its claws at the big knife that pinned the other. Failing to move the blade, it tore its own wing to pull it off the knife.

"Take it alive," Aprian called out.

The crusaders and sellswords ran to surround the tree even as the fiend beat its wings and began to fly. I had no scroll left to trap it between the branches, but I did have something that might let me duplicate Radovan's trick. Enhancing my strike with the last scroll of its type, I flung the Shadowless Sword. The point struck true, stapling the demon's ear to the tree trunk.

Pulling his big knife out of the tree, Radovan ensured the destruction of the fiend's death gaze with two quick strikes to the eyes. The demon screamed and clutched at its face before reaching and kicking blindly for its attacker. Pinned by its enormous ear, it could not follow as Radovan darted away.

It tried baffling us by summoning a cloud of darkness, but within a minute we had it bound fast to the tree.

With the fiend's head and limbs secured, Radovan went to work with his fists. Jelani turned away, and a few of the others blanched to witness the brutality.

I understood their reactions, but I had long ago divested myself of sympathy for demons. It was as pointless to sympathize with hatred, cruelty, or cowardice.

Once the fiend was prepared, Radovan clutched its throat just below the jaw. We had done this before, far too many times to count. At my nod, he would choke the demon rather than allow it to summon an ally or utter a word of Abyssal magic.

I explained this situation to the fiend. "Now, tell us what we wish to know, and you shall have a clean death."

The fiend uttered a dangerous word. Even before I could signal him, Radovan closed the demon's windpipe. With his other hand, he removed a throwing dart from his battered jacket and found a painful place for it.

More crusaders and even a few of the Kellids gasped and walked away.

"You might want to walk away," Radovan said to those remaining. "Cover your ears. Think about puppies or something. This is going to get a lot worse before it gets any better."

Most heeded his warning, but Roga and Valki remained, as did Aprian and two of his crusaders. Dragomir stood clenching his fists, staring his hatred into the demon's face as if he could inflict pain by force of will alone. Naia drew her curved dagger and said, "Say the word if you need some help."

At her cool pronouncement, even Aprian raised his brows.

We continued for a while. Radovan performed the dirtiest of the work while I listened for any syllable of magic and interrogated the fiend in its own language.

"Kill me and be done," croaked the death demon. "My kind have no fear of death."

"We will cut off your wings and your hands and your feet, but we will not let you die. We will leave you here, bound to this tree, for all the vescavors to peck at you. You will be days dying, perhaps weeks."

"Shaorhaz will return to destroy you all."

"What is this Shaorhaz?"

"The greatest among death demons, with four fists of black fire to tear your bodies to pieces even as he devours your souls."

"Where does this Shaorhaz lair?"

"At Greengrave Keep, although you will not find him there."

"What is this Greengrave Keep, and where can we find it?"

The demon laughed. "We built it from the stones of your holiest site, the Circle!"

It was not my holiest site, but I knew the demon must speak of the Circle of Hierophants, thought by many to be the first druidic circle, and the birthplace of worship of the Green. "Did Shaorhaz command the destruction of these forests?"

"At first he did. Then he sent us out to gather what remained of the druids' lore. We gathered the stones we had shattered, sifted through the bark of the trees we had burned. Whatever we found with runes upon it, we returned to the Circle."

"You lie, demon. Perhaps we should start with the feet."

"No, I tell the truth! And I laugh at your feeble efforts. You're too late—others have already come to the Circle of Hierophants. You may have escaped death at my hands, but you will never overcome the new mistress of Undarin. Yavalliska will destroy you all."

Chapter Nineteen
The Prince of Bats

Oparal

Behind a dense cloud of vescavors, the prince's chariot flew above the Worldwound.

Kasiya clutched the rail and leaned forward, oblivious to the foul exhalations of the pestilent demons. He cast another spell to hasten their flight, heedless of the fact that exhaustion killed more of them each hour. His eyes were locked upon the pole star, Cynosure, using it to navigate us northeast toward our destination. I could not help but cast my eyes downward, into the endless yawning maw of the Abyss.

Diseased spires of stone thrust up from those occluded depths, forming small islands of stability. From some poured endless falls of tainted waters. On others, small bands of demons formed brief alliances to fend off challengers to their territory. We had taken shelter on one of them the day before. I stood guard, weaponless, as the prince slept within a grave I had dug for him with my hands.

I could have slain him then, if I had been willing to remain marooned upon a spear of earth within the mouth of the Worldwound after exposing his body to the sun. Several times, I had almost done so.

But then I thought of Gemma and the hope that she remained alive. I promised myself I would go back for her, but first I needed to escape. Until then, I would have to survive.

Below the spires and hoodoos, the rift fell away much farther than my elven eyes could see. In the light of the crescent moon I glimpsed ridges glistening like the inside of a gullet rather than cliff walls. Oozes climbed up or drizzled down the crannies, disappearing into cavernous openings. From some of them emanated the glow of fires, yellow and red. I could hear distant clamors, some of metal, others of voices or the clash of hard demon carapaces.

Flights of death demons, shadow demons, fire demons, and Deskari's favored locust demons crisscrossed the chasm. One of the latter peeled away from its patrol to approach us. Two wasp-like constructs of metal and chitin moved to follow it.

"I have no time for this," said Kasiya. "Hand me a flame. Prepare the thunder."

I passed him one of the red javelins from the quiver built into the chariot's shield. He raised it to his lips, whispered a word of arcana, and hurled it at the demons moving to intercept us. The javelin burst into flames as it left his hand, growing larger and larger until it exploded within feet of one of the wasp-constructs. That one fell flaming into the Abyss while the locust demon and its other servitor veered away, unwilling to further test the charioteer's patience.

Silently, I replaced the thunder javelin in its compartment, suppressing the desire to thrust it through the vampire's back to pierce his undead heart.

Slaying him would cost my life, if I could not control his chariot—and I had no idea how to begin directing the chaotic vescavors drawing the vehicle. But plunging into the Abyss might be a fair cost to pay for ridding the world of the vampire-sorcerer, not to mention the fell tomes he carried on his hip.

And yet doubts lingered in my mind. Though free from the dominating power of his mesmerizing eyes, I had not yet found a way to destroy him without sacrificing my life and thus abandoning Gemma to the depravations of the vivisectionists in the Tower of Zura. Yet with every mile we drew closer to the Circle of Hierophants, my chance of destroying him before he could use the power of the *Lexicon of Paradox* grew slimmer.

Yavalliska's message had arrived only a few hours earlier. Upon hearing it, Kasiya flew into a rage, incinerating the messenger with a spell. The succubus had gone on before us, to prepare the way, she said, for Kasiya's great ritual at a place called the Circle of Hierophants. One of her demon allies had been combing the ruins of the northern forests for the lost lore of the druids. This same ally was also the one responsible for first razing the land, an irony that Kasiya did not appreciate as fully as Yavalliska might have done.

We left Undarin at once, driving the vescavors without mercy. Every hour or so, a few more died at the jaws of their fellows. I began to fear we would not reach our destination before falling into the Worldwound and all the way down into the Abyss itself.

Yet somehow we endured and continued to fly ever northward. We landed an hour before dawn, whereupon Kasiya spoke the words that returned his chariot to miniature form. I wondered what became of the vescavors, but when he rose again after sunset and threw the chariot upon the ground, they remained tethered to the full-sized vehicle.

At last we spied solid ground once more. Even from a great height, I could see the ruination of the woods. They had been felled and razed, in most places their lands tainted beyond regeneration. Fires still smoldered here and there, vile fumes rising from what might once have been hot springs before the demons had polluted them with the foul discharge of their bodies. Only a few sad stretches of new growth dared to strive against the desolation.

We flew deep into the ruins before the anomaly appeared: In the center of the ruined forest lay a tangle of new growth, little of it green. Weed-choked woods of black trees formed an outer barrier around a labyrinth of demon-tainted foliage. Giant briars with blood-red teeth formed twisting walls around a huge, spiral-shaped hill.

Where the thorns thinned, mounds of moss or fungus poked up misshapen heads. Gargantuan heaps of rotten vegetation steamed in the cool night air, while plantlike hulks shambled out from under their flaccid leaves to wander the twisting avenues.

Here and there a true clearing emerged around a circle of stones. Even with my limited experience among the Green-worshiping druids, I recognized something wrong in the configuration of the monoliths. They were not set in patterns reflective of the stars, the planets, or the chambers of the sun or moon. Instead, the five-pointed figures suggested the asymmetrical circles of evil cultists. They had been set not by druids but by demons.

In the center of it all rose a pinwheel-shaped hill, its top flat to accommodate a hectic fortress. The walls appeared to have been scavenged from hundreds of druid's circles. The blue-gray stones absorbed more than reflected the moonlight, except where the deep runes carved into their faces glowed sulfurous yellow. Craggy towers rose toward the sky, some of them tilted at such improbable angles that only fiendish magic could have held them in place.

Enormous insects emerged from hives pasted between gaps in the stones. They floated wasp-like into the night air, reminiscent of nothing so much as the temples of Calistria in Kyonin. The difference was that these giant insects glittered with clockwork mechanisms, and their stingers left sizzling puddles of venom in their wake.

A vulture demon leaped from a filthy aerie to swoop down on one of the wasps. It struck its prey hard, bearing it down to the ground while rending the flesh out from beneath its carapace and steel armor. The wasp's fellows swarmed to its aid, but the demon sent them reeling with a shriek so loud and piercing that it scattered our vescavors, sending us into a dive.

With a silent command, Kasiya regained control of the fiends in time to smooth our flight. We circled the shambled tower twice before someone on the ground set alight a flaming symbol of Zura on the ground. The vampire guided the chariot down to the site, where we saw Yavalliska standing before a cowering mob of cultists and demons. Directly behind her, the daemon Ommors made a noisy mess of a felled blood demon.

The chariot touched down, and Kasiya reined in the vescavor with an arcane word. With another, he returned the chariot to its diminutive state and hung it from his belt, beside the *Codex* and *Lexicon*, which floated at his hip by some enchantment of their chains.

We stood at the base of Greengrave Keep. Upon the ground beside the flaming symbol of Zura lay a pentagonal design. Nearby, stacks of bark and stone lay on the backs of brimoraks who knelt to form a table.

Kasiya drew his khopesh and marched toward Yavalliska. The instant he spoke, the curved blade glowed with crimson magic. "How dare you leave Undarin without me?"

"And interrupt your studies, my prince? That is what I dared not do." She stood with utter nonchalance, even raising her chin in an unspoken invitation to his blade. "I thought it better to surprise you with my acquisition of the last pages you require for your ascension."

Kasiya raised his sword, but the succubus held her ground. As the vampire threatened Yavalliska, a vulture demon plunged down to land behind her. A buzzing miasma surrounded its foul and lanky body. It approached, pausing as it noticed Ommors sucking at the carcass of the blood demon. It screeched in offense, but Yavalliska waved it back with a casual gesture.

"I am, of course, yours to dispose of as you will, my prince," said Yavalliska. "Yet in my absence, I fear there are no others here who can advise you as to which of the recovered pages you require. Also, while the dread Shaorhaz will not mind my visit, should he return to find me damaged, I am afraid he will be quite uncooperative."

"Whoever this Shaorhaz may be, I do not fear him."

"No, princes never know the fear that resides in common men," she said. "Thus are they pitted one against the other, often to unfortunate conclusions. Shaorhaz is a prince among the death demons. You have seen some of the minions he sent to Undarin as a favor to me."

Kasiya hesitated, torn between executing his threat and learning more from Yavalliska.

What a fool he was. In Undarin she had mocked him to his face, and moments later wrapped his fragile ego around her finger. Whatever happened next, it was by her design, not his.

Then I knew that it was by the grace of Iomedae that I had not slain him sooner. His death was not worth my life, but hers might be. Killing her would surely cost my life, here beneath the shadow of her death demon's castle. The only decision I had left was when to strike.

"Tell me, then," said Kasiya. He returned the khopesh to his half-scabbard. "Tell me what preparations you have made."

"The restless dead of the northern groves have drawn his attention for a while," said Yavalliska. "But he shall dispense with them soon, and I fear he would not look kindly on our use of his library."

"You call this a library?" said Kasiya.

"The embarrassing truth is that he had nearly annihilated this forest before realizing the treasures it contained. Only in recent years has he set his minions to salvaging what remains of the ancient lore the druids carved upon the trees and stones. Precious little remains. Fortunately, I was able to recognize enough of the ancient figures you showed me in the *Lexicon* to narrow the salvage to these dozens." The succubus gestured to the sheets of stone and bark lying upon the table of brimoraks.

"The figures I showed you?" Beguiled by the succubus's offering, Kasiya trailed from suspicion to distraction.

"I might have peeked once or twice." Yavalliska dimpled. As Kasiya glided toward the haul, she turned to me and winked.

Surprised, I fought to keep my expression neutral.

Obviously, Yavalliska would not allow Kasiya to use the books' power to gather the aspect of a god or greater demon about him—not alone, anyway. The question was not whether she meant to betray him, but how and when. If I struck too soon, her mob of demons would surely overwhelm me. Even without their help, she might be capable of fending off my attack, lacking as I did a weapon. She was no common succubus, just as Kasiya was no common vampire.

As the prince sifted through the salvaged druid lore, Yavalliska turned to receive the compliments of her fawning minions. I moved to stand near Kasiya, adopting the posture of a bodyguard even as I kept in mind his relative position and the several ways I might steal away his sword or snap his neck before he could cast a spell.

A desire for justice told me to act now, but a deeper wisdom cautioned me to wait. It was still too soon.

Or was that the voice of cowardice wringing another moment of life out of my will? Was I willing to make a martyr of myself here, alone, surrounded by the most abominable foes imaginable? Could I face with peace the prospect of an obscure demise, my last sacrifice unknown to those I left behind?

Yes, I decided. I could face that fate. And still the doubts niggled at my mind. Was it enough to slay Kasiya? Was there any hope that I could kill him and Yavalliska both before the horde dragged me to pieces? Could the death demons destroy my soul before Pharasma weighed and judged my life?

Despite my resolve, I was afraid.

Kasiya selected pages of wood and stone from the texts Shaorhaz's demons had gathered. He laid his choices upon the *Lexicon of Paradox*, seeing which best fit the torn binding.

To me the process appeared to be an idiot's mimicry of a scholar's work, yet the magic of the *Lexicon* responded to the proximity of its missing contents. Each time Kasiya lay a page beside it, the book's rough binding swelled with violet energy. Soon it reached out arcane tendrils, leading Kasiya's hand to pages chosen not by the vampire but by the book itself.

When it was done, the cover of the *Lexicon* regenerated, the bark cradling its missing pages and sending out green shoots to bind the missing pages back into its spine.

Kasiya held open the *Lacuna Codex* and lay the *Lexicon* upon it. The text of both tomes glowed white and red in affinity for each other and their bearer. Behind the golden mask, the vampire's eyes reflected the writing.

"I shall require a sacrifice." Kasiya spoke the words as plainly as a diner asking another to pass the salt.

"Did you not yourself bring the perfect offering?"

The flames of the symbol of Zura flickered on Kasiya's golden mask as he looked at me. "Indeed, I did."

I had not known the true depth of fear until that moment.

It was not time. I was not ready, and yet now Kasiya looked upon me not as his spear-bearer but as his sacrifice. If I were to act now, I could never take his weapon away before his undead reflexes allowed him to cut my throat and drink my blood.

"My prince," I said. Bright goddess, I prayed, give me the strength for one last deception. Fleetingly I thought of Aprian and his advice that deceiving the enemy was not only just but obligatory. "My life is yours. I await your command."

Kasiya's head moved. Even obscured by his mask, his gesture told me he was pleased with my response. He turned to Yavalliska.

"Such lovely submission," said the succubus. "Your spear-bearer's gesture makes me jealous that I have no further gift to offer you. Or perhaps I have: Take Ommors. The daemon will do as I bid. Test your ritual upon a disposable subject before endangering yourself with the undertaking."

Kasiya lowered his chin, considering the succubus's offer.

"My prince," I said on impulse. Yavalliska was too subtle to use such a simple ruse again. However she intended to manipulate Kasiya, I had to ensure the opposite outcome, even if it meant placing myself in the position of a sacrifice before striking my enslavers. "Do not believe her. The succubus tries to fool you again, as she did with the hearts of her rivals. If you make a god of Ommors, the daemon will remain in her thrall. She will use him to destroy you and then use the ritual upon herself."

"Silence, slave!" hissed Yavalliska. "You would say anything to save your wretched life."

"No," said Kasiya. "She warned me about you before, and I have seen the proof of your treachery. No, you will stand back and witness my ascension. Afterward, we shall see whether I am in a forgiving vein. I no longer see you at my side, Yavalliska. After this new deception, you may pray to me that I allow you a place at my feet."

"My prince, I assure you—"

"Silence, harlot!" said Kasiya.

My body tensed, preparing for the succubus to unleash her minions upon us. Instead, she bowed and backed away, the very picture of contrition.

I did not need to see a secret smile upon her face to realize what had happened. Yavalliska had anticipated that I would persuade Kasiya to refuse her suggestion. She had manipulated me as well as the imbecile vampire.

"I shall have as my sacrifice this insect." Kasiya pointed at Ommors, who continued gnawing at the blood demon.

"What?" said the daemon.

"Do as the prince commands," said Yavalliska.

"As you wish."

After falling into the succubus's trap, I could not escape. To reverse my warning now would only put me back in danger of becoming the sacrifice. Besides, I thought, what did it matter which of them destroyed the other first? I would spend the last moments of my life destroying the other.

Or failing.

"Here," said Kasiya. He stood beside the rebuilt druid's circle and pointed to its center. "Prostrate yourself, daemon."

Ommors did as Kasiya bade, laying down its swollen red body and letting its eight wet legs droop upon the stones. "If Yavalliska wishes it."

Kasiya beckoned to me. I went to him, but he beckoned me closer still. Suppressing a shudder, I leaned close to his mask. I smelled his grave-sour breath, felt its cold upon my face. "You, my spear-bearer, keep your eyes on the succubus. At the first sign of treachery, break her neck. Under no circumstances is she to approach me until the ritual is complete."

In his bloodshot eyes I saw no recognition that he had already been betrayed. The succubus had a far greater hold on him than I had realized, or else by deflecting his trust from herself to me, she was a more subtle manipulator. Perhaps she was content to remain the power behind the throne—or, in this case, behind the god. "Yes, my prince."

I turned my back to him, watching as Yavalliska gestured for her demons to surround the circle. At her signal, they prostrated themselves before Kasiya.

At the first sign of their obeisance, Kasiya cast a spell upon himself and read from the *Lacuna Codex*. The words were none that I knew, not even the babble of the Abyss which I had come to recognize from the mouths of demons. As he completed the first phrase, the book rose to hover before him, leaving only the *Lexicon* in his hand.

As he recited more of the ritual, demonic energy illuminated the pages. The figures from the page reflected off his golden mask, the beams of their unholy light tracing across the stones of the summoning circle. Once they touched the stone, the lights moved as of their own accord, swirling around the daemon at the center, drawing closer and closer until they entered Ommors's blood-swollen body to illuminate it from within.

"Kasiya!" called Yavalliska. I watched her carefully, but she did not approach. Instead, she continued calling the vampire's name. Her demons joined her in the chant.

I glanced over my shoulder to see the ritual. The vampire turned his attention to the *Lexicon*. As with the *Codex* before it, his first reading caused the book to rise before him, its text glowing as he activated its powers by reciting each passage. Both books cast lighted characters onto his mask, which reflected them onto the circle. He was not simply speaking the words—he was summoning them into the world from their prison on the pages.

A red aurora appeared in the southern sky, dancing above the Worldwound. As the light grew brighter, I realized it was approaching the circle, rising up from the mouth of the Abyss to plunge back down into the circle behind me.

Once more I looked. This time I saw the blinding red light of chaos pouring into Ommors's body, swelling the daemon to gigantic proportions. In an instant the fiend's body burst, painting Kasiya and the bindings of his books in fresh blood.

"We are privileged to witness the birth of a new god," said Yavalliska. She knelt and raised her arms to praise the vampire. "No longer shall we commend our sacrifices to Zura. After tonight, we make them in the name of Kasiya, God of Blood."

I could wait no longer. I offered a silent prayer to Iomedae that Gemma's soul might find rest, for I knew now it was not my fate to liberate her from the Tower of Zura. Turning, I reached for the sword at Kasiya's side. No sooner did I touch the hilt than his hand clamped down on my wrist.

He turned gracefully, the blazing pages of the book casting him in silhouette. His body levitated half a foot from the ground. From beneath his golden mask, red light shone out the eyes and mouth.

Releasing me, he took his mask in both hands and raised it from his face. The red light dazzled my eyes. For an instant I saw a ruined visage, but his old face melted away to reveal the perfect features of an exquisitely handsome Osirian man, brown skin suffused with the glow of blood.

"You, too?" His voice filled the air and shook the ground beneath my feet. He raised a hand, the bandages falling away to reveal perfect skin beneath. He slapped me, the blow more powerful than an ogre's. I fell to the ground, my head reeling.

Vaguely I saw Kasiya turn around to bask in the warm radiance of the energies pouring into the circle from the Worldwound. I struggled to stand, my thoughts as deranged as if I had been surrounded by vescavors.

"You cannot defeat him . . . not outside the circle," someone whispered in my ear. I turned, recognizing Yavalliska's voice. The succubus remained kneeling some distance from me, her hand cupped by her mouth. She winked at me.

Kasiya resumed his recitation from the tomes. I staggered to my feet, shook my head, and rushed him. Throwing all my weight and strength against his body,

I bore him to the ground inside the stone circle. As we fell, I pulled the khopesh from its half-scabbard and rolled away.

Kasiya's recitation interrupted, the lights from the books cast spears of light into the night sky.

Kasiya leaped to his feet, nimble as a cat. The rest of his bandages had fallen away to reveal a fully regenerated body, flush with the vigor of youth and health. Only his red eyes betrayed his undead nature.

I lunged, sweeping the unfamiliar weapon in an arc toward his neck. He slapped away the blade as easily as he had knocked me to the ground earlier. The weapon flew from my hand. "You cannot turn my blade against me," he said. "Your own holy blade is drowned. You have no weapon to defeat me."

I threw myself upon him, fingers encircling his neck. The sinews beneath were tough and strong. Even as I squeezed, I realized my giant's strength was not enough to break his neck.

And yet, I realized then, I was not the Inheritor's warrior.

I was her weapon.

"Iomedae!"

The goddess filled me with her radiance. It pulsed through my veins and poured out of my fingers and into the vampire's throat.

Kasiya struggled and choked. His implacable grip crushed my arms, but only for an instant before the light of the Inheritor withered his strength.

His sensuous lips moved in silence. The light shriveled his skin, cracking his fleetingly perfect face. I held him down until his struggles slowed. Before he stilled completely, the demonic light burst out of him once more. The force of it hurled me aside, but I did not fall to the stones. Instead, I floated above them as ruddy light poured from Kasiya's body toward the place where he had stood.

"I told him you were perfect," said Yavalliska. I looked up to see her standing in Kasiya's place before the *Codex* and the *Lexicon*, her bare feet floating inches above the ground, her expansive wings opened behind her in exultation. The Abyssal energies flowed into her.

The demons about us altered their chant from the vampire's name to hers: "Yavalliska! Yavalliska! Yavalliska!"

The succubus took up Kasiya's recitation. The text of the books shone now on her face, and from their pages came a chorus of insane verses. Vescavors swarmed above us, adding their mad jabbering to the celebration of a new goddess of blood.

All around, flames rose from the labyrinth of thorns. Behind the conflagration rumbled a sound of thunder, closing in like doom.

Chapter Twenty
The Five Devils

Radovan

I was hoping we'd showed up just in time, but it was looking like we were just too late. Sometimes they look about the same.

Through the flames, I saw Oparal's body floating a couple feet over a stone circle. There was another body lying beside her, red energy flowing out of it and into a succubus standing beside the circle. Surrounding them, demons waggled their limbs in what I guess passed for worship among the fiends.

The boss had landed to fight beside Jelani. Together they'd thrown so much fire into the maze of brambles that the whole thing had gone up in flames. These days I wasn't fireproof, and I was willing to bet no one else was, either.

All around us, the Kellids and crusaders fought to control their horses, which reared and shied away from the fire. Even Arnisant was feeling antsy, shifting around at the boss's feet as he whimpered and moaned.

Tonbarse handled it better, but Alase couldn't stop wiping her eyes for all the smoke.

"Boss, we got to get up there," I said.

He pulled a few more riffle scrolls from his bandolier and shook his head as he looked down at them. Time was, he knew where every one of them was stored, but he was losing his touch. It was hard to blame him, since he was running out of spells. He wasn't bad with that Shadowless Sword, but it was spells that made him dangerous in the field, not his blade.

He called Jelani over. "I can lay down a sheet of ice, but that's the best I can muster. Do you have anything to douse the fire?"

"Nothing strong," she said. "Fire and sand are my—"

The boss snapped off his scroll and sketched a rectangle with his hand. Where his fingers traced the shape, a wall of ice formed over the fire he and Jelani had started. The flames hissed on the ice. A cloud of steam rose up from the fight between fire and water.

Aprian's horse shifted side to side, ready to rush in.

"Wait," said the boss. "It's still dangerous. You'll be scalded to death."

Soon we couldn't see a damned thing on the other side of the fog. The crusaders with lances tucked them under their arms. The Kellids raised their swords and shouted their own names or those of their clans. A few looked back over their shoulders, no doubt wishing they'd never left Gundrun.

The boss and Jelani saddled up. I pulled the last of my phony pony scrolls out of my pocket and thought about a horse. I snapped off the scroll.

Nothing happened.

"Desna wee—" Another wave of smoke rolled over us, choking me.

"They come!" shouted big Kronug.

Out of the steam flew the first of the fiends.

I recognized the death demons first and looked away from their eyes. The boss had already warned me that wouldn't protect me from their soul-stealing gaze, but I couldn't help it. The Kellids did the same as me.

The crusaders charged the ones that came close enough. Tonbarse ran in to help, while Arnisant stayed close to the boss, who snapped a scroll, pointed a finger, and shot a ray of ice at a demon. Jelani did the same, but I could tell they were both running out of their best stuff.

Me, I filled my hands with darts and waited for my shot. The first one came when a big vulture demon swooped close to me, screeching to panic the horses. The spores coming off its wings filled my eyes with tears. I threw the blades, but I didn't hold out any hope I'd hit it anywhere that hurt.

Brimoraks came running down the hill next. The little fiends didn't give a damn about the fire still licking at the brambles. Their cloven hooves left burning prints wherever they stepped. Naia knocked one down with a short charge. Before it could get back up, I put the big knife through its eyes a couple or six times until it stopped squirming. My hands came away raw from burns.

That was an awful lot of effort to kill such a little demon.

Around me, the others weren't having any easier a time. Some horse-shaped demon charged out of the steam. It overran Barek and his mount together, pausing only to stab two scorpionlike tails into the

Kellid. Blood and scalding venom splashed across my chin on the back-stroke of the tails.

Venom, I thought. Smoke and flame. And, judging from the Kellids and me, more than enough fear to go around.

Sigils, I thought. The sigils of my devils.

In the middle of the fight, I couldn't remember the others off hand, but those might be enough.

"All right, the timing couldn't be worse, but here goes: I, Radovan Virholt, summon my ancestors to me." I took a deep breath, hoping as much as fearing my gamble would pay off the way I hoped. Quang wanted me to call only his name, but I had a surprise for him. "Fell Viridio Dokange the Flaying Tongue Gharalon Eriakne and Quang you little shit."

I don't know what I was expecting, but like with my last riffle scroll, all I got was a lot of nothing.

"That little huckster tricked me. When I get my hands on you, you little imp—"

Something hit me hard. I was on the ground before I heard the boss call out my name in warning. Stunned, I rolled away until I hit the burning hooves of another brimorak. The goat-faced jerk raised a flaming sword to cut me a new groove. I shot an elbow to its knee and felt the joint snap under my spur.

The demon dropped its flaming sword and bleated in pain.

I screamed louder than the brimorak as my arm swelled up, tearing through the shrinking sleeve of my jacket. The skin wasn't red-brown like Viridio's. Instead it was blue-gray, with ridged whorls and lines running across it.

Nice shot, said a voice inside my skull.

"Quang."

And nice going with the summoning, he said. *I don't care what anyone else says, I still think you're smarter than you look.*

The rest of the jacket pulled away, tight across my chest as wings pushed out from my back. My spine twisted in spasms as I felt the tail grow out the bottom.

The pain of transforming cleared my vision enough to see a demon stalking toward me. It had the body of a pale musclebound man with rusty plates of armor nailed into its flesh, blood still flowing from the wounds. Bat wings hung folded across its back. Its horned and hairless wolf's head snarled as it reached down for me.

I tried rolling away, but it caught me by the wings and swung me back like a half-filled sack of grain. Twisting to escape, I felt my body slip out of its grip. It didn't feel like I'd pulled free so much as I'd turned myself into water or mist, if only for a second.

That is exactly what we did, said an oozing voice. I'd never seen the devil before, but I remembered the greasy feeling his voice gave me.

"Gharalon!"

Something between a growl and a roar sounded behind me. I turned to see the bloody-armored demon crouched, a lion's tail twitching behind it. It pounced, wings spread.

I jumped up right after it, my own wings snapping open behind me. I caught a glimpse of black feathers to either side. Those came from Eriakne, I thought. The fallen angel.

Concentrate on your foe, you idiot, came her husky voice.

The wolf-lion-man demon proved her point by clobbering me in the face. I reached for its throat but managed only to put my hand in its jaws. It bit down and savaged my fingers.

We fell together, its fists beating on my ribs. I grabbed its throat with my free hand. Instead of pulling my bitten hand out, I shoved it deeper into its throat. It started to choke, and we hit the ground. I wanted to roll away, but it kept its jaws clamped hard on my hand.

Is your attention so fleeting? said Gharalon. *Surrender to my will, and I will free us.*

No! cried out four other voices, one rough, one high, one sensual, and one that sounded both like a boy and the sound of nails on slate.

Give in to me, piped Quang. *I can fly us out of here, buddy.*

None of the others has flown higher than I, said Eriakne. *Let my wings carry us away. Just give your soul to me, and I will keep it safe.*

We will consume the demons, said the double voice. Hearing it reminded me of the image of a young boy wreathed in purple flames, a pair of tiny mouths where the devil's eyes should have been, a veil covering whatever it had instead of a mouth.

Say, "Dokange the Flaying Tongue, I surrender my soul to you."

Just how stupid do you think he is? said Quang. Then he snorted and giggled. *Sometimes I crack myself up.*

I will tear them to pieces, said Viridio. *You have seen what I can do on the battlefield.*

Gharalon, said Gharalon.

While the devils bickered, I wrestled with the lion-wolf demon. Thinking hard about *not* giving up my soul, I remembered what Gharalon said and concentrated on pulling my hand out of the demon's mouth.

The long gray fingers slipped out easy, wavering like mist for a second before turning solid again. I watched as dark purple flames licked along the ridges on its—*my*—skin. The deep gouges from the wolf fangs didn't look half so bad anymore.

With a snarl-roar, the demon leaped at me again. This time I caught it by the throat. We took turns grabbing and twisting, kneeing and biting. It damned near broke my leg with a kick from an iron hoof. We exchanged some harsh language. We battered each other with our wings.

I remembered I had a tail, too.

All it took was to think about hitting it in the back, and the heavy tip of my scorpion's tail snapped over our heads to curl around into the demon's spine. This time it howled and whined, losing its grip on me.

Fly, cooed Eriakne's voice. *Let us view the fray from a height.*

That seemed like a damned fine idea. I jumped up, thought about flapping my wings, flew barely above Tonbarse and Alase, and crashed straight into Aprian, knocking him from his horse.

"Sorry, pal," I told him as he staggered to his feet. One of the brimoraks he'd been fighting rushed toward him. I grabbed it by its smoking horns, shook it hard a couple of times, and left it dead on the ground.

Dragomir came running at me. He'd lost his shield and picked up somebody else's sword in his other hand. But it wasn't the shining crusader blades that bothered me. It was the look in his eyes. He was scarier than any of the demons.

I held up one of my creepy hands. "Hey, take it easy! It's me, Radovan!"

Dragomir snarled, but he changed direction and cut down a demon instead of me. "Thank you, Desna!"

"Radovan?" said Aprian. "You look . . . different."

"Yeah," I said. "Don't let it bother you none. I'm still pretty on the inside."

Inside, I heard Quang cackling and got a clear image of Eriakne sneering. *He can't even fly!*

"Do me a favor and tell the others not to hit me. I'm going to— Hey, you can understand me?"

While I ride you, you speak all tongues, said Dokange.

"Handy," I said. "Maybe we can—"

Wolf-lion demon crashed down on me. I caught a hoof in the breadbasket. I batted away its thick white fingers before the demon could put one in my eye. It shifted its grip and grabbed something on my head. It didn't feel like hair, but it let the demon jerk my head around.

"Dammit! I've got horns!" That was the only thing that could have been worse than a tail.

Well, maybe it wasn't the worst. I remembered what I'd found when I took a peek down below the year that Norge had been riding my soul.

Wolf-lion shook me around until I got my hands on its wrists. Then it beat its bat wings and pulled us both up into the sky.

My tail snapped overhead again and again, but the demon's wings kept blocking the stinger. A stain crept up over the demon's white shoulder, swelling the dark veins in its neck. Maybe the venom would numb the wings enough to put us back on the ground.

Soon we were high enough that I struck that wish off my list.

Between twisting to catch the bruising kicks from my dance partner's hooves on my arms and legs, I finally got a good look at where we were. The boss and Jelani had managed to burn all the way through the briar maze, but his ice wall was still boiling off into a thick cloud. They couldn't see how close they were to Oparal.

She was struggling to reach a succubus standing in front of a couple of glowing books hanging in the air just outside a five-sided stone ring. A big stream of red light was flowing into the circle from somewhere far to the south.

No, I realized. It wasn't going into the circle, but into the ruined body of some *thing* lying at its center. The energy hopped from that body into that of a man lying beside Oparal, then into the succubus. It was feeding her, filling her with power.

Even from a distance, I could tell she was seven or eight feet tall and growing. She was also changing, her skin twisting up in dark red patterns, the dark skin of her wings turning transparent, like red glass.

Another hoof to the gut brought my attention back to the party.

"I've had about enough of this," I growled. With my head held fast, I swung high but hit only hooves and knees. My tail kept lashing, but apart from a few poisoned holes in the demon's wings, it wasn't doing much good.

Devour it, said Dokange. Just the "sound" of its voice in my head made me queasy. *Burn it in the flames of your hunger.*

I didn't feel hungry, but I was plenty mad. It had worked before, so I focused my thoughts on fire, trying to burn the demon.

For my troubles, all I got was another kick, this time in the chest.

Let me do it, said Dokange. *Surrender yourself to me.*

I gave him some advice of my own, the kind the boss calls "pithy."

Something kicked loose inside me. Maybe it was on account of my irritation with Dokange. Maybe it was because I'd looked straight down and realized how high we'd flown. Anger or fear or something else pushed through a dam I hadn't known was in me.

Purple flames rushed out of my eyes, and for the first time I realized they weren't eyes but mouths. For a second, I wondered how I could still see but decided it didn't matter. The lion-wolf demon howled in pain and let go of my horns. I was falling.

For another crazy second, I thought I saw the boss flying past me, going up as I was falling down. That was no delusion, I figured. He must have kept one last flying scroll in case of emergency.

I figured I qualified as an emergency.

Fly, idiot! said Eriakne. *Spread our wings.*

Since she put it like that, I stretched them wide. The black feathers caught the hot air rising from the boiling ice.

I still felt like I was falling, but my direction shifted with every yard, a little more to the side, a little less down. I swooped over the wilted ruins of the burned hedge, the thorns scraping my face and chest as I curved the fallen angel's wings, rising.

With a feeling like shrugging, I beat the wings and felt the air beneath me like water in my palms while swimming. They were *my* wings, now, a part of me, not just something borrowed from Eriakne. I turned, circling the battlefield.

Kronug was down, and Roga was missing—no, not missing. I saw pieces of him passing from demon to demon. Tollivel slumped against the body of his horse, clutching his belly with one hand, stroking the dying animal's nose with the other. Bolivar lay on the ground, blank eyes staring up at me.

Covered in gore and standing in front of fallen comrades, Dragomir was the one the demons couldn't stop. He own eyes blacker than Hell or the Abyss, he kept cutting them down as fast as they came.

Aprian channeled light from his god, scorching the fiends nearest him. As the demons reeled and veered away from him, the paladin ran to his fallen comrades.

The boss and Jelani fought side by side. She kept flinging spells, but he clutched a riffle scroll in his hand while defending her with the Shadowless Sword. When he swung the blade, I could hardly see it move.

He hacked the hand off a tusked boar demon. Then he snapped off his scroll and threw the sword. It flew end over end through a swarm of those babbling bat demons. By the time the sword came back to his hand, three of them fell to the ground in six halves, their mouths still yammering nonsense.

Me, I could barely hear the gibbering fiends. I had plenty of babble going on inside my skull.

We must flee, said Eriakne. *She will ascend any moment. We must not be here when she does!*

Let me loose, said Viridio. *The others are holding us back. I will crush them all like insects.*

You're a fine one to talk, said Quang. *You're nothing but a big insect.*

Arachnid, said Gharalon. *Scorpions aren't insects.*

371

Useless pedantry, said Dokange. *What we* should *do is—*

"Shut it, all of you!" I shouted.

Getting the hang of this flying business, I tried climbing higher. It felt weird, like straining muscles I never knew I had—which made sense, since I'd never had them before.

Once I had some height, I took another quick glance down at the battle. Everybody was on foot, the horses scattered, most of them running back to the west, where we'd left the drivers, carriage, and wagon. With any luck, the animals would find their way back without running into more demons.

The people weren't looking so lucky. Aprian and the boss tried rallying the Kellids and crusaders together, but a few were cut off. Urno and Naia fought back to back, his axe and her sword gleaming crusader silver as their enchantments sparked off of demon hide. They fought like heroes in a painting, the kind where you know the hero dies a second later.

I swooped down, thinking of all the stuff my devil body could do. First my tail shot through the neck of a lean flayed-looking demon. I slapped a couple of ratty hunchbacked fiends with the purple fire from my eyes—or mouths, or whatever the hell they were. The last one, a crocodile-headed thing, I grabbed by the head, snapping its neck as I rose back up above the fight.

Naia looked up, her mouth twisting in fear when she saw me. I threw her a jaunty wave and flew on.

You're getting the hang of this, said Quang. *Now everything's going to be fine, as long as you keep us away from that succubus on the hill.*

I wondered why he sounded so cheerful.

Be silent, you fool! hissed Eriakne.

The others growled and spat at each other, but I wasn't paying attention. I climbed higher, beating my wings as I spiraled around for a better look at the hill.

The succubus with the stained-glass wings had to be almost nine feet tall by now. Either that or she'd shrunk Oparal, but the paladin looked her usual size compared to the burned and bloody corpse lying on the stone circle. She had her feet on the ground now, her open hands crossed in front of her chest in the sunburst symbol of Iomedae. I'd never seen her do that before, because before she'd always had her sword to pray on.

It occurred to me then that she was in one hell of a lot of trouble without that sword, not that you'd know it by how bold she walked up to the succubus. They were too far away to hear, but I could see they were shouting at each other.

Oparal stepped into the light streaming from the fallen guy to the succubus. She blocked the stream of energy, her body convulsing as it poured into her. Her black hair floated up behind her, and her gray eyes glowed red. Her hands shook, but she forced them back together in the sign of Iomedae. Then I realized what she was shouting. It wasn't an argument with the succubus.

It was a prayer to her god.

The red light surrounded her body, denting what was left of her armor like some invisible hand was crushing her. She threw back her head and screamed.

"Hold on!" I shouted. "I'm coming!"

Don't do it, said Quang. *I'm telling you to stay away.*

Stay back, said Gharalon. His oozing voice seemed calm considering the situation.

I glanced down. The good guys were moving slowly up the field. With Aprian and the boss up front, they cut their way foot by foot through the demon cultists. At their rate, it was going to take them a month, except for the fact they'd be dead within ten minutes.

I needed to help them, too.

There was one way to do both.

I swooped down low over the crusaders and Kellids. The boss looked up, and I yelled, "Follow me!"

I poured out the purple fire, burning every demon in a line from my guys all the way to the top of the hill. There, for an instant, I saw Oparal screaming to the sky, her back arched in agony as her arms shook useless at her sides. From her mouth, the red light turned gold, shooting up to spill away in a fading fountain of dying sparks.

The succubus screamed something at Oparal. She reached out with claws the size of garden rakes, black fingers tipped in blood-red talons. But as I flew close, she turned her head to stare at me. Even before she saw me, she was hissing, a steam of blood surging out from between teeth that made mine look dainty.

Flying through the scalding blood, I crashed straight into Oparal. I held her close, shielding her from the bloody blast with my wings. Only then did I feel the flames on the black feathers.

A guy who's been on fire as much as I have knows what to do in that situation. Tucking all my bits and parts, I rolled over and over, across the stone circle and into the cool grass beyond. And I kept rolling, as much to get away from that succubus as to put out the flames.

Oparal started struggling in my arms. I unfolded everything and let her go. When she looked at me, her eyes widened. Her hands clenched in fists.

"Relax, Captain Sweetheart. It's me."

She blinked once and accepted it. "Get the books. I'll draw her attention."

"No dice. You look worse than me."

She looked—what's the boss's word?—incredulous.

"I mean you look pretty banged up. You get the books. I'm going to give the tart something to think about."

Oparal nodded. "Her name is Yavalliska. She wants to become the blood god."

"Got it."

We scrambled to our feet.

Yavalliska was already coming for us. I shot her the tines beneath my jaw. She sneered back at me. I stuck out my tongue.

What came out over my fist and between my fingers, we ain't never going to talk about. Let's just say I disgusted myself more than the succubus.

Once I sucked it all back in, I showed her my neck and said, "You thirsty, girl? I hear once you go devil, you never go back."

She took a step toward me and hesitated. She was bigger than I'd thought from the air. Or maybe I wasn't as big as I expected. I was a head above Oparal, anyway, so at least I wasn't little.

She hissed again. This time the blood spray wet the grassy ground. Everywhere a drop fell, the earth burped and sent up a slender red tendril. I'd seen enough of druid magic that I knew I didn't want to hang around to see what they turned into.

Beating my wings, I rose up and backward. Yavalliska spread hers, but she didn't beat them. She rose up like something under one of the boss's spells, using the wings for guidance, or maybe just for show. They glistened—not with sweat, but with blood.

"What are you?" she said. "You smell like a sister."

"Hey, I'm all man. Ask anybody."

Somewhere in my skull, Eriakne chuckled. Quang's cackling voice joined in.

"All right," I added. It was hard to move backward while flying, but I inched away. Across the circle, I saw Yavalliska's demon worshipers falling back as the boss and company approached the edge of the hill. "At the moment it's a little more complicated than that, but there's no call to disparage my manliness."

"I've never seen your kind before," she said. "But you *are* a devil, aren't you?"

"More than one, actually."

"Then you have more than one reason to die!"

She reached out both of her claws. Black fire curdled in her palms, but only for a second before beams shot out to hit me in the face, the chest—everywhere. The blackness covered me, and then it shattered into a million shards of all the colors. Each of them shone brighter and brighter until it was all white.

I felt myself torn to pieces, each one falling in a different direction until they landed hard on the cool wet evening grass. Looking up, all I could see was the constellation called the Stair of Stars.

My gaze climbed the steps, one by one, until at last it reached the pole star, Cynosure.

"Desna weeps."

Chapter Twenty-One
The King of Chaos

Varian

A cloud of blood expanded behind Oparal as she ran toward us. In her arms she clutched a pair of books, the lingering energies of their magic still flickering across the edges. I recognized them as the *Lacuna Codex* and the *Lexicon of Paradox*—the latter filled with its previously missing pages.

As Oparal drew near, she saw that my eyes and those of all the others not presently engaged in fighting for their lives lay not on her miraculous return but on the plume of blood where Radovan's devil body had only moments earlier hovered beyond the stone circle.

"He is not dead," I said to anyone who could hear. "I have thought him dead before, and I was wrong each time. There is no point in thinking he is dead."

Even as I said the words, I felt ice forming in my heart. As I raised my eyes to look upon the wings of the transfigured succubus, the cold crept into my every limb and digit. It did not paralyze me.

It made me hard enough for murder.

At my side, Arnisant growled. He pressed his shoulder against my hip, and I felt the heat and trembling inside him. He too wanted the sign to kill.

"Count Jeggare," said Oparal. She pushed the books toward me. I sheathed my sword to accept them. "Do something."

The *Lexicon* was warm to the touch, the *Codex* even colder than my hatred. The hairs on my arms rose where their arcane energies licked over my arm. I resisted the urge to throw the useless things away. "It is no use," I said. "There is no time to study them, no time to set their spells in mind."

"But you've read them already," said Jelani. "You studied the *Lexicon* for days. You copied spell after spell from your grimoire. All you need now is to trust that the power resides within you."

"No. For all your good intentions, you are wrong. I am a wizard, not a sorcerer. The world operates on principles of reason, not intuition." I opened my clenched hand and looked down at my last remaining riffle scroll. Why I had drawn it, I could not say. It was next to useless.

Yet perhaps not entirely so.

Riffling the pages across my thumb, I evoked a gust of wind, letting the spent riffle scroll fly away as the blast raised sand and dust from the ground, blowing back the bloody mist to reveal what lay upon the ground.

The scorpionlike giant Viridio was the first to emerge. It stood even taller than when incarnated on Radovan's soul, nearly fifteen feet tall at the shoulder. Its features were far less human, its heavy carapace sheltering a retracting head. Its arachnid eyes scanned the field, lingering only briefly on my party before fixing on the transformed succubus. It crouched low, tail curling as it considered its next move. Then it bounded away, leaping to plunge into a gang of demons loping down from Greengrave Keep looming above the circle.

Two devils flew up from the cloud of dust and blood.

One was an imp whose name I knew was Quang. I had encountered hundreds of its type, usually as familiars to the diabolists of Cheliax or our western holdings. The little terrors flew freely over the skies of Korvosa, where they battled with house drakes for territory. This one tumbled head over spurs in my blast of air, clutching its potbelly. A pair of coiled horns curved up from its angular face. At chin and toe and tail, black hooks curved from its scarlet flesh.

The other flyer was a dark angel, one of hell's winged archers. Her kind I had seen most recently at the Gate of Heaven and Hell in distant Tian Xia. From Radovan's description, I knew this one was named Eriakne. Heavy scars formed whorls and paths across her blue-gray skin, and the wind blew traces of ash off her blackened wings.

A fourth devil rose from the ground. Its aspect was that of a small boy wreathed in purple flames. Even at a distance, I could see it had mouths for eyes, and before it could raise its fallen veil, I saw a long, wet horror drooping from the ragged sphincter of its mouth. It raised a hand as if to ward off a blow from above and vanished in a flicker of its own fire.

There should have been a fifth—some shapeless fiend known as Gharalon—but of that devil I saw no sign. An instant after that thought, a thick mist blew back against the direction of my spell. It pushed us back on our heels. At my side, Arnisant whimpered. The Kellids murmured and clutched their totems. The crusaders made the sign of Iomedae. Even Tonbarse called out a prayer in some ineffable language.

Eriakne screeched like an eagle and flew away to the east.

The imp flew toward us, careful to remain well beyond the range of our blades. It threw a jaunty wave at us and cried, "So long, saps!"

The succubus turned toward us. Her ruby eyes fixed on Oparal, who stood at my side. Aprian handed her a bloody sword, freshly scavenged from the hand of one of his fallen crusaders.

"Yavalliska," Oparal said to me. "By the grace of Iomedae, I was able to disperse the stream of chaos from the Worldwound. Let us pray it was in time."

"In time for what? For her to summon a hundred more fiends?" said Urno. The dwarf's face was striped with blood and ichor.

"To stop her from becoming the god of blood."

"Oh, is that all?" said the dwarf, hefting his axe. His brave tone didn't quite disguise his fear.

As my windy spell subsided, the bloody dust pooled at Yavalliska's feet. I could see no other bodies lying on the ground behind her, but something stirred in the obscuring cloud. Without thinking, I gestured as I might have done had I prepared another scroll with the same spell.

Another blast of air blew forth, scattering the dust. It did not reveal Radovan, as I had half-consciously hoped. Instead, dozens of young succubi rose from the ground, their damp wings unfolding like flower petals.

There were no two of them alike in form or coloration. They resembled all the beauties I had ever seen, dark or light of skin, ample or slim, fair or black or gold of hair. Their eyes were gems, deep waters, clear skies, and spring buds. Their wings spread wide, drying in the night air. Most were the color of coal dust or rich soil. A few were pale or spotted, but even in such plentiful comparison, every one remained a beauty unparalleled.

All of them looked to me and smiled like secrets, winked more than a hint of sin.

"They're peering right into all my guilt," Urno cried. "Away, ye damned temptresses!"

"Turn away," said Oparal, casting her own gaze to the ground.

I looked away, but only to set my eyes on Yavalliska. Desna favored me, for the succubus did not capture me with her gaze. Instead, she looked down at the legion of succubi born of her blood. "My daughters," she said, in a mockery of maternal affection.

Aprian intoned a prayer, but his exhausted voice conveyed no more divine magic. He was as depleted as I.

"Destroy them, Varian!" said Jelani. "Cast your most powerful spell! Look, the books are feeding you!"

Baffled, I looked down at the *Codex* and *Lexicon*. As Jelani said, each of them pulsed with arcane power— far more than they had moments earlier. But what drew my attention more was my empty hand, the one from which I had just cast another gust of wind.

My empty hand.

"Dry your wings, my children," said Yavalliska. "Bring them all here to worship at my feet. We shall have the Chelaxian complete the ritual that Osirian bungler could not, and this time the prince's pet shall be our first sacrifice. Then shall we feast."

Extending my hand, I imagined the formula for the most powerful frost spell I knew. My fingers traced the esoteric signs as I murmured the evocation.

Nothing resulted.

"I cannot do it," I said. "I remember the spell perfectly. It simply will not work without prepar—"

"Don't remember how it *works*, you fool," Jelani slapped me across the face. "Remember how it *feels*!"

Only a long lifetime of propriety prevented me from striking her back. Gritting my teeth, I turned away from her and cast all my anger at Yavalliska, thrusting out my hand in a gesture similar but not identical to the one I had learned from my grimoire.

A narrow cone of ice shot forth, striking the transformed succubus in the face. She reeled backward, nearly falling to the stone of the circle before catching herself on one hand. Frost whitened her face, sealing her eyes and stopping her mouth with ice.

Her succubi stepped forth.

One of them came for me. "Varian," she said. "Stop this foolishness. Come to me. Lay your head in my lap, and let me soothe your heated brow."

I felt the tug of unbidden desire, as much within my heart as within my loins.

Yet my fury still superseded my lust. I shook off the unwelcome pangs and tore my gaze from my temptress.

Beside me, I saw others do the same, or fail.

Aprian and Oparal raised their blades and stepped toward the succubi.

"Ye bastards!" roared Urno. He leaped at Aprian, axe high. "I'll not let you hurt these girls!"

Naia shuddered, her gaze switching between Oparal and another of the succubi. "No, Captain. I'm sorry, but I can't let you do this." She raised her sword.

Dragomir rushed toward me, his dark eyes wet with tears. "This is all your fault, you miserable Chel."

Arnisant intercepted him, clamping his jaws around one wrist and bearing the Ustalav to the ground.

Everything was falling apart.

"Radovan!" I cried, knowing even as I said his name that it was useless. I saw him nowhere on the hill. In freeing his devils, the demon must have obliterated him. Rolling all my anger into a single point of fury, I turned back to the erstwhile god of blood. "Yavalliska!"

She blinked open her eyes just in time to receive a fireball to the face. The flames barely singed her glassy hair, but by the time she cupped her palms and pointed them toward me, I had impaled her with lightning.

She shrugged it off, although she could not hide the burns left upon her glistening body. "Oh, how you will suffer as you learn to adore me."

Black flames flickered in her palms. She raised them above her head and lowered them in my direction. Yet as she did so, her eyes widened in surprise.

From behind us came a sound of thunder and a cool wind that smelled of smoke and pine needles.

At first sight, it appeared a mist rose all across the western half of the spiral hill. Then I made out the shapes of hundreds of unicorns charging toward us. Those who poured up through the path we had carved were obviously tangible beings, their bodies steaming in the cool summer night. At their head ran Bastiel between Alunelsheas and Caedaynenlo.

Through the brambles on either side charged the ghosts of unicorns slain by demons over a century's depredations. I ached to look upon their sorrowful eyes, but when they tossed their manes and lowered their heads, I saw not misery but yearning.

A yearning for revenge.

As the unicorns crested the hill, the succubi screamed in chorus.

"Bastiel!" cried Oparal.

The unicorn charged past her without a glance, racing with his fellows toward the succubi.

A few of the demons retained the wherewithal to lock their eyes upon a unicorn and speak soothing words, but none of them finished articulating a temptation before a storm of hooves trampled them to the ground.

Yavalliska shrieked, raising one foot like a housemaid flinching from a rat. After a nonplussed instant, she composed herself and turned once more toward us.

"Help them," Alase cried to Tonbarse.

The eidolon said, "Let me at the mother."

The god caller's blue eyes lit up. The sigil blazed upon her forehead, Tonbarse's responding. Her lips widened in a determined grin. "Go!"

"Arnisant, kill!" I pointed at Yavalliska. Arnisant became a pewter blur.

The *Codex* and *Lexicon* trembling in my arms, I followed the command with another blast of frost. It was enough to shake Yavalliska, if not put her down.

As the succubi fell to the horns and hooves of the unicorns, the stricken crusaders and sellswords came to their senses.

"Forgive me, Sergeant," said Urno, backing away from the injured Aprian.

"Kill that succubus," he said. "And all's forgiven."

"Aye, Sergeant!"

Aprian and Oparal led the charge together. Their crusader swords struck hard but left barely more evidence of their passing than a careless ring upon a crystal goblet.

Urno leaped to the attack, bringing the full weight of his body down behind his axe. His blow cracked Yavalliska's glassy skin.

Behind them all, the unicorns wheeled around. A few mangled succubi struggled to rise, but they were no longer a present threat. The ghosts among the herd stood still, fading from view even as their descendants moved from a trot to a full gallop. Bastiel had fallen back, but the twins led the unicorns straight toward Yavalliska.

Her hands moved in a strange yet familiar pattern. I recognized it at once, but it was a summoning I had never dared cast myself. Nonetheless, I raised my hands, pausing only briefly to remember Jelani's admonition: I let my fingers improvise the somatic diagram I remembered. As though guided by unheard music, the gestures felt not so much correct as *true*.

"Ahh!" Yavalliska thrashed her hands, frustrated at the failure of her conjuration. Her eyes fell upon me. She saw by my gestures that I had countered her spell. She tried another, this time directed at me.

The unicorns reached her first. Alunelsheas and Caedaynenlo were the first to dip their horns and crack her crystalline skin. At last, crimson ichor oozed from the wounds, but not nearly enough.

The image of cracked glass gave me an idea. Again I blasted her with pure cold, this time focusing my spell upon her legs. As I had hoped, the succubus winced in pain.

Bastiel ran up behind her. A rider leaped from the unicorn's back, falling upon the succubus's shoulders as Bastiel crashed into Yavalliska from behind.

It was Radovan, naked as a newborn.

He hooked an elbow around the succubus's neck and drove a fist into her face. The blow barely cracked her nose. She grasped him by the hair and pulled him off, throwing him down as easily as a fishwife might fling away a housecat.

Thinking of all the times I had cast spells to enhance his strength or swiftness, I did the same for myself, only this time by feeling rather than thought. As I did so, the *Codex* and *Lexicon* responded. I felt their energies adding their strength to the source that lay within me—that had always lain within me, neglected by my lifelong pursuit of the wrong arcane calling.

As I bolstered myself and then my blade, the others threw themselves at Yavalliska. She battered them away with hand or wing. Once she turned a black-flamed palm toward Barek. It was no spell I knew how to counter, so I watched in horror with the others as the dark energy sheared away the top of the Kellid's head.

With a last spell to consummate its flight, I flung the Shadowless Sword. Perhaps because of the magic speeding my own limbs, time seemed to slow to a crawl as it turned end over end.

As the blade's point pierced her heart, Yavalliska opened her mouth to scream. Blood-red energy shot out, boiling with black motes and bubbles. The force of the stream jerked her head around to face south, where the fleeing light arced down to return from whence it came, into the mouth of the Worldwound.

"Get away from her!" shouted Jelani.

All obeyed with varying degrees of speed—all except Urno, who continued smashing at the succubus's knee with his axe.

"Get out of there!" yelled Radovan. He grabbed the dwarf by the collar and pulled him away. After a brief exchange of snarls and a surprised glance down at Radovan's exposed nether region, the dwarf nodded curtly and ran by his side.

Yavalliska's glassy skin darkened and cracked, soon resembling the crust of a burned sheet of sugar candy. Dark ichor oozed out between the cracks to solidify in tumorous clumps. We threw ourselves to the ground at the first deafening crack. An instant later, molten globs of bloody effluvium fell down upon us.

Naia screamed as one fell upon her shoulder. Oparal grabbed her, tearing away her pauldron and using the unburned edge of the metal to scrape away the rest.

I stood and saw the Shadowless Sword standing up from a large chunk of Yavalliska's chest. Extending my hand, I called the weapon back to me, but it did not budge. I tried again, shaking my hand impatiently.

"What spell is that?" asked Jelani.

"No spell at all, but a wizard's trick."

"Ah," she said.

"What do you mean by 'ah'?"

Her smile was half mischief, half triumph. I knew what she meant. She meant that she had told me I was not a wizard, and now I knew that she was right.

"Master," called a squeaky voice behind me.

A pair of hunchbacked, rat-faced demons scurried forward to prostrate themselves before me. Their beady eyes shifted from the sight of the books in my arms to my face.

I raised a hand and spoke a few arcane words. One of the demons fell lifeless to the ground, while the other scampered away, squealing in fear until Arnisant caught it by the neck, shook his mighty head, and ended its abominable life.

Aprian led a triage for our wounded while Selka and Urno led the rest in dispatching the injured demons.

Looking up at Greengrave Keep, I glimpsed a pair of vulture demons watching us with wary eyes. An empty nest stood between their perches.

"They might fear us for a short while," said Oparal. "But I don't know when their master will return."

"Let us make haste," I said. "Where's Radovan?"

She shrugged.

I gave her a tired smile. "Fetching some trousers, let's hope."

She let out the barest laugh at that, but she almost choked as she looked past me. Turning, I saw Bastiel standing beside Alunelsheas. Nearby, Caedaynenlo bowed his head and turned to lead the rest of the unicorns toward the west.

Bastiel stared at Oparal. Then he nuzzled Alunelsheas.

Oparal's eyes glistened. Several times she tried to speak. I put a hand upon her arm and said, "Shall I leave you to say farewell?"

Mutely, she nodded.

Glancing back only once to see her cautiously approaching the unicorns, I walked down the hill with the others. Halfway down, I found Radovan searching the ground. He already had his big knife in hand.

"What is it?" I asked. I twisted my light ring to illuminate the ground.

"My lucky copper," he said. "It's got to be here somewhere."

I helped him search until Oparal came down the hill alone. Radovan looked up at her, utterly uninhibited by his nudity. "Hey, sweetheart," he said. "You all right?"

"Let her be," I whispered.

He watched her walk past us to join the others. We returned our attention to the ground and searched for a few more minutes before he said, "Desna weeps. It's not here. Well, you got the books. Anything else we need before we blow out of this joint?"

A dreadful weight formed in my stomach. I could barely believe I had not thought of it sooner. "Oh no."

I ran up the hill, Radovan close behind me. Arnisant woofed and ran to join us, sensing a chase. He came to sit by my heel as I looked down at the ashes, bones, and golden mask that lay upon the stone circle.

"That's something, anyway," said Radovan.

Sifting through the remains, I found the clasps from which the *Lexicon* and *Codex* had once hung. I took Kasiya's miniature chariot and shook off the ashes. "Fetch a couple of men," I said. "We are taking the corpse."

"What, you going to put him in a glass case in your library?"

"I shall return his remains to the royal family. But first I shall see them blessed by the highest priest of Iomedae and drowned in the purest holy water money can buy."

Radovan grinned. "Because he don't know when to quit."

"And I intend to teach him."

Epilogue

Oparal

A hush fell over the camp. Emerging from my tent, where I had finished donning my repaired and restored armor, I looked around for the source of the sudden change.

Despite the continuing exodus of demons unwilling to defend their city in the absence of Areelu Vorlesh, a constant clamor of preparation had run throughout our growing camp. Since we had taken up a position just east of Undarin two days before, more crusaders joined us almost hourly: infantry, cavalry, inquisitors, battle-clerics, and war-wizards from Nerosyan.

The survivors of our expedition were now but a small fraction of a far larger company. Hundreds strong, we had assembled for a single purpose: to free the captives of the Tower of Zura. Every demon we slew in pursuit of that goal was an additional triumph.

Afterward, the expanded company would return to Nerosyan to escort our precious cargo: the original and restored *Lexicon of Paradox*. Count Jeggare had once again astonished me by agreeing to return the fell volume to Queen Galfrey.

A month earlier I would have suspected treachery, waiting for him at any moment to snatch away the *Lexicon* and deliver it to his despicable Queen Abrogail. But now, after the shared trials and perils of our journey around the Worldwound, I believed the Chelish count truly was as good as his word.

Even with his grimoire destroyed, Count Jeggare's newfound sorcerous ability allowed him to convey a message to an old acquaintance in Nerosyan. He could barely contain his excitement at the revelation Jelani had given him. It was as though he had become an apprentice again, discovering a talent for magic for the first time.

I spied a mass of crusaders gathering at the southwestern corner of camp, the one nearest the cliff below which ran the poisoned river. Somewhere beneath its tainted currents lay my sword, the Ray of Lymirin.

The first thing I had done upon reaching the shore was to plunge into those waters, only to rush out again, unable to stifle my own screams. The polluted current burned my flesh with unholy power. The Ray was lost to me, until one day the engineers could divert the river long enough to mount a search for its recovery.

I pushed past other crusaders to see what had caused the commotion. Most of them were strangers to me, but they saluted my rank. A few addressed me by name, surprising me because I knew none of them. I began to wonder exactly what else Count Jeggare had communicated to Nerosyan.

Aprian ran up beside me. "What is it?"

"I don't know."

The answer revealed itself to both of us at once. The soldiers before us parted to reveal Radovan, walking unclothed through the camp. Spying me, he approached with a grin.

I saw that his borrowed clothes lay draped over his shoulder as filthy water dripped off his naked body. In his arms he bore a long, narrow object covered in burlap.

When he approached, I said, "What's so important that you couldn't put on your pants first?"

"I brought a towel," he said, unwrapping the object in his arms. "But I needed it for this."

The Ray of Lymirin lay within the folds of the cloth.

"But how did you—?" I knew the answer even as I spoke the words. While his actions had often proved anything but evil, Radovan was born of a uniquely fiendish bloodline. The unholy river might burn me and the other crusaders, but it didn't harm him.

The burlap had wiped away much of the river slime, but as I took the hilt in hand, the Ray blazed white, disintegrating the remaining muck. Radovan winced and stepped away from the radiance, causing a stir among the assembled crusaders.

"Calm down, boys and girls," said Radovan. "I'm the devil you know."

A few of the soldiers looked to me. I nodded to them. "Despite appearances, Radovan is most certainly our ally. Look what he's done." I held the Ray high for all to see. The crowd's appreciative murmur reassured me that they wouldn't seize and try the hellspawn anytime soon.

Radovan rubbed himself dry with the burlap. As he donned his clothes, I saw burns on his hands and arms.

For the same reason the river had not burned him, the Ray had.

"You mad fool," I said. "Why did you hurt yourself?"

"Oh, you know. Anything for a friend."

I handed the sword to Aprian. "Here, Radovan. Give me your hands."

"I knew you'd come around one day." He leered at me, and I almost changed my mind.

Instead, I held his hands in mine and prayed to Iomedae. "Peerless Inheritor, though his blood and heritage are strange, I beg you to grant this wretched hellspawn your healing light."

"Hey, what's with the 'wretched hellspawn'?" he complained.

One might argue that we had both blasphemed with our childish banter, but the goddess didn't mind, or else she forgave us both. The radiance flowed from Iomedae into my heart, through my hands and into his. Soon, Radovan's copper skin was once again unmarked by injury.

"Thanks, Captain—" he said with a wink. "Captain."

A soldier ran up to deliver a message to Aprian. When he was done, I overheard the sergeant instruct the man to fetch me a scabbard and shield. As the messenger ran off to obey, Aprian returned the Ray to me. "Captain, I am informed that the commander wishes you to have the honor of leading the first charge."

Pride swelled within my heart, but it was tempered with sadness. Without Bastiel, I would need to borrow a steed from the cavalry. Perhaps it was my pride that had cost me the unicorn's companionship. I had insisted on going into Undarin the first time, knowing I couldn't take him with me. If I had remained behind, letting Aprian take my place—

No, I decided. That decision was not a mistake of pride. If I had not gone into the tower, I would not have fallen into the hands of Prince Kasiya, and thus I would not have been present to slay him before he completed his ritual.

Of course, Yavalliska had also used my presence to her own ends. Perhaps if I had never been there—

No, it was too much for my mortal wisdom to comprehend. I would place my doubts and pride alike in the hands of Iomedae and trust her light to guide me in the future, even though I faced that future alone, without Bastiel.

When we last met beneath Greengrave Keep, Bastiel told me of the bargain he had made: For their aid against Yavalliska, he promised the noble twins that he would return to the Shroud of Unicorns to help them defend their shrinking territory and replenish their numbers.

He had taken a mate, leaving no more room in his heart for me.

Radovan

Heading back from giving Oparal her sword, I wondered what else was wrong with me that the river wouldn't burn me but the holy sword would.

It wasn't too hard to figure out.

The devils waiting on the other side of the portal—which was me, but which was also an actual gate in Hell, and apparently another one in the Abyss—they'd all spilled out to enjoy their freedom. That I could live with, as long as they stayed clear of me and mine. There were a lot worse things than five devils already running lose in the world.

Problem was, their coming through didn't change me. Two nights after we left Greengrave Keep, it was my turn to cook. Second or third time I shook the skillet, I felt something different—something familiar. Which is to say, I hardly felt the heat coming off the iron, even though it was hot enough for cooking.

Just like the bad old days.

The first devil that ever came through me was Norge, a big spiky beast with fire for his sigil. I wasn't surprised I hadn't seen or heard him back at Greengrave Keep. He'd "died" in our world about a year ago. The one time

I'd seen him since, he was sleeping it off in a nasty little alcove near the Hell side of me.

With all the other devils gone, after I didn't feel the heat of the skillet, I figured Norge was next in line again, just waiting to wake up and for me to get myself burned bad enough to invite him over. As long as I was still connected to Hell that way, I figured paladins and unicorns were still going to hate me on first sight. Unholy water still wasn't going to hurt me, and holy swords were still going to burn me.

That was the one thing I'd figured out, but it was a pretty big, bad thing.

Thinking about that, I lost track of where I was going. I couldn't figure out which tent was mine. The damned crusaders made them all alike, white canvas boxes with a little flag only on the officers' tents. I should have stayed with the boss in the carriage.

Looking around, I tried to snag a soldier to give me directions, but everybody was in a hurry. Besides, despite what Oparal had said when I bought back her sword, most of the crusaders took one look at me and hurried off. The brave ones shot me a sneer before they went. I shot them the tines.

"Can't find your tent?"

Alase snuck up behind me, quiet as a mouse. She looked just about small as one whenever Tonbarse was around, but I didn't see the big black wolf anywhere.

What I did see was that the god caller had found a bath somewhere, and not in the nasty river I'd just swum. Not that Alase was all that smelly before, but she cleaned up real nice. She'd even parted her usually shaggy hair, showing off the glowing blue rune she and Tonbarse shared.

And she had that look in her eye.

I knew that look better than anybody, and ordinarily I was plenty happy to oblige. "Yeah, I just got to get ready for the fight."

"They won't be ready for an hour," said Alase.

It was a real good point she had.

"Radovan? I was hoping to find you before—" Jelani clammed up when she saw Alase on the other side of me. She squinted down at the little god caller, but I could tell she'd just had that same look in her eye, at least until she saw the competition.

Alase glared right back at her. "Go away," she said. "I found him first."

"Please," said Jelani. "You're only embarrassing yourself."

"Hey, I've got a great idea," I said.

"Do you?" said Jelani, raising an eyebrow crossing her arms.

That wasn't a good sign.

"Well, it's just a thought. You know, two birds with one . . . kind of . . ."

Alase walked around me to stand beside Jelani. With a glance at the taller woman, she crossed her arms and looked at me, too. "What's this great idea, hm? I think we'd both like to hear what it is you're thinking."

To the west, I saw the crusaders were already forming ranks. They looked plenty brave with their shining armor and colorful shields. But all they were facing was demons.

"On the other hand," I said, "maybe I should save my strength for the fight."

"Oh?" said Jelani. "And here I thought you were about to invite both of us into your tent to prepare for that battle."

"To get our blood up," Alase nodded. "Isn't that what you were going to suggest?"

"Well, now that you mention it, it's always a good idea to warm up before—"

"Radovan," the boss's voice whispered in my ear. "Come to the carriage at once."

"Seriously, boss?" I remembered to cup my hand by my mouth and whispered, "Now's not a good time. I'm in a delicate sort of—"

"Must I remind you the attack is imminent?"

I sighed. "All right, all right. I'm coming."

Jelani looked down at Alase. "Now he'll tell us the count has summoned him."

"He's full of big talk," Alase agreed. "Perhaps you and I should go without him."

"Oh, come on. That's just mean."

"As you said," Jelani purred. "It's always best to warm up."

"You're putting me on, right? You're just making fun of me."

Alase took Jelani by the hand and led her away.

"Radovan!" insisted the boss.

"Oh, Desna weeps." I watched the girls disappear into a tent, still wondering whether they were serious.

"You daft juggler!" said Urno. I was so focused on the women, even an armored dwarf could sneak up on me. "You're not just going to let them go, are you?"

"The boss just called for me," I said.

"It's just as well," said Urno. "They're probably just yanking your—well, your chain."

"Yeah, you're probably right."

"I mean, unless they're in there waiting for you, stripping off each other's clothes."

"You don't think . . . ?"

Urno shrugged, but he couldn't hide the smile growing beneath his beard.

"You're a mean, mean dwarf," I yelled at him before running off to the carriage.

By the time I got there, the boss was wrapping up some business with the high priest of Iomedae. I hung back, waiting for them to finish, but I couldn't stop myself from looking back and craning my neck to see whether Alase and Jelani were still in that tent.

They were probably just putting me on, in which case Desna smiled on me before I got myself into any worse trouble.

On the other hand, if they weren't just teasing . . .

Desna weeps.

Varian

"May the light of the Inheritor ever guide you, Your Excellency." The priest bowed as he received the package containing the *Lexicon of Paradox*. His hands trembled to receive it. To his credit, he restrained himself from opening the wrapping to confirm its contents. While Radovan and I would accompany the crusaders on their return to Nerosyan, the man was clearly relieved to take the book into his own hands rather than to leave it a moment longer in my custody.

Although I knew full well that it meant inviting the displeasure of my own monarch, I had resolved to relinquish the original *Lexicon of Paradox* to Queen Galfrey's sorcerers. Queens Abrogail and Telandia would have to content themselves with copies of the tome, as would I.

Whether I would send a third to the Decemvirate, I had yet to decide. The question of how Kasiya had obtained the *Lacuna Codex* only deepened my growing suspicions about the Pathfinder Society's inner circle.

Despite my long and often rewarding association with the Society, I had begun harboring thoughts of following the example of Ollysta Zadrian and resigning my commission. Unlike the leader of the Shining Crusade, I had no interest in reforming the organization or forming my own. Fortunately, my personal resources allowed me to travel and explore as ever. I had never relied upon the Society for resources, only for colleagues.

The *Codex* would remain in my custody, along with my copy of the *Lexicon*. Securing them at my home might be dangerous, but I could entrust them to no others.

The priest of Iomedae and his paladins bowed their respects and left me beside the Red Carriage. Arnisant sat to my left, while Radovan fidgeted nearby, occasionally craning his neck to peer among the tents.

"Are you looking for someone?"

"You don't even want to know, boss. Anyway, I'm here now. What's up?"

"I noticed you have been uncomfortable in your borrowed clothing," I said. "My friend in Nerosyan kindly sent you a new set of leathers."

"Really?" Despite his casual tone, I could see I had piqued Radovan's interest.

"In the carriage."

I waited while he went inside to change, smiling as I heard a joyous exclamation from inside the vehicle. He emerged moments later, shrugging his shoulders and moving his arms to feel the fit. "It's perfect," he said. "You're the best boss ever."

"Turn around," I said, admiring the enchanted armor.

The deep red leather jacket was no match for the one he had lost in Kyonin, but it compared favorably with the one he had destroyed in Ustalav. Hand-tooled, the leather depicted a variety of demonic figures, which

I suspected would appeal to him even more after he discovered the designs were based on the badges granted for heroism among the Mendevian crusaders. He had already found the sheath in the jacket's spine. His big knife fit perfectly inside, once more giving him the appearance of a short tail.

The darker trousers and boots were similarly adorned, and only the latter needed adjustment. I recalled a minor spell I had learned decades ago, a utilitarian enchantment I had never seen fit to consign to a riffle scroll. Relaxing my thoughts, I spoke the words and performed the gestures as I felt they should be.

"Careful!" said Radovan as his boots contracted to fit his feet.

"Too tight?"

He walked a few steps. "No, perfect."

Retrieving a few scrolls from my pocket, I turned them over to him.

"Ponies?" he said.

I nodded. "And a pair of lesser fire spells. If your theory is correct—"

"I can light myself up," he said, wincing at the thought. He put the scrolls in a side pocket. "You'll understand if I don't try that one anytime soon."

"Of course," I said. "Nevertheless, I have asked Captain Celverian to warn the troops not to kill you if you suddenly transform into a devil."

"Thanks," he said. Frowning, he looked at something he had found in his pocket. "What the hell?"

"What is it?"

He held up a stained and half-melted Ustalavic copper piece. Peering at it, he said, "It's the same damned one I lost up north!"

"Curious," I said. "Did you not tell me you had lost it once or twice before?"

He breathed a curse while holding the coin at arm's length. He flipped it and caught it on the back of one hand. Lifting his fingers, he revealed the disfigured head of an ancient Ustalavic king. "What is this? Good luck or bad?"

I shook my head, wondering at the mystery.

All around us, the camp hushed. To one side of the assembly area, I saw an impromptu crowd gather around some point of interest. Without a word, Radovan snapped off his riffle scroll. His steed appeared, its flanks molten red, its fetlocks trailing gray smoke. I conjured my own, a sleek destrier with a blue-black coat. Arnisant followed us as we rode through tents toward the origin of the commotion.

Halfway to our destination, Dragomir joined us on his own mortal steed. He had abandoned his shield in favor of a second sword, and he had thrown off the crusader's tabard in favor of his own dark steel and leather armor. Aprian had told me earlier that the Ustalav had tendered his resignation, effective after this final action to recover any surviving prisoners from Undarin. Broken hearts usually drove men into the crusade, I thought. This one seemed to drive Dragomir out of it.

We found the crusaders gathered murmuring around an unexpected sight. We dismounted and joined them in a circle around Oparal and the unicorns.

Bastiel had returned. I saw that the last scars had vanished from his neck and throat, no doubt the result of his return to a community of his kin. The noble Alunelsheas stood by his side, shy of all the humans around her, nuzzling Bastiel's neck for comfort.

Oparal stood a short distance away, staring at the unicorns with an expression of mingled hope and disbelief. No one dared speak, until Bastiel moved his equine lips and broke the silence in a voice like summer honey. "Someone bring me a saddle."

"Why?" said Oparal. "Why have you returned?"

"I never knew my sire," said Bastiel. "And my mother died soon after I was born. I never had a name until you gave me one."

Her face ever stoic, Oparal's dark gray eyes glittered with barely restrained emotion.

"I got no idea what that means," said Radovan.

"If I may," I said, stepping in front of him in a vain effort to silence him before he spoiled the moment with a crass remark. "Unicorns name with a combination of the grandparents' names, do they not? And the best possible omen for a foal's birth is the presence of those grandparents."

Bastiel nodded, his steady gaze assuring me that he wished me to continue.

"Alunelsheas, for instance. Her sire's mother had Alunel as part of her name. Her dam's mother, Sheas, as the other half. Or perhaps the opposite."

Alunelsheas bowed her head in agreement.

"I still don't understand," said Oparal.

"There will be a foal," I told her. "One with Oparal in its name."

"She's going to be a granny," Radovan whispered, not quite snickering.

Gradually, carefully, gently, Oparal went to Bastiel. As she put her arms around his neck, Sergeant Aprian began shooing away the onlookers. "Back to your places!"

"Come on, boss." Radovan pulled at my elbow as I pulled a handkerchief from my sleeve. "Let's get out of here before you embarrass the both of us."

Soon we were composed, mounted, and ready to join the crusaders on the first drive into Undarin. The Tower of Zura and its twin were our first goals. We would harrow the halls of demons and free as many of the captives as remained. We prayed that Gemma was among them, and perhaps Erastus, although we held out faint hope that either had survived so long.

While the officers mustered their troops, Aprian rode by once more to check on us. He pointed to Captain Celverian, the grim crusader I had met only briefly. At his side rode Jelani, who pointed across the ranks to indicate Oparal at the head of the vanguard.

"Before the battle, I wanted to thank you both," said Aprian. "Especially you, Radovan, for recovering the captain's sword."

"Aw, that was no big deal," said Radovan. "With the unicorn back, she would have been all right."

"Maybe so," said Aprian, shading his eyes from the light as Oparal raised the Ray of Lymirin to signal the charge. "But now she's perfect."

About the Author

Dave Gross is the author of numerous other Pathfinder Tales stories featuring Radovan and Jeggare, including the novels *Prince of Wolves, Master of Devils,* and *Queen of Thorns;* the short stories "A Lesson in Taxonomy," "A Passage to Absalom," "Killing Time," and "The Lost Pathfinder"; and the serial novellas *Hell's Pawns* and *Husks.* He also contributed to Elaine Cunningham's *Winter Witch.* His first full-length novel was *Black Wolf,* followed by the final volume of the Sembia series, *Lord of Stormweather,* both set in the Forgotten Realms. He has since written for a variety of settings in novels and fantasy, horror, and SF anthologies, including *Tales of the Far West, Shotguns v. Cthulhu, The Lion and the Aardvark,* and a little series pitch in Robin D. Laws's *Hillfolk.* His most recent publications are *The Devil's Buy* and *Dark Convergence,* both set in the Iron Kingdoms. In desperate times, Dave has taught English and other subjects, and he is a former editor of various magazines, notably *Dragon, Star Wars Insider,* and *Amazing Stories.* He lives in Alberta, Canada, with his wife, their cats, and a miniature giant space buffalo.

Acknowledgments

For a thousand keen questions, suggestions, and encouragement on the manuscript for this novel, I am grateful to Clint Barkley, Jesse Benner, Elaine Cunningham, Jaym Gates, John D Halpin, Chris A. Jackson, Jen LaFace, and Carlos Ovalle.

Glossary

All Pathfinder Tales novels are set in the rich and vibrant world of the Pathfinder campaign setting. Below are explanations of several key terms used in this book. For more information on the world of Golarion and the strange monsters, people, and deities that make it their home, see *The Inner Sea World Guide*, or dive into the game and begin playing your own adventures with the *Pathfinder Roleplaying Game Core Rulebook* or the *Pathfinder Roleplaying Game Beginner Box*, all available at **paizo.com**. Those readers particularly interested in exploring the Worldwound further should check out *Pathfinder Campaign Setting: The Worldwound*, learn more about demons with *Pathfinder Campaign Setting: Demons Revisited*, or confront the demonic menace personally in the Wrath of the Righteous Adventure Path. Fans of Varian and Jeggare can follow the duo's previous adventures in the novels *Prince of Wolves*, *Master of Devils*, and *Queen of Thorns*.

Absalom: Largest city in the Inner Sea region.
Abyss: Plane of evil and chaos ruled by demons, where many evil souls go after they die.

Abyssal: Of or pertaining to the Abyss.

Acadamae: Notoriously effective and amoral school of magic in Korvosa.

Acts of Iomedae: Holy text of the church of Iomedae.

Anaphexis: Deadly cult devoted to keeping secrets at all costs. For more information, see *Prince of Wolves* and *Pathfinder Campaign Setting: Rule of Fear*.

Andoran: Democratic and freedom-loving nation formerly controlled by Cheliax.

Andoren: Of or pertaining to Andoran; someone from Andoran.

Arcane: Magic that comes from mystical sources rather than the direct intervention of a god; secular magic.

Aroden: The god of humanity, who died mysteriously a hundred years ago, causing widespread chaos.

Asmodeus: Devil-god of tyranny, slavery, pride, and contracts; lord of Hell and current patron deity of Cheliax.

Avistan: The continent north of the Inner Sea, on which Cheliax, Andoran, the Worldwound, and many other nations and regions lie.

Azlant: The first human empire, which sank beneath the waves long ago.

Azlanti: Of or pertaining to Azlant; someone from Azlant.

Bloodwater Betrayals: Massacres caused when Ustalavs refused to harbor Sarkorians fleeing from the newly opened Worldwound, instead forcing them back across the border to be slaughtered.

Bones Fall in a Spiral: The holy text of Pharasma.

Brimorak: Goat-headed demon with a burning sword and hooves.

Calistria: Also known as the Savored Sting; the goddess of trickery, lust, and revenge.

Chel: Derogatory term for a citizen of Cheliax.

Chelaxian: Someone from Cheliax.

Cheliax: A nation in southwestern Avistan that gained power by allying with Hell.

Chelish: Of or relating to the nation of Cheliax.

Children of Westcrown: A resistance movement in Cheliax dedicated to overthrowing the diabolical House of Thrune and breaking the nation's alliance with Hell.

Daemons: Evil, nihilistic beings who exist to devour mortal souls.

Dawnflower: Sarenrae.

Decemvirate: Masked and anonymous ruling council of the Pathfinder Society.

Demon Lord: A particularly powerful demon capable of granting magical powers to its followers. One of the rulers of the Abyss.

Demonblooded: A humanoid who bears demonic traits due to interbreeding between demons and his or her ancestors.

Demons: Evil denizens of the Abyss, who seek only to maim, ruin, and feed on mortal souls.

Demontongue: The language of demons.

Deskari: The principle demon lord responsible for the demonic invasion through the Worldwound. Also known as the Lord of the Locust Host.

Desna: Good-natured goddess of dreams, stars, travelers, and luck.

Devils: Evil denizens of Hell who seek to corrupt mortals in order to claim their souls.

Diabolist: A spellcaster who specializes in binding devils and making infernal pacts.

Drezen: Fallen crusader city in the northern Worldwound.

Druid: Someone who reveres nature and draws magical power from the boundless energy of the natural world.

Dwarves: Short, stocky humanoids who excel at physical labor, mining, and craftsmanship.

Dyinglight: Demonic city in the northern Worldwound, ruled by marsh giants.

Eagle Knights: Military order in Andoran devoted to spreading the virtues of justice, equality, and freedom.

Egorian: Capital of Cheliax.

Eidolon: A unique mystical creature called from another plane of existence and bound to serve its summoner, usually willingly. Revered as gods by Sarkorians.

Elven: Of or pertaining to elves.

Elves: Long-lived, beautiful humanoids identifiable by their pointed ears, lithe bodies, and pupils so large their eyes appear to be one color.

Familiar: Small creature that assists a wizard, witch, or sorcerer, often developing greater powers and intelligence than normal members of its kind.

Fiends: Creatures native to the evil planes of existence, such as demons, devils, and daemons, among others.

Fierani Forest: Ancient forest that occupies most of Kyonin.

First World: The rough draft of existence, which still exists behind the Material Plane. Original home of fey creatures and gnomes.

Frostmire: Enormous demon-haunted fen in the northern reaches of the Worldwound.

Gallowspire: The unhallowed former stronghold of the Whispering Tyrant, now turned into his prison.

Garund: Continent south of the Inner Sea, renowned for its deserts and jungles.

General Arnisant: Taldan general who sacrificed himself to imprison the Whispering Tyrant beneath his tower in Gallowspire.

God Callers: Sarkorian summoners who worship the eidolons they summon, seeing the creatures as patron deities.

Golarion: The planet on which the Pathfinder campaign setting focuses.

Gorum: God of battle, strength, and weapons. Also known as Our Lord in Iron.

Gozreh: God of nature, the sea, and weather. Depicted as a dual deity, with both male and female aspects.

Grand Lodge: The headquarters of the Pathfinder Society, located in Absalom.

Green: Also called the Green Faith; the worship of nature from which druids draw their magical powers.

Gundrun: City in the southern reaches of the Worldwound where humanoids still manage to defend themselves against the demonic horde.

Half-Elves: The children of unions between elves and humans. Taller, longer-lived, and generally more graceful and attractive than the average human, yet not nearly so much so as their full elven kin. Often regarded as having the best qualities of both races, yet still see a certain amount of prejudice, particularly from their pure elven relations.

Half-Fiend: Someone whose ancestry includes crossbreeding with evil extraplanar creatures such as demons, devils, and daemons. Often bear physical signs of their lineage.

Hallit: Northern language spoken primarily by Kellids.

Harrow Deck: Deck of illustrated cards sometimes used to divine the future.

Harrower: Fortune-teller who uses a harrow deck to tell the future—or pretends to.

Hell: Plane of evil and tyrannical order ruled by devils, where many evil souls go after they die.

Hellspawn: A humanoid who bears devilish traits due to interbreeding between devils and his or her ancestors.

Imp: A weak devil resembling a tiny, winged humanoid with fiendish features.

Infernal: Of or related to Hell.

Inheritor: One of Iomedae's titles, due to her taking over of much of Aroden's congregation after his death.

Inner Sea: Heavily traveled sea at the center of the Pathfinder campaign setting.

Iomedae: Goddess of valor, rulership, justice, and honor, who started life as a human before attaining godhood.

Irori: God of history, knowledge, self-perfection, and enlightenment.

Isger: Vassal nation of Cheliax.

Isgeri: Someone or something from Isger.

Iz: Demonic capital city of the Worldwound.

Kellids: Traditionally uncivilized and violent human ethnicity from the northern reaches of the Inner Sea region.

Kenabres: Fortified crusader city along Mendev's border with the Worldwound.

Korvosa: Largest city in Varisia and outpost of former Chelish loyalists, now self-governed.

Kyonin: An elven forest-kingdom in eastern Avistan. The center of elven power in the Inner Sea region. Largely forbidden to non-elven travelers.

Lady Luck: Desna.

Lady of Graves: Pharasma.

Landshark: Ferocious monster that burrows through solid earth and eats almost anything.

Lich: A spellcaster who manages to extend his existence by magically transforming himself into a powerful undead creature.

Lord of the Locust Host: Deskari.

Low Templars: Crusaders who flock to the Mendevian Crusade in hopes of fame and loot rather than for more altruistic reasons.

Mammoth Lord: The ruler of a following of Kellid tribes in the Realm of the Mammoth Lords.

Marsh Giants: Brutish, backward giants fond of swamps and marshes.

Mendev: Cold, northern crusader nation that provides the primary force defending the rest of the Inner Sea region from the demonic infestation of the Worldwound.

Mendevian: Of or pertaining to Mendev.

Mwangi: Of or pertaining to the southern jungle region known as the Mwangi Expanse; someone from that region.

Nerosyan: Fortress city and capital of Mendev, situated along the nation's southwestern border. Also called the Diamond of the North, after its shining towers and diamond-shaped layout.

Orc: A bestial, warlike race of savage humanoids from deep underground who now roam the surface in barbaric bands.

Osirian: Of or relating to the region of Osirion, or a resident of Osirion.

Osiriani: The native language of Osirion.

Osirion: Desert kingdom ruled by pharaohs south of the Inner Sea, in northeastern Garund.

Paladin: A holy warrior in the service of a good and lawful god. Ruled by a strict code of conduct and granted special magical powers by his or her deity.

Pathfinder Chronicles: Books published by the Pathfinder Society detailing the most interesting and educational discoveries of their members.

Pathfinder Lodge: Meeting house where members of the Pathfinder Society can buy provisions and swap stories.

Pathfinder Society: Organization of traveling scholars and adventurers who seek to document the world's wonders. Based out of Absalom and run by a mysterious and masked group called the Decemvirate.

Pathfinder: A member of the Pathfinder Society.

Pharasma: The goddess of birth, death, and prophecy, who judges mortal souls after their deaths and sends them on to the appropriate afterlife.

Pharasmin: Of or related to the goddess Pharasma or her worshipers.

Plane: One of the realms of existence, such as the mortal world, Heaven, Hell, the Abyss, and many others.

Prince of Law: Asmodeus.

Qadira: Desert nation on the eastern side of the Inner Sea.

Rasping Rifts: Deskari's personal domain in the Abyss.

Razmiran: Nation ruled by a self-proclaimed living god.

Razmir: Ruler of Razmiran, worshiped by his subjects as a living god.

Razmiri: Worshipers and subjects of Razmir.

Riffle Scroll: Magical scroll shaped like a flipbook, which is activated by flipping the pages rapidly.

River Kingdoms: A region of tiny, feuding fiefdoms and bandit strongholds, where borders change frequently.

Riverspire: Elven tower-city in southern Kyonin.

Saint Lymirin: Former priestess of Iomedae, now honored as a saint by the faithful; often depicted as an eagle-headed woman with wings.

Sarenrae: Goddess of the sun, honesty, and redemption. Often seen as a fiery crusader and redeemer.

Sarkorian: Of or relating to the region of Sarkoris.

Sarkoris: Northern nation destroyed and overrun by the Worldwound.

Scroll: Magical document in which a spell is recorded so that it can be released when read, even if the reader doesn't know how to cast that spell. Destroyed as part of the casting process.

Sczarni: A subgroup of the Varisian ethnicity known for being wandering thieves and criminals.

Silver Crusade: Organization of Pathfinders dedicated to using their abilities for righteous purposes. Led by the paladin Ollysta Zadrian.

Sorcerer: Someone who casts spells through natural ability rather than faith or study.

Starknife: A set of four tapering blades resembling compass points extending from a metal ring with a handle; the holy weapon of Desna.

Storasta: River city in the southern portion of the Worldwound, currently overrun by demons, hags, and twisted plant creatures.

Succubus: Female demon devoted to seduction and manipulation.

Summoner: A particular type of spellcaster who can cast a variety of spells, but focuses on the ability to call a specific creature from another plane to act as a companion.

Taldan: Of or pertaining to Taldor; a citizen of Taldor.

Taldane: The common trade language of Golarion's Inner Sea region.

Taldor: A formerly glorious nation that has lost many of its holdings in recent years to neglect and decadence.

Thassilon: Ancient empire which crumbled long ago.

Thassilonian: Of or related to ancient Thassilon, as well as the name of its language.

Three, The: The three spellcasters responsible for opening the original gate to the Abyss that became the Worldwound.

Thrune: Ruling house of Cheliax, which took power and stabilized the nation by making an alliance with Hell.

Thuvia: Desert nation on the Inner Sea, famous for the production of a magical elixir which grants immortality.

Thuvian: Of or related to Thuvia.

Tian Xia: Continent on the opposite side of the world from the Inner Sea region.

Tian: Someone or something from Tian Xia, the Dragon Empires of the distant east.

Tien: The common trade language of the Tian peoples of the Dragon Empires.

Tines: Raised fork on which Chelish criminals are sometimes impaled. Also the name of a rude hand gesture from Cheliax, which suggests that the recipient should be impaled in such a manner.

Torag: Stoic and serious dwarven god of the forge, protection, and strategy. Viewed by dwarves as the Father of Creation.

Treefolk: Race of long-lived and intelligent plant creatures that resemble vaguely humanoid trees.

Treerazer: A powerful demon that resides in the Fierani Forest.

Tymon: City-state in the southwestern River Kingdoms.

Undarin: City near the center of the Worldwound, inhabited by demons and cultists.

Urgathoa: Evil goddess of gluttony, disease, and undeath.

Ustalav: Fog-shrouded gothic nation of the Inner Sea region, with a reputation for strange beasts, ancient superstitions, and moral decay.

Ustalavic: Of or related to the nation of Ustalav.

Valahuv: Town of humanoids in the Worldwound that manages to survive due to the protection of a mysterious patron deity.

Varisia: Frontier region at the northwestern edge of the Inner Sea region.

Varisian: Of or relating to the frontier region of Varisia, or a resident of that region. Ethnic Varisians tend to organize in clans and wander in caravans, acting as tinkers, musicians, dancers, or performers.

Venture-Captain: A rank in the Pathfinder Society above that of a standard field agent but below the Decemvirate. In charge of directing and assisting lesser agents.

Vermleks: Worm-demons that inhabit corpses and move them around like puppets.

Vescavors: Small flying demons that are mostly wings and jaws, and whose chatter can drive people mad.

Wardstone: Magically imbued obelisks that line the Worldwound's border and help hold back the tide of demons.

Westcrown: Former capital of Cheliax, now overrun with shadow beasts and despair.

Whispering Tyrant: Incredibly powerful lich who terrorized Avistan for hundreds of years before being sealed beneath his fortress of Gallowspire a millennium ago.

Wight: An undead humanoid creature brought back to a semblance of life through necromancy, a violent death, or an extremely malevolent personality.

Wiscrani: Someone from Westcrown.

Witch: Spellcaster who draws magic from a pact made with an otherworldly power, using a familiar as a conduit.

Witchbole: Twisted tree-fortress of the demon Treerazer.

Wizard: Someone who casts spells through careful study and rigorous scientific methods rather than faith or innate talent, recording the necessary incantations in a spellbook.

Worldwound: Constantly expanding region overrun by demons a century ago. Held at bay by the efforts of the Mendevian crusaders. Refers to both the central rift to the Abyss at the region's heart and the greater territory currently held by demons (formerly the nation of Sarkoris),

Yath: Strange demonic tower-entity which recently arose in the Worldwound and was then destroyed by adventurers. For more information, see the Pathfinder Tales novel *The Worldwound Gambit*.

Zura: Demon lord of vampires, cannibalism, and blood.

In the war-torn lands of Molthune and Nirmathas, where rebels fight an endless war of secession against an oppressive military government, the constant fighting can make for strange alliances. Such is the case for the man known only as the Masked—the victim of a magical curse that forces him to hide his face—and an escaped halfling slave named Tantaerra. Thrown together by chance, the two fugitives find themselves conscripted by both sides of the conflict and forced to search for a magical artifact that could help shift the balance of power and end the bloodshed for good. But in order to survive, the thieves will first need to learn to the one thing none of their adventures have taught them: how to trust each other.

From *New York Times* bestselling author and legendary game designer Ed Greenwood comes a new adventure of magic, monsters, and unlikely friendships, set in the award-winning world of the Pathfinder Roleplaying Game.

The Wizard's Mask print edition: $9.99
ISBN: 978-1-60125-530-3

The Wizard's Mask ebook edition:
ISBN: 978-1-60125-531-0

The Wizard's Mask

Ed Greenwood

PATHFINDER TALES

When a mysterious monster carves a path of destruction across the southern River Kingdoms, desperate townsfolk look to the famed elven ranger Elyana and her half-orc companion Drelm for salvation. For Drelm, however, the mission is about more than simple justice, as without a great victory proving his worth, a prejudiced populace will never allow him to marry the human woman he loves. Together with a fresh band of allies, including the mysterious gunslinger Lisette, the heroes must set off into the wilderness, hunting a terrifying beast that will test their abilities—and their friendships—to the breaking point and beyond.

From acclaimed author Howard Andrew Jones comes a new adventure of love, death, and unnatural creatures, set in the award-winning world of the Pathfinder Roleplaying Game.

Stalking the Beast print edition: $9.99
ISBN: 978-1-60125-572-3

Stalking the Beast ebook edition:
ISBN: 978-1-60125-573-0

Stalking the Beast

Howard Andrew Jones

You've delved into the Pathfinder campaign setting with Pathfinder Tales novels—now take your adventures even further! *The Inner Sea World Guide* is a full-color, 320-page hardcover guide featuring everything you need to know about the exciting world of Pathfinder: overviews of every major nation, religion, race, and adventure location around the Inner Sea, plus a giant poster map! Read it as a travelogue, or use it to flesh out your roleplaying game—it's your world now!

EXPLORE YOUR WORLD!